# DREAMSPELL

# DREAMSPELL

A Medieval Time Travel Romance

TAMARA LEIGH

The characters and events portrayed in this book are fictitious. Any similarity to real persons, living or dead, is coincidental and not intended by the author.

Text copyright © 2015 Tamara Leigh
All rights reserved.
No part of this book may be reproduced, or stored in a retrieval system, or transmitted in any form or by any means, electronic, mechanical, photocopying, recording, or otherwise, without express written permission of the publisher.

ISBN: 1942326173
ISBN 13: 9781942326175

# TAMARA LEIGH NOVELS

## CLEAN READ HISTORICAL ROMANCE
### The Feud: A Medieval Romance Series
*Baron Of Godsmere:* Book One 02/15
*Baron Of Emberly:* Book Two 12/15
*Baron of Blackwood:* Book Three 2016

### Medieval Romance Series
*Lady At Arms:* Book One 01/14 (1994 Bantam Books bestseller *Warrior Bride* clean read rewrite)
*Lady Of Eve:* Book Two 06/14 (1994 Bantam Books bestseller *Virgin Bride* clean read rewrite)

### Stand-Alone Medieval Romance Novels
*Lady Of Fire* 11/14 (1995 Bantam Books bestseller *Pagan Bride* clean read rewrite)
*Lady Of Conquest* 06/15 (1996 Bantam Books bestseller *Saxon Bride* clean read rewrite)
*Lady Undaunted* Late Winter 2016 (1996 HarperCollins bestseller *Misbegotten* clean read rewrite)
*Dreamspell:* A Medieval Time Travel Romance 03/12

## INSPIRATIONAL HISTORICAL ROMANCE
### Age of Faith: A Medieval Romance Series
*The Unveiling:* Book One 08/12
*The Yielding:* Book Two 12/12
*The Redeeming:* Book Three 05/13
*The Kindling:* Book Four 11/13
*The Longing:* Book Five 05/14

**INSPIRATIONAL CONTEMPORARY ROMANCE**
**Head Over Heels: Stand-Alone Romance Novels**
*Stealing Adda* 05/12 (ebook); 2006 (print): NavPress
*Perfecting Kate* 03/15 (ebook); 2007 (print): RandomHouse/Multnomah
*Splitting Harriet* 06/15 (ebook); 2007 (print): RandomHouse/Multnomah
*Faking Grace* 2015 (ebook); 2008 (print edition): RandomHouse/Multnomah

**Southern Discomfort: A Contemporary Romance Series**
*Leaving Carolina:* **Book One** 11/15 (ebook); 2009 (print): RandomHouse/Multnomah
*Nowhere, Carolina:* **Book Two** 12/15 (ebook); 2010 (print): RandomHouse/Multnomah
*Restless in Carolina:* **Book Three** Mid-Winter 2016 (ebook); 2011 (print): RandomHouse/Multnomah

**OUT-OF-PRINT GENERAL MARKET TITLES**
*Warrior Bride* 1994: Bantam Books
*\*Virgin Bride* 1994: Bantam Books
*Pagan Bride* 1995: Bantam Books
*Saxon Bride* 1995: Bantam Books
*Misbegotten* 1996: HarperCollins
*Unforgotten* 1997: HarperCollins
*Blackheart* 2001: Dorchester Leisure

\**Virgin Bride* is the sequel to *Warrior Bride*
*Pagan Pride* and *Saxon Bride* are stand-alone novels

www.tamaraleigh.com

# Prologue

**London, 1376**

*Even I would have killed for thee.*

Dawn lit the words etched in stone, bade him draw near. Aye, he would have killed for her, though not as it was told he had done. Still, this day he would die. For three years, he had languished in this wretched cell awaiting a trial that was only a formality, and yesterday he had been brought before his peers. Now, with the newborn day, the Lieutenant would take him through the city to Smithfield where a noose awaited him.

He rose from his pallet and crossed his cell to where he had carved the words by which he would soon die. Head and shoulders blocking the light that shone through the small window, he traced each letter through to *thee*.

"Nedy," he whispered, remembering everything about her, from the gentle curve of her lips to her long legs to mannerisms not of this world. More, he remembered the last time they had kissed and the promise she had made him—a promise not kept. But at least he had loved.

The door opened, but it was not the Lieutenant who came for him. Though the years had cruelly aged the man who stepped inside, rounding shoulders that had once been broad, there was no mistaking the third King Edward.

"Wynland." The king inclined his head.

It was three years since Fulke had been granted such an audience, but he remembered himself and bowed. "Your majesty."

Edward peered into his prisoner's face. "You are prepared to die?"

"I am."

"Yet still you say it was not you?"

Fulke stared at him, those few moments all the confirmation needed of the idle talk of guards. Edward's mind was on the wane. Was the recent death of his son, the Black Prince, responsible? Though not since the queen's passing seven years ago could he be said to be right in the head, this was worse, as evidenced by his neglect of affairs of state. The great King Edward was no longer worthy of the crown, the power he had once wielded now in the hands of his greedy mistress, Alice Perrers.

"I trusted you," Edward said, his jaw quivering in his fleshy face. "When all opposed your wardship of your nephews, I granted it. When my fair Lark was attacked, I would not believe 'twas you."

It was an opening for Fulke to defend himself, but he was done with that.

"Have you naught to say?" Edward demanded.

"I have had my say, my liege. There is no more."

Edward cursed, turned to leave, and came back around. "Beg my forgiveness and mayhap I shall allow you an easier death."

"There is naught for which I require your forgiveness." This did not mean he did not seek the forgiveness of others. But it was too late for that.

Anger staining the king's face, he looked around the cell and lingered on the words that covered the walls. "I was told of this. The troubadours pay well for the guards to bring them these words by which they compose songs of love."

Fulke considered all he had carved into the stone these past years—words never spoken.

"Why do you do it?"

Feeling a pang at his center, Fulke said, "That she might know."

Edward shook his head. "You loved wrong in choosing a woman such as that when you could have had—" His voice broke. "I would have forgiven you anything, except my Lark." He stepped from the cell.

As the door swung closed, Fulke stood motionless, each moment that passed drawing him nearer his last. Finally, he crossed to his pallet and retrieved the worn spoon that was only one of many to have lent itself to his writings. Thumbing the rough edge of all that remained of its handle, he eyed the last words he had inscribed: *Even I would have killed for thee.* They said much, but there was more.

When they came for him an hour later, the final line read: *And now I shall die for thee.* As he stood to be shackled, he considered his words carved around the walls. They were for Nedy, wherever she was.

# 1

**University Sleep Disorders Clinic**
**Los Angeles, California**

"I was there," Mac said amid the tick and hum of instruments. "Really there."

Kennedy waited for his eyes to brighten and a grin to surface his weary face. Nothing. Not even a flicker of humor. Dropping the smile that was as false as the hair sweeping her brow, she said, "Sorry, Mac, I'm not buying it." She turned to the bedside table and peered at the machine that would monitor his sleep cycles.

"You think I'm joking?"

Of course he was. For all the horror MacArthur Crosley had endured during the Gulf War, he was an incorrigible joker, but this time he had gone too far. She unbundled the electrodes.

"I'm serious, Ken."

Her other subjects called her Dr. Plain, but she and Mac went back to when she had been a doctoral student and he was her first subject in a study of the effects of sleep deprivation on dreams. That was four years ago and, at this rate, it might be another four before she was able to present her latest findings. If she had that long...

Feeling the snugness of the knit cap covering her head, she said, "Serious, huh? I've heard that one before."

The familiar squeak of wheels announced his approach. "It happened."

Meanwhile, the clock kept ticking, the minute hand climbing toward midnight.

"Listen to me, Ken. What I have to tell you is important—"

"Time travel through dreams, Mac?" She uncapped a tube of fixative and squeezed a dab onto the electrodes' disks. "How on earth did you hatch that one?" Though she might concede some dreams prophesied the future, time travel was too far out there. "Let's get you hooked up."

"That's not what I'm here for."

She turned and found herself sandwiched between the table and the wheelchair that served as his legs.

"I've been holding out on you, Ken. I would have told you sooner, but I couldn't—not until I was certain it wasn't just an incredibly real dream."

"Come on, Mac. It's midnight, I haven't had dinner yet, and I'm tired."

He clamped a hand around her arm. "I'm dead serious."

Though she knew she had nothing to fear from him, alarm leapt through her when a tremor passed from him to her. Never had she seen Mac like this, and certainly he had never taken his jokes this far. Was it possible that what he said was true—rather, he *believed* it was true? If so, he was hallucinating, a side-effect not uncommon among her subjects, especially beyond sixty hours of sleep deprivation. But she had never known Mac to succumb to hallucinations, not even during an episode four months back when his consecutive waking hours broke the two hundred mark. That had complications all its own.

He released her and pushed back. "Sorry."

Kennedy stared at him. The whites of his eyes blazed red, the circles beneath shone like bruises, the lines canyoning his face went deeper. Forty-five years old, yet he looked sixty, just as he had when his two hundred and two waking hours had put him into a sleep so deep he had gone comatose. But he had reported eighty-seven waking hours when he called an hour ago.

He had lied. Kennedy nearly cursed. She knew what extreme sleep deprivation looked like, especially on Mac. True, he had cried wolf before, convinced her of the unimaginable to the point she would have bet her life he was telling the truth, but this came down to negligence. And she was guilty as charged.

She consulted her clipboard and scanned the previous entry. Five weeks since his last episode, a stretch considering he rarely made it three weeks without going a round with his souvenir from the war. But why would he under-report his waking hours? Because of the safeguard that was put in place following his coma, one that stipulated all subjects who exceeded one hundred fifty waking hours were to be monitored by a medical doctor?

Knowing her own sleep would have to wait—not necessarily that she would have slept since she was also intimate with insomnia—she said, "How many hours, Mac?"

He pushed a hand through his silvered red hair. "Eighty…nine."

"Not *one hundred* eighty nine?"

"Why would I lie?"

"You tell me."

"I would if you'd listen."

Realizing she was picking an argument when she should be collecting data, she rolled a stool beneath her. "Okay, talk."

He dragged a tattooed hand down his face. "The dreams aren't dreams. Not anymore. When I went comatose, I truly crossed over, and that's when I realized it was more than a dream. And I could have stayed." He slammed his fists on the arms of his wheelchair. "If not for the doctors and their machines, I *would* have stayed!"

Pain stirred at the back of Kennedy's head. "You would have died."

"In this time. There I would have lived."

Then he truly believed he had been transported to the Middle Ages of his serial dream. Interesting. "I see."

"Do you?"

Was this more than sleep deprivation? Had Mac snapped? "I know it seems real—"

"Cut with the psychobabble! Sleep deprivation is the key to the past. It's a bridge. A way back. A way out."

She took a deep breath. "Out of what?"

"This." He looked to the stumps of his legs, wheeled forward, and tapped her forehead. "And this."

Stunned by his trespass, Kennedy caught her breath.

He sank back in his wheelchair. "In my dreams, I have legs again. Have I told you that?"

She gave herself a mental shake. "Many times."

"I walk. I run. I feel my legs down to my toes. It's as if the war never happened."

She laid a hand on his shoulder. "It did happen."

"Not six hundred years ago."

She lowered her hand. "What makes you believe this isn't just an incredibly real dream?"

"I don't know the places in this dream, and I've never seen any of the people."

*That* was his proof? Though dreams were often forged of acquaintances and familiar landscapes, it wasn't unusual to encounter seemingly unfamiliar ones.

He reached behind his wheelchair, pulled a book from his knapsack, and pushed it into her hands. "I found this in an antique book shop a while back."

It was old, its black cover worn white along the edges, all that remained of its title a barely legible stamped impression. She put her glasses on. "The Sins of the Earl of...?"

"Sinwell," Mac supplied.

Kennedy forced a laugh. "Catchy title." She ran her fingers across the numbers beneath. "1373 to 1399. History...never my best subject."

"He's the one."

"Who?"

"Fulke Wynland, the man who murdered his nephews so he could claim Sinwell for himself."

Mac's dream adversary. Though he had told her the dream arose from a historical account, he hadn't named the infamous earl or the British earldom for which Wynland had committed murder.

"I'm in there." Mac nodded at the book.

Kennedy raised an eyebrow.

"Look at the pages I marked."

A half dozen slips protruded from the book. She opened to the first and skimmed the text. There it was: Sir Arthur Crosley. Okay, so someone in the past had first claim to a semblance of MacArthur Crosley's name. What proof was that? She read on. With the King of England's blessing, the errant knight pledged himself to the safekeeping of orphaned brothers John and Harold Wynland. She read the remaining passages, the last a single sentence that told of Sir Arthur's disappearance prior to the boys' fiery deaths.

Kennedy set the book on the bedside table. "You're telling me you're Sir Arthur?"

"I am."

"Mac, just because your name—"

"When I first read it, there was no mention of Crosley. His name—my name—appeared only after the dreams began. And when the book says I disappeared, guess where I went."

*Pound,* went her headache.

"That's when I came out of the coma, Ken."

Worse and worse. "But you've reported having these dreams since then. If what you say is true, where are *those* experiences documented?"

"They're not. Though I've returned four times since the coma, the present keeps pulling me back before I can save the boys from that murderer." Fury brightened his eyes a moment before his gaze emptied.

"Mac?"

"Fifty waking hours isn't enough, not even a hundred. It takes more."

This explained the man before her whose years came nowhere near the age grooving his face. "Two hundred?"

"It's a start."

She held up a hand. "The truth. How many hours?"

"Two hundred seventeen."

She came off the stool as if slung from it. "You know how dangerous—"

"Better than anyone."

He didn't look like a madman, but he had to be. "You're forcing it, aren't you? You could have slept days ago, but you won't let yourself."

"Dead on."

Kennedy reached to rake fingers through her hair, but stopped mid-air. There was too little left beneath the cap, stragglers that served as painful reminders of her former self. She laid a hand to Mac's arm. "You're going to kill yourself."

His smile was almost genuine. "That's the idea."

Over-the-edge crazy. Deciding her efforts were better spent admitting him to the university hospital, she straightened.

"I'm not going," Mac said.

For all his delusions, he could still read her like a book. "Please, Mac, you have to."

"It's my way out."

*Pound. Pound.* "You think I'm just going to stand by and let you die?"

"You don't have a say in it."

"But you're my patient. I can't—"

"You think I like living in this thing?" He gripped the arms of his wheelchair. "When I lost my legs, I lost everything—my wife, my boys, my career. All I do is take up space, and I'm tired of it. You have no idea what it's like."

Didn't she? Her world was crumbling, and though she had no choice as to whether tomorrow came, he did.

His gaze swept to her cap, and he muttered a curse. "I'm sorry, Ken."

She crossed the observation room and stared through the window at the monitoring equipment.

"How's the chemo going?"

She tossed her head and achingly acknowledged how much she missed the weight of her hair. "It's going well." A lie. There had been progress early on, but the tumor was gaining ground.

"The truth, Ken," he turned her own words against her.

She swung around. "This isn't about me."

"You're wrong." He wheeled toward her. "My dream is a way out of the hell I'm living. And it could be yours."

Nuts. Positively nuts.

He rolled to a halt. "Not my dream, of course. Something of your own choosing."

*Pound. Pound. Pound.* She stepped around him. "I need to take something for this headache."

"You think I'm crazy."

She looked over her shoulder. "I'll be back in a few minutes, and we'll discuss this some more."

After a long moment, he said, "Sure. Can I borrow your pen?"

She tossed it to him and steered a course to the washroom where she gulped down the pills prescribed for just such reminders of her tumor.

Though she rarely did more than glance in the mirror, she searched her features: sunken eyes, ashen skin, pinched mouth, the hollows beneath her cheeks evidence of her twenty-pound weight loss. As for the hair sweeping her brow, it and the knit cap to which the strands were attached was a gift from her well-meaning mother. She looked almost as bad as Mac, far from the green-eyed "looker" she had been called before...

Almost wishing she was as crazy as Mac, she hurried to her office. After being reassured two orderlies were on their way, she returned to the sleep room. It was empty. "No." She groaned. "Don't do this, Mac."

She ran down the corridor, through the reception area, and out the glass doors into the balm of a Los Angeles summer night, but there was no sign of Mac or the cab that had delivered him to the clinic. Where had he gone? It would be a place where no one knew him, where he wouldn't be bothered if he didn't show his face for days. Unfortunately, the possibilities could run into the thousands.

What about the cab? If she could find the company he had used, perhaps she could discover where they had taken him.

She went back inside and, in the sleep room, saw the pen Mac had borrowed on the bedside table, beneath it his book. He had forgotten it. Or had he?

She opened *The Sins of the Earl of Sinwell*. If not that she recognized Mac's handwriting, she would have flipped past the inscription on the inside cover. She slid her glasses on. *Ken*, it read, *think of this as a postcard. Your friend, Mac*

"Oh, Mac." Try though she might, she knew that if she found him it would be too late. But knowing it and accepting it were two different things. Keeping an eye closed against the pain hammering at her head, she tucked the book under an arm and hurried to her office.

# 2

*A WAY OUT.*

Mac's words of a month ago whispered to Kennedy as she stared at the reflection of a woman she recognized less each day. Radiation and chemotherapy had taken the last of her hair. And for what? The hope she could beat unbeatable odds. Four weeks, eight at the outside, Kennedy Plain, twenty-eight years young, would go out with a whimper.

"A way out," she muttered. "Crazy Mac."

She tightened the belt of her robe and crossed her living room to the glass doors of her condo. A quarter mile out, waves battered the rocky beach, swept sand in and dragged it out again. Stepping onto the balcony, she sighed as cool morning air caressed her bare scalp. It was just what she needed to get through another waking hour. How many was she up to? She glanced at her watch. Seventy-two, meaning it was Monday.

Since forced to take medical leave two weeks ago, she had found it increasingly difficult to track her days—until this past Friday when she began marking time by the hour.

She turned back inside. The journal lay on her desk on a pile of paperwork that represented eighteen months of research. Research that would molder in some forgotten closet if the clinic director had his way. But she wouldn't let that happen. If it killed her—ha!—she would conclude her study with data culled from her own dream experiences.

She dropped into the desk chair and reached for the journal. It would be her fourth entry, likely the last before her self-imposed sleep deprivation compelled her to sleep. With a quaking hand, she wrote:

*8:25 a.m. Seventy-two waking hours. Not sure I can make it to ninety-six. Hands trembling, eyes burning, headache worsening, nauseated. No hallucinations, some memory lapses. Can't stop thinking about Mac.*

She lifted the pen and recalled the night he had borrowed it. For four days she had clung to the hope he lived, but on the fifth day, his lifeless body was found in an abandoned warehouse.

Kennedy swallowed hard. "Wherever you are, I pray you've finally found peace." She rested her forehead in her hand and squeezed her eyes closed. Like a thief, sleep reached for her.

She jumped up and steadied herself with a hand on the chair. "Twenty-four hours," she murmured. Could she do it? Her chronic insomnia having never exceeded sixty, she was ahead by twelve, but another twenty-four?

What she needed was a good book. Unfortunately, as her library consisted mostly of textbooks and periodicals, the best she could do was *The Sins of the Earl of Sinwell*. She eyed it where it lay on the sofa table. It had to be less dry than her other choices.

Sliding on her glasses, she retrieved the book and fingered the ridges and recesses of the worn title, then opened past Mac's inscription to the first chapter. "1373," she read aloud as she began to walk the room.

An hour later, she gave up. Not because the reading was dry, but her comprehension was nearly nil. One thing was clear from the little she had learned about Fulke Wynland, the Earl of Sinwell: he had no conscience. Not only was he suspected of having a hand in the accident that killed his brother, the Earl of Sinwell, but as a military advisor during the "Hundred Years War," he had been party to the atrocious massacre of men, women, and children following a siege on the city of Limoges. So what chance had two little boys, aged four and six?

She trudged into the kitchen, opened the freezer, and stuck her face into it. Frigid air returning her to wakefulness, she congratulated herself on that bit of genius and closed the door. "And caffeine will do it one better," she murmured.

After the coffee maker sputtered its last, putting an exclamation mark on the smell of freshly brewed coffee, Kennedy carried the pot to her cup with a hand that shook so violently that nearly as much made it on the counter as in the cup. When the caffeine kicked in on her third serving, she reached for Mac's book.

The seventh chapter, marked by a slip of paper, held a scant introduction to Sir Arthur Crosley. Then came the mysterious Lady Lark and a color illustration of the type of clothing a fourteenth-century lady might wear—a pale yellow gown with fitted bodice and long flowing sleeves, a hair veil secured by a tiara set with red and blue jewels, and flat-soled shoes with ridiculously long toes.

Kennedy returned to the text. According to the author, Lady Lark made her first appearance at King Edward III's court in 1372. No one knew where she came from, her surname, age, or whether she was of the nobility. The only thing for certain was that the king wasted no time numbering her among his mistresses.

During the summer of 1373, two months after appointing Sir Arthur Crosley to watch over the Wynland boys, King Edward dispatched Lady Lark to Sinwell to care for the motherless children. Though it was suggested his other mistress, the ambitious Alice Perrers, had worked her influence over Edward in order to rid herself of a rival, the author was more given to the belief that the king had simply tired of Lady Lark.

Kennedy trudged past the sofa, pushed her glasses up, and rubbed her eyes. She resettled the glasses.

On the approach to the castle of Brynwood Spire where the boys resided, Lady Lark's baggage train was attacked and her entourage murdered. Of the lady herself, no trace was ever found. The one responsible for the carnage: Fulke Wynland, the author suggested. Sir Arthur Crosley, fearing for the boys' lives, spirited them away that very day...

Kennedy didn't recall reading this particular passage at the clinic, and there was no slip of paper to mark its reference to Sir Arthur. Likely,

Mac had lost the marker without realizing it. However, when she dug further into the book, she found three other unmarked references. Odd, especially as they were more significant than the ones Mac had asked her to read. But nothing compared to the final reference near the end of the book. She read it twice. Hadn't Sir Arthur disappeared at book's end? Not according to this passage that stated that, following two weeks of pursuit, Wynland overtook him. Swords were drawn and the knight's life severed by the man who would be earl.

Of course, it *was* a month since she had read the passages. Was that it? Or was she delusional? She shrugged off the niggling at the back of her mind and, a short while later, slammed the book on Wynland's ascension to "earl" following the deaths of his nephews in a fire of unknown origin.

"Murderer," she muttered. And caught her toe on the sofa table. The book flew from her hand and landed on the floor at about the same time she did. It should have hurt, but she was too numb to feel anything but relief at gaining a prone position.

*Get up, walk it off. Only ten hours to go.* She forced her head up. Seeing the book had fallen open to Mac's inscription, she pulled it toward her, read his scrawled inscription, and pressed her forehead to the carpet. "A postcard, Mac?"

*Don't close your eyes.* But she was too busy melting into the carpet to give more than a glancing thought to hooking herself up to the EEG she had borrowed from the clinic. Sleep descended, scattering her thoughts here, there, everywhere—until they met the enigmatic Lady Lark.

What would it have been like to live in an era of knights and castles? To have been of the privileged class? To dress in gowns with beautiful bodices and long flowing sleeves? To be the mistress of a mighty king? To travel across country in a baggage train with an entourage? Imagine that…

The sweet smell of earth, the breath of a breeze, a gentle tapping against her cheek. Wondering who disturbed her, Kennedy opened her eyes. Not who, but what. She stared through the hair fluttering across her face—thick, dark, sprung with wave, the likes of which she hadn't seen in a long time. A tremor of expectation swept her, but she let it go no further.

This was a dream. When she awakened, not a single strand would remain. She fingered the darkness and lingeringly pushed it out of her eyes. There was something silken at her forehead and, above that, a metal band encircled her head. She drew the former forward and stared at what appeared to be a veil.

A moan sounded from somewhere nearby, and she pushed the veil aside. Only then, with a forest spread before her, did she realize she was prostrate. Where had her dreaming taken her to this time? And what was the vibration beneath her cheek?

She rolled onto her back and stared up at a canopy of trees. It was beautiful the way the sunlight pierced the leaves, thrusting shafts of light into a place that might otherwise appear sinister. There was the twitter of birds and, somewhere, the babble of a brook. It was vibrant, as if—

A mordant scent struck her, causing the dream to veer in a direction she preferred it didn't go. She sat up and caught her breath. Twenty or more feet out, the bodies of a dozen men were gored and grotesquely bent, most conspicuously two draped across an overturned wagon. And there was more. She felt it, feared it, tried to ignore it, but looked around. Behind her lay a horse, its teeth bared in death, its rider pinned beneath, the man's chest sliced open and his arm nearly severed.

Kennedy clenched her teeth and lowered her gaze to where the blood of beast and man pooled on the ground. It spread outward, running in rivulets toward her. Nausea rose as she followed its path to the skirt of her dress. Knee to ankle, crimson saturated the pale yellow fabric, causing it to adhere to her skin.

Not a dream. A nightmare.

She scrambled to her feet.

"My lady?" someone croaked.

Kennedy forced herself to look among the bodies. Had she ever before had such a vivid dream? Swallowing hard, she settled her gaze on the man beneath the horse who stared at her through half-hooded eyes.

"My lady…are you…?" He reached with his uninjured arm.

She knew she ought to flee before her imagination transformed him into something more heinous, but she couldn't turn her back on him. Too, this was only a dream. Though it might cause her to awaken in a cold sweat, that was the worst she would suffer.

When she dropped to her knees beside the man, she saw that, though he had closed his eyes, his wheezing chest told he still lived.

"What can I do?" she asked.

"I saw the miscreant's…device." His thick accent sounded almost British.

"Device?"

"Had his medallion…in my hand." He spread his empty fingers. "Upon it a wyvern…two-headed…above a shield…bend sinister."

"I'm sorry, I don't understand."

He lifted his lids. His eyes, pinpoints of pain, traced her face. "You are not my lady."

"No, I—"

He caught hold of her arm. "What have you done with her?"

For a man about to die, he exhibited incredible strength. "I don't know what you're talking about."

He dragged her toward him, affording her a close-up of his death mask. "You come to steal from the dead," he spat, flecking her with saliva.

A more morbid dream Kennedy could not recall. She wrenched backward and broke free, but not before he tore the veil from her hair.

She shot to her feet and nearly tripped over her hem. Why was the dress so long? And why was she wearing something like this in the middle of a forest?

Once more, she felt the vibration through the ground. It was stronger. Nearer. Horses? From which direction?

She whipped her head to the side and the breeze caught her hair, sifting it across her face and into her eyes. Though she longed to pause and relish the feel of it, something bad was coming.

*It's only a dream. Stay put and get it over with, and you'll be awake in no time.* But she couldn't. Heart pounding, she gathered her hair high at the back of her head, knotted it, and hiked up her skirt.

As in the days before her illness, she sped across the ground, vaulted over debris and fallen trees, and nearly forgot the reason she ran. She thrilled to the rush of blood and tightening of her lungs, the strength in her calves and thighs. The only thing missing was a decent pair of running shoes.

When a shout resounded through the trees, she glanced over her shoulder. A horse and rider bore down on her. She pumped her legs harder, but she was no match for the four-legged beast that drew so near she could hear its breath.

*Wake up!* she silently called to where she lay sleeping. *Open your eyes!* Though a thread of consciousness often allowed her to talk her way out of disturbing dreams, her pleas went unanswered. Thus, she veered right, seized a branch from the ground, and whirled around.

Her pursuer reined in his horse, scattering leaves and dirt, and guided the animal sideways to look down at her. Clad in metal neck to toe—a jangling, clanking get-up that sounded with each quiver of his horse—he stared at her out of eyes so blue she knew her imagination was in overdrive. Though her dream had neglected to place a helmet on his head, it had made sure there was a sword at his side.

*Only a dream. He can cut you in two and you'll awaken whole.* At least, as whole as a person with a death sentence hanging over her head...

"You do not need that." His voice was deep and accented, though of a more precise nature than the dying man who had mistaken her for his lady. "You have naught to fear from me."

Of course she didn't. He was only a figment, though from where he had originated she had no idea. But with those cheekbones, shoulder-length blond hair, and closely clipped beard and moustache, he was likely a belly-button-bearing model from a billboard she passed on her way to the university.

"Lady Lark?"

She blinked, then nearly laughed at the realization she had dreamed herself into the mysterious lady of Mac's book. What was the year? 1373? As for this behemoth, was he Fulke Wynland? He had to be. Forget that he was blonde rather than darkly sinister as she had imagined, that his eyes were blue, rather than bottomless black. He was surely the one responsible for the carnage to which she had awakened, not to mention the death of his nephews and the disappearance of the king's mistress—the same woman he mistook her for.

She jabbed the branch at him in hopes it would send horse and rider back to wherever they had come from.

The animal rolled its huge eyes, reminding her of the one time she had ridden a horse, a mistake that culminated in her missing a barbed wire fence by inches.

"I am Lord Wynland of Brynwood Spire."

And beneath his armor he probably wore a medallion with a two-headed—what was it? Wyvern? "Stay back!"

"I am King Edward's man. Be assured, no harm will befall you."

She swung the branch. "I'll brain you!"

He frowned deeply, as if her words were foreign, as if her subconscious had not formed him from the pages of an old book. "After what you have seen, my lady, 'tis natural you would suffer hysterics."

"Oh, puh-lease!"

He lowered his gaze over her. "You are injured?"

No sooner did she follow his gaze to her bloodied skirt than he lunged, seized hold of the branch, and used it to haul her toward him.

Kennedy let go, but not before he caught her arm. Handling her as if she were a child rather than a woman who topped out at five foot eight, Wynland lifted her off her feet and deposited her on his saddle between his thighs.

She reached for his face. Unlike her hair, she hadn't dreamed herself a set of long nails, and she fell short by the split second it took him to capture her wrist and grip it with the other.

"Calm yourself!"

She strained, kicked, bit—and got a mouthful of metal links that made her teeth peal with pain.

"Cease, else I shall bind you hand and foot!"

Before or after he killed her? She threw her head back and got a closer look at her version of Fulke Wynland. Not model material after all. As blue as his eyes were, his face was flawed. A scar split his left eyebrow, nose had a slight bend, and the jaw visible beneath his beard was mildly pocked as if from adolescent acne or a childhood illness. Handsome? Definitely not. Rugged? Beyond. Deadly? Ever so.

Realizing her best hope was to catch him off guard, she forced herself to relax.

Wynland gave a grunt of satisfaction, reached down, and yanked up her skirt.

Horrified that her dream was taking a more lurid turn, she renewed her struggle.

The horse snorted and danced around, but neither Kennedy nor the skittish animal turned Wynland from his intent. His large hand slid from her ankle to her calf to her knee.

It was then she felt the draft and realized that, somewhere between reality and dream, she had lost her underwear.

When his hand spanned her thigh, she opened her mouth to scream, but just as quickly as the assault began, it ended. He thrust her skirt down and smiled—if that wicked twist of his lips could be called a smile. "Worry not, my lady, I place too high a value on my health to risk it with you."

What, exactly, did he mean? That she was promiscuous? Diseased? Of course, she did portray a king's mistress...

"Whose blood if not yours?" Wynland asked.

That was why he had touched her? She didn't know the man's name, only that he had rejected her as being his lady. She frowned. How was that? If she was Lady Lark, why had one of the players in this dream not recognized her?

"Whose?" he growled.

She shifted around to fully face Wynland. "What does it matter?"

His lids narrowed. "A soldier—nay, a dozen—bled their last to defend you. What does it matter who they were? Who their wives and children are?"

When he put it that way...But she wasn't the villain, *he* was. Those men were dead because he had ordered it. Or done it himself. "Put me down."

"What befell your escort?"

Why the pretense when he meant to kill her? Or did he? According to Mac's book, no trace of Lady Lark was ever found. Had Wynland allowed her to live—for a while, at least?

*It's a dream!*

Though she knew he was only smoke floating about her mind, she detested him for the sins of the man after whom she had fashioned him. "Why don't *you* tell *me* what happened to my escort?" She was bold, and it felt good, so like her old self before this thing in her head pulled the life out from under her.

Wynland's face darkened. "You think I am responsible?"

"If the shoe fits..."

Confusion slipped through his anger. "What shoe?"

One would think she had truly hopped back in time. If this was anything like what Mac experienced, no wonder he thought it was real. She only hoped that when she awakened she would remember the outlandish dream long enough to record it. "You don't want me at Burnwood."

"*Brynwood*, and, nay, I do not. But I assure you, had I wished you dead, we would not be having this conversation."

Nothing came between him and what he wanted, including his nephews. The deaths those little boys had suffered incited Kennedy further. "Just goes to show that if you want something done right, do it yourself."

He puller her closer. "If you have anything else to say to me, my lady, you would do well to choose your words carefully."

His hands on her, thighs on either side of her, and breath on her face, were almost enough to make her believe he was real. *Only a figment. He holds no more power over you than the next dream.*

"Do you understand?"

"What is there not to understand?"

He stared at her, then released her arms and turned her forward. Before she could gulp down the view from atop the horse, he gripped an arm around her waist and spurred the animal through the trees.

She was riding sidesaddle. How much worse could it get? Though she tried to shut out memories of her last horse ride, she remembered exactly how bad it could get. She squeezed her eyes closed. Where was Wynland taking her? And if murder was on his mind, why the stay of execution? No one would hear if she cried out—

He wasn't alone. The thundering of hooves had surely been of many riders, meaning others could have seen her flight. Fortunate for her, unfortunate for Wynland.

She opened her eyes. Trees sped by at breakneck blur, the forest floor rose and fell, shafts of sunlight blinded.

She retreated behind her lids again and was all the more aware of the hard body at her back and the muscled arm against her abdomen, the sensation so real she felt the beat of Wynland's heart through his armor. She chalked it up to it being a long time since she had been in a man's arms, which was more her fault than her ex-husband's. Graham would have held her if she had let him, but the marriage had coughed its last long before the onset of her illness. Kennedy Huntworth was no more—not that she had gone by her married name. At the urging of Graham's mother, she had retained her maiden name for "professional purposes." In the end, it had worked out for the best. Or was it the worst?

Wynland dragged his horse to a halt, and a grateful Kennedy opened her eyes, only to wish she hadn't.

# 3

He had returned her to the gore, the smell of butchery. Add to that twenty armored men who moved among the dead, impervious to the horror, it should have awakened her in a cold sweat. Instead, the dream gripped her more fiercely.

One of the soldiers, a man who aspired to just over five feet, stepped from the upset wagon. Like several of the others, but unlike Wynland, he wore a white sleeveless shirt over his armor, the breast embroidered with a green shield dissected by a black cross. Perched on the shield was something like a dragon.

The man shook his head. "All dead, my lord."

Kennedy searched out the one who had spoken of the medallion. He stared wide, but he had seen his last living day.

"Thieves?' Wynland asked.

The soldier strained his neck to look up at him. "'Twould appear so, my lord. The king's men have been stripped of armor and weaponry, their horses taken and, excepting a trunk beneath the wagon, all of the lady's belongings are gone."

"You have searched the attackers' bodies?"

"There are none to search, my lord. More, the ground is bloodied only where the king's men lie."

Kennedy felt Wynland's disbelief. He probably hadn't expected his hitmen to fare so well against the king's soldiers. How convenient for him.

"'Tis like nothing I have seen," the soldier said. "As if—"

"—they knew their attackers," Wynland finished, then more gruffly, "Is that how 'twas, Lady Lark?"

His charade was for the benefit of his men, but as much as she wanted to set the fools right, she knew it was a battle best left for when Wynland wasn't so near. She looked over her shoulder. "I don't recall."

His left eyebrow arched on either side of the scar, forming a sinister M. "Do you not?"

"I...hit my head." She rubbed a spot above her right ear.

"You were attacked?"

Kennedy feigned offense. "You ask that with all this carnage?"

"I ask it when none but you survived."

It was strange, but this *was* a dream. "My injury occurred when the wagon overturned." She pointed at it.

"You were in *that* wagon?"

Apparently not. A carriage, then? She didn't see one, though that didn't mean there hadn't been a carriage prior to the attack. What about a horse? Had ladies in this age travelled on the beasts?

"Lady Lark?"

She sighed. "Yes, that wagon."

"Regardless of what you are, have been, or nevermore will be to the king," Wynland bit, "'tis difficult to believe Edward would have so little regard for the woman he chose to care for my nephews that he sent her to Brynwood in a baggage wagon."

Kennedy shrugged. "I'm not a horse person."

His regard sharpened as if he saw Kennedy Plain past Lady Lark. Then, with one fluid move, he swung out of the saddle and dropped to the ground. Tall as a smoggy Los Angeles day was long, he strode toward the wagon.

That was it? He was going to leave her sidesaddle on an animal that surely sensed her fear? However, as much as she wanted to call him back and ask for help in dismounting, pride wouldn't allow it. Nor the possibility of escape.

She eyed the horse. Surely she need only nudge it with her heels? Though she hated the idea, she had nothing to lose but the fast-fading memory she would have upon awakening. She grabbed the saddle horn and swung a leg over the other side of the horse. When the long dress fought her, making a good case for riding sidesaddle, she hitched up the skirt, scooted back, and reached her feet to the stirrups. She was on the tall side, but Wynland's legs outdistanced hers.

The stirrups weren't necessary, were they? She lifted the reins and jabbed her heels into the horse's sides. Nothing. She snapped the reins, dug her heels deeper. The horse shifted its weight. She leaned forward. "Come on, big guy, show me how it's done."

The horse tossed its massive head and issued a snort suggestive of laughter.

"You are thinking of leaving?"

Kennedy looked around and saw Wynland approach at a leisurely pace indicative of the confidence he placed in his trusty steed.

He halted alongside her. "He answers only to me."

Kennedy straightened. "I had to try."

He lowered his gaze down her leg. "The king may enjoy such brazen displays, Lady Lark, but you are at Sinwell and such behavior will not be tolerated."

She looked down her leg and did a double-take, though not because of any sort of indecency. The shoes that had served so poorly during her flight from Wynland were pointed and three inches too long, just like the ones illustrated in *The Sins of the Earl of Sinwell*. So that was where her imagination had gone to outfit her...

"Cover yourself," Wynland ordered.

She glanced at him, then looked down again. Above the shoe, a thick sock pooled around her ankle. Higher, a stretch of bare calf was visible. She could use a shave, but she was hardly brazen. Certainly not by twenty-first century standards. The prude! She reached down and tugged the hem of her skirt, but it was no use. In straddling the horse, there wasn't enough material to cover her legs.

She shrugged. "I tried."

Wynland scowled and thrust something at her. "Your veil and circlet, I presume."

Air trembled through the white gossamer, sunlight ignited red and blue jewels set in the gold wire band he called a circlet. Remembering how she had lost them, Kennedy glanced at the soldier. His eyes were no longer open. Had Wynland closed them?

"I am curious as to how the king's man came to be in possession of these," Wynland said.

She took them. "I was trying to help him." She tried, but failed, to put images of the encounter from her mind.

"Continue."

She pulled the veil through her fingers. "And I removed them."

"For what purpose?"

She draped the veil over her upswept hair and settled the circlet over it.

His lids narrowed again. "Clearly, you are unaccustomed to such manner of headdress, my lady. Tell me of your maid."

Lady Lark had one?

"Surely you did not set out from London without one."

"I...yes, I had one."

"Where is she?"

Kennedy looked past Wynland, but searched no further than the nearest fallen soldier, a man far from whole. She swept her gaze back to blue.

"Thirteen lie dead," Wynland said, "but none amongst them is a woman. What befell your maid?"

"I must not have brought her with me after all."

His teeth snapped. "You wish me to believe the king not only set you upon the road in a wagon, but did not have a maid accompany you?"

He thought her a flake or a liar—or disoriented. Falling back on her feigned injury, she touched her head. "I'm not thinking straight right now."

Clouds stormed his eyes. "You fear the wrong one."

So he thought she played dumb because of her distrust of him. That would work. "*Do I?*"

A humorless rumble rose from him. "You think you have no enemies, Lady Lark? A woman who tried to displace the grasping Alice Perrers?"

Though Mac's book had speculated that the king's favored mistress might have been responsible for Lady Lark being sent from court, there the speculation ended. Had this Perrers woman taken it a step further? A possibility, but Kennedy thought it was more likely Wynland's attempt to throw her off his scent.

"How convenient you were in the neighborhood and able to come to my aid so quickly," she hazarded.

With what sounded like an obscenity, though she had never heard the word, he caught her wrist. "Neither I, nor my men, were near when this happened. A villager brought tale of the attack to Brynwood."

As she looked into his anger, she had the feeling it cost him dearly to defend himself. Odd he should feel the need to do so with a woman for whom he had such low regard. Of course, Lady Lark was the king's mistress. He wouldn't want Edward gunning for him.

He released her and put a foot in a stirrup. Like rain on a metal roof, his armor rang against the quiet of the forest as he swung up behind her.

Expecting him to try to turn her back to sidesaddle, Kennedy clamped her thighs against the horse. However, Wynland put an arm on either side of her, took the reins, and guided his horse to where his men gathered near the wagon.

Kennedy was disturbed by the looks that came her way, from surprise to lewd appreciation to affront.

"Sir George," Wynland called.

The man stepped forward. "My lord?"

"Divide your men and search the demesne. I want the murdering thieves found."

Tempted to tell the man to look no further than his lord, Kennedy bit her tongue.

"After I have delivered the lady to Brynwood, I will return with more men."

How stilted Wynland's speech sounded. A few contractions here and there would go a long way to remedying the problem.

As Sir George returned to his men, Kennedy was surprised to discover that none of them was any more familiar than Wynland. Odd. Where had she seen these faces that she would unknowingly store them in her memory? And what about their voices? Though, on occasion, she had been around British accents, these weren't quite the same.

Mac had said he didn't know the people in his dreams. Though Kennedy hadn't achieved his level of sleep deprivation, she guessed this was analogous to what he had experienced.

*Oh, please, let me remember just one tenth of this when I wake!* Unfortunately, the likelihood of doing so was hampered by the fact she hadn't hooked up to the EEG. If she had, the alarm rigged to awaken her following REM sleep would have facilitated her recall. Now she was dependent on luck.

"Gain your mount, Squire James," Wynland called.

Kennedy saw a young man hasten from the gathering and swing into his saddle. He also wore a sleeveless shirt, but it bore a beast that was half-eagle, half-lion. Why two different coat of arms? Did the eagle-lion belong to Wynland, the dragon to his deceased brother?

Wynland guided his horse through the maze of dead and, once clear, fastened an arm around Kennedy and let the animal run.

Kennedy watched as they passed from forest to open meadow. To the edge in the distance, lush vegetation filled the eye and was capped by skies so blue that the cirrus streaking it could not dampen its radiance. Blankets of wildflowers undulated color amid greater green, towering trees stood sentinel over the bordering forest, sheep dotted a hill like a thousand tiny clouds come to ground. And the scent? Like a hundred Carolina mornings rolled into one. How incredibly removed it was from the glass, concrete, and metal that sprouted from Los Angeles, the smog that burned her eyes. But nothing prepared her for the fairy tale edifice that jagged the sky. Gait by gait, its white walls grew to immense proportions, beat by beat, its spires sharpened. Brynwood Spire.

Built on a hill, the castle stood guard over a walled city jutting to the left. Black on green flags flapped from spires, sunlight on armor flashed silver atop the walls, and from the center of the castle arose a building with towers in each corner. Although the structure should have appeared out of place against the pristine countryside, it seemed as much a part of the scenery as the grass and trees. Storybook perfect—except for the two little boys murdered within those walls.

Kennedy pondered the man who held her. How could he order the deaths of innocent children? It was evil. To have lived during the Middle Ages must have been to live a nightmare. She couldn't imagine—

Couldn't she? This *was* a dream, every crumb fallen from things and people forgotten in some deep crack in her memory.

As Wynland guided his horse onto a forty-foot span of bridge raised above a rushing river, Kennedy remembered the young man who had trailed them throughout the ride, and only because of the clatter of hooves that joined theirs.

A soldier was at the far end of the bridge, motionless until they were nearly upon him. His gaze on Wynland, he said with a deferential nod, "All is quiet, my lord."

With a spur of heels, Wynland guided the horse onto the beaten path that wended upward to the castle. Shortly, they crossed another bridge over what Kennedy guessed was a moat. That was where the fairy tale took a sharp turn off the page. Who knew what pestilence the fetid muck harbored?

Shouts drew her regard overhead. Several men leaned out of recesses in the upper wall and called greetings to Wynland, welcoming his return as if he had been gone days rather than hours. In silence, he directed his horse beneath the arched entrance and through a shaft outfitted with not one but three sets of doors three times the height of a man and bounded by soldiers.

If the rest of the castle was as well-manned, no one came or went unchecked. That included Kennedy. Though all were quick to give Wynland their attention, they stole furtive glances at her. Did they know of the attack on Lady Lark's entourage? Was that behind their interest? Or was it her appearance? The blood on her skirt and her straddling of the horse that revealed a bit of leg?

A clamor reached Kennedy in advance of their exit from the shaft, but she was unprepared for the flurry of activity in the courtyard they entered. People dressed in the clothes of common folk were everywhere, along with dogs, horses, wagons, contraptions—one that looked like an enormous grinding wheel. From the far left came the sound of metal being struck. To the right, a glowing fire radiated enough heat to work up a sweat.

Kennedy could hardly believe the depth of imagination that had concocted such a fabulous dream, especially considering her limited knowledge of history.

There were more shouted greetings, nods, gap-toothed smiles, arms raised in recognition of the man who plotted a heinous act to assure his ascendancy to earl. Although Kennedy couldn't imagine these people cared for him, he certainly had their respect—likely through fear.

Wynland ushered his horse beneath a portal and into another courtyard. It also teemed with laborers. In one corner, women bent over immense barrels, some stirring, others scrubbing on what looked like washboards. Opposite, teenage girls hung strips of red cloth from a clothesline stretched overhead. In the middle of the courtyard stood a small building open on one side, the man inside working amid rows of candles.

"M'lord, m'lord!" A smudge-faced, wild-haired boy bounded into Wynland's path.

He jerked the reins and Kennedy wondered what harsh words he would speak.

"Tell the tale, m'lord," the boy implored with lit blue eyes. "How many did ye kill?"

*Oh, about a dozen.*

To her surprise, Wynland leaned down and ruffled the child's fair hair. "None yet, Jeremy."

Disappointment shrunk the boy's brow, reminding her of someone. Finally, she had placed a person in her dream—sort of. Jeremy was familiar, but she didn't know where she had seen him.

"Not even one, m'lord?"

"There were none to kill."

Jeremy propped his hands on his hips. "Ye'll not let the brigands go, will ye?"

"You know I will not."

With a grin that revealed he was short a front tooth, the boy turned his gaze on Kennedy. "Who is that, m'lord?"

"'Tis Lady Lark come to care for John and Harold."

With wide eyes and a mouth to match, Jeremy said, "M'lady is most fair. Not at all what John and Harry feared."

Kennedy had to smile. Not since before her illness had she received such a sincere compliment.

"Have ye something for me, m'lord?"

Wynland tossed a coin to him, and the boy snatched it from the air with a greasy fist. Hooting with joy, he spun and disappeared among the many.

"Your new home," Wynland said, "Brynwood Spire."

Kennedy looked up at the building at the center of the castle. Though impossible to overlook, that was what she had done, engrossed as she was with the activity before the grandiose structure. Six stories high, as many wide, its top edge notched all around, it gave new meaning to her notion of how a castle should look.

"It's…" She shook her head. "…big."

"You expected less?"

She looked around. "Actually, I hadn't thought much about it."

"Then you ought to. The earldom of Sinwell is vital to England—strategically located, fertile, and among the wealthiest."

*And aren't you just dying to get your hands on it?* "I'll keep that in mind."

Wynland urged his horse forward and reined in before a long flight of steps that led up to what she assumed was the entrance. He dismounted and passed the reins to Squire James who waited for him. "I will be gone but a few minutes. See that my horse is watered and ready to ride when I return."

"Aye, my lord."

My lord this, my lord that. Was it really necessary?

"Lady Lark." Wynland raised his arms.

Tempted as she was to refuse his help, Kennedy leaned toward him. His great hands gripped her waist and lifted her down. No sooner did her feet touch ground than he released her and turned toward the steps.

He probably feared he would catch something from her as he had earlier alluded. Trying not to feel the warm imprint of his hands, she lifted her skirt and followed him. Dozens of steep steps later, she caught up with him at the top landing. Feeling deep appreciation for whoever had invented the elevator, she looked to Wynland and found him studying her as if she were a one-thousand piece puzzle he must put together without a picture to guide him.

"A moment," he said and lifted the circlet from her head. He adjusted the veil that hung longer on one side and resettled the circlet.

"Thank you," Kennedy murmured.

He looked like he might smile. "So you do know something of propriety." Before she could concoct a comeback, he turned his back on her. "Come, my mother will wish to receive you."

Had Mac's book mentioned Wynland's mother? If so, either the reference was obscure or Kennedy had been too tired to store the information.

The two soldiers who stood guard at the massive doors offered the usual "My lord," gave Kennedy the once-over, and pulled the doors open.

Inside, Wynland allowed her only a cursory examination of her surroundings before he struck out across the stone floor—not that more was needed. The entrance hall was stark, nothing extraordinary about it. So what had happened to the run of imagination that had brought her this far?

"Brother!" someone called. Descending a stairway was a man whose resemblance to the one he called "brother" seemed limited to hair color and build. Younger than Wynland by five or so years, his features were more handsome, eyes darker, and when he stepped off the stairs she saw he was shorter by several inches. "What news do you bring?"

"They are all dead, excepting Lady Lark." Wynland stepped to the side to reveal Kennedy.

Surprise shot across the man's face. "Lady Lark?" His gaze traveled down her, but when it returned to her face he had regained his composure.

"Lady Lark," Wynland said, "my brother, Richard Wynland, Baron of Kinsey."

Before Kennedy could respond, Richard demanded, "What of the attackers?"

"Gone." Wynland began to ascend the stairs.

Richard looked to Kennedy again, allowed her a glimpse of what might pass as dislike, then motioned her to precede him.

*Don't take it personally. It's just the stuff of dreams.* She stepped forward. This stairway was less imposing than the first, and she soon found herself in a room so immense, so fabulously furnished, and so alive with the people of this era that she halted.

Brightly painted pillars supported an arched ceiling splashed with vibrant green, black, and gold. Tapestries around the walls depicted lovers in a garden, battling knights, and a dragon perched on a shield like those on the shirts worn by Sinwell's men. A fireplace the size of her spare bedroom was fueled by enormous logs. And the men and women, with their aristocratic deportment and splendid costumes—the men in shirts over hose and pointed shoes—looked as if they had walked off a movie set. But what was hay doing on the floor? Were they expecting cows?

An older woman wearing an ivory dress with sleeves that fell from her wrists to her calves, appeared in a fog of perfume that made Kennedy wince. "Lady Lark?" Her voice was so melodious it could have been an instrument.

This had to be Wynland's mother. She was petite, but there was no mistaking the resemblance, from the blonde hair encased in strange wire cylinders on either side of her head to intense blue eyes to soaring cheekbones.

Kennedy stuck out a hand. "Yes, I'm Lady Lark."

As if a handshake was beneath her, the woman frowned.

Remembering another time, another place, another woman who had made her feel ten inches tall, Kennedy stole a glance at Wynland where he stood beside his mother. His expression was all the confirmation needed that a handshake was not how things were done here.

She lowered her arm. If they hadn't shook hands back then—now—how had they greeted one another?

"I am Lady Aveline, Lord Wynland's mother."

"A pleasure to meet you."

Another frown, then a sniff as she noticed Kennedy's bloodied skirt. "My son has assured me you are uninjured."

"I was fortunate."

Something flashed in the woman's eyes that gave Kennedy's memory a painful stir. Her ex-mother-in-law, Celia Huntworth, hadn't liked her either. But then, the woman's carefully laid plans for her debutante-destined son had been ruined when he stepped out of his "class" by marrying Kennedy.

"I am sure King Edward will be relieved to learn of your well-being," Celia's fourteenth-century counterpart said.

Kennedy nodded. "Yes, he will."

Wynland's mother waved someone forward, and a woman rose from a chair before the fire. Though her dress was less fine than Lady Aveline's, her sleeves also trailed. "This is my daughter, Marion."

Unlike her mother, the thirty-fiveish Marion was no little thing. Though she wasn't tall by twenty-first century standards, she topped her mother by half a foot and carried ten to fifteen pounds more on her big-boned frame than insurance companies liked. Eyes blackest brown, hair straight and dishwater blonde beneath a veil, mouth wide, she was as different from Lady Aveline as summer was from winter. Not homely, but plain. From her posture to the color staining her cheeks, she appeared to lack her mother's self-possession.

Marion inclined her head. "Lady Lark."

"Lady Marion." Had she got that right?

"My daughter will show you to your chamber where you can bathe and rest," Lady Aveline said.

Happy to put distance between herself and Wynland, Kennedy followed the woman. Although the others in the room resumed their conversations, she remained an object of interest. Not until she was before a winding stair did it occur to her something was missing. She spun around, scattering hay, and saw that Wynland strode opposite with his brother.

"Mr. Wynland, what about..." What were their names? "...John and Henry?"

He turned. "John and *Harold*."

Right. "When do I get to meet the boys?"

"Later." He resumed his course.

"Come, Lady Lark," Marion beckoned.

Kennedy lifted her skirt and climbed the stairs. Up and around and around they went, to a stone-laid corridor.

"You have been given the east tower room," Marion said as she led the way forward, a spring in her step that had not been there before. At the end of the corridor, she pushed a door inward and stepped aside to allow Kennedy to precede her.

The furnishings consisted of a bed, a stool, a small table with a bowl and pitcher, a raised iron pot that looked like a small barbecue, and a lit candle. Kennedy chuckled. She had dreamed herself into a place over which any self-respecting twenty-first century inmate would have filed a lawsuit.

"Is there anything you require, Lady Lark?"

A bath? She searched the room again and noticed a narrow door that had to be the bathroom. She opened it. The room measured three by three feet and was bare except for a ledge against the back wall. And in the center of that ledge was a hole. An indoor outhouse. Wrinkling her nose at the odor, she closed the door.

"Something is amiss, my lady?"

Kennedy looked to the woman in the doorway. "I was hoping for a bath."

Marion frowned. "I directed the servants in the preparation of your chamber. All should be in readiness." She crossed to the table and dipped a finger in the pitcher. "The water is still warm." She poured some into the bowl. "And here is your towel."

A bowl of tepid water and a hand towel was her idea of a bath? Hoping she didn't sound ungrateful, Kennedy said, "I was thinking of a long soak."

"In a tub?"

"You have one, don't you?"

"Two, in fact." That last was spoken with pride. "Unfortunately, all of the fires in the kitchen are taken with preparations for the nooning meal, so 'tis not possible to warm water for a bath."

No plumbing. Kennedy sighed. "Of course."

"I will leave you to your ablutions." At the door, Marion turned back. "I hope we shall be friends."

Her words seemed so genuine Kennedy smiled. "So do I."

A grin brightened Marion's face. "Then we shall."

Obviously, this Marion and the one she had first met were not the same.

"Mayhap you will share with me tales of your life at court."

Never before out of the twenty-first century Kennedy Plain? Whose only experience with "life at court" was two hours spent in traffic court last summer? "I'd love to." Chances were she would be long awakened from this dream before she had to make good on that.

"Rest well, my lady." Marion stepped into the corridor and pulled the door closed.

Kennedy crossed to the left of the bed and opened the single shutter. A shaft of light slanted across the floor, lighting the dust motes and the stain on her skirt. Though she didn't have clothes to change into, she decided the slip beneath would suffice. As it hit just below the knee, it had escaped the fate of the dress.

To her frustration, she soon discovered there were no buttons or zippers to release her from the dress, only laces at the back. After much contorting and grunting, she captured the trailing end of one lace and pulled. The bodice loosened, and she quickly vacated the dress. Surprisingly, the slip was pleated, embroidered around the neck, had long sleeves, and was made of what felt like silk.

Kennedy slipped out of the shoes and tugged off the socks. As she washed the blood from her calves, she pondered the boys. "Later," Wynland had said. Could he do that? Or, as the king had appointed Lady Lark to care for them, could she demand to see them immediately? Of course, it wasn't as if the boys were without a protector. They had Sir Arthur Crosley. For a moment, she wondered if he bore any resemblance to Mac. Ridiculous—unless her subconscious decided to cast Mac in the role he had tried to convince her was his.

Kennedy unknotted her hair and raked fingers through it. It took time to get it to the place where she could braid it, but she enjoyed every moment. Funny, only now that she had it all back did she appreciate what she had too long taken for granted. Day in, day out, she had confined her long hair to a bun or ponytail and silently threatened to whack it off each time it fell into her eyes. Leave it to cancer to take care of the problem...

Kennedy let her sectioned hair slip through her fingers. Deciding to enjoy it for the short time she had it, she shook her head and let the waves fall over her shoulders. No wonder Mac had wanted to believe his dreams were real. If she were just a bit mad, she might herself.

She lay down on the bed and, certain she would awaken on her living room floor, mumbled, "Good riddance, Mr. Wynland."

# 4

No woman he had ever known was worth dying for. Yet thirteen men had given their lives to protect this one—the king's leman.

A lovely leman, Fulke admitted as candlelight danced through dark hair and skipped across a face rendered innocent in sleep. Though he knew he should not, he pushed the door wider. The movement made the links of his hauberk ring, but Lady Lark did not awaken. Gaining a full view of where she lay on the bed, Fulke slid his gaze to her throat, then over the thin material of her chemise.

He clenched his hands in an attempt to turn back the attraction he had first felt when he had carried her before him on his horse. The effort was in vain, for the sight of her, looking as if she had fallen asleep awaiting a lover, stirred him to discomfort.

One could hardly fault Edward for taking her to mistress, for she was beyond lovely, and without aid of rouge or powder. And her scent... No perfume had assailed him when he breathed her during the ride to Brynwood. She had smelled of light and air—

He berated himself for such fanciful thoughts. Fulke Wynland, Baron of Trune, protector of Sinwell, was not fanciful—though once he had been. He lifted a hand to knock as he had earlier done, but Lark murmured and turned fully toward him, causing her chemise to rise.

What Fulke's hand had known his eyes quickly learned—muscled calves and firm thighs. It was as if her days were not spent at needlework, but on the training field. Not possible, but he *had* seen her run. Never had he known a woman to move as she did, and while wearing a gown lifted high. Such strength and stamina were not acquired running around a king's bedchamber.

He considered the dwindling candle and reflected deeper on this woman thrust into his life by an aging king determined to upset his vassal's ordered life—first with the appointment of Sir Arthur Crosley, now this woman. Why had Edward done it? It was something Fulke had questioned a dozen times since receiving word of Lady Lark's impending arrival. How many nursemaids did two children require?

Of course, if he was honest, the boys had been adrift until the coming of Sir Arthur. Following the death of Fulke's half-brother, the earl, it had been necessary to discharge the woman who had cared for John and Harold since birth. For two months, Fulke had disregarded the woman's impertinence and reports of her speculation over his role in his brother's death, but when he had come upon her warning the boys against him, his forbearance had shattered.

Determining his mother should care for the boys, he had sent to Trune for Aveline, but they were not her grandchildren and she had been unable to hide her disdain. As for Marion, in her uncertain state she was unfit for such responsibility, though she did spend much of her day in their company. However, he had but to advance the possibility of wedding his sister away and she deteriorated more rapidly than a rose in frost. He oft wondered about that.

With none to properly mother the boys, the king had twice taken it upon himself to ensure Sinwell's heir was cared for. But why *this* woman? Though surely apt at putting a man to bed, it was far different from tucking children in at night and soothing away their worries and fears. It must be as it was said: Edward had simply used the opportunity to rid himself of her. But what had wearied him? Her peculiar behavior? Her forward disposition? Her sharp tongue? Surely not those legs.

Stirred again, Fulke forced himself to recognize another reason Edward might have sent her. No, the king would not presume so far.

Lady Lark was stained, and not even Edward could make her clean again. Still, if she came to him, and she might now that her bed was cold, could he send her away?

He cursed. If she was as free with other men as she had been with Edward, she was likely diseased. If not, there was the matter of her refusal to tell him what had befallen her escort, her claim to a head injury of which he saw no evidence, and her allusion to him being responsible for the attack.

Regardless, this was not the place to question a woman like her. Fulke turned away.

"Graham?"

He looked around and saw she spoke out of her sleep. Was Graham another lover?

"Too late..." she breathed.

For what?

Was it light? A scent? A sound? The chill in the air? Whatever it was, it woke Kennedy. She lifted her lids and caught her breath at the sight of the man who filled the shadowed doorway head to toe, shoulder to shoulder.

She was still in the fourteenth century of a dream that had turned night, and no amount of shadow could disguise her visitor. It was Wynland, and she doubted he was here to ask whether the accommodations were to her liking.

In the flickering light of the candle, she sat up. In spite of the chill from the open window, she resisted the temptation to drag the slip over her bare legs. After all, as the king's mistress she had a reputation to live up to. And it wasn't as if she didn't show more skin in a bikini.

She tucked her feet under her. "What do you want?"

He stepped into the light. Still wearing armor, the small room magnified his size, making him appear even more a behemoth. "'Tis time we spoke." Metal on metal, he strode to the window and closed the shutter.

"About?"

His gaze lingered on her legs. "Has no one ever told you, Lady Lark, that which is kept hidden from a man is more intriguing?"

If she understood him to mean it was better to leave something to the imagination, it would be her mother who had told her that. Kennedy curled her fingers into her palms. "What do you want to speak to me about?"

Though clearly displeased by her disregard for his suggestion that she cover herself, he said, "Your attackers have gone from Brynwood as if they never were. If I am to run them to ground, I need to know what befell your escort."

She supposed he did have to expend some effort to throw suspicion off himself. "You think that whatever I saw may be of use in apprehending the…murderers?"

"Perhaps."

She touched her left temple. "I'm afraid I still don't recall—my head injury, you know."

His lids narrowed. "It has spread to that side, my lady?"

Caught. Not that he had believed her the first go around. "Hmm. It seems so."

His hands clenched. Would he keep them to himself?

A scuffling arose in the corridor.

Wynland snatched up the cover and whipped it over her legs and chest. "Due modesty, my lady, lest my men take your wantonness for an invitation."

Wantonness? She, who had been a virgin until the age of twenty when she met Graham, the man she later married?

Two soldiers appeared in the doorway, a trunk between them. "My lord," they spoke in unison.

Wynland motioned them inside. "There."

Eyes averted, they set the trunk at the foot of the bed. As suddenly as they had appeared, they disappeared, leaving Kennedy alone with a man she would have feared if he were real.

"When you *do* recall what happened," he said, "I trust you will come to me."

"*If* I recall." She sighed. "I suppose this means the end of your search?"

A muscle in his jaw jumped. "Half my men are still out there. At first light, I will lead a second contingent to the eastern border."

She frowned. "Why did you come back?"

"I answer to no one, Lady Lark, but for you I shall make an exception. As I told you, Sinwell is vital to England. Thus, until John comes of age, *I* am lord and responsible for the demesne and its people. What happened today is serious, but I will not leave Brynwood Spire too long to avenge men whose lives are already forfeit."

End of story, and so convincingly told that if she didn't know better, she might believe him.

"Now clothe yourself." He pivoted. "My mother will expect you at table for supper."

"How am I supposed to do that when my dress is bloodied?"

When he came back around, his left eyebrow once more formed an M. "The trunk would be a good place to start."

She looked to the end of the bed. This must be the trunk that had been trapped beneath the wagon. She tossed the cover back, swung her feet to the floor, and padded to it. "Lady Lark's?"

Silence. Had he gone? She looked around and met his suspicious gaze.

"You speak of yourself as if you are not present, *Lady Lark*." He leaned a shoulder against the door frame. "Why is that?"

*Because she is not present, and I am having a hard time keeping her hat on.* But she couldn't tell him that. Or could she? How would this man of her dreams react? What words would her subconscious put in his mouth? Tempted as she was to find out, she didn't dare.

Hadn't Mac's book said no one knew where Lady Lark came from? And her surname, age, and social standing were as much a mystery. "Hardly a world traveler, are you, Mr. Wynland?" Kennedy said with renewed confidence. "Where I come from, one often uses the formal to refer to one's self."

Disbelief. "Where is it you come from, Lady Lark? Not England, I wager."

"You are right."

"And certainly not France with an accent such as yours."

Had he picked up on the drawl that had once mapped her Southern roots? As she had left North Carolina at the age of thirteen following her parents' divorce, she had thought it long gone.

"Where?" he pressed.

"That is between the king and me."

His gaze held hers long and hard, then he straightened and strode down the corridor.

Obviously, the king was a good card to play with Wynland. Come to think of it…

She ran to the door. "Mr. Wynland, I will expect your nephews at supper."

He turned, retraced his footsteps, and set his six foot three of bone and muscle over her. "Will you?"

"They *are* the reason King Edward sent me."

"As I heard tale, you were sent that he might rid himself of a tedious mistress."

Kennedy raised her chin. "My relationship with *Edward* is none of your business. Suffice it to say that I am here to carry out his orders that I care for your nephews."

"And how do you intend to do that? By exposing yourself?" He caught the neck of her slip and pulled her forward. "By going about wearing naught but your chemise? Tempting my men?"

Though Kennedy reminded herself this was only a dream, there was nothing dream-like about Wynland—the condemnation in his eyes, the masculine scent of his sweat, the prickling sensation where his rough fingers brushed her throat, the body heat radiating across the space between them.

She swallowed. "I assure you, no harm will come to John and Harold while they are in my care. Can you say as much?" That last slipped out. How a dream could rub her so wrong, she didn't know, but this one—this man—did.

Wynland reeled her in until they were nose to nose. "I was wrong. You *should* fear me, Lady Lark."

As much as she tried to convince herself her fear was unfounded, it was all she could do not to put it out there for him to see. "Let me go."

He released her.

"The king will hear of this, Mr. Wynland."

"I am *Lord* Wynland. See that you afford me my title in future." Once again, he strode opposite.

Kennedy glared at his back. He would never be *her* lord. If he didn't like "Mr." she had some choice alternatives.

When he entered a room halfway down the corridor, she grimaced at the realization it was likely his bedroom. She closed the door and returned to the trunk. Kneeling, she lifted the heavy lid. Inside were two dresses made from bright cloth, a long slip—or chemise, as Wynland called it—a pair of thin-soled pointed shoes, thick socks, two belts, a veil, a silver circlet, and a comb.

Kennedy chose the emerald green dress over the red. Fortunately, it had laces down both sides, but how on earth would she manage the dozen buttons running the sleeves from elbow to wrist? She eyed the red dress. It didn't have buttons, just those long sleeves, but it laced in back. No wonder ladies of this age had needed maids.

Kennedy pulled off the slip, reached for the clean one in the trunk, and froze. She had breasts. Though her weight loss had robbed her of their fullness to the point she hadn't needed to wear a bra in months, there they were. She was whole again. No headaches, no illness, everything the way it had been. She could get used to this.

But that was the trap Mac had fallen into. If she wasn't careful, *she* would end up marked for the loony bin. Not that her sentence would be lengthy...

Kennedy pulled the slip on, followed by the green dress, and discovered the buttons were the least of her worries. The dress didn't fit. The sleeves were short by an inch, the skirt hit above her ankles in contrast to the trailing length worn by Wynland's mother and sister, and even if she didn't lace up the sides, it would be snug.

What to do? By twenty-first century standards, the slip could pass for a light dress, but from Wynland's reaction, it was inappropriate. She held the red dress against her. Same size. The green would have to do. She snugged up the side laces as much as possible, tied them off, and struggled through the buttons on the sleeves. Since the shoes were too small, she pulled on the ones that had served her so poorly during her flight from Wynland. Lastly, she tackled her hair. And despite the mess, it was a joy.

The draft alerted him, its chill pricking his bare feet and legs. Fulke dropped the hose he had been in the process of donning and pulled his misericorde from the belt that lay on the bed. The dagger's blade reflecting torchlight, he pivoted, swept the tapestry aside, and fell on the intruder.

The man cried out, but not until the misericorde was at his neck did Fulke realize it was Marion.

"God's patience!" He lowered the dagger. "For what are you skulking about my chamber?"

Though it was dim behind the tapestry, torchlight slipped in and curved around the hand she held to her throat. "Remind me not to steal upon you ever again, brother."

He looked to the door through which she had entered the solar. Behind it and a dozen more lay the passages that ran the inner walls of the keep. It was years since he had negotiated them himself, and usually it had been with Marion close behind.

"If I must remind you not to steal upon me again, you will deserve what ill befalls you."

She scowled. "I do so miss the boy."

The boy he had been and would never be again. Their days of mischief, games, and shared imaginings were long over. He thrust the tapestry back, tossed the misericorde on the bed, and returned to his hose.

"My!" Marion feigned shock. "Had I known you were without dress, I would not have entered your chamber."

She made it sound as if he was nude when he had but to don hose and boots. He rolled the left hose up his leg.

She lowered to the edge of the bed. "Did you think I was Cardell?"

Cardell who would prefer him dead. "In such circumstances, Marion, one does not think. One acts." He tied the top of the hose to the braie girdle beneath his tunic. "But had you been him, you would be no more." As he pulled on the opposite hose, he rued the responsibility bequeathed to him by the death of his half-brother—especially the dissension that had risen from it.

"The people like you," Marion slipped into his thoughts as she was still able to do, "as do several of the barons."

But not Cardell and half a dozen others. Fulke jerked his above-knee tunic down over his hose. "What do you want?"

She rose and crossed to the trunk, removed a jeweled belt and shoes, and held them out to him.

Fulke turned away. His sword belt would better serve, as would boots. He slid the misericorde in its sheath, girded the belt, and dropped the lid on the trunk. Seating himself, he reached for his short boots.

Marion lowered beside him. "I am wondering what you think of Lady Lark."

He shoved his feet into the boots. "She is the reason for your trespass?"

"One of the reasons. What do you think of her?"

"Naught."

"I think she is lovely."

"You expected the king's leman to be otherwise?"

Marion leaned back on her hands and gazed at the ceiling as if it were a canopy of stars. "Do you remember when, as children, we dreamed of the one we would one day wed—all the while mother and father spat at one another?" She turned her gaze to him. "We were going to be different."

"They were dreams, Marion. Never meant to be."

"Perhaps."

He stood. "Supper awaits."

She eyed him. "You would make a fine husband, Fulke."

Unfortunately, he could not say she would make a fine wife. "When you are wed, dear Marion, mayhap I shall get me an heir." In which case, it might never happen.

The sister he knew disappeared from her eyes and was replaced by one he preferred not to know—someone whose mind had twisted long ago.

Casting her emptied gaze down, hands beginning to tremble, she muttered, "Aye, supper awaits."

An ache in his chest, Fulke slid a hand beneath her elbow and raised her to her feet. "Come."

# 5

KENNEDY STEPPED OFF the torch-lit stairs and into a room she hardly recognized. Had she taken a wrong turn? She remembered the tapestries, the painted ceiling, and the fireplace. It was the place Wynland had brought her through earlier, but transformed by tables, benches, servants bearing platters of food, a multitude of people who had not been present upon her arrival, and a clamor that was almost deafening—until a hush fell.

Heads turned and eyes widened. Did she look *that* bad? There hadn't been a mirror.

Although she longed to head back upstairs, she determined she would face these people and their disapproval, and do it with style—hopefully. Sensing Wynland's gaze, she looked past rows of tables to a table raised above the others. He sat at its center, as if in judgment of her, and beside him was his brother.

She put her shoulders back and walked forward. There were whispers, snickers, snide comments, a lewd grunt, but she didn't falter.

Nearing Wynland, she noted he had changed into a black shirt embroidered around the neck and his unruly hair was secured at his nape. He cleaned up well, appearing less sinister than he had in armor. Until she looked into his eyes. His silent regard was all the warning she needed that he would extract payment for whatever sin she had committed. Let him try.

She stopped before him. "Where would you like me to sit?"

When he didn't speak, Marion said, "Beside me, Lady Lark."

Since the woman was three places removed from her brother, one from her disagreeable mother, Kennedy said, "Thank you." She stepped onto the raised platform, skirted the table, and lowered to the bench.

Marion turned to her. "Were you able to rest?"

"Yes, I got some sleep."

"Splendid." Marion lifted a metal goblet and sipped.

Realizing how thirsty she was, Kennedy looked to the table. No goblet, but the good news was that interest in her was waning.

"How was your bath?" Marion asked.

"It was...different."

"I imagine at court you had the luxury of a tub bath once a sennight. I enjoy them myself, but I am able to indulge only once a fortnight."

However long that was, it didn't sound good.

Lady Aveline leaned forward, stirring the air with perfume, the abundance of which probably had something to do with bathing being a luxury. "For all the horrors you endured this day, you appear to have fared well, Lady Lark."

Kennedy wondered how to respond. Though she didn't think she would ever forget the terrible images, it could be nothing compared to what the real Lady Lark must have endured. "I was fortunate." Lame.

"Lady Lark sustained a head injury, Mother." Wynland netted Kennedy's gaze. "She is unable to recall the incident."

"Is that so?" Lady Aveline mused.

"How terrible," Marion murmured.

Richard Wynland merely shined his dislike on Kennedy.

A server appeared. Cheeks pink from exertion, the woman set a goblet in front of Kennedy and poured a dark liquid into it.

Wine? Though, on occasion, Kennedy enjoyed a glass of wine, water was her poison. "Excuse me, can I get a glass of water?"

Surprise came at her from all sides, though it was most prominent on the servant's face. "Water, m'lady?"

"From the tap is fine."

The woman's confusion deepened. "But…"

"Surely you jest, Lady Lark," Marion said. "Everyone knows water is an evil drink."

Now Kennedy was confused—until she recalled the advice for traveling in third world countries. Water must not be safe in medieval England either. She smiled at the server. "Milk?"

Still the woman looked disconcerted. "I shall fetch some, m'lady." She hurried away.

Lady Aveline harrumphed. "Even John and Harold choose wine over milk."

Children drank wine?

"Where *are* John and Harold?" Wynland asked.

"'Tis likely Sir Arthur again," Lady Aveline grumbled.

"Squire James!" Wynland called.

The young man rose from a lower table. "My lord?"

"Collect my nephews and bring them and Sir Arthur to the hall."

"Aye, my lord."

Marion leaned near Kennedy. "They hate each other."

"They" being Wynland and Arthur Crosley. Pretending ignorance, Kennedy asked, "Why?"

Before Marion could answer, a plate was set between her and her mother, on it a large scooped out round of bread filled with what looked like stew. Marion picked up a spoon and took a bite. As did her mother.

They were not the only ones to share a meal, a practice that was hardly hygienic. But when a plate was set between Kennedy and the heavy man beside her and she realized he was to be her partner, she was too hungry to object.

"For some reason," Marion finally said, "Sir Arthur believes my brother plans to out the heir that he might take the earldom for himself. Try though I do to convince him he is wrong, he refuses to believe me."

If only she knew. Kennedy looked to her shared meal. Seeing the man was halfway through it, she snagged a spoonful of chunked vegetables.

And was surprised. Though she hadn't held much hope for the offering, it was tasty.

"Unfortunately," Marion whispered, "he is not the only one to believe ill of my brother."

Kennedy spooned up another bite of her rapidly diminishing meal.

"Come mirth, come woe, Baron Cardell opposes Fulke." She inclined her head opposite. "You see him? He sits two past Richard."

Kennedy looked beyond Wynland's brother to an older man who made her startle. The mass of curling black hair that sprouted from his jaw resembled a skunk's tail—black on either side of a gray streak that ran chin to chest. "The one with the beard?"

"That is him. Ere our brother's death, the baron was the earl's confidante. He does not boast such an esteemed position with Fulke."

"Why?"

"He and Fulke do not like one another—never have, methinks never shall."

Tempted as Kennedy was to suggest Baron Cardell might have a good reason, she said, "Why don't they like one another?"

From Marion's eyes rose a depth of wisdom far different from the face she had thus far revealed. "Because Fulke cannot be controlled. Of course"—her voice grew more hushed—"the baron's true enmity lies in the king's decision to grant wardship of John and—"

"Hush, Marion," Lady Aveline snapped. "Eat your meal."

Back into her shell Marion went.

Kennedy took a spoonful of the stew, but hardly had the vegetables hit the back of her tongue than her partner cleared his throat and turned his flushed face to her.

"Careful lest ye strain yer seams even more, my lady."

He was one to talk! Two—maybe three—of her could fit into him. Kennedy dug deeper. When her milk arrived, she took a gulp and nearly spit it out. It was thick and tasted as if sweetener had been added.

"About your clothes," Marion said a while later.

"Yes?"

"Your gown is beautiful, but rather lacking." She smiled apologetically. "Unless it is the new mode at court?"

Could she get away with that? Perhaps with Marion, but not with her mother who also awaited an explanation. And though Wynland's attention appeared to be elsewhere, she wouldn't be surprised if he was tuned in.

"Nothing like that. It's just that I'm a bit of a yo-yo with my weight. Size six, eight, sometimes ten." Actually, with the onset of cancer, the opposite was true—eight to six to four. But that was in the real world, a place to which she didn't have to return for however long this dream lasted.

From the confusion on Marion's face, it was as if Kennedy spoke a foreign language. "It's a weight thing," she tried again. "I gain some. I lose some."

Marion nodded. "What of the surcoat?"

"Surcoat?"

"Your overgown." She touched her own garment with its trailing sleeves, beneath which tight-fitting sleeves buttoned down to her wrists.

Now Kennedy understood. The red dress with its back lacing was to be worn over the green. "I...don't care for layering."

Marion frowned. "And of the length?" She leaned in. "I could see your ankles."

What a shock she would have if she were dreaming in Kennedy's world. "Terrible, isn't it? If I've told my maid once, I've told her a hundred times—cold water."

"She caused your gown to shrink?"

"It would appear so."

Lady Aveline looked around her daughter. "Could it be the dress is not yours, Lady Lark?"

"Of course it's mine."

Lady Aveline's lids narrowed. "My son tells me you were not traveling with a maid. Can that be?"

Where was this second degree going? To the lie about the maid shrinking her dress or her assumed identity? In the next instant, Kennedy was struck by the possibility she was playing the part of someone other than Lady Lark. It would certainly explain the dying soldier's rejection and the contents of the trunk.

That was probably it, but she couldn't admit it since it would mean Wynland's wrath and questions she couldn't answer. She would have to play along, especially as it seemed far better to be a lady than a maid—or a criminal.

"That's correct. My maid was unable to accompany me."

The dragon lady's plucked eyebrows arched.

Kennedy turned her regard to Marion. "Do you know what a wyvern is?"

Once more, puzzlement came to roost. "A type of dragon. Surely you know that?"

Kennedy nearly laughed at her recent assessment of Lady Aveline. "Of course." She glanced at the enormous tapestry on the wall behind. "Like that one."

"Nay, a wyvern has but two legs. A true dragon has four, like the one on Sinwell's shield of arms."

"Oh." And it wasn't two-headed as the dying soldier had spoken of. So much for evidence of Wynland's guilt. "Your brother's shield of arms is different from Sinwell's, is that right?"

"Aye, Fulke bears the gryphon."

The half-eagle half-lion Kennedy had glimpsed on his squire's shirt and several others' when she had come downstairs.

"My lord, my lord!" A woman ran across the hall, the veil on her head askew, eyes wide, Squire James following. "He has taken the children!" She stumbled to a halt before Wynland. "Taken them and gone from Brynwood!"

He stood. "How?" he roared above the buzz caused by the woman's words.

She raised a hand to reveal the rope dangling from her wrist, grasped the cloth encircling her neck. "He bound and gagged me, my lord."

"The beast!" Lady Aveline hissed.

Kennedy looked to Wynland's sister and thought she glimpsed hurt in the woman's eyes. What was going on? Hardly had the question formed than the pieces fell into place—Squire James, who had returned empty handed...the book that said Sir Arthur had stolen the boys from Brynwood following the attack on Lady Lark. How could she have forgotten?

"When?" Wynland demanded.

"After you rode from Brynwood this morn, my lord."

His nostrils flared. "I shall wash my hands in his blood!"

Not an idle threat. Poor Sir Arthur. His only crime was trying to prevent the murder of two innocents. "He won't hurt them," Kennedy said.

Wynland's eyes pinned her like a fly to fly paper. "How do you know that?"

Because she knew Mac and—no! Mac had nothing to do with this. It was the account she had read of Crosley. This, in a way, made her something of an authority. "Because I know Sir Arthur."

Wynland's lips curved, but it was hardly a smile. "I am sure you do."

Amid snickering, Kennedy said, "He wants only to protect your nephews."

"And who, do you think, seeks to harm them?"

The murmur grew louder.

Kennedy glanced at the people, saw dislike in some of their eyes, uncertainty in others. They had no idea what their "lord" was capable of. "Whoever has the most to gain, of course."

Wynland's gaze hardened further. There had never been a possibility they would be friends, but still she had blasted the nonexistent bridge to kingdom come.

He strode from behind the table, causing Kennedy to startle at the sight of him. If ever a man looked good in hose, it was Fulke Wynland.

"All of you"—he swept a hand around the room—"to your horses!"

Richard Wynland and thirty or more men stood, several in hose and above-knee shirts, though none cut quite the figure their lord did.

"Lord Wynland!" a booming voice halted them. Baron Cardell unfolded his stout frame.

"Cardell?" Wynland said.

"What of Brynwood?"

"In my absence, it will not be without. Richard!" Wynland searched out his brother. "Though I know you were to return to Kinsley on the morrow and would prefer to aid in my search, I ask that you remain here in my stead."

The younger man's jaw tightened. "As you wish."

Wynland returned his attention to Cardell. "Ready yourself and your men."

"I would remain here."

"You ride with me."

"I—"

"Else await my return in a prison cell."

Time stretched, but finally the baron said, "I am your man, *my lord*."

It didn't take a genius to fathom the lie just told. And from Wynland's caustic smile, he was aware of it. He resumed his course.

A hand closed around Kennedy's wrist, nails dug into her that she traced to the woman who reached past Marion.

"How dare you accuse my son of seeking to harm those boys," Lady Aveline hissed. "You know naught!"

No mother wanted to believe her child capable of the atrocity hers had committed—would commit. Deciding the best way to defuse the situation was to appeal to the grandmother in her, Kennedy said, "All I know is that your grandsons—"

"John and Harold are not of my blood, just as their father was not of my body." The words flew off her tongue with such passion there was no doubt she felt no love for the boys.

So she had been a second wife—maybe a third or fourth. "My apologies, Lady Aveline. I am simply concerned for the welfare of your son's nephews."

"Then look to the one who has taken them from their beds!" Lady Aveline released her.

Kennedy glanced at the half moons scoring her flesh.

"Is it true you know Sir Arthur?" Marion whispered.

"I...yes, I do."

"You are friends?"

Did she detect jealousy? "In a manner of speaking."

"In a what?"

"Well, we—"

"Make ready, Lady Lark," Wynland's voice skinned Kennedy's.

He was advancing on her. Unsettled by his return and this stuff about "making ready" she said, "What?"

"You shall come with me." He stepped onto the platform and put his palms on the table. "As you profess to know Crosley, methinks you may prove useful in our search."

She knew from historical account that Crosley's flight would take him to the monastery of Farfallow where he would be slain, but she had no intention of aiding this man. "I don't see how I can be of help."

"Still, you will come."

Another wild ride? "Are we talking horses?"

He leaned so near she could smell wine on his breath. "Time is of the utmost, Lady Lark. Thus, there will be no carriage or, in your case, baggage wagon."

"I told you, I'm not a horse person. I can't ride. I—"

"You cannot ride?" Marion exclaimed. "How can that be?"

"Pray tell, *Lady Lark*," Lady Aveline said.

Surprisingly, Wynland came to her rescue—in a manner of speaking. "Five minutes. If you are not ready, I will take you as you are." He stalked away.

# 6

SIDESADDLE AGAIN. THOUGH Kennedy had thought it was bad before, she realized how good she'd had it with Wynland. He had held her securely, without threat of losing his hold on her, but the man to whom he had entrusted her an hour ago lacked the strength and size of Wynland. Time and again she caught air, slammed to the saddle, slid sideways, bumped her head against the knight's chin. It was miserable. And Wynland was going to hear about it.

Teeth clenched to keep them from chattering in the chill night, Kennedy glared at her nemesis where he rode ahead of his men. The full moon shone on his pale hair and caused light to undulate across the cape that flew from his shoulders. A regular Paul Revere.

Kennedy sank deeper into the cape she had been given. Where was Wynland headed? Did he have a clue as to where Sir Arthur might have fled? Before leaving the castle, he had divided his men. One group he sent to retrieve those searching for Lady Lark's attackers to turn their efforts to his nephews. That left two contingents, one he headed up, the other led by a man whom Marion had said was the most trusted of her brother's knights. Once over the stinking moat, the two contingents had ridden opposite one another.

The horse veered, once more snapping Kennedy's head back against her escort's chin. She yelped.

The knight shouted, then spewed words so charged with anger they tripped over one another in their haste to be the first to exit his mouth.

Feeling herself slipping, knowing the horse's pounding hooves were her next stop in this nightmare, Kennedy grabbed for something to hold onto and came up with a handful of mane.

The horse careened, tossed its head, and reared. Then she was falling.

*Now would be a good time to wake up.* Her only lifeline the coarse hair her fingers tangled around, she held on as she twisted and slammed against the horse. Then her feet hit the ground as the animal came back to earth.

Though she risked being trampled, she knew that if she held on she would be dragged. She thrust backward, landed on her rear, rolled to her back, and was spared the beast's hooves by inches.

With a whinny, the horse galloped away.

Kennedy closed her eyes and let her aching muscles sink into the earth. It was a relief to feel the still ground beneath her. Though this dream had given her back her health, she tired of its gore, wild horse rides, uppity Lady Aveline, and temperamental "lord."

"Lady Lark!"

In that moment, she would have welcomed a visit from an obnoxious salesman were he to awaken her from this dream.

Armor pealed its familiar chime, feet landed with a thud, and a warm hand felt for the pulse in her neck.

The louse probably had his fingers crossed in hopes she was dead. She opened her eyes. Before a scathing word could pass her lips, his hands felt downward—over her collarbone, around her ribs, then her hips.

Kennedy pushed onto her elbows. "I'm fine."

He turned his gaze on her.

For an instant, she thought she might have mistaken him, but it was Wynland, a man transformed by moonlight that gentled his features and forgave him nearly every flaw—even the kink in his eyebrow.

"You are uninjured?"

Nothing felt broken, but she was one massive ache. "No thanks to you."

His eyes caught the bare light and turned chill again. "Then let us delay no more." He straightened and motioned someone forward.

When she saw who it was, she scrambled to her feet. "If you think I'm getting back on that horse"—she jabbed a finger toward the advancing knight—"think again!"

The knight dismounted and stepped before Wynland.

"Sir Malcolm, what befell you that the lady with whom you were entrusted lost the saddle?"

"Forgive me, my lord. In all my years in your service, never have I taken my duties without due seriousness." He glanced at Kennedy. "The lady does not move with the horse, but against it such that my mount grew anxious. Thus, when we rounded the road, my horse reared. As the lady was sidesaddle, I was unable to keep hold of her."

Sidesaddle because he wouldn't have it any other way. Kennedy had tried to convince Sir Malcolm it would be better if she rode astride. Failing that, she had thrown a leg over the horse, but he had lifted her and plunked her down sideways. Maybe the next time he would listen to her. Not that there would be a next time.

"I shall deal with you later," Wynland said.

As irked as Kennedy was, she feared for the knight, as her father had said those same words to her. Later, he had pared a willow branch and "tanned her hide," criss-crossing her rear with welts. With Wynland, punishment was bound to be more harsh than a willow branch.

"Make ready to ride," he ordered the knight and started for his own horse. "Come, Lady Lark."

She hurried after him. "Mr. Wynland."

His stride never broke.

"All right. *Lord* Wynland!" She caught his arm.

He halted, though only because he had reached his horse.

"What happened was my fault, not Sir Malcolm's."

"That I do not doubt."

"Then why—?"

"Because he is a knight, a distinction attained through strength and stamina, courage and honor, blood and war. In giving you into his care, I asked little of him and, no matter the reason, he failed me. Thus, he will answer for his negligence." He looked to her hand on him. "Now that I have explained myself, which I need not do, 'tis time we continue our search."

When he lifted her onto the horse, Kennedy untangled a leg from her skirt and swung it over the opposite side. Wynland didn't oppose her refusal to ride sidesaddle, but mounted behind and settled his hard thighs alongside hers.

Kennedy looked over her shoulder. "You won't...kill Sir Malcolm, will you?"

Dry laughter rumbled from him. "You are hardly precious to me, Lady Lark."

It was the wake-up call she needed. Likely, his anger with the knight stemmed from her not having broken her neck.

Gripping her securely around the waist, Wynland spurred his horse into the night.

He liked her best in sleep. And what man would not? Unless, of course, the accusations in her eyes was replaced with passion, those on her lips captured by a meeting of mouths.

She drew a deep breath where she had curled against his chest when hours of discomfort and fatigue made her surrender to riding sidesaddle, and opened her eyes. They stared at each other.

Fulke felt it, was sure she felt it too, searched to put a name to the awareness that strained between them. Thirst, he decided, and not the kind eased with drink.

In the murk of dawn, a smile touched her mouth, but she blinked and it was gone. Once more, she looked at him as if he were the basest of men. Though she was but one among several who believed him responsible for his brother's death, she had gone further in not only accusing him of the attack on her baggage train but of intending to harm John and Harold.

Curse her! He wanted her gone from Sinwell. As soon as Sir Arthur and the boys were found, he would ride to London to speak with Edward on the matter.

Lark straightened. "Where are we?"

"We have stopped to take food and water the horses."

She looked to the others who remained mounted while their animals drank from the stream. "I'd like to stretch my legs."

"You need to relieve yourself?"

"No."

"Then you shall remain astride."

Her chin came around. "In that case, I do need to *relieve* myself."

"Then you will have to wait until we stop again." As she sputtered, he reached behind, retrieved a bundle from one of his packs, and turned back the folded cloth. "Here."

She stared at the hard biscuits and dried meat. "No, thank you. I'm not hungry."

"As you will." He bit into a biscuit.

"While you enjoy your meal, surely I can take a little walk?"

"Nay."

She glared.

He reached for another biscuit. "Do not sulk. I abhor sullen women."

"All the more reason I should sulk."

Fulke was surprised to feel a smile at his mouth. "Methinks if you slept more, my lady, I might grow fond of you."

"Pardon me?"

"Naught." He offered the bundle again. "'Tis all there will be to eat until we arrive at Castle Cirque."

"When will that be?"

"When we are done searching the neighboring villages."

She muttered something beneath her breath.

"Do you not eat it, I shall," he warned.

She snatched a piece of meat and a biscuit and turned her back to him.

Fulke smiled.

A sunrise and three villages later, Kennedy lifted her face from the huddle of her hood and peered at the looming castle. It was smaller than Brynwood Spire. As she watched, the drawbridge descended with a creak of timber and a clatter of chains. "Castle Cirque?" she asked.

"Aye."

The drawbridge touched down, the metal grate over the entrance rose, and a half dozen riders sprang from beneath it. Most conspicuous was the one who rode before the others—a woman, her blue dress and white veil fluttering. And she rode sidesaddle. As she and her escort neared, Kennedy saw she guided her horse with one hand, while the other supported what looked like a bird.

When the woman reined in before Wynland and his men, it was indeed a bird she held, but not of the garden variety. Its head was hidden beneath a hood topped with bright feathers, it wore bells on its legs, and was strapped to the woman's gloved wrist.

"Welcome to Castle Cirque, Lord Wynland."

Kennedy eyed the woman. A vision of blonde hair and twinkling brown eyes, full breasts and a teeny waist, she looked like a fairy tale princess—until she smiled, revealing yellowed teeth and receding gums. Did these people know nothing about oral hygiene?

The woman laid a hand on Wynland's arm. "Pray, why did you not send word of your arrival that I might prepare for you?"

"'Twas not planned, Lady Jaspar."

Was this woman mentioned in Mac's book?

"I come with ill fortune upon my house," Wynland said.

"What has happened, Fulke?"

How quickly she dispensed with formality, and how strange to hear Wynland called by something other than his surname, which in Kennedy's mind better served his villainous character.

"John and Harold have been taken."

"Taken?" Shrill disbelief caused the bird to turn its hooded head toward the woman. "By whom?"

"By the man Edward sent to protect them, Sir Arthur Crosley."

A movement beyond the lady drew Kennedy's gaze to a young man who sat tall in his saddle. As handsome as Lady Jaspar was beautiful, the marked resemblance was surely no coincidence—golden hair cut to his jaw, bright brown eyes, good cheekbones. A prince to Jaspar's princess. But he did his sister one better when he smiled at Kennedy, revealing strong white teeth.

At last, a friendly face. She returned the smile.

"Why would Sir Arthur do such a thing?' Lady Jaspar asked. "What gain for him?"

Kennedy returned her attention to the woman and saw she only had eyes for Wynland. Resisting the urge to pat herself to make sure she hadn't turned invisible, Kennedy pushed the hood off her head.

"According to Lady Lark," Wynland said, "he took the boys to protect them from me."

Lady Jaspar broadened her horizons to include Kennedy. "You are Lady Lark?"

"I am."

The self-assured woman of moments earlier twitched. "Excuse me if I am…surprised. Though I heard you were to be sent to care for John and Harold, I did not know you had arrived."

"I almost didn't."

"Pray, tell."

"My…" Once again, Kennedy's gaze was drawn to the young man. As if he also awaited an explanation, he leaned forward, gaze intent. "My baggage train was attacked."

Lady Jaspar's eyes widened. "'Tis true, Lord Wynland?"

"It is. Have you word of a knight traveling with two small boys?"

"I fear not."

"Then I shall need all the men you can spare."

"They are yours to command."

This place was under his rule? It seemed so. Until, of course, Sinwell's heir came of age. Not that either boy would.

"Come to my hall," Lady Jaspar said, "While you and your men refresh yourselves, I will send garrison to the village to inquire if any have heard or seen anything unusual."

"My thanks, Lady Jaspar, but we have already inquired."

Her lids fluttered. "Still you will come inside, will you not?"

"Aye, though only long enough to rest ourselves and our mounts that we might set out again."

There was no mistaking her disappointment. "As you will, my lord." She looked beyond him and inclined her head. "Lord Cardell."

"My lady."

Lady Jaspar turned her horse and the young man fell in beside his sister. Together, they led the way to the castle.

When Wynland lifted Kennedy down from his horse, she was tempted to kiss the ground. And might have if not that she was so sore. Slowly, she followed Wynland and Lady Jaspar up a dozen steps and into a room that resembled Brynwood's great hall, complete with hay on the floor.

Using her study of the room as an opportunity to rest her legs, she stepped to the side. Wynland's men filed past, eager to accept the drink offered to them. As for the beauteous Lady Jaspar and Wynland, the two stood center, deep in conversation.

"Lady Lark." The young man, whose looks were testament to the shared blood between him and his sister, halted alongside Kennedy.

"Yes?"

He gave a curt bow. "I am Sir Leonel Aimery, cousin to Lady Jaspar." Cousin... "It's a pleasure to meet you." How old was he? Twenty-five?

"May I?" he offered his arm.

"Certainly."

"You are surely blessed to have survived the attack," he said as he led her forward.

"I am. It was..." Memories of the carnage flashed before her. "It was horrid."

"There were no survivors?"

"None."

Regret shone in his warm brown eyes. "I am sorry."

As they passed a cavernous fireplace, Kennedy was struck by its heat. It had to be eighty-five degrees in here. Of course, it didn't help that, before leaving Brynwood, she had pulled the red dress on over the green. She reached to the brooch that held her cape closed, but the clasp Marion had secured resisted her efforts.

"Mayhap I can assist?" Leonel offered.

"I can manage." But she was still struggling with it when they halted before Wynland and Lady Jaspar.

In spite of the other woman's hand on Wynland's arm, it was obvious he had been watching Kennedy—and that she had done something to displease him. Abandoning the brooch, she lowered her arms. It was then she saw the gryphon on the sleeveless shirt Wynland wore over his armor, the same as that worn by his squire. As his cape had covered it during the ride, the lapels of which were now thrown over his shoulders, it was the first she had seen of it.

"Lord Wynland, you remember my cousin, Sir Leonel Aimery."

Wynland lowered the goblet he had tipped to his lips and inclined his head. "Sir Leonel."

"My lord."

The bird on Lady Jaspar's wrist ruffled its feathers.

She stroked it. "Leonel received knighthood this past spring, a year early due to an act of bravery that saved the life of his lord, Baron Brom. To show his appreciation, the baron awarded my cousin—"

"'Twas naught," Sir Leonel said.

Wynland considered the knight for some moments as if to determine if he was worthy of his new title, then said, "What do you at Castle Cirque, Sir Leonel?"

"I have no lands of my own. Thus, I have given myself into the service of my cousin."

"What of Baron Brom?"

"He gave me leave to do so, my lord."

Wynland opened his mouth to say something more, but closed it when his regard was captured by the armed soldier who strode into the hall.

"'Tis the captain of the guard," Lady Jaspar said. "I shall not be long." She turned to her cousin. "Leonel."

He looked to Kennedy and bowed again. "My lady." Led by the captain of the guard, he and his cousin withdrew from the hall.

"I wager you are sore," Wynland said.

"What makes you think that?"

He swept his gaze over Kennedy. "You are not quite as tall as you were ere we rode from Brynwood."

She narrowed her eyes. "Have you ever considered a career in stand-up comedy?"

He frowned.

"Never mind." She lifted the brooch and searched the underside for the clasp.

"Do not remove your mantle."

Context telling her it was the cape he referred to, she said, "It's hot in here." An instant later, the clasp revealed its secret.

He gripped her hand. "Do as I say."

"I will not."

"Lest you forget, you are more out of your clothes than in them."

So they were on the tight side. She wasn't the first to squeeze into clothes a size or three too small.

"I have warned you about your wanton displays." He leaned near. "Though I cannot say my own men would turn from whatever temptation you place before them, those of Cirque are to be trusted even less." His gaze intensified. "Have you ever been ravished, Lady Lark?"

As in raped? When he put it that way...But was it her well-being he was concerned about, or was he just giving her a hard time?

— 68 —

"Of course, mayhap a man would not have to resort to force to have you."

Taking the dream to heart as if it was Kennedy Plain he smeared and not a woman whose reputation preceded her, she said, "How dare you!"

He put his head to the side. "Such outrage, Lady Lark. Surely you do not think to convince me you are untouched?"

"Of course not!" Immediately, she regretted the denial. It was none of his business that she and Graham had tumbled around the bed—on the rare occasion they were under the same roof. Hating the glint in Wynland's eyes, she said, "Think what you will."

"I do. Hence, the mantle stays."

And if she defied him?

His grip tightened. "It stays."

Grudgingly, she nodded.

He released her and carried the goblet to his lips.

A servant handed Kennedy a goblet. Too thirsty to reject the purplish-red contents, she took a long drink and nearly gagged. Not only was the wine watered down, but it was warm.

She blew hair up off her brow and affected a high wavering voice, "I'm melting."

Her impersonation of the Wicked Witch earned her Wynland's frowning regard.

She shrugged. "Never heard of the land of Oz?"

"That is where you are from? Oz?"

Why not? "Yes."

His lids narrowed. "I have not heard of it. It is on the continent?"

"Uh...yes."

"Where?"

Thankfully, a young woman dressed in a rough wool dress appeared. "My lord, they say you are looking for two small boys and a knight."

Wynland turned to her. "What have you to tell me?"

"Methinks I saw them this morn on my way to the castle."

"Continue."

"I heard laughter and followed it to the river. There I saw two boys and a man clothed not as a knight, but who had a horse worthy of one—a black stallion fit with a fine saddle."

Kennedy sensed Wynland's agitation, was certain it was all he could do to keep his feet rooted to the floor.

"How old were the boys?"

"Four and...seven?"

"What of the knight?"

"He was of an age, my lord. Tall."

"What color his hair?"

"Red, my lord."

It sounded like Mac. The thought forced Kennedy to regroup. This was a dream. Of her own making. Thus, she shouldn't be surprised if MacArthur Crosley played a part.

Wynland stepped nearer the girl. "Were you seen?"

She had to look so far up that her eyes nearly rolled back in her head. "Nay, my lord. I hid. All know the wood is traveled by men of ill repute."

"You will take me to where you saw them."

"But what of my lady? Forsooth, she will not like—"

"What is your name?"

"Joan, my lord."

"Worry not, Joan. Lady Jaspar will understand." He took her arm and called to his men.

The thought of getting back on a horse causing her aches to multiply, Kennedy started to follow.

"You shall remain, Lady Lark," Wynland said. "I will not have you slowing me."

Then he was abandoning her. Not a bad thing. She smiled. "Drive safe."

Questioning came and went on his face, then he was striding from the hall with the serving girl in tow.

All that remained were those of Lady Jaspar's household—predominantly men. And they were watching Kennedy. She shrugged, lifted the goblet, and sipped its wretched contents.

# 7

As the only remaining occupant of the hall, Kennedy turned her attention to the skin-and-bone dogs that snuffled amid the hay in search of fallen morsels. Poor things. They looked ready to lie down and give it all up.

"Lady Lark." Jaspar had returned with her bird. "I trust you fared well in my absence."

"I have." Kennedy noted the woman's flushed cheeks and the tic at a corner of her mouth as she advanced. "I suppose you know Wynland has taken Joan and gone in search of his nephews?"

Jaspar's disposition soured further. "Though I warned him the wench lies with the tongue of a snake, he would not be turned from his course."

Wench...Kennedy didn't like that word.

Jaspar sighed. "I will have to deal with the trollop when she comes skulking back."

From wench to trollop. "What makes you think she's lying?"

The woman stroked her bird. "Likely, she fancies Lord Wynland, as does many a woman."

*Not this one.*

"'Tis curious that he attracts them so." Jaspar slid her gaze to Kennedy. "He is hardly handsome, is he? I wonder that any woman would welcome his embrace."

*Looks aren't everything,* Kennedy silently defended him, surprising herself.

Watchful, Jaspar said, "I pity the woman who must take him to husband."

A lie if ever Kennedy had heard one. From the body language that fairly shouted from this woman, she would not only welcome Wynland's embrace but pity herself if another were to "take him to husband."

The lady puffed her chest with new breath. "Enough, though. Let us speak of you, Lady Lark."

Not a good topic. "After that horrendous ride, I'd like to clean up and rest."

Jaspar put a hand on her arm. "Once your chamber has been made ready, you may do so."

"No need to put yourself out for me. Whatever you have will work fine."

"Nay, Lady Lark, 'twould be remiss of me to not provide for a *friend* of the king."

She was as suspicious of Kennedy as Lady Aveline had been. "Really, I don't mind—"

"Surely you can spare me a few minutes?"

Kennedy swallowed her sigh. "All right."

"Now, with regards to your gown..."

Not where Kennedy wanted to go. "Is your bird blind?"

Jaspar frowned. "He is a hawk and, nay, he is not blind. Why do you ask?"

"The thing over his head."

"'Tis a hood." She laughed. "I am surprised, Lady Lark. Know you naught of hawking?"

"I've led a rather sheltered life." Or *had*. It was a long way from the grits and gravy of North Carolina to the grit and grime of Los Angeles.

Jaspar's gaze reflected her deepening suspicion, and suddenly the topic of Kennedy's clothing didn't sound as bad.

"About my gown," she said.

The woman clung to her misgivings a moment longer, then took the bait. "Lord Wynland said it does not fit well, that you have..." She smiled faintly. "...added weight."

Kennedy clucked her tongue. "It's all that fancy food they serve at court."

The woman smoothed a hand across her eighteen-inch waist. "I fear none of my gowns will fit you."

"Then I'll have to make do with what I have."

"My maid, Esther, is a large woman, though mayhap not as large as you. She may have a gown you can borrow."

Never had Kennedy been called a "large" woman. She was no waif—at least, not in this dream—but one hundred thirty five pounds on a five foot eight frame was nothing to fuss about. In fact, she would give anything to be this weight again when she awoke.

"Are you not warm, Lady Lark?"

So much that the gown and hair at the back of her neck clung. However, as much as she wanted to throw off the cape, not only would her snug outfit elevate the woman's suspicions, it would invite further insult. "Actually, I'm chilled."

"You must be ailing." Jaspar turned so abruptly her pet flapped its wings. "Come, let us draw near the fire."

Kicking herself all the way, Kennedy followed her to the hearth where the woman passed her hawk onto a perch and lowered into the largest of three chairs.

As Kennedy settled onto the chair beside hers, Sir Leonel entered the hall.

"Leonel, dear," Lady Jaspar said, "join us."

"All is well, ladies?" He halted alongside the fireplace and raised a booted foot to the hearth.

"Quite," Jaspar said.

Kennedy felt perspiration trickle down her back.

"You are not what I expected, Lady Lark," Jaspar said, looking cool in spite of the heat beating on her. But then, the material of her gown was light and her hair braided off her neck.

Trying not to squirm, Kennedy said, "How is that?"

"Your peculiar speech, mannerisms, lack of...well, gentility."

Kennedy glanced at Leonel who looked suddenly uncomfortable. Before Kennedy's mother divorced her abusive husband, Kennedy had often felt the sting of such cruelty, especially from other children. Then she and her mother moved to California. For years, her mother put in twelve-hour days in hopes of raising her daughter above an eighth grade education. For the first time in Kennedy's life, she had worn halfway decent clothes, made friends, and competed in school athletics that earned her a scholarship. Her mother's selflessness had leveled the playing field so Kennedy would never again feel inferior to anyone. But then came Graham's mother, an American blue-blood who had done her best to keep Kennedy off the playing field, even when marriage to her son had made an undesirable her daughter-in-law.

"I have heard you have not a surname," Jaspar fueled the fire, "that you are not of the nobility."

Kennedy rose. "If you would tell me where my room is, I will leave you to your needlepoint—or whatever you do for intellectual stimulation."

Jaspar feigned surprise. "Why, Lady Lark, have I offended you? I vow 'twas not intended."

"I'm tired. Where's my room?"

"Come now, do not be so—"

"I'll find it myself." Kennedy started for the doorway. Gentility! She had more class in her little finger than Miss High and Mighty had in her entire body. So if she thought—

Kennedy applied brakes to her indignation. Was that what this dream was about? Dealing with the demons of her past? Coming to terms with the child in her, the insecurity she had worked to overcome?

"Do you think you can satisfy him?" Jaspar called.

Kennedy had been too caught up in self-analysis to realize she was followed. She turned. "Satisfy who?"

"You know I speak of Fulke."

"What are you talking about?"

"Your marriage, Lady Lark." A feline smile curved her mouth. "Surely you have not forgotten?"

# 8

MARRIAGE TO WYNLAND? It made no sense. The book had said Lady Lark was sent to care for his nephews. Could there be more to it? More that was never known due to her disappearance? Or was this a set up?

"Poor Fulke," Jaspar lamented. "I wonder how he shall feel when he learns he is to wed the leavings of another man."

Sir Leonel appeared over Jaspar's shoulder. "Cousin!"

"Quiet, Leonel!"

He closed his mouth.

Letting Jaspar's gibe roll off her, Kennedy focused on the bigger picture. If the woman was telling the truth, how did she know of the marriage when Wynland did not? Why wouldn't it have gone down in history? *Because this is only a dream.*

"Naught to say, Lady Lark?"

Kennedy knew what the woman implied, but she wasn't letting any figment of her imagination get the better of her. "I'm merely curious about how you learned of the marriage."

The woman's poise faltered. "I have friends at court. As there was talk the king might match me with Fulke, word was sent when you were chosen."

To Kennedy, the thought of someone choosing her life partner was deplorable. It was a good thing she had been born during a more enlightened time. In the midst of congratulating herself, she remembered her divorce. Kennedy Plain was no poster child for wedded bliss.

"The...arrangements are between the king and me," she said. "It is not common knowledge." If the marriage had been fabricated to expose her as a fraud, that should throw a wrench in the works.

Lady Jaspar tried on a smile a size too large. "There are no secrets at court, Lady Lark. Surely you know that. Even the walls have ears."

It sounded like Washington, D.C. "I must remember to warn the king the next time we meet."

That unsettled Jaspar enough to drop her chin a notch. But what about Wynland? When he returned, would Jaspar tell him of the marriage that might not even be? That could get sticky.

Kennedy tugged at the neck of her cape. "If you don't mind, Lady—"

"Why you?" Tears brightened Jaspar's eyes. "Why did the king choose you?"

Then her disparaging comments about Wynland's looks *were* a smokescreen behind which to hide her wounded pride. Still, it was a good question. If Lady Lark was to have married Wynland, why had the king chosen a woman of her reputation? A reputation he knew first hand?

"I thought it might be my age," Jaspar said, "but now that I have seen you, it cannot be. You must be at least twenty and five."

Twenty eight, soon to be twenty nine, but it was no compliment Kennedy had received. From the woman's tone, she considered twenty-five old, as if she herself had not attained that age several years earlier. Thinking this might be another test and not knowing how old the real Lady Lark would have been, Kennedy put the question back on the woman. "How old are you?"

For a moment, it looked as if Lady Jaspar would refuse to answer, but she said, "I have attained my twenty-third winter."

Was she lying? Pretty as she was—providing she didn't show her teeth—she looked nearer thirty. "Just out of curiosity, how old is Mr.—Lord Wynland?"

"Fulke is seven years older than I."

Thirty. Again, Kennedy was off in her estimation, having guessed he was mid-thirties. It seemed people of the past had aged more rapidly.

"The chamber is ready, Lady Jaspar," someone said.

Over her shoulder, Kennedy saw a woman on the stairway.

"You have not answered me," Jaspar said. "Why would the king choose a woman of low birth and morals to wed his finest vassal?"

They were back to name calling. "I'm just unlucky, I guess."

Stunned silence.

"Lead the way," Kennedy said to the woman on the stairs. Only when she was out of sight of Jaspar did she allow her shoulders to relax.

"Lady Lark," Leonel called as she stepped off the stairs into a passageway.

She turned. "Yes?'

"I pray you will accept my apology. My cousin means no harm. She is merely pained by her loss."

The woman had no idea that a favor was being done her. "I understand."

"I thank you, my lady."

"No problem." She turned from the confusion she had a knack for putting on the face of most everyone she encountered in this dream and entered a room smaller than the one she had been given at Brynwood Spire. Again, there was only a bowl and a pitcher of water for bathing.

"I am Esther," the servant said.

Kennedy looked more closely at Jaspar's maid who might have a gown she could borrow. She was not as tall as Kennedy, but there would be plenty of swimming room in any garment she might loan.

"My mistress has given me to serve as your maid for the duration of your stay."

What was behind the generosity? From Esther's white linen cap to the hem of the dowdy wool skirt packaging her five foot seven frame, she looked harmless enough, but looks could be deceiving.

"Do you need anything, you have but to ask. *Is* there anything you require, my lady?"

— 78 —

Kennedy considered the bed, the stool, and the three-legged table. "You have no idea," she muttered. "No, thank you. I require nothing—or 'naught' as you people say."

As the woman turned to the door, Kennedy ran her tongue across her teeth and grimaced. "I take that back."

Esther looked around.

"I could use a toothbrush and paste."

"I shall see what I can find."

As for the perpetual draft up Kennedy's skirt... "I don't suppose you have any extra underwear laying around?"

"Underwear, my lady?"

"To cover your...private parts."

The woman gasped. "Surely you do not mean braies?"

Was that what they were called? "Yes, braies."

"But, my lady, 'tis unseemly for a woman to wear braies."

Only men wore them? No, Esther just didn't understand. "What do you call a woman's braies?"

"You do not, my lady. Though, mayhap, where you come from women wear these...underwear, 'tis not done in England."

"You're telling me *you* are wearing nothing under your skirt?"

"Indeed, my lady. What need have I for the like?"

Kennedy rubbed a hand across her face. Men were behind this. "I'll need some material, needle and thread, and scissors." Not that she knew much about sewing, but how hard could it be?

Esther made a sound in her throat. "I shall return anon, my lady."

When she was gone, Kennedy lowered her aching bones to the feather mattress. Now if she could stay awake long enough to brush her teeth and remedy this pesky draft.

*How hard could it be?* Kennedy silently mocked as she sucked a finger. Though the needle was so dull it could barely pierce cloth, it suffered no such difficulty where flesh was concerned.

— 79 —

"Mayhap you ought to leave it for later, my lady," suggested the woman whose threadbare gown hung shapeless on Kennedy.

Kennedy considered the woman perched on the stool, then the crude garment. Excepting a drawstring that would have to do in place of elastic, it was finished. "Tell me about Lady Jaspar."

"Ah. I fear my mistress does not like you, Lady Lark."

"That's obvious." As Kennedy picked up the material she hoped to transform into a drawstring, she tongued her lower front teeth in hopes of dislodging the bristle there. The "toothbrush" Esther had brought—a miniature broom—had left behind several such reminders of its crudity.

"You must forgive my lady," Esther said. "Her life has not been easy."

Didn't Jaspar take responsibility for anything? First Leonel, now her maid apologizing for her.

"She should never have been wed to a man old enough to be her grandfather twice."

Kennedy blinked. "Lady Jaspar is married?"

"Lord Thurford died last summer. Four score, he was."

Eighty. Talk about robbing the cradle.

"My lady had hoped the king would match her with Lord Wynland. They were once to have wed, you know."

The needle slipped and caught in the flesh beneath Kennedy's thumbnail. She grunted and pulled it out. "Come again?"

Confusion.

"I mean...say that again."

"They were betrothed. You did not know?"

Never a dull moment. "What happened?"

"Six months ere the wedding, Lord Wynland went to France to help put order to the king's war. Following the recapture of Limoges, word of Lord Wynland's death was brought to my lady. While she grieved, her father made a marriage between her and Lord Thurford."

Though Kennedy didn't want to pity the woman who had tried to make her feel like scum, sympathy crept in. So did suspicion. Why was the maid so forthcoming?

Esther cleared her throat. "Hardly were the vows spoken and the marriage bed warmed than Lord Wynland returned to make a lie of his demise. Broke my lady's heart, she so loved Lord Wynland."

Was this what had soured him—put him on the road to murder? Kennedy scratched a thigh chafed by Esther's wool gown. "When did this happen?"

"My lady was fifteen when she wed the old baron and is now twenty and three."

Fifteen years old! There were laws against that—in the twenty-first century. Kennedy threaded the drawstring through the casing.

"My poor Jaspar, she who should have been wife to an earl wasted on an old fool."

The story grew muddier. "Jaspar was to have been the wife of an earl? But you said she was betrothed to Wynland."

"Aye, and he would have been earl if his older brother had not turned from the monkhood to take his father's title."

Following this was about as easy as wrestling a Rubik's cube.

Esther frowned. "'Tis strange you know naught of this."

"As I'm sure you know, King Edward is a busy man. Since my betrothed didn't become earl, he must not have thought it important to mention. So what made Wynland's brother change his mind?"

Though Esther looked skeptical, she said, "'Twas the earl's mother who convinced him to take his birthright."

"She's not dead?"

"She is now. Let me explain. After five years of marriage to his first wife, Fulke's father sent the woman to a convent in France where he had her take vows to become a nun. That done, the church granted him an annulment that allowed him to wed Fulke's mother, Lady Aveline. Thus, had Fulke become earl, he would not have attended the king's war and would now be wed to my Jaspar."

Kennedy congratulated herself on wading through the mishmash. But though she knew she should accept the pats on the back and run, it would be foolish to not take advantage of Esther's knowledge. "I understand the earl of Sinwell may have been murdered. What do you think?"

"You are asking if I believe your betrothed murdered his brother?" A hint of a smile wrinkled her upper lip.

She seemed pleased with herself, as if she had led Kennedy down a path her mistress had said she should.

"'Twas likely he did it. 'Tis not beyond one such as Lord Wynland."

A ruthless military advisor. Still, Kennedy had the feeling Jaspar was behind Esther's revelations, that all the woman said was designed to send Kennedy scurrying for cover. "For argument's sake, let's say it wasn't Lord Wynland. Who else could it have been?"

The question seemed to set Esther back. After some moments, she allowed, "I suppose 'tis possible it was simply an accident."

"And if not?"

Esther shrugged. "Mayhap you ought to look to the one who attacked your baggage train, my lady."

Fulke Wynland.

"Too, it could have been Baron Cardell."

Kennedy frowned. "Why would he do such a thing?"

"He covets wardship of John and Harold, which the earl promised him in the event of his death. 'Tis a position of great power."

Sticky. "How did Fulke Wynland gain wardship of the boys?"

"By the king's decree. Lord Wynland is a favorite of his."

"But if Cardell may have killed the earl, why does Wynland allow the man to accompany him?"

Esther smiled. "Better at his side than his back, eh?"

True. "One more thing, Esther, did Wynland ever marry?"

Laughter escaped the old woman. "Nay, though many a match the king has tried to make."

Was he mooning over Jaspar? If so, what held him back when there seemed no more barriers?

Esther leaned near. "I pray that all I have told you will help you better understand my lady and the reasons for the things she says and does."

There was more to the maid than met the eye. Perhaps Jaspar hadn't put her up to this chat. "You must care very much for her."

"We have been together since her birth when I was given to be her wet nurse."

Whatever that was.

Esther stood. "I shall come for you ere the nooning meal."

Only then did Kennedy realize how hungry she was, her last meal having consisted of a biscuit and a piece of meat. Transported back to the stream, she remembered awakening to find herself curled against Wynland, his face above hers, gaze intent. It had been as if seeing him for the first time, and for a moment she had found it hard to believe that he and the villain of Mac's book were the same.

A creak and groan returned Kennedy to Castle Cirque and the woman slipping out the door.

"Esther!"

She poked her head back inside. "My lady?"

Though the question of whether or not Wynland had returned Lady Jaspar's love was on Kennedy's mind, she held up her handiwork. "What do you think?"

Esther grimaced. "'Tis true that where you come from women wear these...underwear?"

"It's all the rage."

Esther shook her head and closed the door.

Kennedy scrutinized the lopsided cut and uneven stitches. The underwear was a far cry from her seamless briefs that molded like a second skin, but this was as good as it was going to get.

Shortly, she wished it got better. She gave the drawstring a final tug, laid down on the bed, and tried not to squirm. At least she didn't feel as exposed. Definitely better, even if the fit was worse than boxers and the material as prickly as her borrowed gown.

She tried to take her mind off the discomfort by pondering the questions tapping at the back of her head: Did Jaspar have anything to do with the earl's death, the attack on Lady Lark, John and Harold's fiery end? She recalled the woman's acknowledgement of Baron Cardell when they first arrived. Partners in crime?

It made more sense that Jaspar and Wynland were working together. Kill off the earl, his sons, and Lady Lark, and Fulke would become earl, opening the door for Jaspar to be his wife. Of course, the murders might be unrelated.

It was a thought, and Kennedy's last before sleep snatched it away.

"What is your name?" a voice rasped.

The woman opened her eyes, searched beyond the grate twelve inches above where she lay. Though there had been no light before, there now shone enough to give shape to the dark one who stood over her. For a moment, she feared it might be death come to call, immured as she was in a cell in which there was only enough room to lie down—not much bigger than a coffin. Nay, she was very much alive, but for how long?

"Who are you?" she croaked, her own voice raw from hours—perhaps days—of calling for help.

"Your name!"

She lifted an arm and shuddered at the sound of scampering. She could hardly rest for keeping the rats from gnawing at her. Swallowing hard, she hooked fingers through the grate and lifted her head from the dirt floor. "Pray, tell me...why do you hold me?"

"I ask again, what is your name?"

She had thought the dark one was a man, but there was a quality about the voice that made her wonder if her captor was a woman disguising her voice. "First, tell me the reason I am here. Why you murdered—"

"Are you thirsty?"

She could not remember ever being so dry. "Aye."

"Hungry?"

Starving. "Aye."

"Then your name."

Naught to bargain with, only a name she would have thought he— or she—already knew.

"Do you know what this hole you are in is called?" He bent down. Eyes catching a cinder of light amid a shadowed hood, he stared at her through the grate. "'Tis an oubliette, meaning a place to be forgotten."

She had known fear before, but nothing compared to that which dragged perspiration from her chilled skin. From the moment she had regained consciousness, a rank odor had pressed upon her that she refused to acknowledge. There was no hiding from it now. She wanted to grovel and plead, but a glimmer of spirit that was her father in her sought assurances. "You will bring me water and food?"

The dark one's eyes glittering large, he straightened, then turned and walked away.

"Lark!" she cried. "I am Lady Lark!"

His footsteps grew louder with his return. "What proof have you?"

Proof? All who had made the journey with her from London were surely dead, excepting perhaps her maid who had run screaming into the wood. "I tell you, I am Lady Lark, sent to Brynwood Spire by King Edward to care for the orphans John and Harold Wynland."

"*That* is your proof? Mayhap you are but a maid."

"I am a lady!"

"I do not hear it in your speech."

Because it wasn't. Though she could affect the speech of the nobility as she had at court, fear made her revert to the commoner. "Am I not clothed as a lady?"

"Aye, but ladies do not always make themselves known when they travel. 'Tis often safer."

He was saying she and her maid had switched clothes? Desperation gripped her more fiercely. She didn't want to die. Not here. Not like this. *Think! You have not come this far to die so young.*

She gripped the grate tighter. "The larger of my trunks has a false bottom. In it is a missive written by the king and addressed to Lord

Wynland." Forget that it was intended for none but Wynland. It was all the proof she had, the only thing that might save her from this place of forgotten souls.

"I have read it," her captor said.

Then he knew?

"Tell me," he said, "what does it say?"

"That I am to wed Lord Wynland."

"That is all?"

Far from it since what was contained in the latter part of the missive was more the reason for its concealment. Feeling as if she betrayed, though her captor already knew the contents, she said, "It says that the marriage is by order of my father, King Edward."

The dark one clapped. "Excellent, Lady Lark."

"You will release me?"

He sighed. "Alas, 'twould seem you are exactly where you belong." He strode opposite.

All for naught. As surely as she breathed, not a crumb of food or a drip of water would be forthcoming. "My father will have your head for this!"

A door creaked open. "First he must find his bastard daughter. I think not."

Lark wailed and shook the grate until blood fell from her fingers and ran with her tears.

# 9

THE GRIM REAPER at her back. Heaving breath, racing heart, pounding fear. The scythe sluicing the air, its death whisper shearing the hair from her nape. A strangled cry. Louder and louder until it wrenched her from the darkness into a day on which the sun was setting.

Kennedy opened her eyes and traced the long shadows that fell across the carpet she sprawled on, in the next instant thanked God her appointment with death had been only a dream. Not that it wouldn't happen soon enough.

As much as she wanted to put the dream behind her, she had to write it down before it faded. She lifted her head and groaned at the pain behind her eyes and the aches sleep had done little to alleviate. What time was it?

She looked at her watch. 4:57 p.m. She had slept close to twenty hours. She needed more sleep, but not until she made a journal entry. As she struggled up from the floor, her gaze fell on Mac's book.

"Wynland." Only a dream, but so vivid it was as if she had truly traveled back in time. It was different from any dream she had ever had, and she recalled every moment though the nightmare from which she had awakened was fast slipping away. Why wasn't she struggling to hold onto the rapidly fading memories of a distant time, a far away place, an imagined man?

It must be sleep deprivation. Time and again her subjects reported that their dreams seemed true to life, and their recall had been incredibly detailed. Too, the dreams were lucid in that the subjects were aware they were dreaming and consciously acknowledged it as Kennedy had. But this...

She made it to her desk and dropped into the chair, but as she opened the journal, nausea sent her lurching to the bathroom. Afterward, she pressed her brow to the cool tile floor and struggled to hold sleep at bay. When it beckoned more forcefully, she dragged herself upright, leaned against the sink, and splashed cold water on her face. It helped, though still she longed to curl up and go to sleep. Lifting her head, she came face to face with her reflection.

One look gave a whole new meaning to "death warmed over." She drew a trembling hand down her gaunt face. How much longer? A month? A week? Days? Fighting tears, she touched her baldness. And she had wanted to come back to this, had been desperate to escape a dream called Wynland so she could return to this real world with all of its ugly truths.

She closed her eyes and remembered how it had felt to run, to breathe deeply, to be free of headaches, to drag fingers through her hair. To feel that way again, she would gladly suffer Fulke Wynland.

"Now I understand, Mac," she whispered. But if she was able to return to the dream, would she begin to believe as he had done? Would she drive herself mad with the certainty that the people and places were real?

She couldn't let that happen. She was an authority on sleep disorders and dreams and knew the difference between reality and fantasy. No matter how appealing the dream was, she would be a fool to believe in it. She trudged back to her desk.

*September 13th, 5:15 p.m.: Following eighty-six hours of deprivation, succumbed to sleep on September 12th at approximately 10:30 p.m. No EEG (too tired to hook up). Awoke September 13th at approximately 5:00 p.m. following 18-1/2 hours of continuous sleep. Recall two dreams: the one I awakened from in which I was chased by the grim reaper (subconscious). I remember the other dream in its entirety, as if I truly lived it. I read Mac's book "The Earl of Sinwell" prior to sleep and dreamed myself into the story. Very detailed, right down to hay on the floor. No clue as to where I came up with the specifics. They weren't in the book, and I know little about medieval life. Another oddity is that I didn't recognize anyone, though one little boy seemed familiar. The dream was lucid, and many times I acknowledged I was dreaming. Though on several occasions I attempted to escape the dream, I was unable to. Events were as follows:*

Over the next hour, Kennedy outlined her experience, beginning with her awakening in the forest and ending with her laying down in her room at Castle Cirque.

She lowered the pen, sat back, and dropped her lids over her burning eyes. Now sleep. Once she was rested, she could begin another cycle. She dreaded it, but if she was to conclude her research—

She opened her eyes. As much as she ached to sleep, it would be a waste of precious time. How much she had remaining, she didn't know, but the mirror didn't lie. She was dying. Four or more days building toward deprivation might be her last. She had to start now while she was still under a sleep deficit. So sick-tired that a sob caught in her throat, she picked up her pen.

*6:30 p.m.: Begin second sleep deprivation cycle. Though all of me hurts, I have to use the balance of my sleep deficit if I'm going to—*

The doorbell rang. Mother? She glanced at the answering machine. Five messages. Fortunately, she'd had the foresight to turn off the ringer and volume to prevent the machine from interfering with her dreams.

The bell rang again. "Kennedy?" Though the Southern lilt was muffled, it was her mother. "Are you home, dear?"

Kennedy jumped up, retrieved the knit cap from the couch, and dragged it on. "Coming!" Though her legs dragged, she made it to the door and opened it to a lovely lavender ball of fluff.

Laurel Jacobsen's smile wavered at the sight of her daughter, but she was too experienced with false gaiety from fourteen years of marriage to Kennedy's father to reveal her true depth of shock. She opened her arms.

Kennedy went into them. "What are you doing here, Mom?"

Laurel wasn't ready to let go, but when she did, her smile was brighter than ever. "Checking on my girl." Her eyes flicked to the knit cap.

Kennedy stepped aside. "Come in."

"Do you know how many times I've phoned?"

Kennedy straightened the cap so the false hair fell evenly across her brow. "Five times?" Feeling the throb of a headache, she closed the door.

"Four. Have you been out?"

"No, I muted my answering machine and haven't checked for messages all day."

"Why?"

"I'm trying to get some work done."

"But you're on leave."

It would have been better to say she had been resting. Affecting an ease that screamed in the face of exhaustion, Kennedy took her mother's lavender handbag and set it on the sofa table. "Just because my project has been shelved doesn't mean I can walk away from it, Mom. The data needs to be compiled for the foundation that awarded the grant. More importantly, if someone decides to complete the study, my work will give them a leg up."

"Look outside, Nedy," her mother reverted to the nickname she had used when Kennedy was a child. "It's a beautiful day." She gestured to the windows. "Well, it was. You should have been taking in the sun. It would have put color in your cheeks."

Kennedy crossed to her desk and stashed the journal in a drawer. "I know, but this is important."

"And your health isn't?"

Her mother knew the diagnosis and that the chemotherapy was unsuccessful but refused to accept it. Though Laurel had never believed in miracles, she professed to believe in them now—was certain her prayers would be answered.

"Nedy?"

Kennedy turned and admonished herself for coming around so quickly. "There are some things I need to do, Mom. I can't just sit around waiting—"

"You need to get more sleep." There was fluster in Laurel's voice.

"Don't worry, I'm taking good care of myself." *Liar, liar.* Trying not to weave, she headed for the kitchen where she kept the pain relievers.

"Graham called me. He's worried about you."

Kennedy opened the refrigerator and pulled out a bottle of water and the vial.

"Oh, what's this?" Laurel asked.

Kennedy looked over her shoulder at where her mother held Mac's book.

"This doesn't look like the usual research tome." She dropped back the cover and flipped through the pages. "Seems pretty old. What's it about?"

For some reason, Kennedy felt as if caught with a naughty magazine. "A fourteenth-century British earl. A friend gave it to me."

Laurel peered at the barely legible title. "The…Sins…of…"

Pained by her mother's struggle that went deeper than far-sightedness, Kennedy finished for her. "…the Earl of Sinwell."

Laurel's eyebrows jumped. "Doesn't sound dry at all. Finished with it?"

"Pretty much."

"Do you mind if I borrow it?"

Inwardly, Kennedy groaned. She should have known where the question was leading, but her mind was too slippery to stand straight. Still, it wouldn't hurt anything. "Go ahead."

"Wonderful. Jack just finished reading one of his thriller-killer books to me. After all that gore, I could use a good biography." Laurel tucked the book under her arm. "Now back to Graham. He says you aren't returning his calls."

"Can I get you something to drink?"

"I'm fine, dear. Why won't you talk to Graham?"

Kennedy removed a cup from the dish rack. "He needs to move on, and so do I." She poured herself water and downed the pills.

"He wants to be here for you."

Kennedy refilled her glass.

Laurel sighed. "Have you been eating enough?"

"I have." *Pants on fire.* "I'm fine, Mom. Really."

"How about I take you to that pizza kitchen you like so much?"

As hungry as Kennedy was, and as empty as her refrigerator stood, she didn't want to go anywhere. How was she going to get out of this? "What about Jack?"

The mention of Laurel's second husband caused a glow to surface her mother's worry-weary face. "He'll understand."

He was a peach, had taken good care of Kennedy's mother these past five years. Just knowing he would be there for Laurel when this was all over was a relief too great for words.

"Please, Nedy."

These *were* their last days together. "All right."

Her mother beamed. "That's my girl. Now let's get you changed. You look as if you slept in your clothes."

She had. She stepped around her mother. "I'll just be a few minutes."

Alone in her bedroom, Kennedy let her shoulders slump and closed her eyes. Sleep pounced on her. Forcing her eyes open, she stumbled to the closet.

Though she longed to stay at the condo, the drive would refresh her and dinner with her mother would be time well spent. Too, the outing should be good for at least a few hours toward her next cycle.

Laurel Jacobsen clenched her teeth to hold back the emotion in her throat. Her baby was sick. Might even—

No, God wouldn't take Kennedy. He wouldn't!

"I'm ready," Kennedy said.

Laurel drew a deep breath and turned. Her daughter wore a denim jumper that had looked lovely on her last year. Now it hung from her.

*Please, God.* Laurel gripped the book tighter and summoned a smile so tight it hurt. "Then we're off."

The entry was made. With an additional seventy-two hours of deprivation, it was time.

Kennedy confirmed that the electrodes attached to her head were secure, then flipped on the machine.

Would this night's dream be as vivid as the other? Lucid? She thought again of Wynland who had yet to fade from memory. Supposing she hadn't awakened, where would the dream have taken her?

She began to slide into herself and out of consciousness. *Think of something else, like snorkeling in the Bahamas, sand between your toes, the political mayhem in Washington, anything but Wynland.* Though it wasn't likely she would find herself back in that crazy dream, there was no need to set the stage when there were so many other places her dreams could take her. Of course, would she be able to run in them? Would her health be restored? Or was she headed for a nightmare?

Fight it though she did, Kennedy's thoughts returned to a man whose strong arms had held her securely. Who hadn't let her fall.

# 10

*Did he appear
because I fell asleep thinking of him?
If only I'd known I was dreaming,
I'd never have awakened.*
~ Ono No Komachi

F ULKE STARED AT Jaspar. "Gone?"

Her gaze flitted to Leonel. "Aye, my lord. Following your departure two days past, Esther saw Lady Lark settled in her chamber. When she went to fetch her for the nooning meal, the lady was gone."

"Impossible."

"But true, my lord."

"Is it?"

Disbelief widened Jaspar's eyes. "Surely you do not believe I—"

"Nay." Or did he? He stared at the woman who would have been his wife if King Edward had not called him to arms, she of beauty, a pleasing disposition, and a cunning streak of which he had quickly become aware during their betrothal. But though Jaspar was spoiled and self-centered, he did not believe she had anything to do with Lark's disappearance.

He looked past his men to Jaspar's knights and men-at-arms who had gathered in the hall to receive him. Had one of them succumbed to Lark's wantonness as he had warned her might happen? "No one saw anything?"

"The entire household was questioned, my lord," Jaspar said. "None saw her leave. She just...disappeared."

A caustic muttering drew Fulke's gaze to the man who stood before an alcove. Cardell. Fury, spurred by the antagonism that had trebled between them these past days, leapt through Fulke. He did not need to hear Cardell's words to know he believed Fulke was responsible for Lark's disappearance—just as he let it be known he believed Fulke was responsible for the death of John and Harold's father.

"If you have something to say, Cardell, speak!"

The baron stood taller. "I was but clearing my throat."

Fulke imagined fitting his hands around the man's neck. He should have sent him from Sinwell at his first utterance of dissension. But he was not finished with his brother's favored vassal. Not yet.

Cirque's senior knight fell next beneath Fulke's regard. "How could this happen?"

The man's brow mapped bewilderment. "It could not have, my lord. All entrances to the castle are guarded. No one comes or goes unchecked."

"Lady Lark did—else she is still here."

"My lord, a thorough search of the castle was made and naught was found of her."

"Then it will be searched again." Fulke motioned a knight forward. "Sir Andrew, organize the men and begin the search."

As the knight turned away, Jaspar touched Fulke's arm. "'Tis not necessary, I tell you. She is gone."

"We shall see."

Jaspar dropped her hand from him. "She makes fools of us. Why, she is likely returned to London and warms the king's bed even now."

Why that possibility should rankle him, Fulke did not know, but he disliked Lark all the more for it. Refusing to examine what was behind his rancor, he dragged himself back. Might Lark have fled to London as

Jaspar suggested? Believing him responsible for the attack on her, she had tried to escape once before.

"Unless, of course, she is not the lady she claims to be," Jaspar submitted on the sly.

The thought had played through Fulke's mind these past days, especially when he recalled her flight through the woods. A lady? Unlike any he had ever encountered. Then there was her speech that was foreign, yet familiar. It had taken a while to place it, but when he had, he had castigated himself for not connecting her with Sir Arthur. With the exception of Lark's barely perceptible drawl, their speech was strikingly similar—flat and without hint of English accent. They must come from the same place. And what of her gown that fit so poorly? If it was hers, it was several years removed from the woman she had become.

"Fulke?" Jaspar said. "What think you?"

That the dark-haired witch was more likely a lady's maid. But as always, he recalled the gown she had worn when first he had come upon her. It had belonged to a lady, not a maid, and unlike that into which she had changed at Brynwood, it had fit every curve.

He met Jaspar's gaze. "'Tis Lady Lark."

"You are certain?"

Certainty had nothing to do with it. How could it? Though rumors had abounded over Edward's newest conquest, Fulke had had better things to do than pay them heed. Now he wished he had, but all would be known once the king received the messenger sent to London to carry news of the attack on Lady Lark. If Fulke knew Edward, and he believed he did, the king would not be long in sending a contingent to investigate the deaths of his men. At that time, Lark's identity would be confirmed or denied.

"'Tis Lady Lark who was sent to care for John and Harold," Fulke said, "and that she will do when she is found." Unless he was able to convince Edward otherwise.

"But the boys are—"

"They will be found." He pinned his gaze to Jaspar, daring her to say different. Two long days of hard riding, searching, and following every scent had led nowhere, but he wasn't done. As soon as he and his men were rested and the thunderously wet day that had driven them inside was past, they would continue the search.

Jaspar put her head to the side. "You do not know, do you?"

What did she have behind her back? "Speak, Jaspar."

"The king sent Lady Lark to care for John and Harold, but more, he sent her to you." Her eyes flashed. "She is to be your wife, Fulke."

Years of self-control held him from revealing his disbelief. He and Lark were to wed? It could not be. After his years of service to the crown, Edward would not do this to him. "She told you this?"

"Aye, though I had already heard tale."

Jaspar and her talebearers. The woman's ears were everywhere.

"'Twas obvious she was unhappy about it."

*Lark* was unhappy? If it was true, she was not alone. Though time and again Edward had suggested matches aimed to increase Fulke's modest land holdings, fill his coffers, and deliver him an heir, never had the king pressed the matter so far as to send him a wife. If that was what he had done, it could prove difficult to convince Edward otherwise. But Fulke would, for his parents had taught him well the folly of an arranged marriage.

"'Tis surely the reason she left." Jaspar sighed. "Mayhap she has not even returned to London but fled elsewhere."

To escape him. Fulke rubbed the back of his neck, kneaded tight, aching muscles. All of his troubles had begun with Lark—first, the attack on her baggage train, then John and Harold's abduction, and now she was missing. What had Edward been thinking to send such a scourge upon him?

"I shall find her," he said. And when he got his hands on her...

She had done it again. Kennedy sat up. Same room. Same dreadful gown. Same makeshift underwear.

She scratched her left side, thigh, calf. The least she could have done was dream herself into something more comfortable, like that first dress. But as she had drifted toward sleep on memories of Fulke Wynland, she had tried to fight him off with reminders of the unpleasantness of the fourteenth-century, including this room and these clothes.

She lowered her feet to the floor. Now what? Wait for someone to come? Considering the days she had just come through, her headaches so severe they had actually aided in keeping her awake, the choice was obvious. Her health once more returned to her, right down to legs that longed to stretch, she stood. Wynland or not, there was a lot to recommend this dream.

Wondering what awaited her in this installment, she crossed to the door and stepped into the passageway. Feeling younger than her twenty-eight years, she hurried down the stairs and into a flurry of activity. A moment later, a hush fell as all eyes found her, excepting Wynland's whose back was turned to her.

He had come back. As for Lady Jaspar, her eyes looked as if they might pop from their sockets. *What faux pas have I committed this time?*

Wynland turned. Surprise reflected in his eyes, then anger.

Kennedy raised her chin, determined he was not going to burst the bubble she had floated in on. "Am I interrupting something?"

"A search," he snarled.

But his nephews were somewhere out there. "I understood you had left. Forget something?"

The way everyone stared at her, she might have grown two heads.

Wynland strode forward, grasped her arm, and pulled her toward the stairway.

She was too surprised to object until the stairs were before her. She strained backward, but he held tight. "Let me go!"

He hauled her up the stairs and didn't stop until halfway down the passageway. "Which one?"

Realizing he referred to the room she had been given, she asked, "Why?"

With a curse, he dragged her forward and into a room that bore no resemblance to her hole in the wall. It was large, its appointments lavish—tapestries, a curtained bed, a beautifully carved trunk, chairs and tables, a fireplace, and a bathtub. Lady Jaspar's room?

Wynland released her and closed the door. "Where have you been?"

She rubbed her arm where he had held her. "Is that a trick question?"

"Two days! Where have you been?"

Two days had passed since she had awakened from this dream? And she had truly been gone—and missed? "Let me get this straight. It's been two days since you left?"

His eyes hardened further. "Two days."

He did look scruffy. What a wild dream. She had assumed she would pick up where the dream left off. "This is strange."

"Where have you been? Lady Jaspar had the entire garrison searching for you."

Kennedy was intrigued by the dream's unexpected twist. "I imagine she's a bit hot under the collar, especially now that I'm back."

"From where?"

*Oh, about six hundred years from here—out of this dream and in the real world with all its real problems.* "Believe me, you don't want to know."

He took hold of her shoulders. "I weary of this game. Now tell me!"

Kennedy stared at him. *Calm down. Remember where you are—inside your mind.*

"I am waiting." His fingers pressed into her flesh. "And not for much longer."

"Alas, I fear I do not remember." How was that for a bit of medieval lingo?

He wrenched her nearer. "You lie."

Curiously reckless, she tossed her head back. "You think I'm afraid of you? This is my dream, and I can make you disappear just as quickly as I made you appear." Not exactly true, as she had discovered the last time she had dreamed the dream, but it sounded good—at least, until she realized what she had revealed. She hadn't meant to let him in on the dream. However, it did the trick. One moment she was all friendly with Wynland, the next a complete stranger.

Fulke stepped back from the woman and felt his anger drain. King Edward had sent a mad woman to care for his nephews, perhaps even to be his wife. How had he missed it? It wasn't as if he didn't know the face of madness. His own sister, Marion, wore it well, had thrice been betrothed and thrice returned before vows bound her to some unfortunate whom no amount of riches could convince to take her to wife.

He frowned at another possibility. Lady Lark had pleaded an injury when he asked about the attack. Was this just another lie? He returned his attention to her and saw a spark of triumph in her eyes. She thought she had won, and perhaps she had, for he still didn't know where she had taken herself to. Mad or not, she couldn't disappear so completely only to suddenly reappear. "You are not going to tell me where you have been?"

"I believe I already have."

"A dream?"

Something—uncertainty?—flickered across her face. "That's right."

Fortunately for her, he did not believe in witches. "And in this dream, did you tell Lady Jaspar that you and I are to wed by order of the king?"

Her eyes widened, then she turned away, walked to the tub, and smoothed a hand over its rim. "So what's on the agenda for tomorrow?"

Fulke glowered. Not only had she evaded his question, but tossed back another that made no sense. "Agenda? Of what do you speak?"

She kept her back to him. "Where will your search for John and Harold take you next?"

"How do you know I did not find them?"

"The book said..." She glanced around. "Never mind. You wouldn't understand."

Likely not, but he wished to know more about this book. "Tell me."

"As I said, this is a dream. It has no bearing on reality."

— 100 —

Mad. Very well, he would let it pass, but not on the matter of their marriage. "Did you tell Lady Jaspar that you and I are to wed by order of the king?"

She stiffened.

He wished she would face him, for what could be read in one's face oft bore little resemblance to the spoken word.

"Actually," she said, "Jaspar broached the subject. I merely confirmed it."

Not what he wished to hear. "Confirmed?"

"You know how Edward is." She looked over her shoulder. "You do, don't you?"

"I do."

She turned and leaned back against the tub. "He gets these ideas into his head and there's no convincing him otherwise. Believe me, I'm not thrilled about it either."

He did believe her. She was no Jaspar, or any number of women willing to look beyond a face scarred by pox and Edward's war with France as long as his coffers bulged—especially now that he controlled an earldom. As an unwed baron he had become accustomed to the attention of women, but now he found himself looked upon with greater interest. They sought him out, smiled at him, touched him with their eyes, those less coy with their hands. But not Lark, a woman used and discarded by at least one man, likely a dozen more. Why? Was it fear of him? The sins she put on him? Whatever it was, she wanted nothing to do with him. And it vexed him.

He strode forward. "Why?"

She looked up with the wariness of a deer caught in the open. Not that she wasn't quick to hide the vulnerability behind one of those "thou dost not frighten me" faces of hers. "Why what?"

"If there is to be a marriage, why are you not *thrilled?*"

She crossed her arms over her chest. "The answer is as plain as the nose on your face."

So it was, though no one had ever had the courage to speak such to him. "Am I truly such a beast, Lady Lark?" He drew a hand down his bearded jaw. "I assure you, I was not born one."

Her eyes traced his scars, lingered over the one that cut his eyebrow. "That is not what I referred to." She sidestepped and crossed to the table beside Jaspar's bed. "Everyone knows what you are—what you did. Or will do."

"Then still you believe I arranged the attack on your baggage train?"

"Didn't you?" She looked over her shoulder. "And what of your brother? What of his unfortunate *accident?*"

She was not the first, would not be the last. "You are right, his death was not an accident." He knew what he implied, saw the fear his words begat. "But as for your escort, what foolishness do you think me capable of that I would murder the king's men?"

"You did not wish Lady Lark at Brynwood."

She had done it again, spoken of herself as if she were not present. "I did not, but murder? There are ways of ridding one's self of an unwanted guest other than by the spilling of blood."

"So how does one rid one's self of an unwanted *wife?*"

"Not by murdering a dozen worthy soldiers, I vow."

She seemed to consider his words.

"And what ill do you believe I have yet to commit?" he asked.

She lifted a hand mirror. "You know better than I."

She believed he intended his nephews harm. Again, she was not the first to suggest it, which was why Edward had yielded to the nobles who objected to the boys being placed under the guardianship of one with so much to gain from their misfortune. Thus, to appease those who had petitioned for guardianship, Edward sent Sir Arthur to serve as personal guard to the boys—a man whose only claim to knighthood seemed his possession of horse and armor. A man now turned abductor. Curse Edward for Crosley! And Lady Lark!

Anger was on Fulke's tongue as he stepped toward her, but it retreated when he saw the awe with which she regarded her reflection. She touched the outside corner of one eye, a cheekbone, and her bottom lip, then tilted the mirror up and pulled strands of darkest hair through her fingers.

It unsettled Fulke, serving as a sharp reminder of the madness he suspected. "Surely you have seen your reflection before, Lady Lark?"

"Of course," she murmured. "I just never put much store in my looks. Grades and athletics were always more important. It's where the scholarships are, you know." She looked over her shoulder. "No, I suppose you don't."

He wished he understood half of what she said.

She looked back at her reflection. "You probably think I'm vain."

He did not. Were she, she would not have donned that gown. Surely Jaspar could have found something more fitting.

"You see, it's just that I've been...ill."

As in mad? "And now you are well?" He watched her face in the mirror.

"Until I awaken. I almost wish that I wouldn't." Lips touched with a smile, she met his gaze in the mirror. "Of course, then I'd be stuck with you—just like Mac."

"Who is Mac?"

She looked away and lowered the mirror. "Someone I once knew. He's dead."

A lover? Feeling a stab of emotion, Fulke reminded himself that the man had been one of many. Still, there was something about the way she said the name that made him wonder if she had felt something for him. Another stab. He didn't care. She meant nothing to him. If Edward had sent her to be his wife—

Something occurred to him that had not before. "Where is the king's missive apprising me of this marriage?"

Her eyes slid away. "He didn't send one. I was to tell you myself. And I would have if not for the attack."

Another lie? "'Tis unheard that the king would not inscribe a decree of marriage beneath his seal."

She sank onto the edge of the bed. "He must have forgotten."

Would Edward have overlooked such an important detail? Years ago he would not have, but he was no longer young, and since the queen's death, he was not always sensible. Still, Fulke might have dismissed Lark's claim, but as tale of the marriage had carried to Jaspar, it was likely the truth. Again, he cursed Edward. Fulke had not remained unwed all these years to now have a wife thrust upon him, especially one such as this, no matter how lovely she was.

He stepped in front of her. "Know this, if 'tis true the king ordered this marriage, still I will not wed thee."

Her shoulders eased. "You don't know what a relief that is. Not being a history buff, I was worried he might have the power to force the marriage."

Edward did. Surely she knew that. What she didn't know was that the king placed a high value on Fulke's military stratagem, one that had earned his gratitude and forbearance in matters such as this.

"No need to make this any more of a nightmare than it already is," Lark added.

It was like being struck in the groin. "A nightmare?"

"You know—it just wouldn't work out between us."

He knew better than to try to salve his man's pride, but this woman pushed him past all sense. He pulled her against him. "I need not speak vows to have what you so brazenly offer."

Her mouth opened, closed, opened. "You mean you'll rape me?"

Fulke frowned. "What has rape to do with this?"

Outrage sprang from her face. "What has...?" She exhaled a sound of disgust. "I warn you, if you try to force yourself on—"

"You speak of ravishment."

Her eyes narrowed. "If it makes you feel better to call it that, fine, but I call it rape."

How odd. "In England, rape is an act of abduction, my lady. I assure you, this is not that."

She rolled her eyes. "Regardless, you are threatening to rape me."

"Again, you put sins on me. Were I to know you, Lady Lark, I vow it would be so only were you willing."

"And I vow I will never be willing. Now let me go."

He should have put her from him as if she were the basest of beings, but he lowered his head and covered her mouth with his, just as he had wanted to do that morn by the stream when the last of night had shone on a face made vulnerable by sleep. Feeling her soften, he drank in the taste of her, the scent...And felt the scrape of her teeth in time to pull back.

Anger flashing from her green eyes, she strained backward. "Try that again and they'll be calling you old lipless!"

He stared at her, the images conjured by "old lipless" making his mouth turn a smile he would not have expected to feel. Then he laughed.

"What's so funny?"

"You are funny, Lady Lark. And I thank you, for it seems a very long time since I have truly laughed." He shook his head. "Mad or no, methinks I like you."

She scowled. "Fine, now get your hands off me."

He released her. "I yield. *This* time."

"Next time you won't?"

"Next time you will come willingly to me."

"Of all the arrogant—!"

"Lord Wynland," a shrill voice sounded. "Lady Lark!"

Following Lark's wide-eyed gaze, Fulke turned to where Jaspar stood in the doorway. She had witnessed what she should not have. And was worse than displeased.

"I believe this concludes our little talk, Mr. Wynland," Lark said, her voice tight.

He looked back at her. "For the moment."

Her lips parted as if to retort, but she shifted her jaw and stepped forward. "Might I impose on you, Lady Jaspar, to point me to your kitchen? I'm suddenly hungry."

"'Tis belowstairs, of course," Jaspar growled.

Without another word, Lark slipped past her into the passageway.

Fulke knew Jaspar's inner raging and felt a pang of regret for being the cause of it. She wanted him. Since her husband's death nearly a year past, she had sent one envoy after another to King Edward to suggest a marriage between her and the man to whom she had once been betrothed. And each time Edward denied her. "My apologies, Lady Jaspar. I should not have trespassed on your private chamber."

"As well you know, 'tis yours for the duration of your stay."

So it was, by right of lordship over Cirque. He strode forward. "My thanks, but I do not require such trappings. Another of your chambers will serve as well."

"You will stay the night?"

"Aye, though only that. We ride at first light."

"Then I insist you take the lord's solar."

"Very well." The sooner he started acting the protector, the sooner he would gather the remainder of his brother's people to his side.

"I would not have believed you were so eager to bed the king's trollop," Jaspar said, "especially as your nephews have yet to be found."

Her words struck hard. Though his attention ought to be on John and Harold, it was divided by a woman of ill repute. A woman he wanted. Why had he allowed her to affect him when there were matters far more pressing? Because, deny it though he did, he knew Sir Arthur would do the boys no harm? That the knight was merely misguided?

"Hear me, Fulke." Jaspar stepped near. "She is a whore."

Why did her words make him want to defend Lark when he ought to agree, to fear what disease he might incur if he laid with one who had been with so many? The answers eluded him, making him feel like a boy of ten and two.

He narrowed his gaze. "If 'tis true she is to be my wife, 'twill be my duty to bed her—after John and Harold are returned to Brynwood."

"Not if you do not wish it." Tears sparkled in her eyes. "Just as you do not wish to wed me, is that not right?"

Of course she knew, just as she had known of the king's decree that he wed Lark. "It is Lady Lark the king has ordered me to wed."

"She is not a lady!"

He couldn't argue that. Wherever Lark came from, she could not be further from English nobility. "She is different, I grant."

She gripped his arm. "I tell you, she is not the one King Edward sent."

"Mayhap. Now I have important business to attend."

Her fingernails bit through his sleeve. "Some say she is a witch."

It would surprise him if the whole castle was not abuzz with talk of her disappearance. It boded no good and was cause to be concerned about what such talk might reap. He removed Jaspar's hand from him. "I had thought you more learned than to believe in witches, my lady."

Desperation dug into her face. "Two days she has been gone from Cirque. Now, upon your return, she reappears as suddenly as she disappeared. What else is there to do but name her a witch?"

"Lady Lark is no more a witch than you," he said, though he was not entirely certain of it. "Now I must leave."

"You will see!"

He bowed curtly. "'Til supper, my lady." He started past her, halted. "Until we learn different, Lady Lark *is* a lady, and the king would have her treated as such. Thus, I trust you will find a more seemly gown to reflect her station."

Jaspar's hands turned into fists. "She is as tall as a man."

"I am sure Esther can add length to one of your gowns."

"Mine? Lady Lark is thicker than I."

Mainly due to generous curves. "Then Esther has a long night ahead of her."

Jaspar's knuckles whitened. "I will see to it."

# 11

THE DARK ONE had returned.

Mouth so parched she could barely move her tongue, skin so chilled she knew no moment's peace from shivering, Lark peered up through the grate at the one who had pronounced death upon her.

Then a miracle. Rain. It splashed her, left her gasping. But she was allowed only one swallow before it slid over her skin and seeped into the ground. Not rain. Wine. Bitter, but so very wet.

Though hope leapt within her, she drew on her remaining sanity to push it down. He was playing with her, just as he had done the last time he had come. How long had it been? Days? A week? More?

"Lady Lark, will you do as I say?"

For what? Another promise broken? However, as much as she longed to deny him, survival whispered that perhaps there would be an opportunity in what he asked of her. *Please, let there be a way out.*

She unstuck her tongue. "Aye, anything." Through thoughts chased with fog, she heard a scrape and click, then the grate was raised.

"Get out!"

It was more than she dared hope. Trembling, she turned onto her belly and levered up on arms that threatened to fail her. When her head was up and out, she looked at the dimly lit cell above the oubliette.

"Make haste!"

She dragged herself from the pit onto the cold stone floor and got a knee beneath her, but could go no further. "I...don't think I can."

"Then you are of no use to me." A booted foot struck her ribs, knocking her back toward the oubliette.

"Nay!" From somewhere, she found the strength to crawl clear of the death pit. "Pray, give me but a moment."

"Now!"

She stumbled to her feet, wove, nearly collapsed.

The sharp point of steel pressed between her shoulder blades. "Death will take you all the sooner do you think to escape me. Understand?"

She nodded.

He thrust something into her arms. "Don that."

Struggling to keep her knees from buckling, she worked the mantle around her shoulders.

The dark one whipped the hood over her head. "Now walk."

Feeling fifty years atop her twenty five, she shuffled forward and was prodded out of the cell, through corridors so dimly lit there seemed no end to them, past a guard who hastened to look elsewhere, and up a tightly-turned stairway upon which she stumbled and fell twice. Still the dark one pressed her onward. Not until the third landing did the agonizing climb end. He pushed her from the stairs to a window and threw open the shutter.

Light poured in, so bright she clapped a hand over her eyes.

"Look!"

"I have been too long without light."

Surprisingly, he allowed her eyes to grow accustomed until she could squint to peer out the window that afforded a view of the outer bailey of a castle.

Nay, not bright at all, but an overcast day that had earlier poured enough rain to cause the inner moat to flood its bank and mire the ground so that those who negotiated it were muddied.

Her captor edged beside her, was silent as if searching for something.

Stealing a sidelong glance, Lark saw his face was hidden by his hood. How was she to escape him when she was scarce able to stand and he held a dagger at her neck? It would take little effort to leave her convulsing in a pool of blood.

Though the likelihood of escape was so far out of her grasp it was not worth the effort of thought, Lark could not resign herself to death. She had to try to escape, and if she died, better here than left to rot in a grated coffin.

"There she is," the dark one said. "Before the smithy."

The one he had brought her to see? Lark put her hands to the sill and leaned forward. Beneath her touch, a stone shifted as she searched out the one of whom he spoke.

Dark hair unbound about the shoulders of a homespun gown, the woman stood in profile before the smithy's shop. Lovely, in spite of her garment, and possibly of some import considering the knight who followed her closely.

"Who is she?" her captor asked.

She was supposed to know? Either she had lost more of her mind than she realized, or the woman discoursing with the blacksmith was the stranger she appeared to be.

"Your maid?"

Hardly. Jillie was not yet twenty, short and round, and cursed with a head full of flaxen hair that defied all attempts to subdue it—as far from this woman as a duck was from a swan.

Lark started to disavow the woman, but it occurred to her it would mean her return to the oubliette. And death. "Why do you wish to know?"

She heard his sharply indrawn breath, felt the dagger's prick.

"Tell me!"

*Almighty God, give me courage.* "Who does she..." She tried to wet her cracked lips with the scant saliva in her mouth. "...say she is?"

Pain. The trickle of blood.

"*I* ask the questions."

"And I...will answer them, but only if you tell me what *I* wish to know." Would he cut her throat, end it all here?

The dagger quivered against her skin, promising a speedy end, but that was not all bad considering what awaited her below.

However, the dark one needed her—for the moment. "That, Lady Lark, is Lady Lark."

Lark jerked her head around, once more felt the stone shift beneath her hands. "What say you?"

"'Tis as the witch claims."

Why? And how? Had the woman been party to the attack on the king's men?

"Now give me the answer I seek."

If she gave it, all would be over. "First, a drink of wine." She guessed he had a skin on his belt.

More pain. More blood. "After you have answered me."

She should not have left court. Should have refused her father as she had wanted to when he told her of his plan to wed her to Wynland. "The wine, else be done with me now and never know what you desire."

The man spewed curses that were so vulgar they called to mind the one who had played at being Lark's father before she escaped him to go in search of revenge on the king who had planted her in her mother's belly.

"I weary of you," the dark one said.

Lark looked to the bailey and saw that the one who had taken her name had moved on to the woodworker's shop. "I will die whether or not I tell you. I but ask for a drink to ease my passing."

As the dagger slackened against her neck, Lark turned her head and watched the dark one search inside his mantle. She could almost taste the wine, feel it wet her dry throat, smell—

Nay! As much as she longed to drink her fill, life was staring her in the face. But how to overpower him? Beneath her convulsing hands, the loose stone grated, answering her as clearly as if it had spoken in her ear.

She did not know how she was able to move so quickly, to swing the stone, to find her mark, but her captor dropped at her feet. Breath caught in her throat, she marveled at how easy it had been and how still he lay. Was he dead? She shuddered, told herself it was no worse than a murderer deserved and what mattered was that her nightmare was over. Or was it? She could not simply walk out of here, wherever she was, for she did not know friend from foe. She took her first breath since felling her captor and panic rushed in with it.

*Calm yourself! Think!*

She considered the form at her feet. Would she recognize the face beneath the hood? If so, it might help her understand why she had been delivered to this hell. She bent and reached, only to snatch her hand back for fear of being seized.

*Run. Now!*

She dropped the stone and, as she skirted the dark one, caught the glint of steel near the stairway. It was the dagger that had flown from her captor's hand when she struck him. She lurched forward, retrieved the weapon she prayed she would not have to use, and started down the stairs.

Behind, the dark one groaned.

Blood thrummed in Lark's ears as she plunged down the steps. *Please, God, deliver me and ever I will do thy bidding.* Now if only He was listening. If only he would forgive her the sin she had thought to commit in the name of revenge.

Kennedy stared at the tower that stood watch over the outer bailey. Nothing. She put a hand to her neck and smoothed the fine hairs that stood on end. She had been sure someone was watching her.

*Just my imagination.*

She looked back at the man who turned a piece of wood into a table leg. Interesting stuff. She couldn't begin to guess from where she had culled such knowledge.

Where to now? The huge cylinder that looked like a silo? The stables? The small building from which came the sound of birds? She decided on the latter as a means to delay her return to the keep—anything to avoid Wynland and what had happened between them an hour earlier.

Though she tried to slam the door on the incident, images pushed through. She remembered his hands on her, his muscled chest against hers, the brush of his hair on her cheek, the graze of his bearded face when he kissed her. She had resisted, but more because she feared his promise that she would willingly give herself to him. She didn't believe it, but never had she felt anything quite like what she did with him—not even with Graham, her first and only love.

Why? Nervous? Out of her element? Needless to say, Wynland had thrown her for a loop when he called her on the marriage thing. She had been so certain her talk with Lady Jaspar wouldn't come back to haunt her.

"Merely confirmed it," she muttered the words she had spoken to Wynland.

Then there was her reflection. The dream had restored her health, but still her image was unexpected. It was such a contrast to the last time she had stood before a mirror that it had been like running into a long lost friend. She had missed herself.

Was this behind her reaction to Wynland? Had she simply been off-kilter? There seemed only one answer: she was warped to feel attraction for a man like him. For all of her training in psychology, this self-analysis thing was getting her nowhere. She needed her head examined by an objective—

*This is not reality.* It was a dream, and though she had been appalled when she put Wynland straight on the matter, it had been liberating. As long as she remembered this for what it was, she had nothing to fear.

She stepped toward the bird building, and the shadow that crossed hers reminded her of the one who had dogged her steps since she had left the keep—Sir Malcolm who had allowed her to fall from his horse. And he looked no worse for whatever punishment Wynland had dealt. In spite of Kennedy's annoyance at being followed, there was relief in that. Had Wynland given the knight this assignment as a chance for the man to redeem himself?

She sidestepped a mud puddle that evidenced the thunderstorm that had been all the talk in Lady Jaspar's cavernous kitchen. Of course, Kennedy had the impression that, prior to her entrance, the talk had been of her disappearance from Cirque. And more than once she had heard "witch" whispered about.

Behind, she heard the squelch of the knight's boots, then muttered curses. Obviously, Sir Malcolm had been too intent on her to notice the mud.

Kennedy turned to the thirty-something knight. "If you must follow me, can you at least make yourself useful?"

He scowled, causing his weathered countenance to age.

"Tell me about this place. What is it?"

He drew alongside her. "A dovecote, my lady. You do not know?"

"We don't have them where I come from."

"It is a place for doves—pigeons."

She stopped before a slatted window set high in the wall. "In other words, a giant birdhouse."

It looked as if he might smile. "Aye, that would be it."

She put a hand on the window ledge and peered at row upon row of birds. Numbering perhaps one hundred, they were mottled gray with the exception of a dozen white. "What are they for?"

"Their dung is of benefit to the crops, but mostly they are for the pot. And for the hawks. The great birds are especially fond of doves."

Wishing she hadn't asked, Kennedy settled back on her heels. She conjured a vision of Lady Jaspar and her hooded bird, imagined the woman serving up a sweet dove to her pet.

"Have you never eaten pigeon, my lady?"

Hadn't and wouldn't, not even in a dream. "No."

"Fair tasty they are. As Lord Wynland has returned, Lady Jaspar's cooks will likely bring doves to the high table this eve. You must try some."

"Tell me about Lady Jaspar's hawk. Why are its eyes covered?"

"To keep it calm. Know you naught of hawking, my lady?"

"Another area of my education sorely neglected."

His puzzlement deepened. "'Tis strange you would not have been introduced to hawking at court. The king delights in falconry and keeps the finest mews."

"That he does." She hoped she wasn't digging herself in too deep. "It's just that there was always something better to do."

The knight's gaze turned knowing and he grinned.

Heat flooded Kennedy's face. Since Lady Lark's reputation as mistress to the king preceded her, Sir Malcolm had taken her words to mean she had been too busy romping around the bedroom to notice something as inconsequential as a hawk.

"Would you like to see Lady Jaspar's mews?" he asked, his tone verging on friendly.

"All right." Kennedy followed him to a long wooden shed.

"The mews," he said. "If the falconer is around, he will tell you all you wish to know about hawking."

It turned out to be interesting. Best of all, it further delayed her next meeting with Wynland.

Laughter.

Fulke arrested his progress across the hall and turned to catch the entrance of Lady Lark accompanied by Sir Malcolm. No manner of peasant wear could lessen the brilliance that shone from Lark's face, just as no manner of finery could make her glow brighter. It was all Lark. No mockery, no contempt, no anger, just laughter. And it returned him to the taste of her mouth.

How had Sir Malcolm made her laugh? And what of the knight's aversion for the lady who had squirmed atop his horse? Was it her comeliness that put a smile on lips that rare turned, that made him forget what all others could not—her disappearance for which there seemed no explanation other than that she was a witch?

Fulke cursed himself for the stink of jealousy that swirled around him. Lark was a harlot, adept at winning men to her. Likely, she hoped to seduce the knight and make him an ally.

"Sir Malcolm," Fulke called.

The man's smile fell. For a moment looking as if caught with his braies down, he slid his gaze past the others who gathered for supper and inclined his head. "Lord Wynland."

"I trust you carried out my instructions."

"Aye, my lord. Never did the lady go from my sight. She but walked the outer bailey."

Fulke had known she would not like being followed but could not risk losing her again. Catching sight of her over Sir Malcolm's shoulder, he said, "Take your leave, Sir Malcolm."

"If it pleases you, my lord, I can—"

"Your leave."

The knight turned toward the tables.

Expecting Lark to avoid him, Fulke was surprised when she came toward him.

"You had a pleasant walk?" he asked.

Her smile was less brilliant than when laughter had earlier put it on her lips. "I did, though I was peeved to discover you had put a tail on me."

Peeved? And what was this about a tail? "A tail?"

"Yes, a…" She made a face. "You had Sir Malcolm follow me."

"To ensure you do not disappear again."

"Oh, I will. But next time I won't be coming back."

Fulke studied her defiant countenance, wondered if her plans included Sir Malcolm whose loyalty there had never been any reason to question—unlike some of the men who had served his deceased brother. "I thank you for the warning, Lady Lark. I shall plan accordingly."

She didn't look concerned, which concerned him all the more.

He gripped her elbow. "To supper."

Jaspar was seated at the high table, her hooded hawk on its perch at her back, when Fulke handed Lark into the chair beside the one reserved for the lord and lowered himself.

With scrapes and screeches, grunts and clearings of throats, those at the lesser tables settled in for the meal as best they could with what they feared was a witch among them.

"My lord," said one of two varlets who appeared at Fulke's side.

Fulke placed his hands over the basin held by the first, turned his palms up as water was poured over them, and held them out to be dried by the second varlet. When they moved on to Lark, Fulke envied the smile she gifted the young men as they washed and dried her hands.

Lark met Fulke's gaze, held up her hands, and turned them front to back. "Just when I was beginning to think you were all uncivilized."

Uncivilized? She, who knew so little of propriety she more often behaved as if she were a villein, should speak thus? As comely as she was, and no matter her play between the sheets, it was no wonder Edward had set her aside.

"Tell me of this Oz you come from," Fulke invited.

Apprehension flashed across her face and was gone. Eyes sparkling, lips parting to reveal even white teeth, she sat back in her chair. "There's this girl named Dorothy. She and her little dog, Toto, live in Kansas, which is tornado alley, as you know—" She wrinkled her nose. "No, you don't know. Anyway, a tornado sweeps up Dorothy's house and lands her and Toto in Oz, a bizarre place populated with munchkins."

Fulke felt as if felled by a quintain. Munchkins, tornados, a dog named Toto, and who was this Dorothy? It was the stuff of too much ale.

"The house lands on the Wicked Witch of the East," Lark continued, "and kills the hag."

Fulke could not believe she would speak thus, especially since so many believed *her* to be a witch.

"East's sister, West, isn't too happy with Dorothy." She swept her hands up. "Fortunately, Glenda the good witch is on the scene—"

He caught one of Lark's hands and pulled her near. "Quiet, woman!"

"What?"

"Speak no more of this...Oz. Do you, you may find yourself staked and burned for being a witch yourself."

She tugged at her hand. "What is this? Salem?"

"This is England where those condemned as witches are burned."

She scoffed. "Uncivilized, just as I thought."

"Lady Lark!"

The derision cleared from her face. "Do I detect concern, Mr. Wynland? I would have laid odds you wouldn't object too loudly to me being burned at the stake."

Just as she believed him responsible for the attack on her baggage train. Still, it *was* curious that he should concern himself over her well-being. Forget that she stirred longing in him. Forget the smiles she so easily bestowed on others. It had everything to do with the king. If anything untoward happened to her, he would answer to Edward.

He arched his scarred eyebrow. "Methinks you would burn most bright, my lady. But then, 'twould be upon me to explain to King Edward what became of his..." He slid his gaze from her lips to her long neck. "...to explain what became of you."

"Hmm. Methinks thou protests overly much."

It was the first time she sounded remotely English.

"Remember," she said, "*you* kissed *me*."

Music sounded from the gallery, heralding the entrance of servants bearing platters. Fulke shot Lark a look of warning, then released her and affected an interest in the victuals, all of which were so lavish they reminded him of his long and dreary days at court. Lady Jaspar had put forth quite an effort.

He looked to her and saw she watched him. How much of his conversation with Lark had she overheard? No, she wasn't watching him. She stared through him, eyes narrowed against the pain of one of her headaches. She had told him that, in her youth, she had suffered them often, sometimes so greatly she could bear only darkness, but he had thought they were resolved. Remorseful at having been curt with her earlier, he said, "'Tis a fine table, my lady."

"For a fine lord." Her smile was hopeful. "Will you share a plate with me?"

He would have to disappoint her further. "If not for my betrothed, I would. But I thank you for the offer."

"Of course." She turned to her cousin.

As if unaware of Jaspar's attention, Sir Leonel lifted his tankard, quaffed it, set it down with a thud, and slumped on an upturned palm. He was likely full up in his cups, the ale he had downed only a small portion of what he must have partaken.

Lady Jaspar's hand on Leonel's sleeve brought his head around so fast his brimmed hat slipped down over one eye. She leaned near, straightened his hat, and whispered something.

Though Fulke was not usually one to listen in on others' conversations, it unsettled him.

"Oh, my," Lady Lark gasped.

Fulke found her gaze held by an enormous platter that two squires set before them. On it was a hoofed leg of stag.

Lark looked at Fulke, her taunting self-assurance that had turned him from her minutes earlier reduced to apprehension. "Is that—?"

"Venison."

"Bambi?"

Was that what they called it in Oz?

The carver laid a thick slice of the steaming meat across the silver plate before Fulke. "My lord."

Fulke cut a piece of venison and offered it to Lark on the point of his meat dagger.

She held up a hand. "I won't have that on my conscience."

What was she talking about? If it had something to do with her witches and magic, he would put a swift end to it. "I vow you will like it. 'Tis fresh—taken this day on our return to Cirque."

She shook her head. "Fish, chicken, pizza, an occasional hamburger, but never Bambi."

He frowned. "You speak most peculiar, Lady Lark."

"And you don't?"

He carried the venison to his mouth and enjoyed every chew of it. "Delicious. Mayhap the next course will be more to your liking."

Platters came and went, but most were so foreign to Kennedy they held little appeal: lamprey—whatever it was, peacock—worse than doves, wild boar—gamey. Nearly as bad, Wynland seemed determined to feed her, time and again thrusting his blade at her with some morsel on it. Mostly, she refused, and the gnawing of her stomach increased.

Finally, a pie was placed between her and Wynland. Chicken pot pie? Fortunately, it was every bit as delicious as its scent promised.

"'Tis to your liking?" Wynland asked.

She met his blue gaze. *Nice eyes, especially when they're not glaring.* "Very much."

He stabbed a piece of chicken and offered his dagger. "'Tis the last real food you will likely see for some days."

"Oh?"

"Come the morrow, we ride again, and this time you go with me."

"You're no longer worried I might slow you down?"

"You shall ride with me."

Lovely. Kennedy plucked the chicken from his dagger and popped it in her mouth.

The fare that followed was less appealing, with the exception of apple tarts that were so tasty Kennedy ate three.

When an end to the meal was called, Sir Leonel was the first to his feet, standing so quickly and crookedly it was impossible to miss him. With tell-tale weaving, he crossed the hall and staggered outside into the gathering darkness. Probably to vomit, Kennedy guessed, and tomorrow there would be a hangover to deal with.

As she stepped from the dais, she glanced behind and saw that Wynland's and Lady Jaspar's heads were bent toward one another.

"Lady Lark?" Jaspar's maid, Esther, approached.

"Yes?"

"My lady has bid me to fit you with a gown more suited to your size."

So Wynland didn't like her in sackcloth. It was almost enough to make her reject the woman's offer. She scratched her thigh. "I'd appreciate that, especially if the fabric isn't as prickly as this."

"I am to alter one of Lady Jaspar's gowns."

And the woman was probably turning cartwheels over that. "Lead the way."

"In truth," Esther said as she and Kennedy neared the stairs, "'tis more likely fleas that bother you than my homespun."

Kennedy halted and stared down the shapeless garment.

"My lady?"

If she had been alone, she would have ripped the gown off. Gritting her teeth, she met Esther's questioning gaze. "I'm right behind you."

# 12

Eighteen buckets. From the doorway of her room, Kennedy counted them, starting with the first that arrived amid the giggles of two maids to the last lugged down the corridor amid grunts and a good deal of slopping.

A hot, steaming, up-to-your-neck bath. But it wasn't for her. It was for the woman behind door number one.

Kennedy groaned. What she wouldn't do for a quick dip, having once more been reduced to a basin of tepid water and a towel hardly big enough to blow her nose on. She scratched her midriff and gazed longingly at the door behind which Jaspar basked. Might she—?

*In your dreams.* In the next instant, she chuckled. It *was* her dream. She looked down at the slip, rather "chemise" that was all she had to wear until alterations to Jaspar's plum-colored surcoat and dark green undergown were completed. Remembering the fitting that had taken over an hour and seen her stuck twice, Kennedy thanked her stars it was over. Though the garments had to be Jaspar's least liked, they were a huge improvement over Esther's tent.

Forgetting her attire, Kennedy padded barefoot down the corridor. As she neared, she heard the sound of lapping water, a crackling fire, and voices—one of them a man's. It wasn't possible to identify Wynland from that bit of muffle, but something told her it was him. And the tinkling laughter had to belong to Jaspar.

An emotion Kennedy tried to fob off as disgust stirred, then churned when the woman's voice sounded through the door. Her words were unintelligible, but there was no mistaking Wynland's reply: "Aye."

In spite of everything Kennedy held against him, her green-eyed monster appeared. Engaged to her and playing footsie with *that* woman! She curled her toes in the water puddle courtesy of the bone-weary maids and pushed the door inward. A glimpse of the room, bathed in firelight, was all she was afforded before a hand clamped around her arm and spun her back against a wall of muscle.

Kennedy's gasp was met by light on steel and a razor-sharp edge at her throat.

"You are fortunate to yet have your pretty head on your shoulders, my lady," Wynland said.

Slowly, she looked around into his face. "I couldn't agree more. Now let me go."

Where there had been anger, amusement crept. "You are certain 'tis what you wish?"

"Of course I am."

He lowered his dagger, released her, and stepped back.

Touching her neck where the blade had worked its threat, Kennedy turned to him. "Oh!" She averted her gaze, but not before every muscle and sinew was imprinted on her memory. Clenching her hands, she searched out Jaspar who knelt beside the tub.

How smug she looked, but at least she was clothed. A washcloth in her lap, soap in her hand, face flushed, she regarded Kennedy.

"Well, isn't this cozy?" Kennedy spoke before she could get a grip on emotions she had no reason to feel.

"Why are you listening at doors, Lady Lark?" Wynland asked as he stepped around her.

Again, she redirected her gaze and peripherally saw him step into the tub.

"Lady Lark?" he prompted.

Braving the sight of his head and shoulders above the rim, Kennedy said, "I was not listening at the door."

"Then for what did you come to Lady Jaspar's chamber in the dark of night?"

Beginning to hum, that woman rose to her knees and soaped his broad shoulders.

Kennedy felt her jaw muscles cramp. "Don't you think that's more a question for you than me, Mr. Wynland?"

"I am bathing."

"And I suppose you need help doing that?"

He looked genuinely puzzled.

Kennedy stepped forward. "I'd like to speak with you. Alone."

He sank more deeply into the warmth that would have incited her envy if she wasn't so occupied with this other emotion. Resting his neck on the rim, he closed his eyes. "You think that would be seemly? After all, we are not yet wed."

*He* played house with Jaspar and talked of being seemly! "Alone," Kennedy said again.

As if he had no intention of sending Jaspar away, he let the silence ride on the melody purring from Jaspar.

Kennedy tried to bring herself back to earth, to pound into her head that none of this was real, but her insides knotted further. If ever there was an ugly emotion, it had to be jealousy, to which she had rarely been moved. She couldn't possibly be right in the head.

"Leave us, Lady Jaspar," Wynland said.

Jaspar drew a sharp breath. "'Twould be most improper, Lord Wynland."

"Leave us."

"Betrothed or not, if Lady Lark does not guard her reputation—"

"I do not believe she concerns herself with such things, do you?" He looked to Kennedy and swept his gaze down her.

Kennedy refused to cross her arms over her chest. She might be wearing something like a nightgown, but he was the one who paraded around naked.

Jaspar stood. "In that you are right." She dropped the washcloth to the floor. "I shall return shortly and wash your hair."

"Nay"—Wynland's eyes never left Kennedy—"'twill not be necessary. Good eve."

Anger mottling Jaspar's lovely face, she brushed past Kennedy and slammed the door behind her.

"We are alone," Wynland said.

"Yes, I..." Kennedy pushed her shoulders back. "What are you doing in Lady Jaspar's room?"

He sat up, exposing biceps and chest played by firelight. "You behave as if cuckolded."

"As if what?"

He grinned. "Surely you do not think I was up the lady's skirts?"

*That* she understood. "What else am I to think when you prance around naked as a jay bird?"

"Naked as a what?"

"As in nude...bare...naked!"

"That I am, but 'tis how I prefer my baths."

He was laughing at her. She knew it as surely as if he had thrown back his head and loosed the offensive sound.

"You have been in England how long, Lady Lark?"

"Long enough."

"Obviously not. Had you been, you would know 'tis not uncommon for the lady of the castle to tend her guest's bath."

"So Lady Jaspar was merely soaping you up, and that's okay?"

"How do you do it in Oz?"

"As our men are able-bodied, they soap and scrub themselves."

"Methinks I would not like this Oz."

"No, you wouldn't."

He nodded. "Now you."

"What?"

"I have told you my reason for being here. I would know yours."

"I heard the maids bringing water for the bath and thought..." She sighed. "It's been a while since I had a bath and—"

"You wished to share mine."

"No! It wasn't until I heard your voice that I realized you were in here."

"You intended to ask Lady Jaspar to allow you to bathe when she finished?"

"Not my idea of a nice bath, but better than a basin."

Wynland crooked a finger. "Come, finish that from which you took Lady Jaspar."

Kennedy dropped back a step. "I told you, we don't do that where I'm from."

Wynland smiled, the distance and shadows transforming his flawed face into borderline handsome. "You do not bathe your guests, but you do magic and wizards and witches."

"Only in the movies."

"The movies?"

She waved a hand. "Just more of my jibber jabber."

He reached over the tub, retrieved the soap, and held it out to her.

Kennedy shook her head. "It's time I left."

"And miss your bath?"

The bait was tempting, but the hook of it was Wynland. "In other words, I soap your back, you soap mine?"

He laughed. "I delight in thy voice, Lady Lark. Your expressions are so...true." He motioned her forward. "If 'tis what you wish, I shall soap your back, but after you soap mine."

"I don't think so."

"Why not? 'Twill be as I shall ask of you when we are wed—the first of many baths you shall attend."

True, but—No, not true. Even if this were real, and it couldn't be, she was fairly certain she was not Lady Lark. Also, what about Wynland's change of heart? "Correct me if I'm wrong, but didn't you say you had no intention of marrying me?"

Something leapt in his eyes. Was it possible he, too, was becoming enmeshed in this crazy dream of hers?

"I said it," he admitted, all humor gone, "and I meant it. Now, if you wish a bath that is passing warm, you will assist me in completing my ablutions."

As if on cue, a stinger of an itch travelled down Kennedy's thigh. Imaginary, she told herself, but it required scratching. Blast! What was a little soaping compared to a long soak that would soon turn cold if she continued to hem and haw? "All right." She stepped to the tub.

His fingers brushed her palm as he passed the soap to her, feeling like a caress when it was nothing of the sort.

She knelt beside the tub. "Ready?"

He sat forward.

Kennedy wet the soap and lifted it to his back. And froze. When he had walked naked from her, she had kept her gaze low. Thus, she hadn't seen the thin scars crossing his back in such abundance they screamed of the pain he had surely endured. Had someone taken a whip to him?

She touched a scar on his shoulder. Though he stiffened, she traced the puckered flesh downward, across his spine, and to the ribs opposite. "Who did this?"

He looked over his shoulder and, in a harsh voice, said, "The water cools."

She shouldn't care since he probably deserved every lash, but she couldn't help herself. "Who?"

"'Twas war."

No name to the hand that had disfigured him. Excepting Kennedy's final meeting with Mac, the Gulf war vet had viewed his life-altering ordeal similarly—holding it to him, referring to all he had witnessed and all that had been done to him by the universal label of "war."

"I'm sorry," she said.

His lids narrowed. "Are you?"

"War is ugly." She saw again Mac in his wheelchair. "So many dead. So many crippled. I think those who survive must suffer more, don't you?"

"How know you of war, Lady Lark?"

"I don't, really. All I know is what I've been told, the little I read in school, and what I've seen on tele—" She shook her head. "Never mind." She pulled her finger from his scarred flesh. "I understand you were a military advisor during the "Hundred Years War." At least, that was what Mac's book said.

"During the what?"

"The Hundred...or was it The Thousand?" She shrugged. "Maybe you call it something else."

"You speak of the war with France?"

"I think that's it."

"Why would one call it the Hundred Years War?"

"Because it lasted that long?"

"'Tis not over with, and though war is not new to England and France, this one is little more than thirty years aged."

Amazing how quickly an innocent remark hung her. "Maybe it just seems like a hundred." She looked down. "Where did that soap go?"

Wynland turned so suddenly the water spilled over the tub and wet the front of her chemise. He captured her wrist. "Are you a witch?"

She tugged at her hand. "Surely you don't believe in witches?"

"I do not. Just as I do not believe this is a dream as you claim."

"Then why ask if I'm a witch?"

He drew her forward until her face was inches from his. "That I might know if I am wrong in believing as I do."

Never would she have thought he could be moved from one side of the fence to the other. It didn't fit the picture of him drawn by the author of *The Sins of the Earl of Sinwell*. But dreams were like that.

"I'm not a witch, but this *is* a dream. You are not real. This room is not real. The fire is not real. None of it is real."

His eyes lowered to her mouth. "None of it?"

Reminded of their earlier encounter in this very room, she searched for an anchor and found it in his own words. "So call me mad. Mad as a hatter, a loon, a nut case. Happy?"

He released her wrist and laid a hand to her throat, causing water to trickle from his skin to hers. "Be you a dream or a witch, Lady Lark, your blood rushes at my touch."

"You did tell me to fear you."

His smile reached his eyes. He was hardly handsome, but when he smiled like that...

"Nay," he murmured, "'tis not fear that makes your heart beat so." He slid his hand to the back of her neck and urged her nearer. "Put your mouth to mine, Lark."

Kennedy knew she should pull away, but something held her. She felt a strange longing to feel him, a precarious tug, a stirring from out of the depths of her illness. It was a long time since she had been aware of her body in ways other than the toll taken by chemotherapy and radiation, but as welcome as the feelings were, they were dangerous. "I can't."

"You want to."

"No, I don't. I know who you are, what you did—or are going to do. I think."

"You *think?*" His voice tightened.

She closed her eyes and rued the mess she had made of herself.

"I am not who you believe me to be, Lark, and though you deny it, you know 'tis true."

Kennedy lifted her lids and saw that though his face remained near, what had shone so brightly from his eyes was gone. "I hope I'm wrong."

He released her and stood. "My towel."

Keeping her eyes low, she said, "What about your bath. I didn't—"

"Had you, I would have had your mouth. And more. Now the towel."

She swept it from the stool. His clothes lay beneath, and atop them a gold medallion suspended from a chain. Her heart almost stopped. However, it was not a two-headed wyvern stamped into the metal, but a curled feather topped by a crown.

"I wait, Lady Lark."

She reached the towel to him. "I was admiring your...medallion. It's beautiful."

He wiped himself down and stepped from the tub.

Glimpsing muscled calves, she returned her attention to the medallion. "What does this mean?" She touched the curled feather.

"You do not recognize the king's markings?"

Of course she didn't. "Well, yes. I'm just curious as to why you have a medallion bearing them."

He reached around her and lifted the medallion by its chain. As it was carried past her, it spun to reveal identical markings on the reverse. "'Twas given to me in appreciation for the retaking of lands in France. I wear it to remind me of the mistakes I made."

Did he refer to his scarred back? She lifted her face and was grateful he had wrapped the towel around his hips. Higher, his gaze awaited hers and allowed a glimpse of what might be pain. He strode toward the bed. "Make haste, Lady Lark, the water cools."

"I won't be long."

He tossed the covers back and laid down as if to stay. "Take however long you require. 'Twill not disturb me."

She took a step toward the bed. "Excuse me, but unlike you medieval people, we in...Oz, regard bathing as a private act."

He plumped a pillow. "Unless you ask it, you need not fear I shall tend you."

As if she would! "You're going to lie there while I—?"

"I am going to sleep. Dawn comes soon and with it a long ride."

"You're sleeping in Jaspar's room?"

"I am." He whipped a sheet over his lower half and closed his eyes. "Good eve."

What of Lady Jaspar? As soon as Kennedy left, would the woman crawl into bed with him?

Kennedy turned to the bath. As much as she longed to absorb the last of its heat and wash away whatever vermin crawled her skin, it was impossible to ignore Wynland. Or was it? She glanced over her shoulder. His eyes remained closed.

To bathe or not to bathe, that was the question. Or was it to itch or not to itch? She glanced around to ensure Wynland wasn't watching, snatched up the hem of her chemise, pulled it over her head, and tossed it to the ground. As she reached to her makeshift undies, she stilled. They would just have to get wet.

She lowered into the tub and stole another peek at Wynland whose chest rose and fell evenly. Relieved, she leaned back and melted up to her chin in water. Forget that it no longer passed for hot and was cloudy. It was a bath.

She fished around for the soap, found a sliver, and soaped herself from toes to scalp. Following a quick dunk to rinse the soap from her hair, she decided a few more minutes couldn't hurt and settled back.

She studied the fireplace. Red and gold leapt, crackled, popped, warmed her face. She relaxed further and mused how quickly something taken for granted attained luxury status. Even cold, she reveled in the feel of the water and its soapy scent that mingled with that of the man who had first tested its depths.

She glanced at the bed on which Wynland was stretched. As the fire had waned, deepening the shadows around the room, she could no longer make out his features.

She peered over the edge of the tub. No towel, Wynland having worn it away. All that was left to her was her chemise. Hating that, as squeaky clean as she was, she had to put that thing back on, she grabbed it. Holding it before her, she stood and, when Wynland didn't stir, stepped from the tub.

Fulke watched her as he had done the past half hour and cursed himself for things never before felt. Not that he knew what they were, so unrecognizable were they. Desire? Aye, he knew that well enough, but it was more.

How had this witch, this mad woman, slipped past his defenses? His thoughts ought to be trained on rooting out John and Harold's abductor, not Lady Lark whose ivory shoulders were swept by dark hair, chemise clasped to her chest.

He watched her struggle to make both ends of the garment meet at her back without donning it. Did she fear his gaze? When he first lay down, sleep had been his aim, but the lapping water and her sighs of contentment had put an end to that. As the shadows settled around the bed, he had watched openly. Obviously, she suspected as much, vainly playing at modesty unbecoming a leman.

A dream, she called this, so sure of it she dared where few dared and pressed him past all patience. How he wearied of her accusations, her belief he would do his nephews harm. Yet for all that, he had taken her mouth to his. He was a fool to lie awake when he could be sleeping, a fool to seek a glimpse of eyes that pierced him each time he looked into them.

Mayhap that was it—her eyes. There was great knowing in them, especially when she spoke of what was to be. It was as if she saw the morrow and knew its secrets. Those eyes made him question himself and his beliefs, so convincingly he entertained the possibility of witches. But if not a witch, how else to explain Lark? A dream, she said, but possible only if this was *his* dream. And he knew it was not. Even mad, as she acceded, that was not all of it.

She started toward the door, then turned and approached the bed.

Vaguely aware he was in need of breath, Fulke watched.

She halted alongside him and peered into the heavy shadows thrown by the bed curtains.

Confident she could not make out his features, Fulke slowly filled his lungs with the scent of her that was not all bath and soap.

Though her own face was in shadow, the last of the firelight lit her eyes, flickered across her nose and mouth, and swept the damp strands of hair about her face.

"Did you do it?" she asked so softly, so unexpectedly, he nearly revealed himself.

She had not come to lie with him, but to ask questions a sleeping man could not answer. Did she refer to the attack on her baggage train, or the fate of his nephews as she believed it to be? Either or both, something made her doubt.

She sighed. "You're just a figment." With a rustle of chemise, she turned and, a moment later, closed the door behind her.

Fulke drew a deep breath and blew it above his head. Never had a woman so disturbed him. He ought to leave her at Cirque, lock her in a tower room if that was what it took to be certain she didn't disappear again. Of course, it wasn't that simple, especially where Jaspar was concerned.

He bunched his pillow and jammed it beneath his head. Sleep was a long time in coming, but when it arrived, he dreamed as he had not done in years—of a woman, elusive, dark-haired, knowing beyond his time.

# 13

Kennedy felt like a child trapped in the back seat of a car. But it was worse than that. Not only were pounding hooves a far cry from tires and shock absorbers, but Wynland was no padded seat. And for a seat belt, she had to make do with his arm curved around her ribs and a hand to her waist.

She closed her stinging eyes against the careening scenery. She was tired, her three or four hours of sleep insufficient for a day that had begun long before the sun showed itself. In the middle of some forgotten dream—strange as it seemed, a dream within a dream—Esther had bustled her out of bed and into the surcoat and undergown she must have spent the night altering. Not that it fit well.

Though Kennedy preferred jeans and basic tops to designer labels, she had hoped the dress would flatter her rediscovered figure. But at least it was itchless.

She opened her eyes and looked over her shoulder into Wynland's face. Mouth a thin line, he trained his gaze ahead. Where was he? In the past with its faces of war, or the future that promised another kind of war—the one between him and Sir Arthur?

Next, she considered Sir Leonel who rode back and to the right of Wynland. He also seemed someplace else. Although Lady Jaspar had opposed her cousin joining the search for the children, Wynland had accepted when the man offered himself and eight of Cirque's men-at-arms. Thus, Jaspar decided she would also accompany them. Fortunately, Wynland had vetoed her. The look she shot Kennedy before disappearing up the stairs was sweltering. And so, with the sun beating on them between clouds that hinted at rain, the day weathered on.

"You are hungry?" Wynland asked.

"I am."

Shortly, he led his men into the bordering wood to a stream, dismounted, and reached to her.

She went into his arms. The brush of her against him turned up the volume on her pulse. His warm breath on her neck and face turned it up further.

"Nay," he murmured, "I did not do it."

What? Then she remembered, and with remembrance came embarrassment. He had been awake last night, had watched as she clasped the chemise to her and asked a question that his answering silence had indicated he slept.

She drew a deep breath. "Well, that makes me feel better."

"Does it?"

Why was he still holding her? "I can manage on my own, Mr. Wynland."

He released her and nodded toward a copse of trees. "'Twill assure your privacy."

To "relieve" herself. Lovely. Not since her failed attempt at "roughing it" as a teen had she made do without a toilet as this dream forced her to do. "Thank you."

He smiled.

She wished he wouldn't do that. His warming toward her was wearing a hole in her defenses and giving rise to traitorous flutterings. She made a beeline for the copse.

When she returned, a man outfitted as a soldier rode toward Wynland where he stood beside the stream. She didn't recognize him, but since he was accompanied by one of the men Wynland had posted at the outer edge of the wood, she guessed he was a newcomer.

"Alfred," Wynland called. "Bring you word from my brother?"

His brother? Kennedy frowned, but then she realized it wasn't his nephews' deceased father of whom he spoke but the disagreeable younger brother she had met at Brynwood Spire. Richard, wasn't it?

"I do, my lord."

Kennedy made it to Wynland's side as the messenger reined in.

The man dismounted, grimaced as if his ride had been as long as the one that made Kennedy's legs shaky. "My lord ordered that I deliver you this missive."

Wynland accepted it. "Refresh yourself ere you return to Brynwood." He jutted his chin to where his men gathered upstream. As if in no hurry to learn what was so important it had to be delivered by pony express, Wynland thumbed the wax seal, then tucked the paper into his belt. He bent to the stream and splashed cold water on his face.

"Aren't you going to read it?" Kennedy asked.

He looked up. "When Squire James returns."

"What does he have to do with it?"

Wynland stood. "For one who gives few answers, you ask many questions."

"Call me inquisitive."

He used his sleeve to wipe the water from his face. "Squire James is my reader."

"I don't understand."

"When I have not my steward to read for me, as when I am gone from the castle, the task falls to James."

Kennedy nearly dropped her jaw. "You don't scrub your own back *and* you don't do your own reading?"

Annoyance skittered across his face. "One by choice, Lady Lark, the other by necessity. Could I read the missive, I would."

An old ache bubbled to her surface. "You don't know how to read?"

He shrugged. "I read poorly. In that there is no shame."

Wasn't there? Her mother had known shame, still did despite coping skills so finely honed that her second husband had yet to discover her struggle. "Do you have a learning problem?"

From his expression, it was as if she had asked if he had three heads. "I mean, was it hard for you to learn how to read or were you just not interested?"

His annoyance returned full force. "Tell me, Lady Lark, for what do I need to read when another can do it for me?" Without waiting for an answer, he turned and began walking downstream.

Wincing at the rough ground under her thin soles, Kennedy hurried after him. "It's surprising, that's all."

He turned. "Nay, that one cannot ride a horse is surprising, especially when one is of the nobility—or claims to be."

Eager to avoid the subject, Kennedy pressed on. "It's not too late. You could still learn to read."

"Why?"

"Everything revolves around the written word. It's...important."

"And riding is not?"

She squirmed in her shoddy undies. "In this day and age, I suppose."

"You live in this *day and age*. Mayhap reading is more important in Oz, but in England, 'tis command of one's horse that calls the battle."

Talk about backward! He had a letter from his brother that was surely important and was held hostage by what she guessed was an unwillingness to learn how to read. "Surely someone else can read it to you?"

"There is no one."

"No one here knows how to read?"

"Some can, but those whom I trust read no better than I."

Interesting. Though, supposedly, these were his "men," it seemed he was watching his back. "What about me?"

His lids narrowed. "You?"

Amazing how he could make a three-letter word ring with the reputation of one of four letters. "I can read it."

He considered her, then held out the missive.

She broke the wax seal and unrolled to the tune of thick, black writing. *Oh no.* Though this dream had returned her health to her, it hadn't done a thing for her far-sightedness. She squinted and found a semblance of focus only to run into another obstacle. The letter wasn't written in English. At least, not English as she knew it. However, it did share a likeness to Shakespearean English—which she had struggled with in an undergraduate class.

"Well?" Wynland asked.

"Just a moment."

"Did you not profess to know how to read?"

"I *do* know how to read. It's just that the handwriting is poor." Did that sound as unconvincing to him as it did to her? "Your brother must have been pressed for time."

"Pressed for time..." Wynland shrugged. "He may have been, but 'twas not likely he who wrote the missive."

"So he doesn't know how to write?"

"He does. Some."

Kennedy lowered her gaze and landed on the word "Farfallow" near the bottom of the page. She knew the name. It was the monastery that hosted the fatal confrontation between Wynland and Sir Arthur.

"Are you going to speak my brother's words or not?"

She swallowed. "It says, 'Brother, I send thee—you'"—she might as well translate it to her own understanding—"'greetings from Brynwood Spire. We yet have...no word of Crosley and the children.'" She affected to clear her throat while silently reading the next passage. *Though it may be naught, one of my men tells of having seen Sir Arthur in private conversation with the monk who passed the night at Brynwood Spire last month. As the monk was from the monastery of Farfallow, a day and a half ride from Cirque, mayhap you ought to stop there.*

"What else does it say?"

This was *her* dream and she wasn't about to have blood shed in it. "It...that..." As Wynland claimed to be a poor reader, meaning he managed to some degree, did she dare skip over Farfallow? If she did and he later looked at the letter, he might recognize the name and have another read it to him—unless she was able to dispose of the missive.

*In your dreams.* Though he might be fool enough to let her read it, he didn't trust her any further than that.

"Continue, Lady Lark."

"He says all is well at Brynwood and wishes you...Godspeed." As she returned the missive to him, she sent up a prayer that he wouldn't have his squire read it.

"Thank you, Lady Lark. You have been of service to me." He strode to his horse, patted its neck, and tucked the missive in one of the packs. "You think you could learn me to read?" he asked over his shoulder.

Though as a teen she had been determined to help her mother break the code, nearly every attempt had ended in frustration. "I don't think so."

A passing breeze flirted with the hair at his brow, lifted it, sifted it, sent strands into his lashes. "Still we shall try, hmm? In exchange, I shall teach you to ride."

She nearly choked. "I don't think so."

"A lady ought to know how to handle a horse."

In the words he had earlier spoken, she found a lifeline. "Why do I need to handle a horse when someone else can do it for me?"

He returned to her side and flashed that new smile that worked miracles on his scarred countenance and caused her fingers to tingle. "Because, my lady, two astride is too intimate for a man and woman who are not yet intimate. 'Tis most uncomfortable, do you not agree?"

She gulped. "Yes."

"Then we shall begin this day. You will take the reins when we ride from here."

"*Your* horse's reins?" She looked to the beast. To her dismay, the horse appeared to be watching her—taunting her with those enormous wet eyes. "I don't think this is a good idea."

His hand closed around her arm. "First overcome fear. If you do not, it will be the horse that rides you." His strength easily conquering her resistance, he pulled her along. "It is the most important lesson. Once you learn it, all else follows."

Her feet skidded over the ground. "What about lunch? I'm thirsty and hungry."

"After I have presented you to my horse."

"We've already met."

"Not properly."

As they neared, the horse snorted.

"No fear," Wynland spoke sharply.

"Oh, believe me"—she strained backward—"I know fear."

"Nay, Lady Lark, *have* no fear." He released her. "Don't move. Just watch." He smoothed a hand down the animal's shoulder, moved to its head and stroked its jowl. "It has been a long day, and you have served me well, my friend."

The horse pushed its muzzle into his palm and blew loudly.

"Aye, you have."

How calming his voice was, almost enough to make Kennedy assume a cross-legged position.

"Know you Lady Lark?" Wynland nodded at where she stood. "She of fair face and long—very long—legs?"

They weren't *that* long!

"She has come to meet you proper." He put his face near the beast's. "Be gentle now." He motioned Kennedy forward.

She unstuck her right foot, then left. *No fear.* Wynland stepped aside when she was face to face with the horse. She swallowed hard. Though she had thought it was bad to bounce around atop the creature, this was worse.

The horse made a low "huh-huh" sound and laid an ear back.

Kennedy flashed Wynland a tight smile. "Satisfied?"

"Talk to him—calmly. As you do, move to his shoulder and smooth your hand down it."

She took a leaden step to the side. "Nice horsie." She grimaced when the animal turned its head to follow her. "Very nice horsie."

"Horsie?" Wynland regurgitated.

"What's wrong with it?"

"It lacks command."

"You never said anything about command. You said to speak calmly. Which is it?"

Impatience lit his eyes. "Think of him as a man, Lady Lark—one from whom you require a favor. Surely you know what to do."

Kennedy cooled her outrage with a reminder of the woman she played. "Aye, I do," she put a medieval spin on her speech, "and very well, thank you."

"Show me."

She held Wynland's gaze, lifted a hand to the horse's shoulder, and said on a husky breath, "Hello, big boy."

She didn't look away when Wynland's incredibly blue eyes turned black, when he stepped forward, when his head lowered, when his mouth closed over hers. It was as if they stared into one another, seeing what no other had seen. This time she didn't resist. She felt his kiss through every part of her, shared his every breath, and melted.

Without realizing she had closed her eyes, she slipped her arms around his neck. He felt so real, as if she had not dreamed him into being. Feeling the rasp of his beard and moustache, she opened her mouth.

He pulled back.

She blinked and, becoming aware of raised voices, saw he had shifted his regard to something on the other side of the horse. She followed his gaze to where a fight had broken out, and for which she ought to be eternally grateful. Ought to be, though regret burrowed within her. Fulke—

What was wrong with her? He was *Wynland*, not Fulke. And it was only a kiss. Wasn't it?

He released her and his strides ate up the distance separating him from those who thrashed on the ground.

How many were there? Three? Four? Amid grunts and curses, above the buzz of onlookers, came the gleam of a knife. Then Wynland was in the fray, throwing the men apart, a moment later standing between the two who panted at his feet—Squire James and a knight Kennedy recognized as one of Baron Cardell's.

Here was her chance…Suppressing her fear of the horse, she moved along its body to a point behind the saddle and laid hands to the pack.

"Sir Waite, for what do you dishonor yourself by scrabbling with my squire?' Wynland threw a hand toward the young man whose face bled a long thin line.

The knight slowly unfolded from the ground. "When one questions a man's honor and loyalty"—he slapped dust from his shirt—"he ought to be prepared to offer up evidence. This *pup* did so charge me before all." He retrieved his knife and held it up for all to see the blood on it. "By my blade, I vow he shall do so no more."

"Sheathe your dagger," Wynland commanded.

The knight glanced at where Baron Cardell stood back from the others.

"Now!"

Sir Waite drove the dagger into its sheathe.

"Squire James, what say you?"

The young man gained his feet, took a step toward Wynland, and swayed. "One ought not to speak ill of his liege." There was a quaver in his voice. "As you are my lord, so you are Sir Waite's through Baron Cardell, and 'tis time he and the others accept it."

As Kennedy stared at Wynland whose brow furrowed as he listened to Sir Waite's denial, she heard the rattle of the missive beneath her fingers. Fortunately, the pack's ties were loosely knotted. As she released them, angry words were exchanged on the other side of the horse. Heart racing, she lifted the flap.

The horse tossed its head and sidestepped.

Kennedy peeked over the animal's back. Thankfully, the horse hadn't called attention to her—yet. She tried again and once more met resistance. Obviously, the horse knew she was up to no good. She patted his haunch. "Good boy."

The horse whinnied.

Fearing she was about to be caught with her hand in the cookie jar, she stole a glance at Wynland who remained in the middle of the altercation. Keeping her gaze on him, she pulled the missive from the pack.

"In future, Squire James," Wynland said, "do not think to defend me. My brother's men, now mine"—he looked to Sir Waite and Baron Cardell—"answer to me."

The boy looked contrite. "Forgive me, my lord."

Kennedy glanced at her ill-gotten gain. Where to hide it? Down her front? In her sock? She shoved it up her sleeve.

Fulke loomed over Cardell's knight. "Are you my man, Sir Waite?"

A hesitation. "I am, my lord."

"Then heed me. Forsake your vow of fealty and by *my* blade your life will be forfeit."

"I am to you as I was to your brother—your faithful servant."

Kennedy turned her attention to how best to dispose of the missive. The copse would be perfect. However, she had only a half dozen steps under her belt when Wynland called to her.

Knowing she was turning the color of guilt, Kennedy looked around and found him striding toward her. "Is everything all right?" she asked.

"No, but it will save until John and Harold are found."

Which brought her back to the missive. She resumed her course.

"We are not finished, Lady Lark."

Did he refer to the riding lesson or the kiss? Was one the lesser of two evils? The horse, she decided as she neared the copse. Definitely the horse.

Fulke stepped into her path. "Where are you going?"

"To take care of a little business." She pretended embarrassment. "You know...that privacy thing."

"Again?"

She put a hand to her abdomen. "I'm not feeling well."

"Not feeling well or..." He lowered his gaze to her mouth. "...running away?"

Actually, she had been feeling a bit crampy, not unlike—No, it couldn't be. Could it? She raised her chin. "What do I have to run away from?"

"You would like me to demonstrate?"

"No, thank you. Now, if you don't mind, I'll take care of my business." She stepped around him.

"Do not make me come after you, Lady Lark."

He thought she might ditch him? "I wouldn't dream of it." She scurried out of sight.

It took longer than expected, but she buried the evidence of her deception. Though she knew that when the missive was discovered missing she would likely be blamed, she would deal with it then.

Upon returning to the stream, she found Wynland deep in conversation with Baron Cardell. She put her hands on her hips and breathed a sigh of relief.

Sir Leonel appeared and regarded her out of bloodshot eyes. "Hungry?"

"Starving."

With a smile that shaved years off a face pained by what was probably a hangover, he presented an apple and a piece of dried meat. "I brought you these—and a skin of wine."

How she missed bottled water, but no chance of that here. Or was there? She looked to the stream.

"Lady Lark?"

She accepted his offering. "Thank you. I was just wondering whether or not the water is fit to drink."

"'Tis a distance from the nearest village. Still, I would not chance it."

She was about to concede it wasn't worth the risk when that old reminder that this was all in her head set down. "I believe I will." She knelt beside the stream.

"Methinks Lord Wynland would not approve," Sir Leonel warned.

She tucked her hair into the neck of her gown. "He can disapprove all he likes. I'm going to have a drink." The water was refreshing, moistening her lips, tongue, and throat, and washing away where Fulke had been.

A half dozen handfuls later, she stood.

"You are most unusual, Lady Lark."

"I'll take that as a compliment, Sir Leonel." She bit into the crisp apple.

"But I do wonder if you are, indeed, King Edward's Lady Lark."

She nearly coughed up the apple. "How is that?"

"My cousin thinks not."

Lady Jaspar, ever the thorn in her side. "And do you believe everything you're told?"

His brow creased. "Are you Lady Lark?"

He asked it with such intensity, such genuine need she considered telling him the truth. But he wouldn't believe her tale any more than Wynland had. "Of course I am."

He smiled a boyishly repentant apology. "I wish that you were not."

Kennedy was jolted. Though, as a professor, she had grown accustomed to the occasional crush, she had missed the signs with this man. "Why?"

He put a hand on his sword hilt and rubbed his palm over it. "Because Lady Lark belongs to another. Do you love him?"

She gasped. "Ful—Lord Wynland? What makes you think that?"

"I saw him kiss you, and you did not look to mind."

So he had witnessed that. She took a bite of the overly salted meat, swallowed. "I am not in love with him."

"But you will wed him."

"The way I understand it, I have no choice."

"Mayhap you do not, but Lord Wynland does."

"That's what he says, but does he?"

"Such a man as he will do whatever is needed to achieve his end. Yet, methinks he will wed you, which makes one wonder if you have cast a spell over him."

If not for Wynland's warning, Kennedy would have shrugged off the allusion to her being a witch. "I assure you, I am not a witch, Sir Leonel."

"Then how is it you disappear with nary a breath to trace your path? How is it you survived an attack that killed your entire escort?"

Deciding his first point was best left alone, Kennedy replied to the second. "I don't know. The attack happened so fast."

"It must have been horrible."

"It was." And she had only seen the aftermath.

"You do not know who attacked you and killed all those men?"

The scene to which she had awakened flashed in her mind, complete with the dying soldier who had denounced her. "No, but before one of the men died, he told—" No. Though Sir Leonel's inquiry seemed genuine enough, there was no reason to show her hand.

"What?"

"I don't want to talk about it."

Concern etched his face. "Forgive me, my lady." He laid a hand on her arm. "I know you grieve—for the king's men and your maid. A terrible loss."

Her maid, whom she just might be. "Yes, terrible. Fortunately, my maid was not among those killed."

Sir Leonel blinked. "None but you survived. If what you say is so, where is the woman?"

*Right in front of you—I think.* "She didn't accompany me."

"You had no maid?" Realization. "Then it was a lady-in-waiting you lost."

Whatever that was. "No. Other than my escort, I traveled alone."

"Surely the king would not allow that."

"I can take care of myself, Sir Leonel."

He stared. "Of that I have little doubt. Now I must ready myself to ride." He inclined his head and came up grimacing.

Kennedy touched his sleeve. "Are you all right?"

He ground fingers into his temple. "'Twas foolish of me to drink so much last eve."

"You have a hangover."

"A what?"

"A headache—burning eyes, nausea, etcetera." She lifted his hand and pinched the flesh between his thumb and forefinger. "This might help."

His pained expression turned suspicious. "Pray, what do you?"

"It's called acupressure. It's worked for me from time to time." Before all hope was lost. "Apply pressure for a minute or so and you should start to feel better."

"Do you speak sorcery, my lady?"

She laughed. "You call a pinch sorcery?"

He considered his hand in hers. "'Tis most unusual."

She smiled. "You'll see."

His uncertainty was soon replaced with wonder. "The pain is passing!"

She released her hold. "I told you."

"You are certain 'tis not sorcery?"

"Positive."

"You are incredible, Lady Lark. Where come you by such knowledge?"

"I pick up things here and there."

He executed a bow that revealed a glimpse of chain at his neck.

Kennedy frowned. Did he wear a medallion beneath his shirt as Wynland did? If so, what markings did it bear? A feather? A crown? A wyvern? Was it possible he was involved in the attack? Though it was hard to believe, she was grateful she hadn't revealed what the dying soldier had said.

"Thank you, my lady." He straightened. "You have been most kind."

"Too kind," Fulke's voice grated on the air.

She looked around and met his gaze. Was he jealous? "I was introducing Sir Leonel to acupressure. He had a headache and I thought—"

"To your mount, Sir Leonel. We are leaving."

The knight sidestepped, caught Kennedy's eye, and winked.

She couldn't help but smile.

Wynland halted before her. "For one who professes to feel poorly, you look and behave remarkably well."

"Amazing, isn't it?"

"Most." He leaned near. "Until such time as King Edward releases me from marriage to you, you will forego such brazen displays. Do you understand?"

She crossed her arms over her chest. "What, exactly, do you consider brazen?"

His blue eyes looked as if they might boil over. "Do you deny you were holding Sir Leonel's hand?"

"I showed him an acupressure point—"

He grabbed her arm and propelled her toward his horse. "No more lest you find yourself staked and burned, from which not even King Edward will be able to save you."

She tried to dig in, but it was futile. "Acupressure has nothing to do with magic. The Chinese have been using—"

"Silence!"

Fine, let him remain in the dark ages.

He lifted her and plunked her down on his horse. "Take the reins."

"You're not really going to make me do this, are you?"

"Take them."

She lifted the leather strap. "Now what?"

"We ride." He swung up behind her.

The intimate press of his body held Kennedy on edge during the six hours of riding instruction that saw them village to village, dead end to dead end.

# 14

It couldn't be. It was, which explained the cramping that had grown steadily during the ride and that she had thought was a nervous stomach caused by Wynland's riding instruction. She should have known, but it was almost a year since she had experienced the symptoms.

Kennedy looked down her front, then grasped the back of her skirt and peered over her shoulder. Nothing. Regardless, it seemed the dream was going all the way. What was she to do in an age where she couldn't beat a retreat to the nearest dispenser of feminine products?

She looked past the warming fire to the tent Wynland had announced she would share with him. In the twilight of a day never to be again, two men were adjusting the stakes they had driven into the ground. Other than that, the tent looked just about ready. How much longer? If she didn't take care of her problem soon, it would get much worse.

Seeking out Wynland, she saw he stood alongside his horse conversing with Squire James. Over his shoulder was the pack that no longer held his missive.

Feeling as if a black cloud were about to burst over her and rain down angry summons and accusations, she lingered over the two men before returning her attention to the tent. If the soft glow that made it look like a paper lantern was anything to go by, it was ready for occupancy. She wove among Wynland's men and pushed through the tent flap.

To the right lay a half dozen packs, at the center a worn rug, at the back a flat rock on which a lantern sat, and to her left a bed of blankets.

Only one bed, meaning Wynland expected her to share it with him. She would set him straight on that, but not before she took care of her problem.

She knelt before the packs. Her rummaging through the contents of the first revealed all manner of items, most foreign to her and of no use. She chose another pack. As she searched it, the tent flap rustled.

She jumped up and spun around.

"Mayhap I can assist?" Fulke said, his voice near frozen.

"I...was looking for something to...Do you have an old shirt you wouldn't mind parting with? Maybe a towel?"

"For what?"

She drew a deep breath. "If you must know, I started my period."

He looked no more enlightened, but at least his puzzlement warmed the chill with which he regarded her. "Pray, what is a period?"

Heat rose to her cheeks. "*That* time of month." Nothing. "Menstruation?"

"Ah, your menses. My apologies. Had I known, I would not have pried."

At least he had the grace to look repentant. "That's why I was looking through your things. I need..."

"I am sure I have something you can use." He pulled the incriminating pack from this shoulder and strode forward.

Then he was going to go through it. When he discovered the missive gone—"Never mind, I can make do without."

"How?"

Good question.

He dropped the pack and reached for another she had not yet plundered.

As relief eased her shoulders, he pulled out a white shirt. "This ought to meet your needs."

She took it and marveled at the silk-like material. "Surely you have something not quite so nice?"

"Naught that is clean."

She was surprised that he would concern himself. "Thank you."

"I shall leave you." He strode from the tent and dropped the flap behind him.

Kennedy rubbed the sleeve's material between her fingers and pondered the man who had given it to her. It seemed the more time she spent in his company, the farther he strayed from who she had read him to be. He was, but was not. Did, but did not. *You're falling for a man who may have murdered his nephews.* She hoped he hadn't, that history had wronged him.

"Oh, Ken," she whispered, "you're dreaming. You made Fulke Wynland, *this* Fulke Wynland. He's only a figment that dies with you." The admission hurt, the rending of the fabric echoing that of her heart.

Dry biscuits, dehydrated fish, watered wine. It was almost enough to make her put aside her disdain for Bambi and now Thumper. Determinedly, Kennedy chewed through a hard biscuit as the others enjoyed succulent rabbit.

Gathered around the campfire, Fulke's men spoke loudly and slapped one another on the back in that tribal dance of men that was beyond women—Kennedy included, though her training had involved a dissection of male behavior.

She shifted on the log that Sir Leonel and another knight had rolled before the fire. Where was Fulke? As with each time he disappeared, she grew nervous. Eventually, he would discover the missive was gone, and when he did she prayed she would pop herself out of this dream.

The campfire having warmed away her chill, Kennedy parted her cape and tossed a flap over each shoulder.

"You say!" exploded a thick man opposite whose lower face was greased with rabbit fat.

"Aye," another said, "'tis what happened."

The greasy one guffawed, spraying the fire with chewed meat that popped and sizzled.

"Lady Lark?"

Kennedy looked around at the man whose beard resembled a skunk and whose loyalty Wynland questioned.

"May I sit?" Baron Cardell asked.

"Sure."

He stepped over the log and lowered himself. "How fare thee, my lady?"

"I'm fine, thank you."

His fire-lit gaze searched hers and brow grew weighted. "Do you know who I am?"

"I've heard."

"Then you know I had the earl's ear—that I was his confidante."

"So I was told."

He looked to the campfire. "'Tis true you are to wed Wynland?"

"If that is what the king orders, that's what I'll do."

"Then you do not wish it yourself?"

"Why do you ask?"

His gaze swung to her. "You were almost killed."

And he believed Wynland was responsible. "Yes, but it doesn't seem I have much say in whether or not I marry."

His mouth edged upward but fell short of a smile. "Unless it could be proven Wynland worked ill upon you, eh, my lady?"

Had he? She was no longer as certain as she had been when first she had walked this mind play. The culprit could be someone else. She lowered her gaze to the tunic the man wore open at the neck. No sign of a chain or medallion.

"What think you, my lady?"

"That it's getting late, and I'm tired. What do you want, Mr. Cardell?"

His eyes hardened. "Only what belongs to me."

Kennedy put a hand on his arm. "Maybe you're wrong about him." Was that her talking?

He considered her hand on him. "If you wish to live, come to me."

"What do you mean?"

"When you are done whoring yourself with Wynland, we shall speak." He stood and, as she struggled with her outrage, returned to the shadows from which he had appeared.

Danger. The question was, from which side did it come? Cardell or Wynland? Both? Regardless, the answer would not be found in the company of men who eyed her as if she were a toothless witch. Leaving her meal to woodland creatures, she returned to the tent and found it empty. She removed her cape. As there had been no opportunity to address the sleeping arrangements, she would have to take matters into her own hands.

Leaving the sweat of the day's ride in the pool, Fulke pulled on his tunic. He frowned as he caught the scent he had cleansed from his body, berated himself for not bringing another tunic. The others also needed laundering, but the odor would not have been as fresh as this. He would have to take Squire James to task for not seeing to the keeping of his clothes. Though a more loyal heart could scarce be found, the young man was remiss in his duties. Of course, if Fulke had not given away the last of his clean tunics the matter would not be as pressing.

He conjured Lark, the surprise on her face when he had handed her the tunic. It was as if he had given her more. But then, his offering did not fit the man of whom she believed ill—just as she scarcely fit the woman he believed her to be. Could it be she was not the only one mistaken?

He thrust his legs into his braies, next his hose. The latter fought him, dragging over damp calves and thighs and straining the seams. He shoved his feet into his boots and girded his sword. As he turned to leave, moonlight on glass returned his gaze to the pool. Though the water had been chill, he had lingered to ponder the woman who might fell him as surely as if by sword. An enchantress.

"Accursed woman!" He tramped through the trees and emerged on the clearing to find his men ringing the fire, arms laid over one another's shoulders as they sang of a tavern wench with many loves. When he came to their notice, they quieted.

Though he knew he ought to order them to their rest, he said, "Continue," and strode to the tent.

Wrapped in one of two blankets that was to have served as their bed, Lark was on her side near the lantern-topped rock.

Fulke stared at her back that rose and fell with sleep. In spite of her earlier response to him, he had known she would object to sharing his bed. But for some reason, he had looked forward to the argument—and winning, for the chill night would turn more chill before morn.

He caught the movement of her long legs. "Lark?"

Her breathing stilled, started up again.

He strode forward and dropped to his haunches. "The day is not done, my lady." Her eyes remained closed, dark lashes throwing long shadows across her cheeks. He leaned near and brushed the hair from her face. "Ought I to kiss you again?"

Her eyes sprang open. "What do you want?"

"Only what is owed me."

"What would that be?"

"Lessons." At her tense silence, he laughed. "Reading lessons for riding."

"Now?"

"'Tis late, but as neither of us is ready for sleep, it seems a good time."

"You may not be tired, but I am." She made a show of yawning, but the pretense ended when her gaze fell to his brow. "You had a bath?"

He pushed fingers through his damp hair. "I did."

"How?"

"There is a pool not far from here."

Her face fell. "You mean a hole in the ground."

"Aye, that." Obviously, she was unaccustomed to the toil of travel, spoiled soft by regular tub baths.

"And it was probably cold," she ventured.

"Very, but if you wish to bathe, I shall take you."

"No, thanks."

He straightened. "Then it is time for a lesson."

She pushed the blanket off, revealing she had not removed her surcoat. "Let's get this over with."

Suddenly modest Lark, Fulke mused. Of course, when she had bathed in Jaspar's solar she had been careful to hide her nudity—so different from the night he had come to her chamber at Brynwood and been allowed to look upon her bared legs.

"What?" she asked.

He was staring. "Your gown would fare better if you did not sleep in it."

She whipped the blanket from her legs and, in spite of a multitude of wrinkles, emerged from it as a butterfly. "I didn't fall off the turnip truck, you know."

He frowned. "I did not know."

She rolled her eyes. "Do you have something to read?"

He turned to his packs, but as he stepped toward them, her hand fell to his arm.

"Scratch that," she said, too quickly and too flustered. "We'll start at the beginning. All we need is a stick to write out the lesson." She hurried to where one lay and motioned him forward. "You probably haven't heard of phonics, but it's a great method for learning to read."

Fulke knew he should pursue what had put her in a tither, but she smiled. He strode to where she knelt on the edge of the rug. "Do show, Lady Lark."

She swept a hand over the dirt, clearing a place to scrape out her lesson. "This is little 'a'."

Did she think him a fool? "That I know."

"Good. What sound does 'a' make?"

"Ah."

"Yes, and that's not all. Listen." She sounded the variant forms, of which he was not unfamiliar. Though he was tempted to advise her of the extent of his knowledge, he was stopped by the tilt of her head, the curve of her jaw, and her full lower lip forming the sounds. Forget the redundancy of the lesson, that for all her ability to read she spelled as one who did not know the English language—not that he spelled much better. He liked being near her, so he suffered an hour of "sounding out" and, surprisingly, learned a few things.

When the revelry outside the tent abated, she looked up. "Had enough for one night?"

He considered her mouth. It would be easy to lose himself in her, so much it might be difficult to find himself again. When he returned to her eyes and saw flight there, he reached to her. "Nay, not enough."

She sprang to her feet and danced away. "Tell me about John and Harold."

What held her from him? Though it was true he was not attractive, she *had* responded to his kiss. He stood. "What is there to tell?"

"They're your nephews. Surely you know something about them."

He advanced on her, and she retreated, only to come up against the tent wall. "Do you care for them at all?"

He halted. Did she truly fear him, or was this a game such as she had played with Edward? "Do you like to be chased, little bird?"

Her eyes widened. "Not one bit."

Not even a blind man could question her sincerity. As much as he longed to know her beyond kisses, this night he would not. He sighed. "What do you want from me, Lark?"

As if surprised to find she was no longer prey, she searched his face. "To understand you."

"Why?"

"Because…" She looked down. "I want to be wrong about you."

What made her doubt what she had accused him of? Desire? "Of John and Harold, I fear I know little, though for that I am more to blame than they." He silently cursed his brother's death that had made him master of all he no longer wished to be. Though King Edward wanted more for him than he wanted for himself, Fulke had been content to exchange the bloody war with France for the modest barony his father had left him. And, for a while, it had seemed he might find peace, but that had been nothing more than a dream. Now he must be father to two little boys who regarded him with trembling and command men who believed him responsible for his brother's death.

What sins the world put on him! Still, some were deserved. Memories of the massacre at Limoges rising, he doused them with a reminder of the sins Lark spoke of that had yet to pass. Not that they would. Never would he harm the boys. Though inept at fathering, he felt for his nephews and might even come to care for them if ever they came out from behind Sir Arthur.

"How are you more to blame?" Lark asked.

"When I came to Brynwood to serve as their protector, they tried to draw near me, but I had naught to give them." He met her gaze. "What do I know of children?"

"So they turned to Sir Arthur."

"Aye."

"You do care for your nephews."

He scowled. "They are my brother's sons."

A smile lifted her mouth.

So she thought she knew him. Far from it, but there was gain to be had in her softening, for with softening came surrender. He stepped forward, bent his head, and brushed his mouth across hers. "I wish to know you, Lark."

She tensed. "Believe me, you don't."

Because she was diseased as he had suggested the day they met? "How many lovers have you had?"

Indignation leapt in her eyes. "Not as many as you think."

He did not believe she was lying. The king's leman, very well, but not to countless lovers as he had thought. After all, he had kissed her, and though that meager joining had awakened his body, her mouth had been less tried than most women he had known.

He turned her face up to his.

"No, Fulke. We're not doing this."

"'Tis only a dream, did you not say?"

She opened her mouth, blinked, and in that moment of confusion, he pressed his lips to hers. But only for a moment. In the next, she broke free and ducked under his arm.

He could have pulled her back, and he wanted to, but something—was it the desperation in her eyes?—told him this was no game she played.

From where she put ten feet between them, Kennedy stared at him. She almost feared her desire as much as his, for the reminder this was only a dream held the promise of pardon. After all, things happened in dreams that one could not control. But this was a lucid dream, more lucid than any she had known.

"Answer me one question," he said. "Why do you refuse what we both desire?"

She pulled her bottom lip through her teeth. "The...time isn't right." It was the truth, in more ways than one.

After a moment, he said, "I vowed you would come to me willingly, and you will—without accusation or regret."

Then it would never happen. Kennedy returned to her bed and watched as he dragged a blanket around him. But sleep did not come soon for either of them. Through the deepening cold that made her long for the warmth of another body, the sound of Fulke's restlessness reached her. A half hour unfolded, and several more before she heard his breath deepen. Only then did she doze.

# 15

Smug. There was no other word for how Kennedy felt. In spite of Fulke's efforts to ensure against her escape, she had foiled him. Awakening at dawn to find him gone, she decided to go in search of the pool he had spoken of. However, one peek past the flap had revealed a soldier stood guard outside.

If not that her "menses" had had a field day with her during the night, that might have been the end of it, but the remains of Fulke's tunic wouldn't hold out much longer. Knowing it could prove dangerous to accept his offer to escort her, she had opened a seam down the rear of the tent by breaking the strong thread with her teeth.

She smiled at the thought of Fulke's reaction when she strolled back into camp. Even if he discovered her missing, he wouldn't expect her to return. Her smile dissolved. Until that moment there had been no question of her returning. Why? Because of a touch? A kiss that made her melt?

She focused on the pool that shimmered in morning's first light. Satisfied she was the only one to brave the chill water, she straightened from the tree and removed her clothes. As it was best to get the shock over with, she rushed the pool and, a few moments later, gasped as she surfaced.

It was as if the pool were fed by a polar ice cap. Teeth chattering, she tried not to dwell on the squish between her toes and whatever brushed her calf as she rubbed her hands over her limbs in place of soap. When she emerged from the water, the morning air felt almost warm in comparison. She pulled the chemise on and dragged the undies up over her goose-bumped legs. As she bent to retrieve the undergown, something hit her from behind.

Her cry was caught in the hand that slammed over her mouth, her attempt to flee squashed by an arm around her waist.

"You are too quick to cover yourself," a graveled voice heated her ear.

She thrust backward, causing her assailant to shift his center of balance and drag her harder against him.

"A pity I must kill you, though I see no reason we cannot delay the inevitable." He pushed her against a tree and held her there with his body.

Kennedy tried to bite the hand that fed her screams back to her, hooked her fingers and swept her arms over her head. She clawed air, her efforts causing her to abrade her cheek on the bark. Hoping to connect with his groin, she kicked a leg back, but he was too near.

He pulled up her chemise, only to still when he reached her undies. "What is this?"

Knowing her attempt at being a seamstress wouldn't keep him from his goal, Kennedy threw her head back and slammed it into his nose. A loud crack was followed by curses. And the release of her mouth.

As her screams resounded through the wood, her assailant grabbed her hair, wrenched her head back, and slammed it into the tree.

Kennedy collapsed. Though the man's face was a blur above her, she could see the bloody mess she had made of it.

A dagger appeared, but as he came at her, so did shouts, thundering feet, and the rustle of ground cover. The blade streaked toward her, but she rolled to her hands and knees and the dagger plowed the ground where she had been.

As he pulled it free, a bellow split the air. He sprang up to meet his attacker, but a sword swept down and sliced through sleeve, muscle, bone. He wailed, dropped his dagger, and slapped a hand over the gushing wound.

The man who was said to have murdered Lady Lark had just saved the woman he thought her to be. Kennedy stared at Fulke. It was over—until another dagger, thrown by someone behind Fulke, caught her assailant in the chest. The man dropped to his knees and stared at the hilt protruding from his tunic like a climber's flag atop Everest.

Fulke swung around. "Cardell!"

Teeth chattering, Kennedy looked to the others who had answered her cry for help. There were more than a dozen, among them Sir Leonel and the baron.

"Why?" Fulke roared.

Baron Cardell stood taller. "I feared he might slay you. As your man, 'tis my duty to protect you."

"I do not need protecting!"

"But, my lord, do you not recognize the miscreant?" Hand on sword hilt, Cardell took a step forward. "'Tis the assassin, Moriel."

A fierce chill gripped Kennedy, and when Sir Leonel knelt beside her and laid a hand on her shoulder, she shrank from him. She didn't want anyone touching her.

Fulke stared at Cardell. He needed none to tell him of Moriel, none to apprise him of what would have happened if Lark had not called out. Her cry yet echoed through him and he longed to go to her. He looked around. Chemise tangled around her thighs, face bloodied, eyes reflecting the horror of the vile thing done to her, she made him long for Moriel's blood, which would have been his *after* the blackguard told all. Curse Cardell!

He turned back to the baron. "I recognize Moriel." At Limoges, Fulke had commanded the knight errant and witnessed his insatiable appetite for killing and unquenchable greed. Thus, he had not been surprised to learn Moriel had turned assassin.

"Then you know his reputation," Cardell said. "A moment more and he would have buried another of his daggers in your heart."

"Or yours, *friend*," Moriel grated.

Fulke strode to the assassin, with a booted foot shoved him onto his back. "Speak, knave!"

Virulent eyes raked him. "'Twould seem I am much in demand where you...are concerned." He dragged breath past a froth of blood, looked to Cardell. "You thought I would reveal you? I would not have, but now..." He heaved the dagger from his chest. "Now I have." Eyes beginning to empty, he looked up at Fulke. "Your brother's death was... not an accident...but you know that."

He did. Though more a man of prayer, his brother had been an excellent horseman and savored the hunt. Thus, when he had been found dead after spurring ahead of his men, Fulke had been certain his broken neck had nothing to do with being thrown from his horse. Here was his proof.

The assassin nodded. "'Twas I who ended him."

Fulke's muscles bunched. Though he and his older brother had been distant much of their lives, they had shared moments of kinship. In fact, months before the earl's death, he had summoned Fulke to advise him on matters of estate. No doubt, Cardell had felt threatened. Fulke looked to the baron who was breathing fast, his shoulders heaving.

"Aye," Moriel rasped, "'twas wardship of your nephews he wished."

"He lies!" the baron burst.

*All of it*, Fulke reminded himself. *When I know all of it, then I will slay Cardell.*

"But you were not given...wardship...were you, baron?" Laughter gurgled from Moriel. "All that coin wasted."

Cardell stepped nearer Fulke, causing the knights left and right of him to take defensive stances. "Lies, I tell you! I loved your brother—"

Fulke trained his sword on the man's convulsing throat. "You loved the power you wielded through him."

Cardell looked to the others, but he stood alone. Even his man, Sir Waite, appeared ready to land a blow to him.

Though Fulke knew his men would defend him, he had never relied on another to keep him alive. Thus, he settled his senses on Cardell before returning his attention to Moriel. "Did Cardell also pay you to murder Lady Lark?"

"I did not!" the baron shouted.

"Ah," Moriel breathed, "the king's trollop..."

"Was it Cardell?" Fulke asked again.

Moriel's eyes rolled.

Turning sideways to keep Cardell in sight, Fulke dropped to his haunches. "Why Lady Lark? Why not me, Moriel?"

"That you could not...wed her."

As it followed that Cardell would have struck at the one who came between him and his prize—Fulke—it made little sense. "Was it Cardell?"

Moriel turned his head, considered Lark through slit eyes, and smiled grimly. It was the face he wore on his descent from life.

Fulke looked to where Lark sat unmoving with Sir Leonel at her side. Though once more gripped with the longing to hold her, to press her face into his neck, he stood and unsheathed his sword.

Kennedy sprang to her feet. "Fulke!"

Sir Leonel pulled her back. "He will prevail, my lady. None stands against Lord Wynland."

Perhaps not, but this time could be different. This time Cardell could be the one left standing. *Please, no. Please don't let Fulke fall.*

The clash of steel on steel, accompanied by grunts and growls, made Kennedy startle and wince and ache to awaken from this nightmare, but she soon found solace in those very sounds. It was the absence of clanging steel that she came to fear as, time and again, the two men circled, swung, and lunged. Though the sound of steel on flesh was deceptively benign, the grunts that evolved into shouts and the blood that stained their clothing and darkened the dirt over which they danced was more vivid than any violence she had ever witnessed. The only blessing was that, in the end, it was Cardell who fell.

A whimper crept from Kennedy's throat, and it was all she could do to keep her knees from buckling.

Fulke swung around. Sweat darkening his blonde hair, chest heaving, he pinned his gaze to her. They stared at one another across the distance for what seemed minutes but, finally, he blinked and his shoulders eased with a great exhalation. It was as if he had returned from some place none of them had been.

He looked to the man over Kennedy's shoulder, "I thank you, Sir Leonel."

Though the knight was dismissed, he didn't ease his hold on her until Fulke thrust his stained sword in its scabbard and strode forward.

Sir Leonel stepped back. "In your service, my lord," he murmured and retreated with the others.

As Fulke neared, Kennedy scrutinized the crimson places on his cheek, his shoulder, and his thigh. There were no gaping wounds that she could see, but that did not mean he was not seriously injured.

He halted before her, and she gasped when he clasped her face between his hands. "You are hurt."

The urgency in his voice made her shudder. "I-I am fine."

"Are you?"

The question went deeper than the cuts, lumps, and bruises. They went to that darkest place that Moriel had meant to take her. "He didn't..." She shook her head. "I wouldn't let him."

Fulke's lids momentarily lowered, and his shoulders dropped a degree more. "Then you will be fine. This I promise."

But would he be fine? "You are bleeding—"

"I will heal soon enough."

She held his gaze. And knew. Though last night she had acknowledged he could not have committed the atrocities history had laid at his feet, she now saw him more clearly than she would have believed possible. There was the warrior, sword sounding a death knell; the brother, steadfast; the uncle, determined; and her redeemer. Fulke Wynland was a man terribly wronged. But all she could think to say was, "I'm sorry."

Without a word, he lifted her high into his arms. As he carried her past Moriel, she forced herself to look at the dead man. Cardell's dagger jutted from the assassin's chest between the lacings of his tunic. Remembering his foul breath and his hands on her, she squeezed her eyes closed. If he was behind the attack on Lady Lark, he couldn't have done it alone, not with so many casualties.

Fulke's arms tightened around her. "'Tis over, Lark."

No, there was something wrong with the equation. Fulke knew it too, as evidenced by his questioning of Moriel about the attempt on Lady Lark's life. And there was more he did not know to ask. Specifically, why would Cardell murder John and Harold when they were his ticket to Sinwell?

She looked up. "It's not over. There's more to it."

"Hush, Lark. I have you."

He did. And he wouldn't let her fall. Knowing there was no safer place, she buried her face against him.

Blood slammed through Fulke's veins. Why had she done it? He looked from where she huddled under the blanket to the seam she had opened in the back of his tent. Not to escape him, but to bathe. She had nearly been killed!

Abruptly, he turned down his inner raging. Her foolishness was not where his thoughts ought to dwell, but on Moriel. If John and Harold were all Cardell sought, why Lark? In the hope her murder would fall upon Fulke, inducing Edward to grant wardship to the baron? Perhaps, for if it had been Fulke marked for death, Cardell's hand in it would show.

"Fulke?" Lark's voice trembled.

He knelt beside her, the sight of her causing his blood to spit and seethe again. Eyes that had snapped at him on the night past were haunted, a face that had been bright and lively was pale, scratched, and bruised. But she was safe now. If he had to bind her to him, no more harm would befall her. He reached for the salve his squire had delivered.

"I shouldn't have gone without you," she said.

He wanted to reprove her that she might never again do something so foolish, but it was not what she needed. "You should not have."

"I'm sorry."

He smoothed salve over her livid cheek. "'Twill heal fine."

"Thank you."

He regarded her a long moment. "I must ask, Lark, was Moriel among those who attacked your baggage train?"

She averted her gaze. "I don't know."

Her head injury again? After all that had happened, still she did not trust him? It was he who ought not to trust her, especially after his discovery this morn that his brother's missive was gone. A moment's analysis of Lark's behavior on the day past had convinced him that she had taken it, meaning the message she had read to him was likely false. Thus, he had returned to the tent to confront her—and found it empty. No sooner had he called to his knights than her scream cut the wood. Though God had sped him to her side, guided his sword arm, delivered her from death, she continued to withhold from him.

"Even after 'tis told who murdered my brother, still you fear me?"

Kennedy looked back at him. "I knew last night you didn't do the things they said you did—that you didn't order the attack on my baggage train, that just about everything I knew about you or thought I knew was false. The author was wrong. History—" Reality slapped her across the face. Not *her* baggage train. Lady Lark's. Since awakening this morning, not once had it crossed her mind this was only a dream. She had lived every moment as if she were truly here. Considering what had happened at the pool, she was grateful for the reminder, but the part of her that was wrapped around Fulke mourned.

"Never have I had such a vivid dream," she breathed. "It's as if Moriel truly happened."

Fulke dragged her to sitting. "He *did* happen! This is not a dream."

She shook her head. "You're part of my research. I made you up—put myself here. You exist only in my mind, just like..." She remembered Moriel. "No. None of you are real. You're six hundred years dead."

Fulke shook her. "I do exist! This moment is now, not in the past, not in a dream."

As much as Kennedy feared what awaited her outside the dream, her encounter with Moriel frightened her more. "It didn't happen."

Fulke thrust his face near hers. "You didn't foolishly go alone to the pool? Expose yourself for any man to look upon? To want? To take?"

She wrenched free. "You think I asked for it? Is that what you're saying?"

Fulke stared at Lark. It *was* what he was saying, and after all she had been through...He closed his eyes. "Forgive me. I did not mean it."

She lowered her face, and he heard her muffled sob. "I don't want to die," she said softly.

He peered at her face through the hair fallen over it and felt a tug in his chest.

"Especially now."

Why? Had it something to do with him? Fulke swept the hair from her face. "Put away your fear, Lark. By my troth, ever shall you be safe at my side."

Derisive laughter bubbled from her, and she looked up. "Until I die?"

They were more than words, something to do with the dream she believed this to be. But he would not be pulled into that mire again. "Until you die a very old woman."

"That I would like to see."

"You shall."

Her smile was bitter. "I know you don't believe me, but this isn't my world, Fulke. I can't stay." A tear streaked her cheek and disappeared into the neck of her chemise.

When he pulled her onto his lap, she buried her face against his neck and silently cried.

Time forgotten, the press to continue the search for his nephews suspended like dust on the air, Fulke held her and felt his chest fill with emotion for the woman who would be his wife. Aye, his wife. He wanted Lark for more than one night, wanted to make her smile as she had done for Sir Malcolm, wanted her passion—even if it meant losing himself in her madness. He drew her heavy hair through his fingers. "No one will hurt you ever again."

She dropped her head back and regarded him past swollen lids. "I still feel his hands on me."

He kissed her forehead and, in that moment, knew that to keep her safe he must send her from him. "He will not touch you again."

She tucked her head beneath his chin, and he held her until it was well past time for them to break camp. "We must needs ride, Lark. I will assist you in dressing." Though he expected her to object, she stood for him while he drew the undergown and surcoat over her head and secured the laces. Leaving her hair to fall down her back, though it would whip about his face during the ride, he clasped her hand and led her outside.

The men were ready. He looked to each and, lastly, Sir Waite. As with the others who had believed him responsible for his brother's death, the accusation was gone from the knight's eyes. They were his men now.

The tent came down quickly and, shortly, Fulke and Lark were mounted.

"You are ready?" he asked.

"Does it matter?"

Uncaring who bore witness, he put his mouth to hers. "It does," he said against her lips, and pulled back. "Now I must know the contents of my brother's missive."

Kennedy's heart slammed into her ribs.

"I do not ask for an explanation, Lark, only the message."

Why was he so understanding when he ought to be raging? Was it because of Moriel? Did he fear she was going to fall apart? As much as she longed to tell him the truth, she couldn't. Dream or not, a man's life was at stake. Fulke hadn't killed his brother, but he *would* slay Sir Arthur.

"I'm sorry. I can't tell you."

"Then I shall know in two days' time," he said gruffly.

Meaning he had sent someone to Brynwood to retrieve his brother's message.

Fulke gathered the reins. "One day," he said, "you will trust me." He looked to his men. "To Farfallow!"

# 16

Farfallow. As Kennedy had done throughout the ride, she worried the name inside out. Was it only coincidence that Fulke was headed there? Or a game he played, asking about the missive when, somehow, he had learned its contents? Regardless, he was going to the monastery and there was nothing she could do.

Head throbbing, reminiscent of the tumor outside her dream, she touched the goose egg in the middle of her forehead. It returned her to Moriel, invoking memories she didn't care to relive. She pulled her hand away.

Maybe Sir Arthur wasn't at Farfallow yet. Hadn't it taken Fulke two weeks to catch up to him? Perhaps they would arrive at the monastery and find him absent. But if he was at—

The orange and blue clad soldiers with their flying flags came at them from the left. Though Kennedy's first thought was that they were being attacked, the small number of soldiers, coupled with Fulke's lack of urgency, dissuaded her. He and his men reined in and the newcomers halted.

"You are Lord Wynland?" asked an armored man with bulging bloodshot eyes.

"I am. What news do you bring?"

"I am Sir Edgar, sent by Baron Howarth to bear the glad tidings that my lord holds your nephews at Glenmar."

Kennedy caught her breath.

"And Crosley?" Fulke demanded.

A knowing smile revealed a mouthful of decayed teeth. "The baron has left the miscreant hurting but whole that you might part him yourself." Confusion flew through Kennedy. This wasn't supposed to happen—not according to *The Sins of the Earl of Sinwell*.

"I will ride escort for you, my lord," Sir Edgar said.

Though Kennedy couldn't be certain, she thought Fulke hesitated. Why didn't he turn and ride pell-mell for Glenmar? She looked around. "What are you waiting for?"

The bitter edge to her voice decided Fulke. Though he had set himself to deliver her to Farfallow for safekeeping while he continued his search, she gave him another reason for putting her from him. What he must do was between Crosley and himself, something for which she need not be present.

Passing over Sir Malcolm who knew too well how to make Lark smile, he ordered four of his most experienced knights forward. "Sir Daniel, you and the others will deliver Lady Lark to Farfallow this eve and remain there with her."

"Aye, my lord." Sir Daniel guided his horse alongside.

Lark shrank back against Fulke. "I want to stay with you."

"You will be safe there."

Her eyes lit. Realizing an argument was forthcoming, and curiously sensitive to the fear that likely put it there, he rumbled, "Hold," and spurred his horse away from the others. At a distance where none might overhear, he turned her to face him. "At Farfallow, you will be cared for. I vow, no harm will come to you."

"What makes you think I need to be cared for?"

"After what happened this morn—"

"Is that why you were going to Farfallow? To leave me there?"

"Aye, and there you shall go."

"You said I would be safe at your side, and now you mean to abandon me?"

It was what he had said, but he could not take her to Glenmar, not with what he must do. "I shall come for you as soon as my business is finished."

Color swept her pale cheeks. "You plan to kill Crosley, don't you?"

"He must answer for what he has done."

"All he did was try to protect John and Harold. For that he has to die?"

"'Tis not that simple, Lark."

She drew a deep breath. "Your nephews are in danger, but not from Crosley. Someone else killed them."

Curse her madness! "They are not dead."

"They will be."

If not for the tripping in his chest, Fulke thought he might put her to the stake himself.

"Though you didn't do it—I know that now—history says you were the one. A despised man. A man who—"

"Did you not tell me this is but a dream? If that is all it is, Lark, then history may, indeed, be accurate."

Confusion, followed by uncertainty, played across her face. Finally, she said, "Yes, a dream," and cupped his face between her hands. "Listen to me, Fulke Wynland of my dreams, Crosley's death is undeserved."

Jealousy twisted inside him. "Do you love him?"

Her eyes grew large. "I..." She struggled, as if it was a question to which there was no answer, then shook her head. "He's only a friend. Retrieve your nephews and let him go."

That the man could plague him evermore? Fulke looked to his men. If he was to hold Sinwell for John's ascension, Crosley must serve as an example of what befell those who went against their lord. "'Tis time I ride on Glenmar."

"Please, don't."

He refused to fall into her eyes. "I will come for you when I am done."

She smiled bitterly. "Don't count on me being there."

Her threat was almost enough to turn him, but his course was set as if fate had long ago foretold it. He lifted her chin and pressed his mouth to hers.

She pulled back. "Goodbye, Mr. Wynland."

So they were back to formalities. It pulled something inside him, forced him to concede he liked his name on her lips. "I will not be long." He guided his horse to his men and drew alongside Sir Daniel. "I trust you will not allow Lady Lark to wander from you."

"I shall keep her ever in my sight, my lord."

With Lark's accusing eyes full on him, Fulke handed her onto the fore of Sir Daniel's saddle. "Take care of her." The absence of her warmth between his thighs gripped Fulke with such longing he glanced one last time at her.

She averted her gaze.

For the best, Fulke told himself and turned toward Glenmar.

Kennedy put her head back against Sir Daniel's shoulder and looked up at the darkening sky. Had Fulke reached Glenmar? Did Sir Arthur lie in a pool of blood?

*Only a dream*, said the increasingly faint voice. But no matter which version of *The Sins of the Earl of Sinwell* played out—hers or the author's—it seemed the end would be the same: death to Sir Arthur, sealing the fate of Fulke's nephews.

If only he would have allowed her to accompany him. Perhaps she could have—

A convulsion rocked Kennedy and, as if from a distance, she heard pounding.

Sir Daniel dragged his horse to a halt. "My lady?"

Someone called her name, but as if from inside her head. She blinked, but the clamor grew more insistent. Louder.

"Are you well, Lady Lark?"

She shook her head. "I need to get down."

"You are ill?"

"I don't know. I—"

"Kennedy!" It was the voice again. Familiar.

"My lady?"

"Please let me down."

Sir Daniel swung out of the saddle and lifted her to the ground. She stumbled against him.

He said something to the others and led her to a tree. "Sit down, my lady."

"Let me in!" The familiar voice again.

"Graham?" She looked at Sir Daniel, read his confusion, and saw him waver. She was awakening, meaning she was about to vanish into thin air.

She pulled her arm free. "I need privacy."

"You must needs relieve yourself?"

"Yes."

He motioned to a thicket and, to her dismay, followed.

"Do you mind?" she shot over her shoulder.

"You are not to go from my sight, my lady."

Counting herself lucky to make it behind the thicket without landing on her face, she met the knight's gaze. He intended to stand there and watch?

He turned his back.

"I know you're in there!" Graham's voice was louder.

Kennedy's feet dropped out from under her, but she wasn't falling. She looked from Sir Daniel to the knights beyond. They blurred and their colors merged into a single bright light.

"Kennedy!"

She opened her eyes to a white plaster ceiling. She was back—rather, awake. Her throat tightened. Fulke was only a dream, but one she remembered as clearly as the first time she had dreamt him.

Amid the buzzing of the doorbell and the scratch of the EEG, she sat up. In contrast to the well-being that marked her dream, she was struck by weakness and a throb between her eyes. She lifted a hand to her head, but no goose egg. Just the tumor ticking her life away.

"I'm counting to ten, then this door is history!"

History. She managed a smile.

"One...two..."

As she dropped her legs over the bed, she remembered the electrodes. As quickly as her trembling fingers would allow, she peeled the disks from her head—and stilled. Her awakening hadn't tripped the EEG's alarm.

"Seven," Graham called.

She stumbled from the bedroom.

"Eight."

Though the living room spun, she made it to the door as number ten exited Graham's mouth. She flipped the deadbolt, but before she could turn the knob, he did it for her. Just barely, she avoided being struck as the door swung inward.

"What took you so—?" He caught his breath.

She must look pretty bad. Of course, he looked his usual handsome self, one of the most attractive men she had ever met. That last thought conjured a vision of Fulke Wynland. Though she had thought him far from attractive when they had first met, and he definitely lacked the beauty of Graham's countenance, he had moved up in her estimation. In fact, she had never been more attracted to a man.

"Oh, Kennedy, look at you," Graham finally spoke.

Her laughter was flat. "Always could turn my head with those sweet nothings of yours."

"Sorry. I just didn't realize—"

"I know. It's been a while." She smoothed a hand back from her temple to the baldness past her ear.

"Can I come in?"

"It's not a good time."

"I need to talk to you."

She sighed. "All right."

He stepped inside and pretended an interest in the living room. "Nice place."

"It's home." She pushed the door closed. Could she make it to the sofa without falling all over her feet?

"Can I help?" Graham reached to her.

She sidestepped. "Really, Graham, I'm no damsel in distress." The words slipped from her without thought, but behind them rolled a memory of Fulke. Though her sickness was rooted in her head, she feared her breaking heart might just beat the tumor to the punch.

"You don't look well."

She sank onto the sofa. "I'm feeling a bit under the weather." Easier to make light of it than be drawn into a discussion of funeral arrangements.

He lowered to the cushion beside her. "You haven't returned my calls."

"I've been busy."

"What are these?" He touched two spots on her forehead.

Realizing he referred to the impressions left by the electrodes, she berated herself for not pulling on the knit cap.

"Electrodes?" he asked.

Wonderful. Though they had lived on separate planes for a long time, he hadn't been totally oblivious to her research. Feigning nonchalance, she said, "They're from a contraption the doctor gave me to relieve the headaches. So, what can I do for you?"

Regret curved his chiseled mouth. "I've been thinking about you a lot."

She stared at him, waited for the rest of it.

"Wondering..." He shook his head. "You know I didn't want the divorce."

She knew. But it wasn't what he wanted that mattered. It was all about what his mother wanted. "You're a bit young to be a widower, Graham." The moment her bitterness was voiced, she regretted it.

He stared at her with such sorrow it made her want to cry. "How did it come to this, Kennedy?"

"Graham..." She drew a deep breath. "If you have to ask, it's all the more reason we never should have married."

"I love you."

Though they were words she had once thrived on, they had long ago lost their depth. "The divorce was for the best. It's what I needed, what you needed, and certainly what your mother needed."

"Forget about my mother. I don't care—"

"Yes, you do. Too much."

He looked away. "I'm all she has. I know she didn't treat you well, but what matters is us."

"There is no 'us.' She made certain of that." No need to go into specifics. He knew them, just refused to accept the truth. Of course, there were things Kennedy had kept from him, such as his mother's investigation of her when she and Graham began dating, then on their wedding day the woman had tried to bribe her to keep her from marrying her son.

"Maybe in time she'll—" Graham began.

"Time?" The word shot off Kennedy's tongue. "Do I look like I have time to waste on a relationship with a woman who would rather die than accept my backwoods blood?"

Graham momentarily closed his eyes. "I'm sorry. I just..." He looked back at her, then slid an arm around her and gently drew her onto his lap.

Though she knew she should scramble away, the arms he wrapped around her were comforting. More, she was worn too thin to waste energy. With a sigh, she laid her head on his shoulder.

"We should have had a child," he murmured. "It would have been a little girl, I think, with dark hair, green eyes, and her mother's smile."

Kennedy clenched her hands. She had wanted children, but there had never been time—after her bachelor's degree, they had agreed, then her master's degree, then her doctorate. All at the urging of a woman who hadn't wanted grandchildren mothered by a "hick." Celia Huntworth always got her way.

Kennedy squashed her anger. It was in the past. Now if only she could be there as well. Mac had it right. Far better a dream than this.

Graham lifted her chin and pressed his mouth to hers. His seeking was sweet, but there was no passion, no heat, no rasp of beard across her skin. She'd had better in her dreams.

She slipped off his lap. "You should go. I need my rest."

Hurt reflected on his face. "I thought we could have lunch together."

"Maybe another time. I'm really tired."

He sank back into the sofa, stared at her as if to impress her on his memory, then stood and strode toward the door.

Kennedy ached for him, and would have called him back if not that she knew this was for the best.

At the door, he looked over his shoulder. "Goodbye, Kennedy."

It truly was goodbye. "Goodbye, Graham."

He lowered his gaze, nodded as if to himself, and walked out.

Kennedy put a hand over her eyes. She hurt for him, for his pain, his loss, his realization come too late that there was more to life than speaking to his mother's every whim. Hopefully, one day he would break free of the woman and rediscover in someone else what he and Kennedy had shared for so brief a time. As for herself, she had her dreams for however long her heart beat. Providing she could, she would return to them, which meant another round of sleep deprivation.

She squared her heavy shoulders and wondered how to while away the hours. The answering machine with its blinking light caught her eye. Doubtless, her mother was awaiting a half dozen returned phone calls.

# 17

"Where are they?"

In the flickering light of wall torches, Baron Howarth smiled pridefully. "Come, Lord Wynland, I will deliver you to the miscreant myself." He turned his horse onto the drawbridge.

Though the embers of Fulke's anger toward Sir Arthur aspired to fire, it was John and Harold he wished to see. "First, my nephews."

"As you wish." The baron spurred his horse forward.

Fulke left his men in the bailey and ascended the steps to the great hall.

"Margaret!" the baron called. "Bring forth Lord Wynland's nephews."

An elderly woman creaked her bones up from before the hearth and urged the children at her feet to rise. "Come, sweetings, your uncle has arrived. Greet him as is proper."

Amid snuffling and a hiccupping sob that reminded Fulke of the distance between him and his nephews, the boys gained their feet.

"Hush now." The old woman turned them toward Fulke.

But it was not John and Harold whose tearful faces halted him. He stared at the boys who no more resembled his nephews than water resembled oil. "What is this?"

Baron Howarth drew up short just past Fulke. "What speak you, my lord? Here are your nephews safe and—"

"They are not my nephews!"

The baron's lids fluttered. "Surely 'tis them. They but require a bath and—"

"Fool! You think I do not know my own nephews even beneath so much filth?"

"Pardon, my lord. I was given to believe these were the boys you sought."

Though Fulke longed to put his hands around the man's neck, he suffered his sword hilt instead. "Who gave you to believe that?"

"Crosley, my lord. He—"

"Crosley? Or another impostor?"

"I...know not."

"Take me to him."

Glenmar's dungeon was dank and foul. There was the smell of urine, feces, rot and mold, the scratching and screeching of rats, the moan and groan of beings that might or might not be human.

At the end of the twisting corridor, the jailer halted and scrambled for the key.

Fulke seethed as he waited alongside Baron Howarth, a man who seemed a good foot shorter than when they had entered the hall.

The key rasped in the lock. "Come forth!" the jailer called, pushing the door inward.

Though Fulke doubted that the man inside was Crosley, still he hoped. That hope died as the prisoner stumbled from the cell. The man's hair and beard were red, and the embroidered and studded tunic belonged to Crosley, but that was all.

He seized the impostor's arm. "Who are you?"

The man peered through twin blackened eyes above a blood-crusted nose and cracked and swollen lips.

*Hurting but whole,* Baron Howarth's knight had said of his lord's capture of Crosley. That the man was, but his pain would be nothing compared to what awaited him if he refused Fulke the answers he sought.

"Who be ye?" the impostor growled.

"Fulke Wynland."

The man's head drooped. "Then me task is done."

"What task is that?"

"The game is over."

It seemed Fulke had moved his playing pieces exactly as Crosley intended. "It is far from over. Tell me your name!"

"I be Tolken and me boys are Edgar and Warren. Ye've done 'em no harm, have ye?"

Baron Howarth lunged forward and stuck his enraged face near the impostor's. "Not yet, we haven't."

Tolken swept pleading eyes to Fulke. "Slay me if ye must, but do me boys no harm. The lads but did what their father asked of them."

In spite of his anger, Fulke would not allow harm to befall them. "Stand down, Baron Howarth."

With a grunt, the man complied.

"Sir Arthur Crosley paid you?" Fulke asked.

"Aye, enough to keep me and me boys in food through winter. I vow I would not have agreed did we not need the coin, me lord."

"What, exactly, did he ask of you?"

"He gave me his horse and—"

"His horse?"

Tolken wiped his sopping brow on his forearm. "A fine destrier, me lord."

Crosley had spared nothing to lead his pursuer astray.

Tolken sought Fulke's gaze. "The horse will fetch a good price— enough to buy a home for me boys."

"Coin and destrier that you wander Sinwell in his name and those of the children he had with him." Anger trembled through Fulke. "Were my nephews well?"

"The older boy seemed so. The younger had a cough somethin' terrible."

What ill had befallen Harold? Struggling to contain his emotions, Fulke asked, "When did you last see Crosley?"

Tolken counted off his fingers. "Five days gone, me lord."

"His destination?"

"I know not, though he turned south."

Did the man lie? Likely not, for Crosley could have no reason to reveal more than the man needed to know.

Heaven's wrath! How much time was lost in this vain chase? More, how much had Crosley gained? Fulke pivoted. South…to London? Mayhap, but what of Harold? If he was ill, Crosley's progress would be hindered.

"Back in there with you!" Howarth shouted.

"Me lord," Tolken called. "Pray, spare me boys."

Fulke halted. As Howarth would surely extract his humiliation from Tolken's flesh, what would become of the man's sons? Might Howarth also work vengeance on them? He shouldn't care, especially as it would take precious time he could ill afford, but he could not leave the children.

"Bring Tolken!" He resumed his stride.

"His flesh is my due!" Howarth sputtered.

Fulke traversed the corridor and mounted the steps. Once more before the sniveling boys, he grudgingly admitted he had done what was best. It was a flaw for which he ought to be whipped.

When Tolken stumbled into the hall, he was met by his sons' joyful cries.

Baron Howarth appeared at Fulke's side. "What is this, Wynland?"

"I am *Lord* Wynland," Fulke reminded him. "Tolken and his sons will accompany me when I depart Glenmar."

"But 'twas I who was first betrayed, I who ought to avenge myself on the knave."

Fulke held the man's stare. "Think well on your words ere you speak another to me, for they shall determine whether you remain keeper of Glenmar."

The man's gaze wavered.

"Food and drink for my men, then we ride." Fulke left the man to his seething and stepped out into the dark of fallen night. Why had he allowed Tolken and the man's sons to come between him and his end?

It was not as if the man did not deserve punishment. But there were children to consider, two little boys who needed their father just as John and Harold—

Fulke closed his eyes. Had he not discouraged their attempts to draw near, they might not have given themselves so wholly to Crosley. No doubt, nary a word of opposition had either boy spoken when taken from Brynwood. As much as Fulke hated to admit it, Crosley was as a father to them.

He shoved a hand through his hair. As for Tolken and his sons, once they were a safe distance from Glenmar, he would release them.

He conjured an image of Lark and thought how strange it was it should sting knowing he would not be soon in coming to her as he had thought. But she was safe at Farfallow. That was all that mattered.

*September 17th, 3:00 p.m.: Awakened by pounding on the door (Graham) at approximately 1:00 p.m. EEG tracing indicates 20 hours of continuous sleep intersected by only six REMS (alarm didn't work). As with Mac's EEGs, the REM periods are significantly longer than normal (see tracing #917). Recall only the dream from which I was awakened—FulkeWynland again. As before, it was detailed, lucid, and so real I recall it in its entirety. Is the tumor responsible? Sleep deprivation? Whatever the answer, I want badly to return to the dream, to Sinwell, to Fulke.*

Cheek pressed to the desktop, Kennedy lifted her pen and stared at the name of a man her spent mind had made real. She didn't need to close her eyes to summon his face, to draw his scent to her, to feel his mouth on hers. Although it seemed too much effort to work her facial muscles, she smiled in remembrance. If only...

Laughter parted her lips. Yes, if only, but she could dream, couldn't she? Sleep descending, she reminded herself of the need to maintain a sleep deficit. It was no use.

He had told himself it could get no worse, but the appearance of Sir Daniel and the accompanying knights dispelled all hope. She was gone, just as she had warned. This time forever?

A thundering inside him, Fulke turned from the villagers who had greeted him a half hour earlier and who professed to know nothing of Crosley and his nephews.

Sir Daniel reined in before Fulke and dismounted. "My lord, I fear I bring you—"

"I know! Tell me how!"

The knight exchanged glances with another of the knights who had accompanied him. "She disappeared, my lord, as if by magic."

Fulke's disquiet deepened. That was not a word to be spoken without thought of consequences. Death was too quick to follow. "You were to keep her ever in your sight, Sir Daniel. Did you slack your duty?"

"I kept her in my sight, my lord, but when she became ill on the ride to Farfallow, it was necessary to stop. She begged a moment of privacy to relieve herself. I stayed near, but turned my back to her as one does a lady. When I looked around, she was gone."

A murmur rose from Fulke's men where they had gathered behind.

"None saw her flee?"

The other knights shook their heads. Only then did Fulke give his regard to the fifth man among Lark's escort—Sir Donald, the knight he had sent to Brynwood Spire to retrieve his brother's message. The missive he drew from his tunic could wait.

Sir Daniel took a step forward. "Methinks she is a witch, my lord, for in her escape she made no sound—no breaking of branches underfoot, no crackle of leaves."

Despite his lowered voice, his words were not lost on the others, as evidenced by their murmurings of "witch," "sorceress," "unholy." Just cause for a burning if ever there was one, and it filled Fulke with fear. However, he quieted it with the reminder that these men were his now that the truth of the earl's death was known.

Sir Daniel shook his head. "'Twas as if the lady had never been."

But she had been. Fulke had the memory of her to attest to it. "You searched for her?"

"For a whole day ere riding to Glenmar where the baron told us of Crosley's trickery. Over the past two days, we have ridden hard to bring you news, ever passing where already you had passed."

Fulke felt as if the world had fallen out from under him, as if his fate were already written.

"Yesterday we met up with Sir Donald. He carries you tidings, my lord."

The knight strode forward and passed the missive to Fulke. "Your brother has entrusted me to deliver his message—written, as well as spoken."

Richard was taking no chances this time. "Then speak."

"He says that, on the month past, Sir Arthur was seen in conversation with the monk who passed the night at Brynwood. As the monk was from the monastery of Farfallow, your brother suggests you stop there."

Remembering Lark's agitation when he had called for his men to ride to the monastery, Fulke almost laughed at the irony of his choice of safekeeping for her. "Sir Daniel, during your search for Lady Lark, did you pause at Farfallow?" Likely not Lark's destination, but perhaps Crosley's.

"Aye, my lord, but the good monks told us they had seen nary of Lady Lark, nor Sir Crosley."

Then not Farfallow. Lark's fear had been for nothing—unless it was, indeed, Crosley's destination and he had yet to reach it.

"There is more, my lord," Sir Donald said. "Your brother bids me to tell you that Lady Lark's maid has been found."

Fulke frowned. Lark had said she did not have a maid traveling with her. A lie? Or was the woman who claimed to be her maid lying? "She is well?"

"Aye, my lord. Your brother questioned her, but I fear there was naught to be learned of the attack. She is most...hysterical."

"Thank you, Sir Donald." Fulke looked again to Sir Daniel, a man in sore need of redemption. "You and the others will return to Farfallow and set up camp outside its walls. If Crosley or Lady Lark comes unto them, you will send word."

"Aye, my lord."

Fulke strode to his destrier. He halted alongside the horse, looked up, and traced the wisps of clouds that floated the sky. Lark was gone. But was she a witch? To accept it would mean believing in something he never had, but what other explanation was there for her ability to appear and disappear? If this was only a dream as she claimed, why did he continue on when she was gone from it?

"Lark," he breathed. Though he knew it would be best if this was the end of her, for if she returned she would likely face fire, it drove a pike through him that he might not hold her again. It was a hard thing to admit, especially considering her deception, but in their short time together he had come to feel something for her.

Love? Though he had never been touched by the elusive emotion, in the deepest place inside him he believed in its existence, which was why he had been relieved when he returned to England and found Jaspar wed to another. He had suffered no sting to his pride, for it had suited him to escape marriage to one for whom he felt little. He wanted to feel more for the woman with whom he would make children, loathed the thought of a marriage such as that which had bound his mother and father. They had never loved, had barely tolerated one another. It was lust for Aveline's youth and beauty that made Fulke's father set aside his first wife to take another. As for Aveline, the marriage her parents forced on her had broken the heart she had given to another. To the earl's dying day, she had bemoaned the loss of her love, uncaring what pain it caused her husband and children.

Fulke met his destrier's steely stare. If he died a childless old man alone in bed, he would choose solitude over wedding one for whom he was unmoved.

But Lark moved him, she who seemed of another world, who spoke of dreams as if nothing in his world were real, who did not trust him. God be with him, like a downy-faced youth he had opened himself to her. Witch or not, he was under her spell. A dreamspell.

# 18

"What are you reading, Nedy?"

Kennedy dropped the cover on her journal and looked to her mother who crossed the living room with a cup and saucer in each hand. "Just some old notes." Actually, they were new, a record of the sleep to which she had succumbed four days ago, and which had cost her the deficit that would have sooner returned her to her research. Still, the twelve hours of seemingly dreamless sleep had refreshed her—not that she wasn't again reduced to trembling and fumbling with this current cycle numbering eighty hours.

"Not that research of yours, I hope."

Kennedy crossed her fingers. "No." She stepped forward and winced at her precarious balance that was compounded by the pounding in her skull. So much for painkillers.

"Nedy?"

She knew from the ache shimmering in her mother's eyes that her infirmity was felt. "Is that tea, Mom?"

The cups rattled. "Y-yes. Come sit down." She placed the saucers on the sofa table.

Amazed at how much concentration it took to cover the short distance, Kennedy lowered to the sofa beside her mother and reached for the tea. Now if she could just get the cup to her lips without scalding herself. Fortunately, the contents were only passing hot, her mother having anticipated she might spill. Funny how tuned in she was to her daughter's condition, yet in breath denied its severity.

Kennedy sipped down half her tea and carefully set her cup on the table.

"You're looking better," Laurel said.

If it wasn't such a pitiful lie, Kennedy might have laughed. No matter how ill she became—and she couldn't get much worse—her mother would cling to hope that would prove a painful pill when she donned black to say farewell.

Kennedy eased her mother's cup from her fingers and set it aside. "No"—she took Laurel's hands in hers—"I don't look better, Mom."

"Of course you do. There's color in your cheeks—"

"There's not. You have to stop pretending that what's happening isn't. It is, and there's nothing you, I, or the doctors can do."

"Nonsense. The chemotherapy—"

"I told you I'm not taking it any more. It wasn't helping."

Her mother's hands shook. "Maybe you should try again."

"No."

"It's mind over body, Nedy."

*Patience.* "I wish it were that simple, but it's not. You have to accept what is happening and prepare yourself."

Laurel jumped up. "God is not going to take you from me. He wouldn't be so cruel."

Kennedy curled her fingers into her palms. "I'm dying, Mom."

"Cancer doesn't run in my family—or your father's. Heart disease, yes, but not cancer."

"It doesn't always run in families." Kennedy started to stand, but it was too much effort. "Sometimes something just goes wrong."

"My prayers will be answered."

"Look at me, Mom." Kennedy pulled the knit cap from her head.

Laurel met her gaze and quickly looked away.

Kennedy reached to her. "Sit with me."

Laurel gripped Kennedy's hand and lowered beside her.

"Mom, it's important—"

"What an interesting man that Fulke Wynland was."

Her attempt to change the subject nearly worked. For a split second, Kennedy swept back to the man she had left behind, longed for his touch—

She wasn't going to think about him. He didn't exist. But how did her mother know about him? The book. Laurel had borrowed it. "He was interesting, but we're not talking about him. We're talking about you and me."

"I'd rather not."

As much as Kennedy wanted to prepare her mother for the inevitable, the desperate pleading in Laurel's eyes made her sigh. "All right. Later."

Her mother settled back and patted her lap. "Like old times?"

Old times when, as a child, Kennedy had laid her head in her mother's lap and they had whiled away the bedtime hour with talk. The memory warmed Kennedy, shunting aside her worry over Laurel's denial. She could almost feel her mother's fingers tugging at her curls, winding them around her fingers. But nevermore.

Kennedy eased her legs onto the sofa and laid her head in her mother's lap.

Laurel curved a hand over her daughter's bare scalp. "My baby."

"My mom." Kennedy closed her eyes and remembered how it had felt to be a child, safe in her mother's arms.

"Graham told me he came to see you."

She should have known they would talk. "Yes, he did."

"And?"

Kennedy opened her eyes. "He wishes things could have turned out differently for us."

Sorrow etched her mother's mouth. "Oh, Nedy, was the divorce really necessary?"

"It was. Now he's free and I'm..." What? A short-lived divorcee?

"He loves you, you know."

That wasn't enough. With the exception of marrying a woman his mother disapproved of, in everything he bent to Celia, excusing his actions with reminders of how fragile and broken she was over her husband's death, allowing her to dictate the terms of his marriage. Bit by bit Kennedy had been pushed to the back of a long bus until she was more roommate than wife. Even when she was first diagnosed with the tumor, little had changed.

Bitterness swept her as she remembered a conversation overheard between Graham and his mother on the night he had told her of Kennedy's illness. Eager to leave Celia's grand home, Kennedy had gone in search of Graham. As she passed the study, she had heard his voice, but before she could announce herself, Celia's words rang clearly to the hallway.

"Better widowed than divorced, I suppose," she said so matter-of-factly Kennedy had felt as if a knife had been put through her.

And all Graham had said was, "Mother!"

Kennedy had finally accepted what she had known for some time—her marriage was over. In spite of Graham's protests, she had filed for divorce.

She sighed away the pain and felt herself begin to drift. She really should get up...

"Do you think Fulke Wynland did it?' Laurel asked.

Though grateful to be pulled back from the edge, Kennedy couldn't bring herself to sit up. "Did what?"

"Murdered his nephews?"

Not the Fulke Wynland she knew, but they weren't talking about a dream. "The evidence points to him."

"That's what the author contends, but I don't believe it."

Kennedy yawned. She should hook up to the EEG, but not until her mother left. "If not Wynland, who?"

"Lady Jaspar, for one."

That awakened Kennedy. *The Sins of the Earl of Sinwell* hadn't mentioned Jaspar. Had it? Wasn't the woman a product of Kennedy's dreaming mind? Or maybe the book had mentioned her and she had forgotten. Her mind *was* falling apart nearly as fast as the rest of her.

"I think he may have been framed, that the woman who passed herself off as Lady Lark was involved."

Kennedy felt as if trampled. "What woman?"

"I don't know her name. No one does, only that she suddenly disappeared and was never seen again, which led Wynland's men to pronounce her a witch." She frowned. "I thought you said you read the book."

Mac's words about the story changing following his travel into it returned to Kennedy. Impossible. "I skimmed it. You're finished with it?"

"No, but as much as I hate to read, I couldn't help but peek ahead."

"And?"

"Poor Wynland, an earl for a day then arrested and hanged for murders he likely didn't commit. But surely you know that."

Surely she did. "Yes, of course." In spite of the shock her mother had delivered, fatigue pulled Kennedy deeper into the sofa. On a stack of Bibles she would attest to Fulke Wynland having come out of the mess smelling like roses—that the deaths of his nephews had earned him the title of earl, not the noose. Had she completely lost it?

"Are you all right, Kennedy?"

"I'm fine. How far along are you in the book?"

"About three-quarters. You know, where Wynland meets up with the king's men who have come to investigate the attack on Lady Lark."

Kennedy didn't know. "The details are a little fuzzy."

"Well, the king's men weren't pleased to learn of Lady Lark's disappearance—rather, the impostor's, though they didn't yet realize that's what she was."

"Go on."

"They accompanied Wynland in his search for his nephews." Laurel shrugged. "That's as far as we've gotten. Would you like the book back?"

"Yes—when you're finished with it." Or maybe she didn't want it back, for it would only prove how much she had deteriorated. Obviously, her mother wasn't the only one suffering from denial.

Nowhere to go but sleep, Kennedy dropped her lids and stared into the darkness. Forget the EEG, forget her research. She was too far gone to gather reliable data. It was over. All she had left was her dreams. That acknowledgment let Fulke in again. She saw him, his ravaged face lit with a smile.

As she relaxed deeper into her mother's lap, she felt his arms come around her and lift her. His breath was on her face, then his mouth on her mouth.

She sighed. Though on occasion she'd had dreams so captivating she had hit the snooze button to pull herself back into them, this went beyond that. More than anything, she longed to return to Fulke—the dream of him, the fantasy, whatever he was—and savor their time together for as long as she had left. Her heart tugged, forcing her to admit that which firmly placed her among the ranks of the mad: she was in love with a dream.

Now the question was whether or not she could dream Fulke one last time. If so, where would the dream take her? Her sinking mind dabbled with the possibilities, pondered what had happened after the king's men joined Fulke's search for John and Harold, and carried her away.

# 19

*Even if I now saw you only once,*
*I would long for you through worlds, worlds.*
~ Izumi Shikibu

STILL NOTHING OF Crosley, Fulke brooded as he sighted the deer over the arrow's shaft. Still nothing of Lark. That made him flinch. Cursing the distraction, he sighted his prey a second time. This night, his men would have meat.

The deer—or Bambi, as Lark called it—stepped into twilight and snuffled amid the fallen leaves.

Sight. Steady. Relea—

The crackle of leaves brought the deer's head up, and it hurtled away.

Cursing what was likely a rodent come between him and his prey, Fulke swung the bow around, followed, and released. At the moment before the arrow gained its mark, a movement to the left caused the deer to veer and the arrow to plow the ground.

Fulke reached over his shoulder, pulled another arrow, nocked it. It was too late for the deer, but there might still be meat. He searched the wood, from amongst the shadows of waning day picked out the movement responsible for his loss. Too large for a rodent. A boar?

String pulled to his cheek, he was rewarded when the animal stepped from behind a screen of bramble. The arrow was a breath from flight when Fulke recognized the one he had thought never to see again.

Clad in Jaspar's dark dress, a color that had nearly delivered her unto death, she halted. "Don't shoot. It's only me."

Only Lark, and lovelier than he remembered. He lowered his bow. She was back, reappearing as if touched by sorcery as his men claimed, as if come out of the mist and into a dream as she claimed. Where had she been? More, how had she—

"Good timing, hmm?" She retrieved the arrow that had missed the deer and resumed her advance.

Eyes filled with the woman he had been unable to shut out, heart hammering, Fulke forsook the mystery of her disappearance. For now, all that mattered was that she had come back to him.

Before she took the last step to his side, he could smell her scent—fresh and clean—and feel the space between them as if it were capable of being held. Lacking the voice to speak her name, he fixed on her face.

She extended the arrow. "This might come in handy later."

His fingers brushed hers as he took it, the brief contact tightening his body.

She smiled. "Miss me?"

As he would miss his heart were it torn from him.

Kennedy searched Fulke's eyes and saw in them the answer he denied his breath. "I'll take that as a yes." Emboldened by regrets that had haunted her these past days, she stepped near, reached her arms around his neck, and pressed her mouth to his.

He dropped the bow and crushed her to him. His beard rasping her face, he kissed her, drinking from her as a man thirsting for water.

Kennedy had no other thought but for him. Only with Fulke did she feel alive, and if tomorrow she died, this one day would be enough to last an eternity.

He swung her into his arms, carried her to a place between the trees that was still warmed by the recently departed sunlight, and lowered her to a bed of grass.

The smell of earth beneath her, Kennedy turned to face him as he lay down beside her. "Dream with me, Fulke." She slid fingers through the tawny hair across his brow. "Even if only for this moment."

"'Tis not a dream."

She pressed fingers to his lips. "Never question a gift."

"You are saying you wish to be one with me, Lark?"

Pained by another's name on his lips, she longed to hear him speak her own name. But did it matter? They were together, and that was enough, because Lady Lark and Kennedy Plain were worlds apart.

"I want to be here with you, but you should know that I was never the king's mistress."

"Then what were you to him?"

Now was the time to set him straight. The problem was, she wasn't certain she was Lark's maid. But that wasn't all. As in her world where the rich rarely hobnobbed with the poor—except for photo ops—here social castes most often dictated one's circle of friends. "Edward and I are friends. That is all."

His jagged eyebrow rose. "You are friends with a man such as he?" Beneath a sky nearing twilight, he picked a leaf from her hair. "I do not think so, but in time you will tell me exactly what you are to him."

That she was a fraud? Only if her deception came to light, and it was not likely as this was surely her last journey into the dream. When she awakened—*if* she awakened—she would not be coming back. As much as she longed to succumb to Mac's fantasy, she still had enough lucidity about her to know Fulke was all in her mind.

"There is something I wish to tell you," he said.

"Yes?"

"I would marry you, Lark."

Lark, not her maid. But Kennedy was determined to live for the moment. She smiled. "You've changed your mind about me."

"Just as you did about me."

"Why? Because I was not Edward's mistress?"

"Forsooth, I am pleased he did not know you, but ere you disappeared again, I determined I would wed you." A frown displaced the tenderness with which he regarded her. "Where have you been? How did you escape my men? And, pray, do not tell me you dreamed yourself away."

"Then I won't. You found Sir Arthur and your nephews at Glenmar?"

For a moment, she didn't think he would let her off so easily, but her question provoked him. "Nay." His faced turned stony. "They were impostors, a man and his sons hired by your *friend*, Sir Arthur, to wander Sinwell in his name."

As much as Kennedy hated Fulke's transformation, she was relieved he wasn't pushing to know where she had gone. He had not killed the knight, but there was a catch. If the dream was staying true, it was only a matter of time before the confrontation. In fact, Sir Arthur was probably at Farfallow now. How much longer before he and Fulke met over swords?

She knew she shouldn't ask, but it was important—even if there wasn't a thing she could do. "I seem to have lost track of time. How many days has it been since you rode to Glenmar?"

"How can you not know?" There remained a harsh edge to his voice.

She ventured a teasing smile. "Time got away from me."

Questioning softened his face. "Six days you have been gone."

Six days! That would place them near the two week mark cited in the book. Hopefully, the author had been off in his estimation of how long it had taken Fulke to catch up with Sir Arthur.

"Now I would know where you have been."

Kennedy laid a hand on his jaw. "Why can't we just enjoy the time we have together?"

"How much time is that?"

"I don't know."

He searched her face, then released a harsh breath. "My men say you are a witch, but methinks it more likely you are simply mad."

This was a dream, plain and simple, but too far out there for him to entertain. "As I don't care to go up in a puff of smoke, I'll have to plead madness."

The admission, if it could be called that, seemed to pain him. "You are not at all like my sister, Marion."

What had sweet, vulnerable Marion to do with anything? "I don't understand."

"She also suffers a malady of the mind."

Kennedy remembered her encounter with the woman. Off-key, perhaps, but mad? It was possible, but from what she had seen, the only thing Marion suffered from was a domineering mother. "Are you sure?"

"Thrice betrothed and thrice returned ere vows were spoken. She has fits."

Unable to reconcile the image with the woman she had met, Kennedy said, "Perhaps she just doesn't care to marry."

Instantly, Fulke pulled back from the darkness of Marion's madness. "If 'tis true you are mad, still it does not explain how you escaped and where you have been for nearly a sennight."

"I know it doesn't." She held his gaze. "You have no idea what it took for me to get back to you."

"Why *did* you come back?"

"For you. You see, a funny thing happened while I was gone…or I suppose it happened while I was here. I came to have feelings for you. Where I'm from, people call it love."

Fulke stared. She loved him? If it was true, how was he to respond? That he loved her in return? After all these empty years, was it possible? He didn't know, but there was no denying what he felt for her went beyond lust—though he wasn't certain how far beyond.

"Crazy, hmm?" She fingered the fleur-de-lis embroidered around the neck of his tunic. "Not that I understand how it happened. I just accept it. Why can't you do the same? Accept me as I am?"

"Lark, you disappeared under escort of four knights. And now, once more, you reappear as if you never left. In the sight of many, it condemns you for a witch."

"You know I'm not."

"'Tis my belief, but one for which I seem to stand alone. As you know, in England witches are burned."

"So unless I come up with a convincing explanation, your men are going to host a wienie roast with me as the guest of honor?" Confusion returned to Fulke's face, but before he could ask her to translate, Kennedy said, "They're going to light a fire under me?"

He shook his head. "You are under my protection. None will challenge me now that Cardell is renounced. Too, whatever your relation to the king, it shields you. But only for so long. Do you persist in disappearing and reappearing, superstitions will continue to mount. In such instances, 'tis not unheard of for men to abandon their vows of fealty in the name of God." He lifted her chin and regarded her with an intensity that caused her heart to ripple. "I may not be able to save you."

*If* she persisted. She might disappear one more time, but that would probably be the end of her. "You have nothing to worry about. The last thing I want is to leave you." The truth, misleading though it was.

"You will stay with me?"

She stared at the man who filled so many empty places inside her. "For as long as I live." Ignoring the ache of their imminent parting and the longing for him to declare his love for her, she said, "I am willing, Fulke."

He levered up, pressed her onto his back, and brushed his mouth across hers. "And I am tempted."

"Only tempted?"

"More, but I made a vow that if ever I saw you again, I would make things different between us. I have waited this long for you. I can wait until we are wed."

Kennedy stared up at him against the darkening sky and wondered if they had that long. She did not think so. Still, she said, "We will wait."

Not wanting their solitude to end, she ran her hands up his back and, through the material of his tunic, felt the ridges she had seen the night she had relieved Lady Jaspar of assisting him with his bath.

"Tell me about these." She traced a scar.

Fulke tensed. For what did she ask? He had told her they were gained in war. No further explanation was needed. "Rain is upon the air." He pulled away. "We ought to return to camp."

Lark glanced at the gathering clouds and sat up. "Why were you whipped?"

All he could think to say was, "It was deserved." Turning back a vision of angry, vengeful faces, he stood and reached a hand to her. "Let us make haste."

"What did you do?"

He stared down at her until she placed her hand in his.

"I'm sorry to pry," she said as she rose alongside him. "I have no right."

He was about to agree when he realized the wrong he did her. As they were to wed, she did have the right to know the truth of the man with whom she would spend the remainder of her years. But how would she react if he told her of Limoges, the heinous crimes committed in the name of England and vainglory, the reason for the flogging that had left him for dead? Would she run from him? Would her love turn to revulsion? Or would she forgive him his sins and love the man he had struggled to become since the bloodletting?

He pulled the medallion from his tunic. "As I told you, this was given to me for the retaking of lands in France. King Edward himself put it around my neck." He lowered it. "But I do not wear it out of pride, Lark. I wear it in remembrance of all who died that it might be cast."

"I don't understand."

"Do you wish to? Do you truly want to know this man you will wed?"

"I do."

He yielded to the images from which he was forever turning. Like faithless old friends come to steal from him, they hastened to his side.

"Do you know of Limoges, the great siege of 1370?"

Kennedy remembered the book had advanced that the blood shed in that city was as much on Fulke's hands as those of the Black Prince, King Edward's son and heir. "I know what happened there."

"What do you know?"

"Hundreds of people died."

"Among them, women and children. Do you know I was responsible?"

She didn't want to hear this, would rather cling to the man she had come back for. If only she hadn't asked about the scars. "I heard you were involved."

He laughed, a sound so void it ached. "The French were advancing into Aquitaine, threatening Edward's holdings. Something had to be done to turn them back—a show of strength, as I suggested to the Black Prince." He stepped back and stared into the trees. "Limoges was to be that show."

His words were barbed with regret. No matter what he had done, there had to be redemption for such remorse.

"The people were revolting against taxation and calling for an end to English rule. Thus, 'twas decided the city must fall. Though the prince was ill, he determined to see it for himself and was carried to Limoges in a litter." Fulke crossed to where his sword glinted amid the leaves and retrieved it. "The siege lasted a month, during which the prince became increasingly hostile. He vowed that when the city was gained, all would die for their faithlessness. I knew he did not threaten without weight, but I pressed on, directed the attack on the walls and the undermining." He looked past his blade to Kennedy. "Pride is a terrible god, Lark. Once you worship it, there is no other. It makes of men what God did not mean them to be." He slid his sword into its sheath. "No matter the cost, I was determined the prince would have his victory, and that I would be the one to give it to him."

"Why?"

"I was military advisor to the crown. Having years earlier lost the earldom to my brother when he assumed the title he had eschewed, it was all I had left."

Kennedy closed the distance between them. Once more able to make out his shadowed features, she asked, "What happened?"

He lingeringly touched her face as if it were the last time he would do so. "A massacre." He stared at her, then through her.

More than anything, Kennedy dreaded his admission to having put men, women, and children to death, but she had asked for it. Still, it did not seem possible that the man she had come to love was capable of such atrocity.

"Finally, the miners broke through. The people of Limoges tried to turn them back, but it was in vain. The prince's army had waited a month for the day, and there was no end to their bloodlust." For a moment, Fulke came back to her and saw her again. "Moriel was there."

The assassin.

"He was among the first to kill, and he did not stop 'til there was no more blood to spill."

"Under your orders?"

He was slow to answer. "'Twas the prince who commanded that all be put to the sword."

Then he hadn't ordered it himself. A seed of hope rooted within her.

"But he did it through me, and so 'twas done."

"You were following orders."

"Orders I should not have followed."

She laid a hand on his arm. "Would it have changed anything if you had refused to give the order?"

"That I have asked myself a thousand times a thousand. The prince trusted me and oft took my advice, but that day he was in so violent a passion I knew it was useless to try to dissuade him. But mayhap I could have."

If only he had tried that the people might have lived, that he would not forever agonize over what might have been. "You were only doing what you were told. Though that doesn't absolve—"

"Only?" he said sharply. "I also killed, Lark. Five? Ten? More? I know not."

She swallowed. "In cold blood?"

Questioning slipped in beside Fulke's pain and drew his eyebrows near.

She had done it again, confused him with her twenty-first century jargon. "Did you kill merely to kill—like Moriel?"

"Nay. Ungodly I may be, but that I have never done. I raised my sword to defend myself and the prince's men."

"And what of the women and children?"

"Though none fell to my sword, they fell by my service to the crown."

And in doing so, had broken his heart that he might discover he had one. "I think you're wrong, Fulke. Men like your Black Prince do as they please no matter how loud the outcry."

He searched her face. "Would that I could believe you."

"You can. Regret what happened at Limoges, yes; learn from it, certainly; but don't let it darken the rest of your life. You have to put it behind you." That last made Kennedy wince. Shrink talk. In spite of her training, it was not her specialty.

Fulke stepped back. "You asked about the scars." Once more, he retreated to that tortured place inside himself. "I had seen enough blood-letting. 'Twas time I returned to England." He drove a hand through his hair. "Though it was foolish to ride across France without an escort, I left the prince's army to its pillaging and burning."

Kennedy glanced at his hands and saw they had become fists.

"A league from Limoges I was set upon by a score of men and women who had fled the city. They brought my horse down and beat me. 'Twas a woman who put the blade to my face." He touched his scarred eyebrow. "They stretched me to a tree and took turns drawing blood from my back until they determined I was dead." He blew out a ragged breath. "I remember their faces, the anger for all they had lost, the need to avenge themselves and their dead even if only on one man. My life was their due—and more."

"But you didn't die, Fulke."

His gaze stabbed, bitterness deepened. "You think that a comfort?"

True. "I imagine it must have been difficult to learn Lady Jaspar had married another when it was believed you were dead."

"How know you of that?"

"Jaspar's maid told me."

"The woman's tongue wags as much as that of her mistress." He shook his head. "'Twas not difficult. It was a blessing—one I did not deserve. With both hands I seized it and vowed to never wed a woman for whom I felt naught."

Kennedy's heart tumbled. "Are you saying you feel something for me?"

His reluctance was palpable, but he stepped before her. "I do feel something for you."

She waited for the rest of it. Nothing.

"After all I have told you, still you profess to love me, Lark?"

As he did not profess to love her. A drop of rain fell to Kennedy's cheek, like a tear rolled to her jaw. Ignoring the ache in her heart, she cupped his bearded face between her hands. "The man you were—the part of you that cared more for glory than lives—is gone. The man with whom I am in love would not do what he did."

"How can you be certain?"

She leaned in and brushed her mouth across his. "Because I have fit nearly all the pieces of the puzzle of you, Fulke Wynland."

"Of what do you speak?"

"There was that little boy—the one who called to you the day you brought me to Brynwood."

"Jeremy, my brother's misbegotten son, John and Harold's half-brother."

Kennedy almost laughed. No wonder the child had seemed familiar, not because he was part of her world but because he was part of Fulke who, doubtless, had the look of his deceased brother. "Yes, Jeremy. You talked to him and gave him a coin. It was so out of character for the man I thought you were. Then there was Sir Malcolm. I imagined all manner of horrible things you would do to him after I fell from his horse, yet he was allowed to redeem himself."

Even though it was dark enough to be called night now, his gaze was intense.

"You could have raped me. I thought you would, but you didn't. Then you started to smile." She let her own lips curve. "But it was that night in the tent when you spoke of your nephews that I knew you could not harm them. And then you saved my life at the pool. I was wrong about you." Her lashes lowered. "I'm sorry."

Fulke longed to believe what she believed of him, to put Limoges from him and go forward with her at his side, but something stood between them. He lowered his face near hers. "And Crosley? How will you feel when he lies dead by my sword?"

She blinked and surprised him with one of her green-eyed smiles. "You won't kill him."

She was wrong. Crosley had challenged him at every opportunity, accused him of seeking to harm the boys, then stolen John and Harold. Such affront could not be disregarded. Unlike the people of Limoges, the knight's death was warranted. He could argue it with Lark, but for what? There was peace between them, and he would take it for however long it lasted. Once Crosley was dead, he would deal with her anger. If she could forgive him the deaths of hundreds, surely the death of one could also be forgiven.

He kissed her until she murmured and bent to him. "Now that I have told you of my past, you will tell me of yours?"

She stiffened.

Then she would not reveal where she had been these past six days. Frustration welled in Fulke, but he forced it down. Eventually, she would trust him enough to tell him all. "Later, then," he said and released her and retrieved his bow and quiver. "'Tis late. We ought to return to camp." He held out his hand.

It felt right, her hand in his, made him feel as if he were the youth who had sat the garden wall with his sister and, for a short while, allowed her dreams to become his.

The hunt having taken him distant from camp, it was a long walk. And wet, the clouds finally emptying their chill rain to satisfy the earth's thirst. In spite of the discomfort, the time with Lark was something he would never forget—their joined hands, the smile in her voice as they talked of little things, her sweet laughter when any other lady would have been whining over her soaked gown, muddied slippers, and dripping hair. She seemed not to notice, though her teeth were chattering by the time the canopied campfire came into view.

Fulke halted and pulled her in front of him. "Promise me something."

Rain running down her face, she nodded.

"Keep your tongue before my men. They will be unsettled by your return and some will name you a witch. Pray, give them naught else with which to stoke their superstitions."

She smiled. "I'll be careful."

Love her? Aye, in that moment he knew it was so. But the words would not be spoken. "Come," he said, "let us be done with this." He pulled her with him over the sodden ground. As expected, a knight cut their path before they reached the clearing.

"Halt! Who goes?"

Fulke pulled Lark against his side. "Your liege."

The man stepped nearer and lowered his sword. "My lord, when you did not return, we feared—"

"I am well, as is Lady Lark."

The man's silence spoke loudly, the night cloaking an expression no doubt born of dismay. "Two parties have gone searching for you, my lord."

"When?"

"An hour past."

Fulke gripped Lark's hand more firmly and resumed his stride. "I must needs see the lady out of the rain."

"Sir Daniel arrived early eve, my lord."

"Sir Daniel?" Fulke's gut tightened. It could mean only one thing.

Beside him, Lark groaned. "I imagine he'll be testy when he sees me."

True, for she had brought dishonor on him. But her discomfort would be nothing compared to that which she would soon face. Despite her belief Fulke would not slay Sir Arthur, she would have to accept the truth of it. Blood *would* be let.

"Return to your post," Fulke said to the knight.

Something was wrong. Kennedy sensed it straight through. Stride fraught with purpose, Fulke's hand tensed around hers as he hurried her forward. When they entered the clearing, a dozen men came out from beneath the canopies and halted at the sight of her.

"Where is Sir Daniel?" Fulke demanded.

"He awaits you in your tent, my lord," Sir Leonel said, his gaze on Kennedy.

Was he among those who would see her staked and burned? She offered a smile.

His lips turned slightly. "Lady Lark."

Fulke urged Kennedy past the knights, flung back the tent flap, and motioned her ahead of him. She ducked into the relative warmth of the tent.

Sir Daniel was the first to rise, eyes widening at the sight of her. The three other men—unrecognizable and outfitted in elaborate wear—also stood.

"Sir Daniel," Fulke said, then turned his regard on the others. "You may deliver word to King Edward that Lady Lark is returned and has suffered no ill."

From the men's expressions, they didn't have a clue as to what he referred.

But Kennedy did. Realization caused her stomach to inch up her throat. The dream had become a nightmare.

# 20

"Where is Lady Lark?" asked the eldest knight, a man whose face was fleshy and lined.

Kennedy swallowed. These were the king's men who, according to her mother, had caught up with Fulke following the disappearance of Lady Lark's pretender. What a web her mind had woven! If there had been any doubt before, here was proof she was off her rocker.

Feeling Fulke's disquiet, she looked at him. Questioning was in his eyes, doubt and distrust. And they cut through her. He returned his attention to the others. "Is this not Lady Lark, Sir Conan?"

The knight's eyes widened. "Lord Wynland, I know the lady myself and this woman is not she." He stepped forward and peered closer at Kennedy. "Even did you wring her out, she would be too tall, too broad, and her hair too dark." He smirked. "You have been deceived, my lord."

As his companions nodded in agreement, Kennedy felt a wall go up between her and Fulke.

Sir Daniel stepped forward. "'Tis true what he speaks, my lord. I bring you tidings that Lady Lark has taken sanctuary at the monastery of Farfallow."

Kennedy's breath caught. Lady Lark lived?

"As has Sir Crosley and your nephews," the knight put the icing on the cake.

Kennedy glanced at Fulke, a man changed from the one to whom she had declared her love. A muscle beating in his jaw, he stared at Sir Daniel. It was over.

Deceived. The vulgar word rolled through Fulke, overturning emotions only just discovered. The woman before him was a charlatan, everything she had made him feel forged of lies. "If she is not Lady Lark, who is she?"

Sir Conan shook his head. "Never have I seen her, my lord."

"One of Lady Lark's ladies?"

"Nay, my lord, Lady Lark had but a maid with her when she left London, and I fear I know not what the woman looks like."

Was it possible the one who had arrived at Brynwood was not the maid she claimed to be? Fool! Though it pained Fulke to accept the truth, *this* woman was the deceiver. "I thank you, Sir Conan." He looked to the others. "We depart in half an hour."

"The rain comes harder," Sir Conan said. 'Twould do no harm to wait 'til the morrow."

"Half an hour!"

The man motioned to the others and stepped into the night.

As the flap fell behind them, Fulke turned to the woman at his side. "Who are you?"

The struggle on her face evidenced her search for a believable lie. She lifted her palms up. "This is only a dream, Fulke. I—"

"Enough! Speak no more of dreams or I shall bind you and set you aflame myself."

She should have been frightened, but she raised her chin. "Not in this weather, you won't."

How did she do it? Where had she learned to speak such that a man's thoughts should scatter so far afield, requiring him to painstakingly gather them back together? "What is your name?"

"Nedy Plain."

As there was too much ache in standing near her, making it hard to think, Fulke stepped away. It followed that Nedy Plain, if that was her name, possessed no virtue whatsoever. "As Crosley hired the man and his sons to pretend themselves to be who they were not, he paid you to be Lady Lark."

Beneath the deepening beat of rain on canvas, in the flickering light thrown by the lantern, she said, "You're wrong."

"Is it not true that your friend, Sir Arthur, is responsible for the attack on Lady Lark's baggage train?"

That knocked the streak of stubborn out of her, lowering her chin a notch. "That's not it at all."

"What I do not understand is what Lady Lark has to do with it. Was she part of Crosley's plan to show me to be a murderer that he might gain wardship of my nephews?"

"No! She had nothing to do with it. She's supposed to be dead. No trace was ever found—"

"She is at Farfallow with Crosley!"

"Neither Crosley nor Lady Lark were behind the attack. You have to believe me."

Never again. "You lied about my brother's missive to keep me from Farfallow because you knew 'twas Crosley's destination. Do you deny it?"

She groaned. "I did know, but—"

"I wonder if 'twas Lady Lark whom Moriel sought to kill at the pond or Nedy Plain. More likely, Crosley was done with you."

"He doesn't know me. We've never met."

Not a breath of truth to anything she said. He returned to her and gripped her chin. "You told me you knew him." He could still smell the wood on her, the grass and leaves. "Now you have never met?"

Tears washed her eyes, dampening his anger before he realized it was happening. Nay, the tears were for herself and the retribution he would visit on her.

She laid a hand on his jaw. "If you have any feelings for me, Fulke—"

He threw off her touch. "I have none."

She stared at him as if she were the one wronged.

"And, henceforth, you will address me as *Lord* Wynland."

Her eyes flashed with an anger so bright it blinded the hurt she had allowed him to glimpse. "Dream on."

As tempted as Fulke was to set her right, he had told the king's men a half hour. He stepped past her and, at the tent flap, looked over his shoulder. "Do you think to escape me, I vow I will find you—no matter where you go, no matter how far you run."

Her retort was lost in the slap of the flap. Drawing on fury to stifle other emotions vying for recognition, Fulke crossed to where Squire James held his horse.

Tomorrow, Farfallow.

*It's only a dream*, Kennedy told herself for the hundredth time since the miserable ride began.

Night having turned to dawn, dawn having turned to noon, noon speeding toward evening, she stared ahead. The last time the scenery had passed so swiftly was when Fulke had been at her back. Now it was Sir Leonel, the only one willing to accept the task of transporting a witch.

She looked to where Fulke rode so far ahead she wouldn't have known it was him if not for his horse. If only his rejection didn't hurt so much. If only he hadn't jumped to conclusions about her character. If only he would have suspended disbelief long enough to hear her out.

Accused, tried, found guilty, and sentenced in a matter of minutes. It followed, though. As Sir Arthur had hired impostors, her own masquerade fell in neatly beside the others. If she was the one trying to make sense of it, she might arrive at the same conclusion.

Her bottom and thighs sore, she shifted and once more felt the medallion between her shoulder blades—at least, she assumed it was a medallion Sir Leonel wore beneath his tunic. She had only seen the chain around his neck, but during the past night and day had suffered the gouge of what felt like a metal disc. Did it bear a two-headed wyvern? Not that it was likely to change Fulke's opinion of her if it proved the one the dying soldier had spoken of.

She looked up and, in the distance, saw enormous walls set with arched windows that reached toward heaven, the mist surrounding the lofty perch making the edifice appear to live among the clouds. The monastery of Farfallow.

"The loveliest of them all," Sir Leonel dropped into her ear. "When God comes to visit, 'tis surely where He stays."

The monastery was, indeed, awesome, but by no means elaborate. In fact, its splendor lay in its simple design.

A bell tolled, resounding above the pounding hooves as they ascended the hill on which the monastery was built.

When Sir Leonel halted his horse before the walls, Fulke had already dismounted. In conversation with a man whose dowdy robes and prayer-clasped hands identified him as a monk, he and the king's men stood in front of wooden doors built to the scale of a giant.

Though fifty feet separated Kennedy from Fulke, it was the nearest she had been to him since he had walked out on her last night. He looked even more hard and unapproachable.

"'Twas foolish of you to love," Sir Leonel said low.

Though it didn't sound like a taunt, Kennedy ignored him. Affable he might be, but what she and Fulke had shared was nobody's business.

"I am sorry," the knight said, his sincerity making her nose tingle.

Fulke's voice rose toward anger, his body language that of a man who was trying to control himself and on the verge of failing.

The monk said something, then stepped away. A small door set at the base of the larger left-hand door opened. Followed by the king's men, the monk stepped through.

Fulke turned, and his gaze slammed into Kennedy. The loathing there took her breath away, and even after he dismissed her, she struggled for air.

"Make camp!" he shouted and swung into his saddle. As his men dismounted, he guided his destrier toward Kennedy. "Sir Leonel"—he looked past her as if she were not there—"this woman is in your charge. Fail me and suffer her fate."

"Aye, my lord."

"She is to be bound and never to go from your sight, not even when she must needs relieve herself."

Kennedy's heart kicked in as he spurred away. "He never even looked at me," she murmured, not realizing she had spoken until Sir Leonel responded.

"Such a man is he. Without heart."

No, he wasn't. She had seen his heart, though it was now returned to that dark place inside him.

"What is your name?" Sir Leonel asked.

"Nedy."

"I knew you could not be Lady Lark."

"What gave me away?"

"Lady Lark may be illegitimate and born into peasantry, but you are...different."

Was it true about Lark? The book's author had lamented the gaping holes in the woman's origins. How did Leonel know what no other seemed to know? Through Jaspar who had heard of Fulke's betrothal long before he had known of it himself?

"You are not a witch, I wager. Who are you?"

She shook her head. "You wouldn't believe me."

"Mayhap I can help."

"You can't."

Argument entered his eyes, but he said, "We will speak again when we are alone."

Not about this.

He guided his horse into the midst of Fulke's men. Though occupied with setting up camp, several took time out of their busy schedules to give her the evil eye.

Kennedy settled back against Sir Leonel only to sit forward when the medallion dug into her spine. If they were going to be spending any more time on a horse, the medallion would have to go. But not before she got a look at it.

Night. And still the king's men had yet to reappear. How much longer?

Fulke straightened from a tree at the edge of Farfallow's orchard and peered past the tents to the doors. Were it not a place of sanctuary, he would scale the walls and bring his nephews and Crosley out himself. But it was God's house and there had been no convincing the abbot to grant him entrance.

If Harold was still ill, as the abbot reported he had been when Crosley brought him and his brother here three days past, it would be different. He must be patient. Soon enough, the boys would be with him and Crosley would be put to the sword.

Try though Fulke did to keep from treading the path of Nedy Plain, she pushed her way into his thoughts and pulled his gaze to where she sat back from the fire. Sir Leonel hovered near.

The knight had bound her hands, but not her feet. Though great was the temptation to order him to fully secure her, Fulke suppressed it. She was going nowhere. Even if the young knight fell to her wiles, the others would ensure she did not escape. They believed there was a witch among them and, if not for Fulke's presence, would likely do as was done to one thought to be the devil's apprentice. Even Sir Malcolm, who had fallen under her spell at Castle Cirque, maintained his distance.

Curse her! Would the memory of her—the longing—forever haunt him? It was as if she was the beginning, middle, and end of him. And he hated himself for it. After Limoges, he had vowed to never again give any part of himself he could not easily retake. He would not allow anyone so near him again.

He strode forward, the ground that the recent rain had turned sodden sucking at his boots and stirring the air with the scent of earth. His men looked up at his approach. Doubtless, they thought him a fool. And they were right.

"Fulke!" Nedy called.

He should have ignored her, but he halted.

Hands bound before her, she stood. "May I speak with you? Five minutes is all I need."

All? And his soul as well. Just the sight of her, the firelight glancing across her face and through her hair, swept him back to when he had laid beside her in the wood and known happiness at the thought she would be his wife.

He crossed to his tent and felt her gaze past the flap he dropped behind him.

"For him, you no longer exist."

Kennedy closed her eyes against the pain of Sir Leonel's words, tried to sew up the tearing inside her. Though she had been determined to ignore Fulke as he ignored her, when she had seen him she had to try to reach him.

"Come," Leonel urged, "'tis late and you ought to sleep."

And if she did, would that be the end of this? Of her?

"Nedy?"

She turned. "I'm ready."

He led her from the campfire to where he had earlier spread blankets. "Yours." He indicated the one on the right.

She settled on it, eyed her bound hands, and tried to pull the blanket around her.

Leonel stepped in. "Lie back. I will help you."

Complying, she grimaced at the cold, damp earth that seeped through the blanket.

"Sleep well, Nedy." He sat down and pulled a blanket around his shoulders for the night vigil.

Kennedy caught a glimpse of the chain around his neck before the blanket fell over it. "Do you always wear that thing?"

"What thing?"

"Wasn't that a medallion that dug into me throughout the ride?"

The moonlight on his face traced his dismay. "I am sorry. I did not realize it caused you discomfort. As I am never without it, I oft forget I wear it."

"It must be special."

He touched the chain. "My former liege, Baron Brom, awarded it to me for saving his life."

"May I see it?"

He considered her, then leaned forward and pulled the medallion from his tunic. The disk spun on its chain, too rapidly for Kennedy to make out the impression in the dim light. Hoping she was wrong, she pushed onto an elbow and reached her bound hands to it.

The medallion stopped in her cupped palms, its metal retaining the warmth of Leonel's body. She tilted the disk to moonlight. Though it wasn't light enough to make out the details, the medallion bore no wyvern, two-headed or otherwise.

Relieved on one hand that the knight was no murderer, frustrated on the other that she could make no connection between what the dying soldier had told and who had attacked Lady Lark, she looked up. "I can't make out what it is."

"'Tis the baron's device—a hand grasping heather. He is proud of it, though not as proud as he is of what his third wife brought to their marriage. She is of royal blood. Do you allow me, I will—"

"I imagine there are hundreds of devices. Do you know who possesses a two-headed wyvern?"

He stared at her, then slipped the medallion from her hands and returned it to his tunic. "For what do you ask?"

Should she tell him? He was as close to an ally as she had. "Before one of the soldiers killed in the attack on Lady Lark died, he told me one of the assailants wore a medallion bearing a wyvern with two heads."

"You thought it was me?" Though his face was in shadow, hurt sounded from his voice.

"No. I just needed...confirmation."

He was silent, as if grappling with feelings of betrayal. "'Twas likely Moriel," he finally spoke.

She revisited her last glimpse of the man and saw the dagger protruding from his bared chest. "Perhaps, but he wasn't wearing a medallion when he attacked me. Besides, he wasn't alone in the attack—not with that many dead."

"You are right. Have you told Lord Wynland of the medallion?"

"No, though I should."

"He will think it a lie."

He was probably right. "Do you think I had anything to do with the attack, Sir Leonel?"

"I do not."

"How can you be certain?"

"Because you and I are much alike. Though I have not known you long, I have watched you. However you came by Lady Lark's baggage train, methinks you cannot have been privy to the attack."

He knew that just from watching her? More than likely it was a case of puppy love. Kennedy laid back. "I'm tired. Good night."

"Nedy?"

"Hmm?"

"Be ready."

She lifted her head. "For what?"

"I shall free you of Wynland."

He would help her in spite of Fulke's threat? "How do you intend to do that?"

"I do not know, only that, at first opportunity, I will take you from here."

He did have a crush on her. Remembering what he had said that day by the stream when she introduced him to acupressure, she realized he had been granted his wish that she not be Lady Lark. Sweet, but it could end in his death. "If I'm going to get out of this"—and she would eventually—"I'll do it myself."

He stared at her. "Upon my vow, I will let Wynland do you no harm."

How gallant. How foolish. "Goodnight, Sir Leonel."

Though the insomnia that had plagued her in the twenty-first century had been firmly on the back burner during her stay in the fourteenth century, it returned. Seconds straggled past, minutes meandered, an hour dragged into the next, but finally she slipped over the edge.

# 21

"Now!" A hand gripped her arm.

Kennedy pared back her lids.

The night framed Leonel's face above hers. "Crosley is coming out!"

Kennedy lifted a hand to rub her eyes and realized it was no longer bound with the other. "But it's still night."

"Aye, and 'twill serve our escape do you make haste." He pulled her to sitting.

She looked past him. Torches lit the monastery and the ground before it where Fulke's men had gathered. And Fulke? Where was he? Doubtless at the front, sword drawn.

"Nedy?"

"I can't go." She pulled her arm from his hold. "I have to stop him."

Leonel shoved his face near hers. "What speak you of?"

"I can't let him kill Crosley." She tossed back the blanket.

"Do not be a fool. We must leave now."

She stood and started forward.

"There is naught you can do, Nedy. Wynland and Crosley will meet and Crosley will die."

She looked over her shoulder. "I have to try." She hiked up her skirt and ran. *Heavenly Father, let there be something I can do to prevent the bloodshed that will forever taint Fulke. He is not a murderer.*

"Nedy!" Leonel called. He was behind her, determined to deliver her from Fulke's wrath—but not as determined as she was to deliver Crosley. Nor as fast. She cranked up the volume on her legs and, nearing the torchlit monastery, tuned into the voices that resounded from the center of the gathering. Angry voices. Familiar voices.

"This night my blade quenches its thirst," Fulke's ominous words sluiced the night air, followed by the ring of steel that announced he had drawn his sword.

Kennedy searched for an opening among the men who were too caught up in the promise of violence to notice her. As for Leonel, he was closing in.

Steel rang again. "It ends here," Crosley dished out his own threat. "To the death."

As Kennedy elbowed her way between two knights, realization hit. She did not need to see the man advancing on Fulke to know who had spoken. She halted and, for one teetering moment, feared she might pass out.

"Mac?" she strangled past the shock.

She felt the punch of Fulke's gaze and heard the murmurings around her, but it was the Gulf War vet who held her attention. Outfitted in armor of mail and plate, sword raised, he spun around. It *was* Mac, minus the wheelchair, less the multitude of years sleep deprivation had aged him.

"Oh, no." She had dreamed him into the role of Sir Arthur Crosley. Just when she was beginning to understand the order of things in this whacked out dream, it threw her for a loop. She should have known what her mind was up to.

From his expression, Mac was just as surprised. He took a halting step toward her. "Is it you, Ken?"

She jerked her chin up and down. "It's me."

Another step toward her, his duel with Fulke forgotten. "What are you doing here?"

"Remove her, Sir Leonel!" Fulke commanded. "And know that I shall deal even more severely with you if she escapes again."

Hands fell to her shoulders and held her so tightly she felt bruises rise. "Come!" Leonel commanded.

He was angry. He had tried to help her and she had repaid him by thrusting his head into the lion's mouth. Still, she couldn't leave Mac to certain death.

"No!" She thrust forward. The release was abrupt, nearly toppling her. She lurched between Mac and death, laying herself open to Fulke's accusing gaze. "Please, don't do this."

Then Leonel had her again, his grip cruel. But as he dragged her back, Fulke called, "Release her."

After a moment's hesitation, Leonel pushed her forward.

Kennedy halted before Fulke. The alternating light and shadow of torches turned his flawed features harsh, making him appear frighteningly diabolic. Still, her heart beat for him.

"You do know Crosley," he ground out, "*Ken.*"

She winced at the loathing with which he spoke her name. What a tangled web. Was there no way to unravel it? "I didn't know Mac was Crosley. I mean...I knew that was who he was in his dreams, but...it's just a dream!" She looked over her shoulder. "Isn't it, Mac?"

"It's real, just as I told you. He *will* kill them."

As if this figment of Mac could be believed! However, in spite of the turn of events, that the man she loved had become her enemy, Kennedy longed for life beyond the voracious tumor. But as close as she was to believing it, the slender thread of reality held.

"Your lies are like disease, Nedy Plain," Fulke said. "Ever reaching, grasping, choking."

"Burn the witch!" someone shouted.

"Burn her!" another called.

"Silence!" Fulke roared. "Do *any* of you think to usurp my vengeance, you shall pay ten-fold." He looked once more at Kennedy. "Are you and Crosley responsible for the attack on Lady Lark?"

"No!" She stepped nearer and laid a hand on his sleeve. "We had nothing to do with it. You have to believe me."

He pulled free. "Did you not, on the night past, deny that you and Crosley had ever met?"

"I didn't know it was—"

"Enough of your lies. Stand aside, your *friend* has a meeting with the devil."

"If 'tis the last thing I do," Mac shot back, "I shall free John and Harold of you and the fiery death you plan for them."

Kennedy turned to him. "He didn't do it, Mac."

"How do you know that?"

"I just do. Fulke couldn't have done such a thing."

"Is that who he is to you—Fulke?" His smile was bitter. "'Tis not your first trip here, is it? You've been before, allowed this devil to seduce you. You always were too gullible." He shifted his gaze past her and swept his sword up. "I am ready, Wynland."

Kennedy surged forward and braced herself before him. "You'll die, Mac."

"Is that what you read?"

"Yes. You can't stand against him. This isn't the Gulf, and that isn't a gun you're holding."

"Perhaps, but now you are here, and that changes everything—it's called the domino effect."

"You don't stand a chance."

"I may not, but it isn't as if I haven't died before."

It was the war he referred to, not sleep deprivation in that abandoned warehouse.

"Should I die this time, 'twill be wholly."

Kennedy turned back to Fulke and dealt what was surely her last card. "Have you forgotten Limoges?"

No amount of night could disguise his darkening face. "This is not Limoges."

"No, but you will regret this as you regret that."

His lids narrowed. "Do not profess to know me, Nedy Plain. Here death is due and here death will be dealt."

"I'm begging you—"

"I do not see you on your knees."

Was that what he wanted? What a terrible, powerful thing pride was, but she crossed to him, dropped to her knees in the moist earth, and turned her face up to him. "If that's what it takes."

He was as stone. "Blood is what it takes." He waved Sir Leonel forward. "She may watch if she wishes. It should not take long."

Kennedy resisted the hands on her, kicked and strained all the way to the sidelines.

Sir Leonel pulled her up. "You wish to watch your friend die?"

She looked into his eyes that were no longer those of an ally. "I'll stay."

It took no more than a single meeting of swords to know Fulke was a force to be reckoned with. Although Mac's handling of his weapon was to be commended, he was no match for one who had been trained up in the blade. Time and again Mac was driven back, time and again Fulke's blade threatened death. And it could have made good the threat more than once, but it was a game of cat and mouse Fulke played. Too soon and his vengeance would be incomplete.

Around they went, Mac grunting and struggling to hold back Fulke's blows until Mac's legs finally went out from under him and his sword skittered out of his hand. Flat on his back, chest heaving, he looked up at judge and executioner.

Fulke hefted his sword high.

"No!" Kennedy screamed.

He stilled, looked to her.

"Please, Fulke."

He was unmoving for what seemed forever, his men's shouts of encouragement echoing around him. Then, with a bellow, he swept his blade downward.

Kennedy jerked her head to the side, unable to watch her friend die and the man she loved shatter.

Mac's shout of pain turned her legs to water and she had to lean against Sir Leonel. She had been wrong about Fulke. She *was* gullible. A hopeless fool, just as she had been with Graham.

"Finish him!" someone shouted.

He wasn't dead? She looked to where Mac lay twenty feet out.

He struggled onto his elbows and stared beyond his waist. "No! End it now, miscreant!"

Blood staining his blade, Fulke looked to Kennedy. "'Tis done."

He hadn't killed. A hum began in her heart as if it might turn over.

"For God's sake," Mac roared, "do not leave me half a man."

"Let me go to him," she pleaded with Sir Leonel.

His mouth tightened. "That I might suffer for you more than already I shall?" He leaned near. "You had your chance."

"Sir Malcolm, Sir Waite!" Fulke shouted.

The knights emerged from the throng.

Fulke looked one last time at the man Nedy Plain called "Mac," undoubtedly the same one she had mentioned the day she had wonderingly beheld her reflection in the mirror. He should have killed Crosley, should not have let the witch dictate his revenge, but she had. At the instant he should have parted Crosley's head from his neck, he had turned his blade down. Unless the injury became infected—and it was possible—Crosley would not die, in which case a prison cell would be his end.

"I give this man into your charge to be returned to Brynwood," he said to his knights. "And the woman." Sir Leonel would not disappoint him again. "Bind them both. We ride at dawn."

They bent and positioned themselves to carry Crosley who cursed and fought them until Sir Waite's fist to his jaw brought silence. They lifted his unconscious form and carried him toward the tents.

Fulke returned his sword to its scabbard and considered the woman who had come back to him only to betray him.

As Crosley was carried past her, she turned her gaze to Fulke. "How could you?"

Were the two lovers? He halted before her. "For what do you complain? He is alive."

"Not without his leg."

Fulke smiled, knew the turn of his lips was cruel, as were his next words. "He still has the other—not that he shall need it where he is going. Now I must needs collect my nephews. And my betrothed."

She closed her eyes and lowered her face as if to hide her pain.

Fulke started toward the monastery door at which one of the king's men awaited him—the knight who had brought him word at middle night that Sir Arthur would challenge him for wardship of his nephews and told that Lady Lark would come unto the victor.

"Wait!" Nedy called.

He nearly stopped, nearly turned, but he was done with her.

"Please, a doctor for Ma—Sir Arthur."

The sooner he forgot her eyes, her mouth, her words of love, the sooner he could turn his efforts to his nephews and the marriage King Edward pressed on him, a marriage to which he was more strongly opposed than ever. Whatever the sacrifice, Lady Lark would return to London an unwed woman. So firm was he in his conviction that he was shaken when the king's men ushered the woman from the monastery.

Harold asleep on her shoulder, John clinging to her side with his face pressed amid the folds of her skirt, she looked the mother they did not have. A mother they ought to have—

Nay! He braced his weakening resolve. This time he would be a father to them. Did they yet require a mother, a kindly village woman would serve.

Fulke halted before her and refused the impulse to take the boys from her. After all they had been through this past fortnight, and that they were only four and six, they would be confused and frightened. If he was to become to them what he had previously refused, he must go slowly.

He surveyed the woman who fell short of Nedy Plain by at least a hand and was smaller in the waist by as much. Here the reason the gowns had poorly fit the impostor. He supposed Lady Lark was lovely with her russet hair confined to a fat braid drawn over her shoulder, her oval face set with sparkling eyes of a color he could not distinguish in the night, her wide curved mouth, but he could not forget darkest hair, greenest eyes, and the sweetest lips perfectly met with his. He would, though.

Lady Lark lifted her chin. "Lord Wynland." The color of her eyes might not shine through, but her dislike did.

Sir Arthur had surely told her all manner of ill about the one she was to wed. It should anger him, but he found good in it—better her aversion than a simpering female bent on taking him to husband. "Lady Lark." He looked to the boy on her shoulder. "How fares Harold?"

"He is improved." She shifted him. "The good monks tell that his malady is well enough past that he may return to Brynwood Spire."

"I will take him."

He was certain her hold on the boy tightened. "He is not heavy."

She did not speak true, but he would not argue it.

She laid a hand on John's head. "John, dear, your uncle has come for you."

He burrowed his face deeper in her skirts.

"Now, then," she gently admonished, "greet him as is proper."

He pushed the skirt aside and showed an eye. From his drooping lids, he longed to return to his child's sleep.

Feeling as awkward as a youth, Fulke dropped to his haunches and forced a smile. "Hello, John."

The boy chewed his bottom lip, then said in a small voice, "Hello."

"Are you well?"

He nodded, showed the rest of his face, and eyed Fulke's tunic. "Is that blood, Uncle?"

Not his, but Sir Arthur's. Fulke cursed himself. He had been too bent on retrieving his nephews to consider it. "I fear I cut myself, but see"—he opened his arms—"I am well."

"Where is Arthur?"

Fulke glanced at Lady Lark and wondered if she or anyone else had been fool enough to tell the boys what had transpired. Hoping John would be too fatigued to pursue the matter, Fulke said, "He is resting."

He heard Lady Lark's muffled gasp of surprise. Had she thought the knave dead?

"I want Arthur," John said.

"When he is finished resting, I will take you to him." Hopefully, come the morrow the boy would forget the promise. "But I am here, and I have missed you, boy." Only after he said it did Fulke realize it was true. Though he'd had little to do with his nephews while at Brynwood, their presence—uncertain smiles and muted laughter—had rooted a place within him.

Perhaps John sensed it, for he released Lady Lark's skirt, took a tentative step forward, and barreled into his uncle's chest.

Fulke gathered the boy to him. The small, warm body felt strangely agreeable and temporarily displaced the woman he had believed would share his life. Nevermore. "We are going home on the morrow. Would you like that?"

John nodded.

"Good. Now 'tis time you slept." Fulke scooped him up and gestured for Lady Lark to precede him. Telling himself he and the lady would talk once the boys were at rest, Fulke followed.

# 22

"It can happen here, too," Mac murmured, the words so embittered they seemed to scorch the air.

Kennedy looked from Sir Leonel who warmed himself before the fire some thirty feet away to the man whose head was in her lap. Though his hand convulsed on his bandaged thigh—made it obvious as to what he referred—she said, "You're awake."

"And yet dead."

She shifted against the tree at her back. "Mac, listen to me—"

"Where are John and Harold?"

"In the tent with Fulke and Lady Lark."

His fingers on his thigh clawed into a fist. "I failed them."

"Fulke won't harm them."

"Won't he?" His slit eyes pierced her. "You're in love with him, aren't you?"

Even now. She eyed Mac's injury that she had cleaned and dressed with strips torn from her chemise. "How does it feel?"

He continued to scrutinize her, but finally levered onto an elbow and regarded his leg. "I'll lose it. Just like before."

Though the bleeding had eased considerably, he was right. Without proper medical attention he *would* lose it, perhaps even his life. His pain slid like a knife between her shoulder blades and made her long to hug him.

"Wynland!" Mac burst. "That devil's spawn!"

The two knights who stood watch over the roped pen between the trees tensed as if expecting Mac to leap to his feet and rush them.

Kennedy laid a hand on Mac's arm and urged him to lie back.

He wrested free and struggled to sitting. "Don't you understand?"

She glanced at the knights and lowered her voice in hopes Mac would do the same. "I do."

His upper lip curled. "You don't believe, do you? You still think it's only a dream."

The irony of it was that, as he said, she didn't believe, and yet she had once more allowed it to become real.

"You're wrong, Ken. It's everything I told you it was. And more."

The knights were listening, their interest punctuating the night like question marks. "Please, lower your voice, Mac."

He laughed. "You're worried about them? If it's only a dream, why concern yourself?"

He was right. It was becoming harder and harder to distinguish dream from reality. But then, she didn't want to. Despite her predicament, despite Fulke turning from her, there was no place else she longed to be. Here there was hope—and love, even if not returned.

"What I don't understand is why you did it," Mac said. "If you don't believe, why are you here?"

"I'm my own subject."

His jaw slackened. "Your research. Why you? What about your other subjects?"

"The university closed me down." She gave a bitter laugh. "I never could leave anything unfinished."

"They shut you down because of me?"

"It had just as much, if not more, to do with my illness. I was having a hard time—" She shook her head. "I can't believe I'm having this conversation."

Mac shifted around to face her, winced, and gripped his thigh. "How many times have you been here?"

"Please, Mac, lie back."

"How many times?"

The knights were taking it in, superstition gaining momentum. She leaned near Mac. "I've had the *dream* three times."

His mouth tightened, but when he spoke his voice was pitched low. "Did you read the book?"

"Yes."

"All of it?"

"Yes." She knew where he was headed, but how to cut him off?

"When did you read it?"

"Before I completed the first cycle of sleep deprivation."

Mac scooted nearer, the effort making him groan.

"You'll start it bleeding again." Kennedy looked to his fingers splayed over his injury. It was then she noticed something was missing. Though there was only moonlight and scattered torches, the tattoo that had wound the back of his hand for as long as she had known him was gone. "What happened to your tattoo?"

"Gone the same as your tumor, the same as any scar you may have had."

Reminded of her discovery before the mirror in Lady Jaspar's chamber, Kennedy fingered the smooth skin at the outside corner of her eye. Though the scar had been small, she'd had it since childhood. But not in the fourteenth century.

"It's like starting over. Being reborn. It's the reason we're here, Ken. Have you read the book since your first journey?"

"No. I let my mother borrow it, though she said..."

"What?"

She rolled her eyes. "This is ridiculous."

"It isn't. The book's the key. It's all there."

"Mac—"

"It changed, didn't it? From the time I showed you the passages at the lab to when you read it through?"

"I...just remembered it differently, but I'm not exactly right in the head, you know."

His gaze slid to her forehead, concern momentarily replacing fervor. "It's really bad?"

Grateful that the intense headaches and her failing motor control were, for the moment, reduced to memories, she forced a smile. "I may not be awakening again."

"Good. Though it's over for me, you still have a chance to make a new life here."

She longed to point out that, as it stood with Fulke, her chance at a new life was highly improbable, but the debate would only lead back down the path of believing something that existed only in her mind. Of course, at this point, what could it hurt?

"Tell me what you read."

Kennedy told him all she remembered, from Sir Arthur and the boys' flight from Brynwood Spire, to the two weeks spent searching him out.

"Everything's changed," Mac said.

"Only because I've lost my marbles."

He gripped her arm. "Take off your doctor's hat, and let yourself believe."

"Come on, Mac. I'm not that naïve graduate student you tortured with pranks and gags. This is a dream, though I admit it's the most amazing one I've ever had."

"Wrong."

She was tired of arguing. "Do you want to hear the rest of it?"

"Continue."

Mac was silent throughout the telling of the confrontation at Farfallow—until she told of his death at Fulke's hands.

"It was as he should have done," he rumbled. "Instead, he left me like this."

Because, dream or not, Kennedy had begged. "I'm sorry."

"So am I." He chuckled, a sound so void it was frightening. "Ironic, isn't it? I came here to be whole again and Wynland sends me straight back to hell."

Kennedy didn't know what possessed her to say what she did next. "You're not going to lose your leg. I'll talk to Fulke—get you a doctor."

His eyebrows shot up. "If you held any sway over him, you would be with him. I don't know what happened between you two, but you're now as much his enemy as I am."

Maybe more.

"Besides, one of the drawbacks of the fourteenth century is that there's no quality healthcare. Leeching is the cure-all."

Bloodsucking worms...

"What about your mother, Ken? What did she read?"

"She said the author referenced a woman who posed as Lady Lark for a short time."

"You? You're the impostor?"

Then he had heard about her charade. "Yours truly. Well, in this dream, that is." Mustn't forget that. "It's all a misunderstanding."

"How's that?"

She told him of awakening at the massacre, of Fulke chasing her down and assuming she was Lady Lark. "Who was I to argue? As I had fallen asleep thinking about her, it followed I had dreamed myself into her." She put her head to the side. "Who told you there was an impostor?"

"Lady Lark."

"How did she know?"

Mac shook his head. "Later. What else did your mother read?"

"That the impostor suddenly disappeared—"

"That would be when you awakened. Just like I disappeared when I came out of the coma."

It made sense. "I suppose—" Kennedy caught her breath, but before she could separate fact from fiction, Mac pulled her back in.

"How did the story end?"

"My mother looked ahead and read that Wynland was hanged for the deaths of his nephews."

"Truly?"

"Yes."

He dragged a hand down his face. "Then my boys will yet die."

He said it with such anguish it was as if he spoke of his own sons. But that was it, wasn't it? Though Kennedy couldn't remember the ages of Mac's sons when his wife ran off with them shortly after his return from the Gulf, they had been young. In this, the fourteenth century, Mac had set out to reclaim what he had lost. The trouble was, John and Harold didn't belong to him.

"I have to stop Wynland!" He tried to rise. "Somehow—"

"He's not the one, Mac." She gripped his arm and glanced at the knights. They would fall on Mac in an instant. "Fulke won't harm them—didn't harm them. I promise you."

"You're a fool, Ken. That greedy knave killed his brother and now—"

"No." She rose to her knees. "Cardell killed the earl. I was there when it was revealed."

For a moment she feared Mac would spurn her, but confusion came to roost. "I was certain 'twas Wynland."

"He's been wronged." And, if possible, she would prove that neither did he have anything to do with the deaths of his nephews. "Now tell me, how did Lady Lark know I was posing as her?"

"She saw you when her captor brought her from her prison to identify you."

"But I never saw—"

"Of course not, as was intended."

A chill crept Kennedy's spine. In Fulke's search for his nephews, they had paused briefly at several castles and numerous villages, so it could be any of them. But it was at Castle Cirque they had lingered, there she had sensed someone watching her while Sir Malcolm tailed her through the outer bailey. "Where was she imprisoned?"

As if shot with sudden pain, Mac grunted and dug the heel of his hand into his thigh. "At a castle. Which one, she doesn't know. By some miracle, she knocked her captor unconscious and escaped. She ran and never looked back."

"What did her captor look like?"

"He—or she—never showed his face, and Lady Lark was too fearful he might regain consciousness to look beneath his hood after felling him."

It was the "or she" that captured Kennedy. Lady Jaspar? The woman had been taken aback when Fulke introduced Kennedy as Lady Lark.

"What is it, Ken?"

"Have you heard of Lady Jaspar?"

"Her name is familiar. I may have heard it mentioned at court."

"She might be the one—at least, the one who arranged the attack on Lady Lark."

A light shone through his pain. "Tell me all of it. From the moment you first arrived."

"If you lie back."

The ultimatum didn't sit well with him, but he settled his head in her lap.

She leaned over him. "It begins with a wyvern."

"Then Sir Arthur is not dead?"

Fulke met Lady Lark's gold-flecked gaze. "Only injured."

"For that, I thank you," she said, stiffly.

Another who liked the miscreant. Fulke glanced at John and Harold where they slept on the pallet that Squire James had stuffed with leaves. "How is it you know Crosley, my lady?"

She began to pace the tent. "I met him at court when he came to petition my...the king for wardship of your nephews. Though Edward refused to grant it, I convinced him to send Sir Arthur to Brynwood to champion the boys." She halted, causing her mantle to swirl about her ankles.

Fulke drove down his resentment. So the king's leman was responsible for the curse of Crosley. Why had she done it? Had she taken Crosley as a lover and rewarded him thus?

She stepped forward and squinted up at him. "You believe as all believe, Lord Wynland, except those who know the truth. And they are truly few."

"Of what do you speak?"

She put her head to the side, inviting shadow to darken her fine features. "The truth of who I am."

"'Tis said you are the king's leman."

"And you believe it."

"I know not what to believe, Lady Lark." That last came hard, as if the name belonged not to her but the one who now called herself Nedy. "I have heard that you were sent to be my wife. Am I to believe that?"

Her eyes widened, but suspicion turned her expression around. She could not have spoken her distrust louder had she shouted it.

"Is it true, Lady Lark?"

"How do you know we are to wed?"

It *was* true, and a less desirable truth than when he believed Nedy Plain was this woman. "'Twas told to me by Lady Jaspar of Castle Cirque. It seems all rumors lead to her."

"Perhaps," she murmured. "As Edward decreed we are to be married, he would have you know I am not his leman."

"You could not steal past Alice Perrers?"

She scowled, the display marring the soft curve of her mouth and thickening her slender neck. "Alice, malice! She was difficult, but that I live is testament that naught comes between Edward and his purpose." She turned away, took two steps, and swung around. "From the moment his gaze picked me from the other courtiers, he knew me, but for a time allowed me to believe my revenge was at hand."

What revenge had she hoped to work? And for what reason?

"To my surprise, Edward was kind. He took me for long walks, sat near, but not near enough to touch me—except my hand on occasion." She laughed. "Have you guessed, Lord Wynland?"

Why had Edward not bedded her? She was lovely, and he a man who could have whatever he wished, a man to whom vows were to be kept only as it pleased him, as evidenced when he had taken Alice Perrers to mistress prior to the queen's death. Was it possible he cared enough for Lady Lark to surmount his lechery? "Do tell, my lady."

"Twenty years ago, my mother worked in the palace kitchens. Her name was Alayna. She was young, beautiful, and betrothed. Then she met Edward."

Fulke needed to hear no more. He knew what had passed between the king and the ingenuous kitchen maid, but he would give the lady her tale.

"He seduced her, and for nearly a year they met at every opportunity. But though the king professed his love, when she revealed she was with child he sent her from the palace with only a purse of coin." Lark swallowed as if to wash down the bitterness. "'Twas not long ere Alayna's mother discovered her daughter was pregnant. As time would reveal to all what manner of woman Alayna was, she was quickly wed to her betrothed and she and her husband were sent from London. Six months later, a child was born in a hovel in the cold north of England." Though the pain of her past glistened in Lark's eyes, she held her chin level. "I was that child."

Edward's misbegotten daughter. Had she not told him, he might not have guessed, but now he could see it in her face.

"As my mother died in birthing me, I never knew her. But I knew my stepfather—a fool of a man. Had not my mother confessed ere she died, he might have believed me to be of his loins though I came too soon." She closed her eyes. "Ten and seven years I suffered his hatred of the woman who betrayed him. Ten and seven years I scraped after him, endured his drunken beatings, and dreamed of revenge. But not upon him—upon the one who discarded my mother."

What kind of woman had Edward sent him? "You sought to seduce your own father?"

"Not so far as consummation. I am not completely godless." A slight smile tipped her lips. "In my mind, I played a thousand times the moment I would reveal myself. Then, in my seventeenth year I took my stepfather's coin and fled. For two years, I toiled as a lady's maid, learning all that might raise me above the common, and when I was ready, I *borrowed* my mistress's finest gown and went to court." She grimaced. "What I did not know was that I had the look of my mother."

How Edward must have enjoyed his game—had likely used it to strike jealousy in Alice's breast.

"So you see, Lord Wynland, I am a lady only because my father deems it."

"Why does he deem it?"

"He sees in me the woman he loved." Her voice softened. "My stepfather's hatred caused me to judge Edward harshly. 'Tis true he indulges overly much and is oft without conscience, but he is old and growing older. In him I have found someone for whom I care, and I have forgiven him."

"Yet he does not acknowledge you as his daughter."

She looked down. "For what? I am yet misbegotten. Too, Alice's fear of being supplanted allows him to bend her more easily to his will."

Of course. "Could she be responsible for the attack on your baggage train?"

"'Tis possible."

But she also feared Fulke might be responsible. "Who knows you are Edward's daughter?"

She stepped nearer, squinted again. "You, Edward, of course, and the dark one who imprisoned me."

What she wished to know was if Fulke and the "dark one" were the same. "Why do you call him the dark one?"

"Never did I see his face—or perhaps *her* face. My captor's voice was strained, as if disguised."

Curious. "How did this dark one learn you were Edward's daughter?"

"He found the missive from my father that I was to deliver to you."

*Was it you?* her eyes asked.

Fulke set his hands on her shoulders. "Search me well, my lady, for I do not lie. By my troth, the attack on you was not of my doing."

"But 'tis true you do not wish to wed me."

"As I wish to wed none." Except one for whom he ought never to have felt. "Still, I would not kill to be free of you, Lady Lark. Rather, I would convince Edward otherwise."

"And if you could not?"

"I would take you to wife."

She wanted to believe—he saw it in her eyes, but she could not let go of whatever Sir Arthur had told her. She put her shoulders back. "You need not worry on wedding me, for I vowed that if the lord delivered me from death, ever I would do his bidding. Thus, I shall enter a convent."

He would not argue that. "Tell me of the attack, Lady Lark."

She stepped from beneath his hands and crossed to the boys to look down at them. "'Twas bloody. They were everywhere, striking life from my escort."

"Who?"

She shook her head.

"There were none dead but the king's men, my lady."

"Aye. They surprised us."

"How?"

She spun around. "They were outfitted as knights and called that they were sent by you to escort us to Brynwood Spire."

Moriel and his band of murderers. "I sent no one."

"They were among us a half hour ere they attacked. 'Twas so sudden, then more came from the wood. My maid ran screaming into the trees. I followed but had not gone far when I was captured."

"You would know your attackers if you saw them again?"

"I saw only a few and not well. My vision is poor. I see fair at distances, but not when one is near."

Then it was not only suspicion that caused her to peer so earnestly at him. "Where were you taken, my lady?"

"I know only that death was to have found me in the oubliette of a castle."

"Which castle?"

"Upon my escape, I did not linger to discover its name, Lord Wynland. I ran as fast and as far as my infirmity would allow, sleeping by day and traveling by night until three days past when I came upon Farfallow."

Then she had arrived in advance of Crosley. "How came you to be here with Sir Arthur?"

"Fate. Only that, though I have questioned it many times." She stepped forward. "Angered though you are that he took your nephews, Sir Arthur is a good and honorable man. No harm did he intend John and Harold."

And she could scarce see the nose between her eyes. "How is it you escaped your captor?"

"He brought me to a tower that overlooked the bailey that I might name the woman who claimed she was me—the same woman whom the king's men tell me you hold."

Then she had been imprisoned at one of the castles at which they had paused during their search. Cirque? Of course, it might not be one of those at which they had paused considering Nedy's disappearances. "When were you taken to the tower?"

"A sennight past, perhaps more, perhaps less. I fear I was not all in my mind having been starved and thirsted for days." She put her head to the side. "How is the woman called who took my name?"

"Nedy Plain. She and Sir Arthur are well acquainted."

She recoiled as if struck. "She told you this?"

"'Tis as they both told me when they conversed this eve ere Crosley and I met at swords." Nedy who had stayed Fulke when he would have made a quick end of Crosley. "If she was a party to the attack, so too would be Sir Arthur."

"No, not him. Never could I believe he ordered it."

Was she in love with him? "Then why does a woman he knows well don your clothes and pretend she is you, Lady Lark?"

She rubbed her temples. "I do not know, but neither did my captor know. For whatever reason this Nedy Plain did what she did, methinks she is not a party to those who killed my escort."

For a traitorous moment, Fulke prayed she was right.

Lark nodded. "Your Nedy Plain is likely a commoner who blundered on the massacre and took advantage of it."

But if a commoner, how had she come upon the gown she had worn when he chased her through the wood? It had fit as if made to her every curve. "Tell me of the castle bailey, Lady Lark. What did you see?"

"I paid little heed to anything but the woman my captor asked me to name."

"What was she wearing?"

"A gown of homespun. An ugly thing and too large."

Esther's gown?

"And there was a knight who followed her as if she were of import."

Sir Malcolm. Then it *was* at Castle Cirque she had been imprisoned, meaning this went beyond Cardell, meaning Jaspar may have determined to rid him of a wife. She *had* known of Edward's plan to wed Fulke to Lady Lark when no other had. Could it be? Jaspar was many things not pleasant, but a murderer? "How did you escape?"

A smile slipped onto Lady Lark's lips as if she found pleasure in the memory. "A stone from the sill was loose. I swung it and God's hand guided it to the dark one's head."

And that eve Lady Jaspar had suffered what Fulke believed was one of her headaches. Coincidence? He strode to the tent flap. "Squire James!"

"My lord?"

"Bring me Sir Leonel."

The squire turned and ran.

Fulke looked to where Nedy Plain sat with Arthur Crosley's head in her lap. He dragged a harsh breath and told himself he was not jealous. Soon all would be revealed.

Curse Nedy Plain! He had given her a chance, and for it punishment would be given him. Leonel pumped his hand on his sword hilt as he followed Squire James across camp. If not that the squire had summoned him to Wynland, he would now be on his horse and headed away from Farfallow. What awaited him in the tent made his heart constrict.

He had been a fool to allow desire to bring him to the place he now found himself. When Nedy had tried to halt the confrontation between

Wynland and Crosley, he ought to have mounted up and gone from here. Instead, he had followed her and been captivated by her acquaintance with Crosley. Fool!

Squire James lifted the tent flap.

Leonel pumped his hilt twice more, resolved he would not take his hand from it, and ducked inside. He looked first to the man whose presence dominated the tent. The hard set of Wynland's face caused a thrill of fear to wind Leonel's innards.

As the flap dropped behind him, he turned his gaze to the other occupants of the tent—John and Harold asleep on the pallet and the woman who sat beside them. He looked back at Wynland. "My lord?"

"Do you know Lady Lark, Sir Leonel?"

A lovely woman, though not beautiful like Nedy. Executing a bow, Leonel sought to compose his face while he kept it turned down. "'Tis my deepest regret we have not met, my lady."

She pulled her mantle more closely around her shoulders, acknowledging him with a lowering of her lids.

Wynland stepped between them. "It has been learned that Lady Lark was imprisoned at Castle Cirque. What do you know of this?"

He jerked, sputtered. "How can that be, my lord? I would have known if the lady was at Castle Cirque."

"And you did not?"

Was that him trembling? Did it show? "The lady is mistaken."

"She is not."

"Surely you cannot believe Jaspar capable of such an atrocity? 'Tis true she wishes you for a husband, but this? I will not believe it."

"If not you nor Jaspar, who?"

"I know not, my lord, but be assured that when I return to Castle Cirque I will discover the truth of it."

"You will not be returning."

Leonel felt every ridge and crevice of his wire-wrapped hilt. "You think 'twas me." Fear, powered by ire, thrust him forward a step. "For what would I do it? I bear this woman no ill and have naught to gain from her death."

Wynland was so unmoving it was as if he had traded flesh for stone. "Perhaps, but until 'tis known who held her at Castle Cirque, you shall remain with me."

"I am to be your prisoner?"

"You may call it such, for which I shall apologize if 'tis found you are innocent."

What chance had he if he drew his sword? Leonel eyed the scabbard on Wynland's belt that was marked by Crosley's blood. No chance.

"This night I shall send an escort to deliver Lady Jaspar to Brynwood Spire that we may hear what she has to say," Wynland said. "Now leave your weapons and go."

Such indignity he was made to suffer, but what else could he do? Loathing making a meal of him, he unfastened his sword belt. "You are wrong, my lord." He lowered the belt to the ground and dropped his dagger alongside. "As you will soon learn."

"'Tis my hope."

The sincerity of Wynland's words were a balm to Leonel's resentment, though slight. He turned away.

"Sir Leonel."

He halted but did not look around.

"Do you think to flee, I will take it as proof of your guilt and hunt you to ground."

"Worry not, my lord. I have no reason to run." He stepped outside, closed his eyes on the night, and felt death's breath on his neck. All would be well. Jaspar would convince Wynland that neither she nor her cousin had committed the heinous crime. But how to explain Lady Lark's stay in the oubliette?

# 23

SHE WAS RETURNING as a prisoner. So different from when she had first marveled at the splendor of Brynwood Spire.

Kennedy considered Fulke where he rode ahead. Lady Lark was at his side, as was to become her permanent place once they were married. As for John and Harold, the former rode with Fulke, the latter with the lady. From time to time, Kennedy caught the sound of their high-pitched voices, but it was as near as she got to the boys. Fulke kept them as far from Mac as possible.

"Take the reins," Mac rasped.

She looked around and saw that perspiration coursed his face. "What's wrong?"

"I have a fever." His lids fluttered. "Take the reins, Ken."

She caught them up and was grateful for the instruction Fulke had given her, brief though it had been. "Hold on, Mac, it's not much farther."

He leaned more heavily against her back as he had done by degree throughout the ride. Kennedy tried to take her mind off the burden and her concern for Mac by rehashing last night's conversation with him. She had told him all that had transpired since her first journey here and done her best to convince him of Fulke's innocence. But with equal zeal, Mac had tried to convince her she wasn't dreaming. Though she continued to deny it, the doubt he planted was sprouting, reaching to the sun, daring to hope for sweet rain. And perhaps it would come, providing she was able to convince Fulke to give her the time of day. Though Mac was still not entirely convinced of Fulke's innocence, he said the wyvern was the key and insisted she tell Fulke about it. But how could she when he wouldn't look her way?

Shortly, they reined in before the keep where Fulke's brother, mother, and sister hurried forward to accept John and Harold as they were handed down.

"We're here, Mac," Kennedy said. When he didn't raise his head from her shoulder, she shifted around. "Mac?"

He slid sideways, but though she grabbed for him, he slipped through her hands and landed hard on the ground.

"Mac!" She scrambled off the horse, dropped down beside him, and thanked God when she saw the flare of his nostrils.

The others who had dismounted moved in, their shadows closing around Kennedy and Mac.

She tossed her head back and glared. "Back, you vultures! Give him room."

They stared.

She curled her hands into fists and started to rise.

"Stand back!" Fulke commanded.

Sunlight falling once more on Mac, Kennedy met Fulke's gaze. It pierced her.

Lady Lark pushed past Fulke. "He is dead?" Concern drew her eyebrows together.

For the first time, Kennedy looked fully into the face of the woman she had played, the one who had befriended Mac when he had gone to court. Seeing how strikingly different she was from Lady Lark, Kennedy wondered how she had gotten away with impersonating her.

"Is he?" Lady Lark asked again.

Kennedy returned her attention to Fulke. "No, but he's very ill. He needs a doctor."

Marion appeared and dropped to her knees beside Mac. "Arthur," she called, "'tis Marion." She stroked the hair back from his brow and pressed her cheek to his forehead. When she looked to Kennedy, her eyes were moist. "What happened, Lady Lark?"

"She is not Lady Lark," Fulke said, "but one who calls herself Nedy Plain."

Though confusion wound her face, Marion said, "He is in a fever, Fulke."

He had the grace to struggle with his enmity, jaw convulsing and hands turning into fists. "Take them to the tower." He turned away.

Hands dragged Kennedy upright. "No, Fulke, please!"

He didn't falter.

She looked to Marion. "Talk to him. Don't let him do this. Mac—Arthur—will die if he doesn't get help."

"I will speak to him. I will."

Kennedy was thrust opposite the keep. Shortly, a hand between her shoulder blades launched her into a small, round room at the top of one of two towers that guarded the entrance to the inner bailey. She looked around at the scant hay on the stone floor, a stool in one corner, and a pot in the other. There were six windows, if they could be called that. Evenly spaced around the perimeter, they were eighteen inches high and all of a hand wide.

A shuffling sound announced the arrival of those who conveyed Mac. The two men laid their burden at the rear of the room and withdrew, then the soldier who had brought Kennedy closed the door with a finality that made her wince.

She knelt beside Mac. He was pale, his cheeks chill. She examined his leg. The bandage was dark with dried blood, the glistening at the center evidence that the wound was bleeding again, likely from his fall.

Kennedy freed the knot with which she had tied off the bandage and carefully lifted Mac's leg to unwind her shredded chemise. The bit of light from the slotted windows showed the injury more clearly than the moon had done. The six inches that sliced diagonally across his upper thigh was ghastly, fresh blood flowing over festered skin.

"All right, then, we do it again." She lifted her skirt, grasped the remains of her chemise, and began to tear.

It was her again. "For what do you once more invade my chamber?"

The tapestry flopped against the wall. "Brooding, brother?"

Fulke sank deeper into the chair and stared harder at the flames. "Where are John and Harold?" Try though he did to forget the boys' fiery deaths of which Crosley had spoken, he could not. The boys were safe, he told himself. It was only a game Crosley and Nedy played.

Marion rounded his chair. "They are in the garden. Mother and... Lady Lark are with them."

He stared through her as if she did not obstruct his view of the fire. "And what does mother think of *this* Lady Lark?"

"She likes her little better than the first."

That would change once she was told this one was of royal, albeit misbegotten, blood. Providing he told her. And for what? There would be no marriage.

Marion sank to her knees before him. "Myself, I like the first better—Nedy Plain, is it not?"

If the woman was not lying about *that*. "Why do you steal into my chamber, Marion?"

"He needs a physician, Fulke. I beg you, send one."

It was a long time since he had seen her so steadfast—as if the madness was gone from her. He reached forward and cupped her jaw. "You believe yourself in love with him?"

She looked down. "I feel for him as I have not felt for another."

Fulke believed her, having thrice taken her back when those with whom she was to have made a marriage rejected her. Where had her madness gone? "Does he feel for you as you feel for him?"

Hope brightening her eyes, she nodded.

"He has told you this?"

"Not in words, but I know 'tis so. The way he looks at me, the things he—"

"You are a fool." Fulke dropped his hand from her. "Crosley cares only for himself." Just as Nedy cared only for herself in spite of her words of love.

"You're wrong." Marion grabbed his hand. "Arthur is a good man."

She saw only through the eyes of depraved love. He pulled his hand free. "Did you know they are acquainted—Sir Arthur and Nedy Plain?"

"'Tis as she told us when first she came."

"As *Lady Lark* she told us—said they met at court. All lies, Marion." He sat forward. "Do you not think it a puzzlement how this woman came to pretend herself a lady—as Crosley pretends himself a knight? 'Tis not to be slighted, especially as they may have been party to the attack on Lady Lark." Not that he could make any connection between them and Castle Cirque.

Marion's mouth dropped open. "It cannot be. As Arthur is mistaken in believing ill of you, you are mistaken in believing ill of him and Nedy."

"He stole John and Harold!"

She sat back on her heels. "Never did he seek to harm them, only to protect."

"From me!"

She winced. "He did not know better. I tell you again, he is a good man."

The next words were past Fulke's lips before he could think better of them. "Even were it so, Marion, do you think he would be with you, a woman thrice betrothed, thrice returned?"

Her mouth trembled, but eyes held steady—no shifting as they did when her madness was broached.

And Fulke knew what he had refused to acknowledge all these years. Relief, intertwined with anger, pushed through him. "You are not mad, are you, Marion? 'Tis merely a game."

She rose and turned to the fire.

Fulke gripped the arms of his chair. Aye, a game he had allowed her to play to keep her dreams alive long after his own had died. Far easier to accept her mind was bent than force her into a loveless marriage. He was weak, the military genius that had gained him a place at the Black Prince's side rendered laughable.

"At least I stayed true," Marion said, her voice so soft it was nearly lost in the crackle of fire. "I did not forsake the vow I made myself." She turned. "But you will, won't you? You'll let her go, tell yourself you feel naught for her, won't allow yourself to believe there is good in her."

The chair creaked beneath Fulke's grip.

"When you are ready to die, you will be alone and bitter, but you will remember her and, if you are honest, regret what you do now."

He shoved to his feet. "Speak no more of that woman."

"I have said all." She stepped forward. "Now, for the love of your sister, I beseech you to send the physician."

He crossed to the wash basin and splashed water on his face.

"Fulke, do you care at all for me—"

"The physician has been sent, Marion." He dragged a towel down his face.

"He is with Arthur?" she squeaked.

"Aye, but do not think I did it for the foolish love you bear him."

"I would not dare think it." She gave a knowing smile. "'Tis most obvious you did it for love of the woman you deny yourself."

Fulke caught back his impassioned denial. He did not need to explain himself to anyone. *Least of all yourself.* "Be gone, Marion, and stay away from the tower."

Sparkling eyes telling she had no intention of heeding his command, she started toward the tapestry.

"Use the door, Marion."

She turned back, opened the door, and paused. "I thank you for not slaying Arthur." She exaggerated a frown. "Or is it Nedy Plain I ought to thank?" She yanked the door closed behind her.

With a string of curses, Fulke slung the towel to the table and strode to the door. Though his brother had assured him all was in order at Brynwood, surely there were matters to attend to. For the first time since attaining wardship of his nephews, he hoped there were.

"Can you save it?"

The physician sighed. "If 'tis not removed, he will likely die."

Kennedy stared at the bared wound. "No, he'll die if he loses it." And as much as she feared for Mac, she knew he would never forgive her if she allowed to be taken from him the one thing that connected him to life.

"Do you not understand what I have said?" The physician's brow grew weightier. "Does he not—"

"I said no. Just stitch it closed and dress it."

"Very well, but his death is upon you."

"I accept that."

He opened his bag and removed various implements and jars of whatever primitive substances he intended to use.

Kennedy sat beside Mac throughout, watching as his severed flesh was sewn closed. Thankfully, he remained unconscious, the only signs of life a groan, some muttering, and an abundance of perspiration.

The physician applied a pungent salve to his handiwork, carefully wrapped Mac's thigh in clean linen, and unstoppered a jar. He took a pinch of its powdered contents and slipped it between Mac's teeth. "For the pain and fever." He handed the jar to her. "Thrice a day."

"Anything else?"

"Does he awaken, keep him still."

"You'll be back?"

"This eve."

"Thank you."

He left the tower room and the guard locked the door behind him. However, not five minutes passed before the door swung inward.

As with the physician's earlier entrance, Kennedy's heart rushed, but it wasn't Fulke who entered. It was Marion, followed by two women servants whose arms were ladened.

Kennedy jumped up. "The physician just left."

"We passed on the stairwell." Marion looked to Mac, then to the servants. "The pallets and blankets there"—she pointed to the back wall as she stepped toward Mac—"the basin there, and—"

"Thank you for speaking to Fulke," Kennedy said.

Marion halted. "I was pleased to do so, though it proved too late."

What did she mean?

Marion swept past. "And the victuals and drink on the stool," she directed the servants.

"You mean—?"

"Nay, Josie," Marion reproved the youngest of the women, "spread the pallets against the walls."

Why had Fulke done it? Though Marion hadn't had a chance to approach him on the matter, was it for his sister he had sent the physician?

"Now come," Marion summoned the women. "We must all lift together."

As the servants bent near Mac's feet, Marion met Kennedy's gaze. "You take his left shoulder, I will take his right."

Surprisingly, the transition from the cold stone floor to the pallet exacted little effort with all of them lifting. Once Mac was down, Marion sent the servants away. "The physician told me you would not allow Arthur's leg to be removed," she said as she draped a light blanket over Mac, "though he believes 'tis what is needed to save him."

"I made the decision, but if you knew Mac—Arthur—you would know it was the only one available to me."

"I do know him, as I know you did what he would demand himself." Marion bit her lower lip. "Has he spoken at all?"

"Not since before our arrival."

Marion poured her gaze into Kennedy's. "Think you he will live?"

Kennedy reached to her, hesitated, then closed her cold fingers around Marion's. "He's a fighter." Cliché though it sounded.

Tears welled in the other woman's eyes. "I love him."

As Kennedy stared at her, she considered what Fulke had told her. *Was* Marion crazy?

"He told you I am mad," Marion said as if she had stepped into Kennedy's thoughts.

"He said you were…fragile."

She shrugged. "'Twas the only way I would not be made to wed a man for whom I felt naught."

Why didn't that come as a surprise? "You pretended to be mad."

"Only when necessary. And three times it was."

"Couldn't you have just said 'no'?"

"No more than you, as Lady Lark, could have refused my brother—had you wished to." She lifted her eyebrows. "But, of course, you are not Lady Lark. Rather amusing, is it not, that we both pretend to be who we are not? Poor Fulke is in such a quandary. First he learns the woman he loves is not the woman he ought to love"—

Had she heard right?

—"then his sister finally admits to deceiving him all these years. Not that he didn't know. He simply preferred to ignore the truth."

"What was that about the woman he loves?"

Marion smiled gently. "Hate himself though he does for it, he loves you."

Kennedy looked to her hands. "I have a difficult time believing he told you that."

"He did not need to. There he sits brooding in his chair before the hearth thinking only of you."

"More likely thinking of how to dispose of me."

"Not the man who told me the physician was already sent." Marion looked pointedly at her. "He did it for you."

"I wish that were true."

"Heed me well, Nedy Plain. When my brother left Brynwood Spire, 'twas to put an end to Arthur. Yet Arthur returns to me alive. You asked it of Fulke and he did it. For you."

"He told you I asked him to spare Arthur's life?"

"Nay, 'twas Sir Malcolm who told me all."

Kennedy looked around the room. "Yet I am imprisoned."

"He will come."

When? No. She wouldn't get her hopes up. "Do you know what has become of Sir Leonel?" She had worried over the knight since this morning when she saw he was stripped of his sword.

"He is being held within the keep until Lady Jaspar arrives."

"Why is she coming?"

"'Twas at Castle Cirque that Lady Lark was imprisoned until she escaped to Farfallow. Thus, Fulke believes Lady Jaspar may have ordered the attack on Lady Lark."

It followed, as Kennedy had already entertained, but was Jaspar capable of such? "As he also believes Ma—Arthur and I were a part of it."

Marion made a sound of disgust. "I know that neither you nor Arthur had anything to do with it, just as Fulke knows it if he will only let himself believe."

Kennedy prayed he would. "Do you think Lady Jaspar could have done it?"

"She is a viper, but this? I suppose 'tis possible."

"Meaning Fulke believes Sir Leonel may also be behind it."

"Aye, though he seems so mild." Marion sat back on her heels. "It is more likely Lady Jaspar who did it, but perhaps both."

What of the incriminating medallion that didn't belong to Sir Leonel? "Lady Marion, would you carry a message to your brother for me?"

"I will, though I cannot promise he will listen."

"There is something I didn't tell him that I should have. When I came upon the massacre of Lady Lark's escort, there was a knight still alive, though barely. He told me that one of the attackers wore a medallion bearing the device of a two-headed wyvern. It's not much, but perhaps it will help Fulke discover the truth."

"A two-headed wyvern. I know of none, but he may." Marion leveled her gaze on Kennedy. "That is the message you would have me deliver? Naught else?"

"Naught else."

"You are sure?"

Kennedy stood. "You're living in a romance novel, Marion."

"A what?"

"Never mind. Just tell him what I've told you."

Marion bent over Mac, touched her mouth to his cheek, and whispered something. "Does he awaken," she said, straightening, "you will tell him I was here and send word to me?"

"I will."

Marion crossed the room and paused at the door. "How is it you know Arthur?"

"We go way back." Or was it forward? No need to confuse Marion with specifics she wouldn't believe.

"You will tell me one day how way back you go?"

"I will, but Arthur and I are only friends."

The woman's shoulders eased. "I will come again. Is there anything you require?"

Only one, but he wasn't talking to her. Kennedy considered the room and mused at how basic a person's needs really were. "We have all we need. Thank you for your kindness."

Marion smiled. "We are friends, are we not?"

"Yes, friends."

# 24

A TWO-HEADED WYVERN. A lie, he told himself as he had done when Marion delivered the message. Yet here he was, past middle night, traversing the inner bailey beneath a full platter moon.

Inside the tower, he waved the guard back to his stool, snatched the keys from their hook, and took the stairs two at a time. Each landing was lit by a single torch, making it a precarious ascent, but his footing was sure. At the uppermost landing, he retrieved the torch from its sconce and strode to the iron-banded door.

Though he did not know which of the keys fit, the second turned the lock. He pushed the door inward and sent the torch ahead of him, revealing the two against the back wall whose pallets were laid end to end.

Fulke halted. Pallets, blankets, the remains of food and drink he had not ordered sent. It had to be of Marion's doing, but though he wanted to be angry, he was twinged with gratitude that she had seen to their needs.

He raised the torch higher and looked from the still form of Crosley on the left to Nedy Plain on the right. She was on her side, her back to him, a blanket up around her shoulders.

He fixed on her dark hair and remembered the feel and sweet smell of it. His chest tightened as other memories crept beneath the doors he had closed. Her skin had been like silk, her mouth like the sweetest flower. Lady Lark turned Nedy Plain was a memory without end, and in that moment he knew she would never let go of him.

"By the saints!" he rasped. If she would not let go of him, he would wrest her hold from him. He thrust the torch into the sconce beside the door and strode forward.

She stirred when he stood over her, then rolled onto her back and opened her eyes. After a long moment, a tentative smile rose to her lips. "You came."

She was pleased to see him, her anger over Crosley's injury having subsided. Why? Because he had sent the physician as she had pleaded for him to do? Aye, and she believed he had done it for her.

Fulke hardened himself against the woman whose hopeful eyes threatened his resolve. "What of the wyvern?"

"The...? Oh, that." She tossed the blanket off and rose from the pallet. "I should have told you, but in the beginning I didn't know who I could tru—"

"Tell me," he interrupted, the nearness of her far too disturbing.

She clasped her hands at her waist and glanced at Crosley. "He hasn't awakened."

"Mayhap he will not. Now tell me of the wyvern that I might return to my rest."

She swept her wide-eyed gaze back to him, and he saw her hope was gone. "Just who do you think you are?"

Vexation, kindled by puzzlement, shot though him. "I am Baron Wynland, keeper of Sinwell, and you are Nedy Plain, a pretender who has taken me from my bed with yet more of your lies. I am done with you."

As he turned away, she caught his arm. When he looked around, there was fire in her eyes.

"I refuse to believe you are so cruel, Fulke Wynland, not when I have known you otherwise. Play the devil if it makes you feel better, but it won't make me hate you, nor will it make you forget what we shared."

He knew he ought to leave, but he also knew she was right. He could not forget her. The wyvern had been little more than an excuse to see her again.

"Please, Fulke, let me tell you what I know of the attack. It won't take long and it's the truth."

He lifted her hand from him and folded his arms over his chest. "Speak."

"There was a soldier, the one who had my veil and circlet. He was alive when I..." It was no use trying to convince him it was a dream, especially when she was no longer certain herself. "...when I happened on the scene. He told me he had seen a medallion worn by one of the attackers."

"Continue."

"He said it bore a two-headed wyvern above a shield and something..." What was it? "...something evil...sinister."

"Bend sinister?"

"That's it."

"'Tis of royalty."

"Then the attacker could be related to the king?"

He turned and stalked opposite. "Mayhap, though more likely it is one who attends royalty and was awarded the medallion for service." He pivoted. "*If* what you speak is true."

"It is."

He returned to her. "'Tis for this you looked so closely at my medallion." New anger edged his voice. "You thought to see a wyvern."

"I did, though I didn't want to. As for Sir Leonel, neither does his medallion depict a wyvern."

His gaze turned accusing. "I did not know he wore one. How know you?"

Jealousy? She hoped so. "He showed it to me last night. It depicted a hand holding wheat, or something like that."

"Then you do not believe he is responsible for the attack on Lady Lark?"

"Perhaps he is, but I don't see it."

"What *do* you see?"

"That neither Sir Arthur nor I had anything to do with it. You must believe me. My only crime is in accepting Lady Lark's identity when you called me by her name, as Sir Arthur's only crime is in wrongly believing you meant to harm John and Harold."

He actually seemed to consider her defense, but then turned away. "Good eve."

"That's it?" Kennedy hurried after him. "What about Mac?"

He looked around. "You speak of Sir Arthur?" Fulke looked to where he lay. "'Tis strange that you call him Mac and, on the night past, he called you Ken."

Ignoring his taunt, Kennedy said, "He needs more. This place is cold and unsanitary."

"I sent the physician. Be content."

She knew she shouldn't say it, but out it flew. "You unfeeling jerk! How can you just walk away?"

His mouth tightened, but it wasn't anger that next passed his lips. "'Tis difficult," he said, so solemn his heart showed, "more difficult than I can say. But does a man not learn from his mistakes, he is a fool without hope of redemption." He reached forward, stopped his hand near her jaw, and lowered his arm. "You made me a fool. I will be a fool no more."

Kennedy felt the burn of tears. "But you are a fool if you go from here and pretend you can forget what you leave."

His crooked eyebrow rose. "Mayhap, but better one of my own making." He strode to the door and retrieved the torch.

"You won't forget me," Kennedy called. Wishful thinking?

"Do I not, 'tis Lady Lark I shall remember." He nodded. "I liked you better when you were she."

"And I liked you better when you had a heart!"

A moment later, the door supplanted him and the lock turned. And Kennedy could only stand there in the dark, her heart crashing to the bottom of her.

Fulke halted when he reached the bailey. Though aware he was watched by the night guards on the walls, he remained unmoving, feeling his way through the words and emotions that had pressed on him as he stood before Nedy. She had infuriated him, but still he had longed to hold and kiss her.

"Nay," he growled. He put a foot forward only to pivot and look up the tower. Why this feeling he had just erred greater than before, that his mistakes were rushing toward one another with heads lowered, that all the ills upon his house would only get worse?

He shook his head. Why this feeling? Because Nedy was right. He could not forget her.

Mac was back. And full tilt going by the contentious light in his eyes.

Kennedy scooted nearer and was warmed by the shaft of afternoon light that fell through one of the narrow windows.

"You're still here." His voice was as coarse as sandpaper.

"As are you." She mothered the blanket higher up his chest. "How are you feeling?"

"How do you think a one-legged man feels?"

"No, Mac, look." She laid the lower edge of the blanket back. "The physician attended your leg and—"

"He wanted to take it, didn't he?"

"He suggested it as a way to deal with the injury, but—"

"The only way. Tell me I'm wrong."

Hope was a powerful healer, so she lied. "You're wrong, and so was the physician. When he came again this morning he said it looked better." The tight-lipped man had said nothing of the sort, but when she had asked for an updated prognosis, he had shrugged. In her opinion, that laid it wide open for interpretation.

Mac pushed onto his elbows, considered his bandaged thigh, and met her gaze. "Did no one ever instruct you in the art of lying?"

He knew her well. "Of course not, but I'm working on it."

"Not hard enough." He laid back heavily. "Do you think you're dead yet?"

"No, I'm still dreaming."

"Are you?"

She stared into his weathered eyes. *Was* she dreaming? Or, by some miracle, was she truly here? As always, logic railed against the reality of this time and place but, increasingly, her heart rallied opposite. Maybe this was a second chance. Maybe her love for Fulke *was* real. "It seems real—everything about it—but it can't be. Time travel isn't possible."

He laid a hand over hers. "It is possible. Now tell me, have you felt the pull?"

"What's that?"

"The feeling of being pulled back to the present."

"Yes, though only the second time. The first time I must have slept through it."

"Then you haven't felt it since your last journey here?"

"No."

"Each time I also felt it, most strongly the last time—three days after I returned—but I fought it and, finally, a peace came over me as if I were ascending." His eyebrows bumped. "I did die, didn't I? I'm not in another coma?"

"You died—in an old warehouse."

He sighed. "Perhaps I could have done it again and corrected the mistakes that put me here."

"What do you mean?"

"You don't have to pick up where you left off, Ken. The dream places you wherever you think yourself, just as it did when you first dreamt it. You see, had I always been disappearing, it would have been impossible for me to serve as protector to John and Harold."

Suspending disbelief, Kennedy bent near him. "You can start over?"

"Of course, though I didn't attempt it until I fell asleep the last time. I brought myself back a week prior to the end of my previous journey, which allowed me to use the time to make certain everything went off without a hitch." The next few seconds seemed to age him ten years. "But it didn't. John and Harold will still die."

Kennedy's thoughts were spinning. "What if *I* repeat the cycle one last time? Perhaps I could—" What was she saying? She sat back. "I've lost it big time."

Mac's eyes pierced hers. "No, you have to believe me."

Therein lay the dilemma. She did believe. She lowered her head. *Dear God, my end must be near.*

Fulke had not felt so awkward since he was a boy. Breath trapped in his throat, he waited as John lifted the lid.

Silence, then a peal of delight echoed by Harold.

"Soldiers!" John picked one from the box.

Harold scooped up one of two dozen carved figures. "A hundred of 'em!"

Fulke let out his breath. Though he felt Marion's gaze where she stood beside the boys' bed, he ignored her as he had done since entering the room. He didn't like what he saw in her eyes each time they fell on him. He almost preferred her supposed madness to this knowing of hers that conjured visions of the woman who had denied him sleep on the long night past.

"Look!" Harold held up a figure. "This one's riding a horse, and his sword is metal."

"Let me see." John reached for it.

Harold hugged the worn, black figure to his chest. "I saw him first."

Fulke prodded himself from the hearth that had surrendered its last ember hours earlier. "There are others," he said.

John searched out one and thrust a white, horsed figure into the air as if it was the only prize to be had. "He looks most fierce, and his destrier as well."

Fulke dropped to his haunches before the boys. "This one and Harold's are knights, and fierce as you say." Unexpected childhood memories rushed at him. "They were my favorites when I was your age."

The disbelief that rose on the boys' faces nearly made him laugh. "Aye, once I was also a child."

"'Tis true." Marion stepped from the bed. "Your uncle and I played out many battles on this very floor."

"You?" John was surprisingly indignant for one so young. "A girl?"

Marion folded her arms over her chest. "One who did not always lose to a boy."

Fulke nearly groaned. Making battle with his sister was something of which he would not have boasted. As his older half-brother had been occupied with his service to God, his younger brother, Richard, was removed by five years, and his mother had not allowed her children to play with those of ignoble blood, there had been only Marion. But the truth was that she, a year older than he, had been a wonderful companion.

Harold rose from the box. "Truly, these were yours, Uncle?"

"Aye. Now they belong to you and John. I trust you will take good care of them."

"Ever so!" Harold wiped his runny nose on his sleeve.

John lifted the box and brought it with him to his feet. "We will be careful with them."

Fulke ruffled his hair. "I am sure you will."

"Thank you, Uncle."

"Aye, thank you," Harold chimed.

Fulke stood. "Belowstairs with both of you. And no warfare until you have broken your fast."

"May we first show our soldiers to Jeremy?" John asked.

They had missed their illegitimate half-brother, as Jeremy had missed them. Still, they should eat first. "After you are done at table."

The boys groaned but didn't argue. However, John paused at the door. "When may we see Sir Arthur?"

The warmth that had begun in Fulke's chest turned chill. That man stood like a wall between him and his nephews. Was there no way over or around him? Through him?

Fulke shook his head. "Not this day, for he is not yet fully recovered."

Disappointment fell from the boys' faces.

"But he is going to be well," John prompted.

Fulke knew the physician's determination, that if the leg was not removed Crosley's life would likely be forfeit, but that was not for children's ears. "He is doing better. Now belowstairs with you."

When the sound of their footfalls in the corridor was all that remained, he looked to Marion.

"Doing better?" she repeated. "You really do not believe it, do you?"

Fulke returned to the hearth and stared at the errant rushes between his feet. When he came around, Marion was waiting with hands on hips. "You would have me tell them the truth of Crosley?" he asked.

She advanced on him. "What truth? That you are wrong about him?"

"You know 'tis his leg of which I speak."

She halted before him. "The two are related, are they not? He has one because of the other."

"Deservedly so."

Anger suffused her cheeks. "I know it's in there." She poked his chest. "Let it out, Fulke."

His heart again. First Nedy Plain, now his sister. But they were wrong. He stepped around her. "Do not go again to the tower room," he called as he quit the chamber.

As he traversed the corridor, he heard her defiant "ha!" His sister was back and, as when they were children, she preferred to stumble and fall rather than bow to him.

"Bloody rood!" he grumbled as he descended the stairs. Was there no end to this tumult and turmoil? Would he never know peace? A vision of Nedy assailed him and caused his absent heart to pound. With her he had known peace, for their short time in the wood had been unfettered and more alive than he had ever felt.

Though he told himself it had all been false, when he reached the hall he was no nearer to ridding himself of unwanted feelings than he was of the woman who had sown them. So he denied them into the nooning hour that came and went with the arrival of Lady Jaspar.

# 25

She denied it, and so convincingly Fulke nearly believed her. He tried to pick the glimmer of a lie from Jaspar's tear-swollen eyes, but if it was there, she was holding it too near to let it be seen.

He rose from the lord's chair and strode past Sir Leonel who sat at the far end of the table with his head in his hand. The knight's own denials had been even more convincingly told than Jaspar's.

Fulke paced the hall. Who had hired Moriel to set upon Lady Lark? Cardell in hopes of making it appear Fulke was responsible for the death of Edward's illegitimate issue? What gain? Fulke's imprisonment or hanging that would see John and Harold once more in need of a protector? That protector being Baron Cardell?

Ignoring his mother's questioning gaze where she sat at the hearth with Marion and Lady Lark, Fulke strode back the way he had come.

What of Alice Perrers? According to Lady Lark, the king's mistress had despised the woman Edward flaunted as her rival. It was not beyond Alice to remove that threat.

"Fulke," Jaspar implored from where she stood on the raised dais, "you must believe me."

Then there was Sir Arthur and Nedy Plain. Had the attack on Lady Lark been but a means to assure the knight's abduction of John and Harold? Why pretend to be Lady Lark? More diversion? Possible, but not as believable as it being Lady Jaspar who had ordered the attack, with or without Sir Leonel's aid. A husband Jaspar wanted, and the arrival of Lady Lark as the king's chosen one was to have laid to rest the possibility she might one day sit at Fulke's side.

It might also have been someone not heretofore considered. What of the two-headed wyvern? *If* it was true what Nedy Plain told. The device was from Edward's paternal side, that much Fulke knew, but there his knowledge waned. Thus, before Lady Jaspar's arrival this noon, Fulke had sent one of the king's men to London to search out the giver of such medallions.

Lady Lark rose from her chair before the hearth. "My lord, I have grown weary. I bid you good eve." She turned to Fulke's mother. "My lady."

The older woman lifted an eyebrow. Two days gone now and she liked Lark no better.

"I apologize for distressing you so, Lady Lark," Fulke said. "Good eve."

Lark stared at him and searched for a response to this man her father would have her wed. It was there, a curious attraction that might grow if she allowed it, but she would not. She had made a vow and would keep it. Bride to Christ, never to man.

Though she tried to ignore the presence of the one she had disregarded throughout Lady Jaspar's pleadings, she glanced at Fulke's brother, Richard, who stood near an alcove. His arms were propped over his chest and legs spread, emphasizing the arrogance on which he seemed erected. Strange, though he had yet to speak a word to her, she was stirred each time their eyes met. If he was the one she was to wed, could she so easily refuse?

Aye, her place was at the convent, and to the convent she would go. Pretending she felt no regret for the keeping of her vow, she looked to Lady Marion.

The woman smiled. "Good eve, Lady Lark."

Lark started toward the stairway. Odd though Marion was at times, especially in the presence of her mother when she turned quiet and passive, Lark liked her. In her mother's absence, she was talkative, especially on the subject of Sir Arthur and Nedy Plain, both of whom Marion had visited twice this day.

Lark ascended the stairs. As she neared the chamber occupied by John and Harold, she heard a sound. Were the boys well? She pushed the door inward. The light within came from the hearth where a fire leapt and crackled. Before it sat John and Harold amid the carved wooden soldiers their uncle had presented this morning. So intent were they on their playthings, they didn't notice her.

She was tempted to slip away and allow them these stolen hours, but it was late and they needed their rest. Crossing the threshold, she winced as the rushes underfoot cracked and popped in time with the logs in the fire. They ought to be replaced. They were too dry and lacked the scent of strewn herbs that only fresh rushes could impart. Her heart tugged. These boys needed a mother to care for them and see to those things a village woman with her own children would care nothing of. *But not me,* Lark reminded herself. Fulke Wynland would have to find another mother for them.

"Boys, you ought to be abed."

They yelped and jerked back, causing the rushes to scatter. Not that they hadn't already made a fine mess of them. The rushes would have to be cleared from the hearth once the boys were abed.

"L-lady Lark." John sheepishly cast his face down. "We were just looking at our soldiers—could not sleep for thinking of them."

She lowered to her knees and lifted a soldier to firelight. "And fine they are, John."

"That one is Sir Arthur," Harold said.

"I do note a certain resemblance." Lark smiled. "Now, 'tis time you and your brother were asleep."

Harold groaned. "One more minute, my lady. Please?"

As he was still somewhat weepy-eyed from the sickness that had laid him abed at Farfallow, it appeared he was near tears. She swept the hair back from his brow. "The sooner you sleep, the sooner you shall awaken and take up your soldiers once more. Now to bed."

Harold thrust his lower lip forward, but John began picking the soldiers from the rushes and settling them in their wooden box.

"May we sleep with them?" Harold asked.

Lark rose. "You will not play with them?"

"Nay, my lady, we shall just hold them."

She smoothed John's hair. "Very well."

Shortly, the boys were snugged deep beneath the blankets.

"Will you stay a while, my lady?" John peered through the shadows at where Lark stood alongside the bed.

"Just until we sleep," Harold said.

"Well—"

"Sir Arthur always sat beside us until we slept," John said.

It seemed nearly all conversations with the boys began and ended with the knight. If only he could be here for them. "You miss Sir Arthur."

Their heads bobbed.

"When can we see him?" Harold asked.

Lark knew she should not speak for Fulke Wynland, but the boys needed reassurance. "When Sir Arthur is recovered, your uncle will bring you to him."

"When will that be?" John asked.

"I do not know. A sennight, mayhap a fortnight." She smiled large. "Now hug your soldiers tight and close your eyes that the morrow will come all the sooner."

"You will sit with us?" Harold pressed.

Five minutes, Lark told herself. "I will." She pulled the chair behind nearer and lowered into it. "Close your eyes."

They complied, but not a minute passed before John's hand crept from beneath the blanket and his small fingers slid over hers.

Poor little soul. Lark laid her head on the mattress. Not that she would be able to sleep draped over the bed, but if the boys thought she did, perhaps they would also go adrift.

John turned onto his side and bent his head near hers. "Good eve, my lady." His sweet, warm breath fanned her brow, making her awkward perch suddenly comfortable.

"Nay!"

The shout tore through Kennedy's dream of flying. "Mac?" She sat up and searched the darkness that was broken by an orange glow.

"Not my boys!" His tormented cry hauled her regard to where he stood before one of the narrow windows that faced the keep. Through it and two others, the orange light entered the room, accompanied by smoke.

Kennedy stumbled to her feet. As she neared Mac, she heard shouts in the bailey below. *Dear Lord, not this.* But it was. She knew it without seeing past Mac. Her hand trembled as she reached to him. "Come away."

His head snapped around, the tears in his eyes reflecting flames. "John and Harold cry for me. Can you hear them?"

Not over the roar and hiss of fire, the gabble of those in the bailey. And neither could he. Kennedy put an arm around him and tried to draw him away.

He wrenched free and reached through the window as if to pull the boys from the flames.

A tear slid down Kennedy's jaw. She swallowed and crossed to the window to the left of the one through which Mac was trying to squeeze himself.

The left front corner of the keep was ablaze, flames shooting from the upper windows, smoke billowing from the rooftop. As the building was made of stone, it would hold, but those within would perish.

She pressed herself back against the wall. Real or not, this terrible night was long ago written and there was no stopping the madman who had once more seen it to its heinous end.

And Fulke? Where was he? Not with the boys—unless that had changed as so many other things had done. No, he was all right. She had to believe it. But what torment the deaths of John and Harold would bring him. Never would he forgive himself. She slumped down the wall.

Mac was raging now, tearing around the room as if his injury did not pain him, and perhaps it didn't, as gripped as he was by this new ache. He cursed, shouted, overturned, and threw the few items he could lay hands to.

Kennedy dragged herself upright. Sinuses stinging from the smoke, she went to where Mac was before the door clawing at the lock and shouting to be let out.

"Mac," she spoke as evenly as her quavering voice allowed, "there's nothing you can do."

He slammed back against the door. "Then why am I here? Why are you?" As when the wheelchair had been the recipient of his fists, the door shook with the anger he landed to it. "I refuse to believe it!"

Kennedy squeezed her emotions into her own fists. "It happened, Mac, just like the book said."

He shoved off the door. "It can be changed. I've seen it, and so have you. It—" He grunted, reeled back, and grabbed his thigh.

Had he torn his stitches? "If you're not careful, you'll—"

"Let him take my leg! He can have both of them. All of me!"

It was time for some shrink talk, and the only place she could think to start was with an acknowledgment of his feelings. Kennedy laid a hand on his shoulder. "You love them, don't you? As if they were your own sons."

He slowly lowered his lids over his pain. "They're my second chance. I can't lose them."

But he had. Barring a miracle, John and Harold were gone as surely as his two sons taken from him by their mother.

"Mac—"

His eyes sprang open, and when he spoke, hope trembled from him. "You can make it right."

His intensity made her step back.

"One last trip, Ken."

She stared at his face that was partially lit by the orange glow. Time travel. Though the slip of reason that was all that remained of her sanity insisted it could not be real, her mad heart believed. "This is crazy."

He gripped her shoulders. "You'll do it?"

She looked down, watched her hands clasp and unclasp. *Go on, stop trying to make sense of it.* Accepting what her heart had known for some time now, she felt a surge of elation, a shower of hope, a soaring in her breast. A second chance. A new start. She had only to let it in.

"Will you do it?"

She focused on his deeply shadowed face. "Yes, providing I haven't..." Why was it so hard to say? She knew it, accepted it. Didn't she? Still, it stuck in her throat. She cleared it. "Providing I haven't died." Just because he had felt the final pull didn't mean she would.

He sighed.

So she would make the journey. When—if—the pull came, she wouldn't fight it. But what if she couldn't make it back? She would never see Fulke again, would die with only a memory that would blow out like a candle with her last breath. "I could die before I reach the level of deprivation needed to return me. You know that, don't you?"

"I know. How many hours does it take you?"

"Eighty-six the first time."

His hands fell from her. "That's all?"

She felt almost ashamed. "I'm no stranger to insomnia, but I'm not conditioned to the level you are—were."

"Do you think you can do it in less?"

"On the second go-around, I got it down to seventy-two."

"How?"

"By not sleeping after the first awakening. I knew I didn't have much time to complete my research, so I started right into the next cycle."

"I tried that but couldn't do it."

She wasn't surprised he had made the attempt. "Two hundred plus hours is a far cry from eighty-six, Mac."

He turned, stumbled, and fell against the door. "My leg. It's..." He pressed a hand to it and showed her his crimson palm. "The stitches are torn."

She eased him to the floor. "I'll send for the physician."

"Nothing can be done for me."

She sat back. "If I can change John and Harold's fate, maybe I can change yours and make it so this never happened." How, she didn't know, but if she made it back to the twenty-first century she would have several days to work it out.

"Not that far back, Ken. This is the night you need to return to. Put yourself in the keep before the fire and bring the boys out."

"But what about your leg?"

His jaw shifted. "What matters is John and Harold. I have lived. It's their turn."

Though she had no intention of leaving him out in the cold, now was not the time to argue. "All right, but don't you think it's cutting it close to return to this night? There's no room for error."

He leaned his head back against the door. "The Dr. Kennedy Plain I knew didn't need room for error. Four-point-oh, wasn't it?"

"This is different, Mac. It's not textbooks and exams. This is more. This is..." She tossed up her hands. "It's life and death."

"It is. But I've tried it the other way. As you know from what happened at Farfallow"—he gripped his leg—"the farther out one goes, the more there is that can go wrong. You have to come back to this night. If I could live it again, it's what I would do. I would forget the heroics and just bring the boys out and..." His face crumpled. "...worry about the loose ends later."

He was right. To return to a time prior to the confrontation between him and Fulke at Farfallow was too great a risk, one that would likely land her right back here with two little boys caught in a fire. "Then this night it is."

"Do it soon, Ken."

As if she could control her awakening. "When the pull comes."

She thought he might sleep, but a few minutes later he said, "Before you return here, get as near your death as you can."

"Why?"

"That way there may be too little left to pull you back to the world you leave behind."

Providing she made it to the fourteenth century. "I understand."

"Didn't you say your first awakening occurred while you were sleeping?"

At Lady Jaspar's castle. "Yes."

"You can't let that happen again. When you return here, you mustn't sleep until after the pull."

"I won't." What was a little more sleep deprivation? "Anything else I should know?"

"Just that it's real, Ken. Don't let that educated head of yours tell you otherwise, and if it does, remember you have nothing to lose and everything to gain."

Including Fulke? Was there a chance she could make things right with him? "I'll remember." She scooted forward and tugged Mac's hand into her lap. "I won't fail you."

"I know."

She sighed and settled her head back against the door to wait for her ride to the twenty-first century.

# 26

Fiery deaths, as foretold by Crosley.

Fulke stood on the threshold he had been unable to breach in the earliest hours of morn when the flames had leapt into the corridor. He had tried, had been determined to go inside though he knew no life breathed within, but Richard had fought him and brought a sconce crashing down on his head.

Now, with the rising sun, came the truth he could hardly bear. John and Harold were dead, and with them Lady Lark, though her death had not been known until the remains of three were brought out.

He dragged a hand down his soot-streaked face. How had Crosley known? He looked again at what remained of the bed and tried to deny a vision of two little boys amid smoke and hungry flames. If it took him the remainder of his days, he would discover the murderer and kill the fiend.

He stared at the ruin, fed off it. Though Lady Lark was also dead, this did not smell of Alice Perrers, but if it was her, nothing would keep him from her throat.

Could it be Jaspar? It was possible, though she had stood for three hours on the night past and maintained she was innocent of the attack on Lady Lark. Had he put her under guard as he should have done, would this not have happened? He cursed himself, swept his thoughts to Crosley and Nedy Plain, and cursed himself again to feel relief at knowing they could not have done this.

Something near where the bed had sat captured Fulke's gaze. He crossed the threshold and drew a sharp breath as heat permeated the soles of his boots. Though the stone floor was still hot from the fire, a chill went through him. He strode forward, sank to his haunches, and lifted an object from the ashes into the light that shyly crept through the window.

He stared at the small metal sword that had adorned one of the mounted knights he had given to the boys.

God have mercy on his soul for the hate that swelled in him. He wanted blood! He shook from the deafening emotion, heard the roaring in his ears, dropped his head back and shouted until it felt as if his throat was torn open. Dropping his chin to his chest, he squeezed his eyes closed.

"Fulke?"

He thought it was the voice of an angel, but there was no mistaking its dulcet tone and curious accent. He jerked his head around and stared at the woman in the doorway where she stood beside the man-at-arms who had been sent to escort her from the tower. So beautiful in spite of her unsmiling mouth and the light emptied from her green eyes.

Fulke drank himself full of her and felt her slip through the cracks and crevices of his emotions. "Leave us," he ordered the man-at-arms.

Nedy was the first to speak. "I'm sorry." She stepped inside.

He swept a hand though the ashes and lifted the blackened remains of the box that had held the tiny soldiers. On the night past, John and Harold had taken their treasure to bed with them—a gift given by a man who had utterly failed them. He dropped the box. "Who did this?"

"I don't know."

He thrust to his feet and strode toward her. "More lies? Crosley knew 'twould happen, just as you did!"

She didn't retreat when he stood over her. "Yes, I knew."

"How?"

The force of his voice made her startle, but she reached up and laid a hand to his jaw. "It's not your fault."

For a moment he slipped free of the rending pain and let himself feel her touch. It healed, wrung longing from him that he had worked hard to deny these past days. Squeezing his eyes closed, he turned his mouth to her palm and breathed her in.

Fool! He jerked his head back. "You will tell me what I wish to know."

She lowered her hand, the soot from his face on her fingers. "Are you ready to believe?"

"No more lies."

"Perhaps we should go someplace else."

"We shall stay here."

"But it's not —" She nodded. "All right. I know you'd prefer to believe me mad or a witch, but I'm neither. It begins with a dream. No!" She raised a hand to stay his sharp words. "Just listen."

He ought to call for the man-at-arms and have her dragged from here, but what had he to lose when all was lost? "I am listening, but I warn you, I am beyond patience."

She crossed to the window from which a blackened shutter hung askew. "An incredible dream brought me and Mac—or Sir Arthur, as you know him. But it's not a dream as I believed." She looked over her shoulder. "It's time travel. The reason Mac and I don't fit is that we're not born yet, and won't be for another six hundred years."

Mad! To travel from one time to another was not possible.

"How else do you explain my disappearances?" she continued. "I vanish into thin air—literally—and that's when I return to my own time. The twenty-first century, Fulke."

He didn't know anything about this thin air of hers, but the rest of it was impossible. And yet how had she done it if not by magic or this time travel?

"Please hear me out, and if you still don't believe me, you can send me back to the tower."

Grudgingly, he said, "I will hear the rest of it, Nedy Plain."

She drew a deep breath. "My name is Kennedy Plain, and I'm a doctor who specializes in the psychology of dreams."

What unwound over the next hour was a tale that made the head injury Richard had dealt Fulke pound more fiercely. Unbelievable, and yet when she spoke of the book and its changes dream to dream, a small part of him began to believe. It was as if he had lived the book through, and through again with the appearance of Lady Lark's impostor. A feeling as if he had once been earl, yet a peculiar tightening about his neck as if he had been hanged. Absurd. Perhaps *he* was the one gone mad.

He grappled with all she told and told himself it could not be, yet something stopped inside him when she said, "I have to go back one last time."

"What do you mean?"

She tested a hand to his arm, and when he did not reject her, settled it. "It's the only way to change what happened tonight."

He looked around the chamber. From its blackened walls to its charred ceiling and floor it reeked of death. "'Tis done."

"Mac says it can be done again." She leaned near. "John and Harold don't have to die, nor Lady Lark. If I return to my time and come back to yours prior to—"

"Nay!" He stepped back and threw his hands up. "What do you think me? A fool? This cannot be undone."

"If it was possible, even if the odds were against you a million to one, wouldn't you try?"

Of course he would, but John and Harold were dead, their little bodies...He longed to curse God in his cruel heaven for what He had allowed to happen.

"Fulke, whether or not you believe what I've told you, I'm leaving, but I will return."

"How long will you stay when next you come?" he asked, hardly able to believe the words he spoke.

She smiled. "Forever, I hope."

"If what you say is true, will you always be appearing and disappearing?"

"Not once I die."

He took back the step he had taken from her. "Of what do you speak?"

"I'm dying, Fulke. I have a brain tumor."

His heart, which he would have sworn no longer existed, jerked.

"Remember what I told you about Mac—Sir Arthur? How he was able to cross over permanently? I can leave my illness behind, too. In your world, I'm healed."

"Then 'tis the reason you wish to return here?" Lord! What was he saying? He did not believe she had come from six hundred years into the morrow.

Kennedy took his hand. "Of course I want to live. I haven't lived nearly enough. But when I return, it will not only be to save two little boys, but for you, Fulke. I know I deceived you, but I meant it when I told you I loved you. If you believe nothing else, believe that." She slid a hand around his neck. "Deny it though you may, I am not alone in these feelings."

The nearness of her was almost too much. He longed to hold her, to press his face to her neck and breathe her, to forget the horror of this place.

"Nedy."

"Fulke."

He clasped her to him and lifted a fistful of her hair to his lips. "Sweet Nedy." He lowered his face to her neck. In spite of her stay in the tower, she smelled as he had only ever dreamed a woman might smell, and when she laid her head on his shoulder, he knew he could not let her go. Having lost so much which he had stubbornly resisted embracing, it was unbearable that he might also lose this strange, beautiful woman.

"Do not go," he spoke against her warm flesh.

Her hands flexed on his shoulders. "I have to."

He drew back. "There is naught you can do for John and Harold. They are dead."

"Next time it will be different."

Was it possible they might live again if she did this thing which he still could not accept? It was even more unbelievable than that she was capable of dreaming herself across the centuries.

"I also need to say goodbye to some people," she said.

"Who?"

"My mother, Graham—"

"Who is Graham?"

She drew a deep breath. "He was my husband."

Fulke released her. "Your husband?"

"We're divorced."

He stared at her. "'Tis nearly impossible to gain dissolution of marriage from the Church."

"In my world, it's not only possible, but almost as common as marriage."

Kennedy watched the emotions war across Fulke's face. He wanted to believe as she had wanted to herself but, like her, he could not accept something so incredible. It was too big to dream. Unfortunately, they had to move on, for she needed answers.

"Marion told me you sent for Jaspar, that you believe she may have ordered the attack on Lady Lark."

It was a long moment before he rose above his emotions. "Thus far, 'tis as near as I can get to finding the one."

"Then you no longer believe Mac and I had anything to do with it?"

"I know you did not."

Relief flooded her. "What made you think it might be Jaspar?"

"Lady Lark was held at Castle Cirque. 'Tis known by all that Jaspar wished to be my wife, and by her own admission she knew of Edward's plans to wed me to Lady Lark ere any knew. Then there was the eve of my return when we sat at meal. It has been determined that Lady Lark escaped earlier that day after knocking her captor unconscious. Beside me, Lady Jaspar suffered what I thought was a headache. Mayhap not."

Kennedy had also noticed that the woman seemed in pain, but something else stirred at the back of her mind. Hadn't—

Her breath caught. There it was, the pull Mac had told her would come. She caught Fulke's sleeve.

"Nedy?"

"It's happening." Her voice trembled. What if she couldn't return? Never saw him again? But she had to go—for John and Harold and Fulke. No peace would he know with the boys' deaths upon him. No happiness. He would die in dishonor, a noose about his neck. But she could change that.

"What is happening, Nedy?"

She wrapped her arms around him. "I'm leaving."

He tilted her chin up. "Of what do you speak? You are not—" His eyes widened. "Nedy!"

"I'll be back. I promise." She touched her mouth to his. "Remember this."

He trapped her face between his hands. "Stay with me."

"I love you, Fulke." Her words echoed around her, then she was torn from him. She saw him as if from a distance, the disbelief and grief on his face, his empty arms.

"Nedy!"

"Fulke…"

"Mom." Kennedy's voice slurred, broke. She raised a heavy arm and touched her mother's face.

Laurel snapped her head up from where it lolled on her neck. "Oh, Nedy." A smile quivered on her lips. "I was afraid…"

She couldn't say it, though Kennedy knew what she had feared. "I'm back." She put an elbow to the sofa and levered up from her mother's lap. She was feeble, possessing hardly more strength than a ragdoll. "You sat here all this time?"

"I had to get up once or twice."

"Thank you for staying with me."

"It's been a long time since I had your head in my lap." Tears wet her eyes. "I was afraid you wouldn't wake."

There, she had said it. Bittersweet progress.

Kennedy eased herself to sitting, lowered her legs to the floor, and sank back into the sofa cushions. "I'm here, Mom." She squeezed a hand over her mother's and winced at the effort required to make the reassuring gesture. "I imagine your legs are numb."

Laurel waved away her concern. "You slept a long time. It's been..." She squinted at the small clock on the opposite wall. "Goodness, a day and a half."

Incredible, but not surprising, as this time she had spent nearly five days in the fourteenth century. But then, she was very ill—which reminded her that, as much as she longed for more sleep, she had no time to lose. "Mom, I need your help."

Laurel sat forward. "What, dear? You're thirsty? Hungry? Well, of course you are." She pushed off the sofa and staggered from the disuse of her legs.

"No, Mom, it's something else."

"What?"

"I need my laptop."

Her eyebrows tacked. "What for?"

"I'd like to do some online research—"

"Research? How can you think about work when—"

"Not dream research. It's British history I'm interested in."

The air went out of her mother's indignation. "Well, if you really want to."

"I do."

"All right, but let me fix you a tray first."

Kennedy wanted to argue, but she was hungry.

While Laurel puttered around the kitchen, Kennedy eyed the laptop on her desk. Would she find the answers there? Could she return to the fourteenth century with a name that would prove Fulke's innocence and save the boys?

A half hour later she was fed—a meager four bites that was all she could choke down—pillows plumped at her back, a blanket snugged up to her chest, glasses on her nose, and the computer online.

"Anything else I can get you?" her mother asked.

"I'm fine, Mom." It almost hurt to talk, her tongue thick and slow. "You should get...home to Jack."

"Don't you worry about Jack. He understands."

Understood that his wife was on death watch. Kennedy pushed the nasty reminder to the back of her mind. It was time to do a search for things medieval, specifically heraldic devices. "All right, Mom, but this could take a while."

"That's fine. I brought plenty of audio books."

Her mother's one vice—books she didn't have to struggle through. Kennedy managed a small smile. "Thank you for staying."

Laurel kissed her daughter's cheek. "What's a mom for?" She turned, curled into the chair beside the sofa, and fit her headphones.

Kennedy swelled with love for the gentle woman. She was going to miss her.

The internet search through medieval heraldic devices proved mind-boggling. Bend sinister this, chevron that, here a dragon, there a lion, everywhere a wyvern. But none two-headed. Her thoughts playing tag amid her pounding head, she squeezed her eyes closed.

"Why don't you rest, dear?"

Kennedy shook her head. "I'm not done."

"But—"

"Please, Mom."

Laurel nodded and repositioned her headphones.

A few minutes later, Kennedy gave up—temporarily. There was something else she needed to know, no matter how much she feared it. Her next search for information on the life of Fulke Wynland turned up a curiously titled book, *The Troubadour in the Tower* that, fortunately, was available in digital format. Too fatigued to read it through, she skimmed. Though written by a different author than the one who had written *The Sins of the Earl of Sinwell*, the early twentieth century account echoed the revised story told by Kennedy's mother. But near the end, the impostor was revealed, a woman known only by the name of Nedy who disappeared following the fire.

Kennedy put her head down and breathed deep. Nuts or not, she accepted her time with Fulke was real, so why did it feel as if she had been slugged in the chest? Because, in the twenty-first century, he was six hundred years dead, and if she didn't return she wouldn't see him alive again. He would remain a man horribly wronged.

*Get a grip, Ken.* She brought the computer screen into focus. There were the deaths of John, Harold, and Lady Lark, a week later the death of Sir Arthur Crosley from an infection that set into his wound. A month later, Fulke was named Earl of Sinwell, the day after arrested and charged with the murder of his nephews and Lady Lark. For nearly three years he had suffered King Edward's imprisonment while awaiting a trial before his peers. When judgment came, he was put to the noose at Smithfield. Unless she returned, this would be his fate.

"Oh, Fulke."

As for the book's title, indistinct pictures of the walls that had been Fulke's prison all those years explained it more clearly and painfully than the accompanying narrative. Carved into stone and preserved to the time of the book's writing, were verses that the author said troubadours had sung of for hundreds of years thereafter, and which he claimed to be among history's greatest testaments to love.

What had Fulke written? Kenny paged forward. There—the back wall of his prison, and carved into it was that which was considered his most exalted tribute to his beloved.

She adjusted her glasses, but poor resolution on her computer screen made it impossible to read. She returned to the text. And was rewarded. Since the poem had been written in Middle English and contained what the author called "a multitude of misspellings indicative of the earl's poor grasp of reading and writing," he provided a translation.

*Are you a dream of mine? Of yours?*
*Did you not run from me, to me, legs bared?*
*Did you not cast a spell to bind me, unveil me?*

*Did your fingers not entwine with mine, nor mine entwine with yours?*
*Did you not embrace me, nor I embrace you?*
*Did you not hold me, nor I hold you?*
*Did your lips not touch mine, nor mine touch yours?*
*Did you not seek me, nor I seek you?*
*Did you not speak words of love, nor breathe them against my lips?*
*Did you not touch me in body, in soul, nor I you?*
*Did you not leave me wanting, nor I you?*
*Did you not smile for me, vowing ever after?*
*Did you not tell tales fantastic, dreaming yourself to me?*
*Did you not make promises, ones answered only in my thoughts?*
*Did you not leave me, disappearing at the stroke upon dawn?*
*You did. You were. You are. But not here.*
*And now I have loved and know the burning, the yearning.*
*All I would have done for you, no matter the cost.*
*Even I would have killed for you.*
*And now I shall die for you.*

A sob slipped from Kennedy, and she glanced at her mother. Head back, headphones askew, Laurel slept.

Kennedy drew a shuddering breath and returned to the computer. The writings were for her, telling of the love Fulke had been unable to speak aloud. She touched the computer screen. "You love me." Or he had...

No! She *was* going back. But not empty-handed. The device of someone, somewhere in the past, boasted a two-headed wyvern.

Kennedy wiped her eyes and looked to the final paragraphs of the book. The author submitted that Fulke's writings were for the mysterious impostor known as Nedy who was believed to have been his accomplice in the murders of his nephews and Lady Lark. In conclusion, Fulke's misguided love for the covetous woman proved his downfall.

It was time to set the record straight. Fingers feeling like pegs on the keyboard, Kennedy returned to the website for heraldic devices.

"That's it." Kennedy stared at the picture of a hand grasping heather that had been the device of a Baron Brom, then shifted her gaze to the two-headed wyvern alongside.

The baron is most proud of it, she recalled Sir Leonel's words when, at Farfallow, he had shown her the medallion his former lord had awarded him, though not as proud as he is of that which his third wife brought to their marriage. She is of royal blood. Do you allow me, I will—

The reverse had undoubtedly borne a two-headed wyvern, the royal device the baron gained through his third marriage. Had Kennedy not interrupted Leonel and alerted him to what the dying soldier had told, she might not have had to leave Fulke.

Her miniscule reserve of energy seeping into the sofa, she removed her glasses. Leonel had been the one all along—but with Jaspar's blessings?

Kennedy trod backward through time. Lady Lark had been held at Castle Cirque, which made it appear Jaspar was involved and, therefore, presented the possibility Leonel was mixed up in it. True, on the evening following Lady Lark's escape, whereby she had knocked her captor silly, Jaspar had appeared pained, but so had Leonel. Wearing a hat Kennedy had not seen before or since, he had imbibed heavily and, afterwards, staggered out of the hall. Had the hangover not been a hangover, but a head injury?

Then there was Leonel's insistence that he accompany Fulke in his search, followed by his questioning of Kennedy about the attack and his near certainty she was not Lady Lark. Had his show of disappointment that she belonged to another been an attempt to charm her into admitting what he already knew? It seemed so. Nevertheless, he had appeared genuinely concerned about her relationship with Fulke. Though he had to have known she was a fraud, he had witnessed their intimacies and must have felt threatened by them. For Lady Jaspar's sake, or his own? Whoever it was, Kennedy guessed the assassin was to have removed that threat when he attacked her by the pond. In his own words, Moriel had admitted he was hired to ensure Fulke did not wed her. Too, Leonel had known quite a bit about the real Lady Lark that no one else seemed to know.

As for the most incriminating piece of evidence, Kennedy had wrongly assumed that, as Fulke's medallion bore identical images on both sides, so did Leonel's. However, when she had asked Leonel if he knew whose device had a two-headed wyvern, he had quickly returned the medallion to his tunic and discouraged her from revealing to Fulke what the dying soldier had told. To top it off, he had tried to flee with her—for fear that, having been clouted into unconsciousness, Lady Lark might be able to identify him as her captor?

What a tangled web! So how did all this piece together? For whatever reason he had done it, it seemed Sir Leonel had hired Moriel and others to do away with Lady Lark. In attending the killing, he had fingered himself. But why John and Harold? What obstacle did they present? If Lady Jaspar was part of it, was it Fulke she wished to wed or an earl unhindered by others' claim to the title? And if Leonel acted alone, for what gain?

Kennedy groaned. She was too tired to work it through, longed to yield to sleep. Unfortunately, forty winks would only lead to more and set her so far back she would never be able to return to Fulke. With hands that shook, she closed her laptop.

"Would you like me to help you to bed?" her mother asked.

When had she awakened? Kennedy looked into the shadows that evidenced the coming of night. "No, Mom, I'm fine here. Would you mind making me some coffee?"

"You need sleep, Nedy."

"I just slept through a day and a half."

Her mother switched on the lamp and scrutinized Kennedy's face. "You're tired. I can see it in your eyes."

Tough love time. She reached a hand to her mother and Laurel took it. "You know it's almost over for me, Mom. Please don't deny me the little bit of time I have left. I want to spend it with you."

Laurel broke eye contact. "Of course." She struggled a long moment, then said, "Coffee it is." She patted Kennedy's hand. "You will call Graham, won't you?"

"I will." If nothing else, she owed him a goodbye. But there was another loose end to tie up. "Would you bring me the blue binder that's on my printer?"

Twenty minutes later, halfway through her second cup of coffee, the final journal entry was complete.

# 27

*Get as near your death as you can.* Mac's advice drifted through Kennedy's consciousness. She had done her best, held on for more than two days, but she had nothing left to give. Her head throbbed, muscles and joints ached, and she was so weak she could barely lift an arm. And the nausea…Though she had given up on food yesterday, the dry heaves were doing her in. Surely she couldn't get any nearer death than this?

"Sleep, baby," her mother said.

She turned her head in Laurel's lap and looked up at her mother's lined face. Since her return, she had twice feigned sleep to allay Laurel's anxiety, but this time it would be real—and final. "Mom, I want you… to have my journal."

Laurel glanced at where it sat on the sofa table.

"Promise me…" Kennedy swallowed in an attempt to moisten her dry throat. "Promise you'll read it."

"Of course I will." Laurel curved a hand around her daughter's scalp. The simple touch eased some of Kennedy's pain. "I love you, Mom."

"I love you, Nedy." Tears floated in her eyes. "Do you remember the prayer you used to say at bedtime?"

"Um hmm." Kennedy closed her eyes as her mother recited it and, on the third verse, joined in. "If I should die…before I wake…" Ironic, she mused as sleep pulled at her, causing her to miss the next verse. "If I should live for other days…" She would, wouldn't she? It was only then she remembered what she needed to do. Dear God, she had nearly fallen asleep without placing herself at Sinwell on the day of the fire previous to Jaspar's arrival.

"...to guide my ways," Laurel finished the prayer, her voice a whisper in the dark behind Kennedy's eyelids.

Kennedy tried to open her eyes, to look one last time at her mother, but they wouldn't open. "Love you," she breathed, then let her mind go to where Fulke waited for her.

Laurel held on, cradled her baby, knew that when she let go it would be forever. The pain made her want to scream. If not for Kennedy's peace found in sleep, she would have. As her daughter slipped away, Laurel kissed her brow. "Send me a sign, Nedy."

Heartstoppingly familiar. So was the dress. Kennedy sat up on the bed in the small chamber she had been given when she first came to Brynwood Spire. She touched the bodice and felt its fine material down to her waist. While putting herself into the dream, she had slipped in a wish that she return in style wearing something flattering like what she had worn at the beginning—absent the blood on its skirt. And so it was.

She hugged her arms to her. She was back, this time forever. No regrets, except for the woman she had left behind. She swallowed the lump of emotion. Mom would be fine. She had Jack. And the journal.

Fulke was somewhere out there. Unfortunately, since he would have no recollection of the alternate past when he had implored her to stay with him, he wouldn't be happy to see her, but they would get past that. Now it was time to put her plan in action, which meant locating John and Harold's chamber and holding vigil over it. Though she had considered trying to get to Fulke to tell him of the medallion, she feared he wouldn't believe her and she would end up with Mac again. He needed proof of what had yet to happen—the perpetrator caught in the act.

She swung her legs over the side of the bed and into the afternoon light spilled through the window. She paused at the sight of the chest at the foot of the bed—the same one that had held Lady Lark's clothes.

On it sat a pack. Whose? She stood. She *had* brought herself back to the correct day, hadn't she?

She breathed the air, tasted it. It was clean, no evidence of the smoke that had rolled from the keep as she and Mac helplessly watched death come to Brynwood. All was well. Though curious as to who owned the pack, it was irrelevant.

She crossed the chamber and nearly got a face full of door when it swung inward.

"Nedy! What...?"

She stepped back from the man who stared wide-eyed at her. "Sir Leonel."

He swept his gaze over the chamber. When his eyes fell on her again, there was knowing in their narrowing. "You are looking for something?"

Of course. He had been given this chamber and, if she guessed right, it was the medallion to which he referred. Inwardly, she groaned over her dismissal of the pack. What if he had stowed the medallion there? But was he such a fool? More likely he had disposed of it.

He closed the door and leaned against it. "I wager Wynland does not know you are absent his prison." He smiled. "You really are a witch, aren't you?"

She almost denied it, but why? Better a witch with supposed powers than a mere mortal whose only defenses were tooth and nail. She shrugged. "You found me out."

He stepped toward her. "As you have found me out."

"I don't know what you're talking about."

He halted before her. "Don't you?"

This was only going to work if the puppy love he had displayed earlier had a grain of truth to it. Though his musty breath offended, she pressed her palms to his chest. "I came to take you up on your offer. You do still want to save me from Wynland's wrath, don't you, Leonel?"

"Save you? I would think you could do that yourself, witch."

"Of course I could, but how much more pleasant to have a traveling companion."

"'Tis too late for that now."

"No, it's not. You tell me where and when and I'll be waiting with bells on." She tilted her face nearer his. "I want to go with you. To be with you. Isn't that what you also want?"

"I want you, aye." He looked to her mouth. "But it's not all I want." It wouldn't be. He *had* murdered. "What else, Leonel?" She hoped she sounded seductive, rather than repulsed as she felt.

His lips curled unbecomingly, reversing his handsome face. He didn't trust her. As if she were a horse he was considering buying, he stepped back and slowly looked her up and down. "I like this gown better. It promises much." He walked around her and stood silent at her back until Kennedy thought she might scream.

She was in over her head. But what else could she do? She could call for help, but would Fulke come? If he did, what hope had she that he would believe her when told of Leonel's medallion, especially now that it seemed likely it no longer existed? Would he return her to the tower, leaving the boys' death sentence in place?

Leonel's hands closed over her shoulders, body pressed against her back, unshaven face brushed her ear. "For now, what I want is what you gave Wynland."

Only her love, though he wouldn't believe that. "That's all?" Kennedy laughed. "You don't ask for much, do you?" She turned to him and slid her arms up around his neck. "Once we're gone from here, we'll have all the time in the world to enjoy each other." If he took her up on her offer, there would be no one to set tonight's killing fire. Later, she would worry about escaping him. "When can we leave?"

He leaned in and lightly rested his mouth on hers. "We cannot. Not so long as Wynland holds me under watch and refuses me my sword."

Hating the feel of his lips, she lowered her face and pretended an interest in his tunic. "Surely you can get around that." She touched the embroidery at his collar.

"Not as easily as you, witch. Now, let me see you." He began prying at her laces.

She jumped away and spun around. "Really, Leonel, now is not the time. Once we leave—"

"You lie, Nedy Plain." His eyes glittered, mouth slanted cruelly. "You did not come here for me, but for Wynland that you might redeem yourself. You love him."

*With every beat of my soul.* "You've got to be kidding. I don't—"

"You told him of the medallion, did you not?" He advanced on her.

He was guessing, Kennedy realized as she retreated from him.

"Aye, you did. Last night when he came to you in the tower, you told him."

Then he was watching Fulke.

"But still he left you there. He believes 'tis just another lie."

"No, he'll look into it—you'll see." She came up against the wall, missing the door by three feet. Could she make it? "Then what will you do, Sir Leonel?"

He took a long stride that placed him in front of her and voided the chance of her making it to the door. "The medallion is gone, as you will be when I am done with you." He placed a hand on the wall on either side of her. "As you should have been had Moriel not desired to lie with you."

It *was* Leonel who hired the assassin. She cringed at the memory of him offering her comfort following Moriel's attack.

"Ironic, is it not," he mused, "that Cardell would also seek Moriel's services?" He laughed. "But then, there is only one Moriel—or was."

"You won't get away with this."

"When Wynland finally learns who bears the two-headed wyvern and heather-in-hand, I shall be in France."

Did his escape plan include Jaspar?

He trailed a finger down Kennedy's throat. "You should have gone with me from Farfallow. Now you know more than you ought to know. Pity."

"Answer me one thing. If you knew I was not Lady Lark, why hire an assassin?"

"Because of the way Wynland watched you"—he pondered her mouth—"touched you"—his finger traced her clavicle—"kissed you. It could have ruined everything."

"For you?"

"Aye."

"And Jaspar?"

Following an absent moment, he said, "And Jaspar." His hand crept lower.

Kennedy knocked it aside and pointed a finger at him. "Back off or I'll cast a spell on you!"

For a moment, he appeared to consider her warning, then grabbed her arms and yanked her around.

The floor skidded out from under her as he propelled her backward. The mattress broke her fall.

"Now, witch," he said, leaning over her, "cast your spell."

Kennedy slammed the heel of her palm into his descending mouth, snapping his head back and causing him to yelp.

"Witch!" He drew back a fist.

She threw up an arm, but the blow was stopped by sounds in the bailey.

Leonel froze. "Jaspar," he said.

She had arrived?

He narrowed his gaze on Kennedy. "Methinks this shall have to wait."

She did a stupid thing then lowered her arm and was rewarded with a fist to her eye. Amid the pain, she was vaguely aware of Leonel's brisk movements about the chamber, then his hands on her again.

She fought him, but he quickly gagged her, bound her hands and feet with rope from his pack, and tossed her over his shoulder.

Kennedy continued to struggle. Night was coming and she was about to be disconnected from it, which would leave John and Harold wide open. She caught a glimpse of Leonel's meat dagger, but there was no way to get to it with her hands at her back.

"You may have escaped Wynland's prison," he said as he lugged her to the indoor outhouse she had come to know as the garderobe, "but you will not escape mine."

He threw open the garderobe and dumped her.

On her descent to the floor, Kennedy's arm hit the rough edge of the stone slab seat, tearing the sleeve of her gown and abrading the flesh beneath. But the sting was nothing compared to her landing. The thrust of her weight on her arms at her back set fire to her joints and shoulders. If not for the gag, her cry would surely have brought someone running.

"We are not done." Leonel looked down on her where she lay crammed in the small space.

Kennedy glared at him, grunted against the gag.

He grunted back, laughed, and slammed the door.

She stared into the semi-darkness that would have been pitch if not for the slotted window that let in a ray of light. Tears of frustration and pain rising, she commanded herself to concentrate. If she didn't get out of here, all she had done would be for nothing. There had to be a way, even if it meant going through Fulke and his disbelief. She surveyed the dim garderobe and stopped on the door. Could she get herself turned around in this impossibly narrow space? Kick at the door and cause enough ruckus to—

The door opened and, for a breathless moment, she thought it was Fulke who stood there.

"It occurs to me, witch, that you will not go easy," Leonel said. "Can't have you rousing a chamber maid, can I?" He booted her alongside the head.

The pain, worse than the blow to the eye, and frighteningly comparable to the worst of the tumor, swept Kennedy toward darkness. *Please, no!*

Angered that he had not been allowed a moment alone with Jaspar since her arrival less than an hour past, Leonel stared at her where she stood before the table at which Wynland was seated. For each question

Wynland put to her, she looked imploringly to Leonel, which made him long to measure her neck with his hands.

Wynland repeated the question he had asked a few minutes earlier, and over which Jaspar had fumbled as if she knew little of the English language. Sensing the swing of her eyes, Leonel set his gaze to the hearth where Lady Aveline, Lady Marion, and Lady Lark were seated. No sooner did he than the latter turned her face toward him. As with each time they drew near one another, he was fearful recognition might hit upon her, be it due to a mannerism or facial feature she might have glimpsed when she struck him with the stone. He leaned forward, put his elbows on the table, and clasped his hands before his face. It was as near a disguise as he could manage.

"Very well," Wynland ground out. "Then tell me this: what know you of a device bearing a two-headed wyvern?"

Leonel's throat constricted. Though he had thought he was prepared if it was proven that Nedy Plain had told Wynland of the medallion, he was wrong. His gaze clashed with Jaspar's, but this time, rather than pleading, disbelief shone from her eyes.

As much as he longed to shake his head to silence her desperate tongue, he knew he was watched. Thus, he gripped his clasped hands to the bones and shifted his gaze to the table.

"I..." Jaspar floundered. "Does not...? Aye, methinks Baron Fulkirk bears a wyvern. Is it...is it two-headed, Leonel?"

"I know not, Cousin."

Wynland's brother, Richard, stepped from the alcove across the hall. "I know the baron's device. 'Tis a wyvern with but one head."

Wynland's gaze pared Jaspar. "'Tis a two-headed one I seek on a medallion seen last by one of Lady Lark's escort who was killed in the attack."

Jaspar stepped nearer the table. "I am sorry, Fulke. I fear I know naught that might aid you. If the lady was held at Cirque, as you say, neither I, nor my cousin know anything of the attack upon her. Is that not true, Leonel?"

"As I have already told Lord Wynland."

The suddenness with which his liege rose from his chair struck fear in Leonel and caused Jaspar to jump back so that she nearly toppled from the dais.

"Someone is lying," Wynland said. "Ere this night is done—" The entrance of one of his knights halted his speech. "What is it, Sir Malcolm?"

The knight ascended the dais. "My lord, she is gone again."

From Wynland's expression, he did not require a name for the one gone missing.

Ah, sweet reprieve. Leonel drank in deliverance. Though it might be of short duration, hopefully it would be enough to see him gone from this place. Unfortunate for poor Jaspar, he might have to leave her behind.

"Is there none competent to hold her?" Fulke shouted as he struggled to contain the emotion that slammed through him, the pain of which demanded a more violent expression.

"'Tis as before, my lord," the knight implored. "She could not have escaped, yet did. Mayhap 'tis true what is said, that she is a—"

"Enough!" Fulke didn't wish it spoken, though he knew he ought not to care. He strode from behind the table. "We are not done, Lady Jaspar, Sir Leonel. When I return, I shall have my answers. Every one of them."

Minutes later, Fulke strode into the tower room and halted before Crosley who sat on his pallet with his back against the wall, hand splayed over his bandaged thigh.

"Surely you are not surprised?" the man said.

He shouldn't be, nor should her absence pain him so. "Where is she?"

"Is it revenge that makes you care? Or is it possible you are...not in love, for that is unheard of for a man like you." He made a show of pondering. "In lust?"

"Where, Crosley?"

"Not in this world, Wynland. No matter how far or long you search, you will only find Kennedy Plain if she decides to return."

Fulke didn't want to believe it, longed to accept Crosley's taunts as merely that, but what the miscreant spoke made truth of what Nedy had tried to convince him. How else to explain all that she was? Fulke pivoted.

"Wynland."

He turned in the doorway.

Crosley sat forward and grimaced at the pain caused by the movement. "I believe she will be back. And soon."

The flickering light that Fulke had tried to extinguish these past days sprang anew, tentatively lighting the dark within him and without. "Why would she want to return to…" He looked around the room. "…this?"

"Because there is still a chance she can change the outcome—that she can save my boys."

Determining he would not dwell on Crosley's possessive attitude toward John and Harold, Fulke reentered the room.

"Too," the man mused, "it seems she loves you."

Fulke remembered the sweet words she had spoken, words he had not spoken in return though he had felt them. "Tell me all of it."

Crosley regarded him with assessing eyes. "As much as I hate to admit it, perhaps Ken is right about you."

"What do you mean?"

"She believes in you, is adamant you didn't do it."

"What?" The boys again? Their fiery deaths?

"Sit down, Wynland. It is a long tale."

Fulke resisted but, in the end, lowered to the pallet.

"You already know what is going to happen," Crosley began, "for you have lived it before. You just do not remember it."

It was almost enough to set Fulke back on his feet, but he knew that if he did not hear it, he would risk losing Nedy forever. "Speak."

And Crosley did.

# 28

"Leonel!"

He halted before his chamber. As the past half hour of waiting had proven Wynland was wholly occupied with Nedy Plain's disappearance, there was time. He turned. "Cousin."

Color in her cheeks, eyes dripping reproach, Jaspar traversed the corridor at such speed he could almost believe she did it on four legs. Chest rising and falling rapidly, she stopped before him. "What have you done?" she demanded as if of a child.

Leonel longed to retaliate, but he reminded himself of all she had suffered since Wynland's summons. First, the merciless pace that had borne her to Brynwood and the uncertainty that must have taunted her throughout. Then, no sooner arrived than she was ushered to the hall to face endless questions that stank of accusation. She had stood throughout, taken in the revelations of Lady Lark and her impostor, Nedy Plain, without a moment to breathe her way past the shock. Thus, her reaction to learning who was responsible for the attack on Lady Lark could be forgiven—for the moment. He pushed the door inward. "Let us speak inside."

She punched her hands to her hips. "We shall speak here."

Fool woman! Though it was not the hour servants were usually about the chambers, due care must be taken with something of such import that it bound his life. Leonel snatched her arm and thrust her into the chamber.

She spun around. "What do you?"

He seated the door and glanced at the garderobe where Nedy Plain surely listened—providing she had regained consciousness. It mattered not. Conscious or otherwise, her tongue would carry no tale of this conversation. Of course, what was he to do with her body? He supposed he could leave it. Or send it down the garderobe shaft. He smiled. If the medallion she sought, the medallion she would find. In death.

Leonel strode past Jaspar, stretched on the bed, and clasped his hands behind his head.

"For what did you do it, Leonel?"

He considered his clipped nails. "For you."

"Me?" Disbelief, but hardly disgust.

He glowered at her. "You could not wed Wynland were he wed to another."

"Of course I could not. But murder?"

"'Twas the only way." The reason he had hired Moriel and his rogue knights—to assure none lived. As Leonel had done a hundred times since the attack, he cursed the vanity that had prompted him to bear witness to what his coin had bought. Had he not, the king's man who had engaged him over swords would not have seen the medallion and told of it. But even that might have been overcome if not for Moriel's lusting after Nedy Plain.

Jaspar stomped a foot. "Fulke will learn 'tis your former liege, Baron Brom, who bears the two-headed wyvern, and to whom the medallion was given."

Not that she was revolted by what he had done. She was merely concerned that, were it discovered who had done the deed, she might be accused of having aided him.

She took a step toward him. "What fool are you, Leonel?"

He sprang to sitting. "I am not a fool!"

"You have accomplished naught but the killing of the king's men. The king's men!"

"Lady Lark was also to have died," he muttered. And would have had her maid not escaped, casting doubt on the identity of the woman Moriel had delivered to him.

"But she did not die," Jaspar snarled, "and now she sits in the hall staring accusation at me!"

He needed none to cast light on the mistakes of that day. "Unfortunate," he growled.

Jaspar stalked to the door, stalked back. "For naught." She jabbed a finger at him. "And now I am dragged to Brynwood to stand accused of your crimes!"

The fire in Leonel's belly rolled to a boil. "Not even a crumb of gratitude, cousin?" He stood from the bed. "I sacrificed all to give you your desire."

Laughter bubbled from her. "'Twas for you that you did it. For Cirque."

She remembered the promise she had made him. But then, their blood *was* near one with the other. "Aye, 'twas not without appeal that you would see me set over Castle Cirque once you and Wynland wed."

He couldn't move fast enough to avoid her palm to his cheek. It landed hard.

"Ill-begotten fool!" she cried.

Rage plowed through him. Never had she called him such, fully aware of the circumstances of his birth though she was.

Too simple to know she ought to flee, she said, "Think you I need any to rid me of the king's leman? I could have—"

Granting himself his wish, Leonel measured her neck with a hand that shut her mouth. Feeling her throat muscles strain, watching shock transform her lovely face, he backed her across the chamber and pushed her against the wall alongside the door.

Desperate for air, she pried at his hand.

He retrieved the key from the hook beside the door, fit it in the lock, and turned it. "You who knows all of the prattle at court know not that Lady Lark is Edward's illegitimate daughter?"

She stilled, eyes bulged.

Not that Leonel had known himself until he found the king's missive to Wynland. It was then he had realized the enormity of his error, known fear as he had never known. But he'd had no choice but to finish what he had begun.

He pushed the key into the pouch on his belt. "As for Nedy Plain who pretended her, Wynland pants for the witch."

He glanced at the garderobe. Not a sound from within, but soon—not that any would hear Nedy's descent to the bottom of the shaft. "Now, Jaspar, do you flee Brynwood with me or remain and bear the blame? Hmm, I must think on it some."

She wheezed a short breath, reached for him with hooked nails, and fell short by inches.

Why did he bother with her? It would be easier if she shared Nedy's fate. Ah, but the blood they had in kind tugged at him. They *were* cousins, though that was not all.

She sagged against the wall.

Was it defeat that dulled her eyes or a lack of air? He sighed. "You will be silent?"

When she jerked her chin, he released her.

With a terrible sucking sound, Jaspar slid down the wall. She filled her lungs, coughed, sucked again.

Leonel spread his legs. "What do you think? You will leave with me or stay?"

Trembling, she touched her throat. She feared him, but did she fear him enough?

"Of course, you realize," he said, "we cannot return to Cirque."

"I...could tell Fulke what you have done."

She didn't fear him enough, but as much as he longed to make her quake, perhaps reasoning would convince her better. "You have lost Fulke—not that you ever had him. Thus, what gain in telling him?"

Her tears evidenced she knew it herself. "I would still have Cirque."

"You dream, Jaspar. He will take it from you."

"Not if I give him you."

He clucked his tongue. "I am disappointed to learn you could be so witless. Even if you were able to give me to him, you think I would not say that all I did was upon your orders?" There was the last bit of fear she had denied him. The fear of knowing all was lost, that her fate—her very life—was not her own.

"How can you do this to me?" she choked.

"Quite easily. Not that I do not feel some remorse. For all the silly, vain woman you are, I do care something for you. But you still have only two choices: leave with me or die with Nedy Plain."

She blinked. "'Twas you who freed her from the tower?"

"The witch freed herself, but I have her now."

"Where?"

He nodded at the garderobe. "Methinks I shall break her neck and drop her down the shaft. A fitting end for an impostor." He pursed his lips. "But fitting for you? That you must decide. Now."

A sob fell from her. "I shall go with you."

The sight of Jaspar in defeat made him smile. No more would she order him to do her bidding. "I thought 'twas as you would choose, but I warn you: reveal me and you shall hang by my side."

"I understand."

He stepped back. "Now let us have done with Nedy."

"I will not help you, Leonel."

"Then you may watch and know your fate if you betray me." He crossed to the garderobe, pulled open the door, and stumbled back.

From her hiding place, Kennedy stared at Leonel's boots.

"She is gone!" he exploded. "Again!"

"What?" Jaspar squeaked, all but her head and shoulders visible from where Kennedy lay beneath the bed.

"The witch is gone—likely to Wynland."

If only she had made it that far. Kennedy glanced at the frayed rope that trailed her right wrist. It had been a nearly insurmountable feat to cut through it, but in spite of a swollen eye and the pain that split her head upon regaining consciousness, she had made it to her knees and backed herself against the toilet's rough, stone edge. Back and forth she had rocked for what seemed hours. Finally, fingers, hands, and wrists scraped and bleeding, the rope had given way. Freeing the gag and her ankles had been relatively easy, but the time required to do so had closed her window of opportunity.

As she had exited the garderobe, Jaspar's voice alerted her to Leonel's presence in the corridor. Scattering rushes, she had nosedived beneath the bed and nearly passed out from the effort required to slow her breathing. Then Leonel's weight had sagged the mattress atop her, and her heart had nearly stopped. But it was almost over. If this played out as she prayed it would, Leonel would be beating a hasty retreat.

"What are you going to do?" Jaspar asked.

"We leave now!" While he moved about the chamber collecting his possessions, Jaspar remained unmoving against the wall.

As much as Kennedy disliked the woman, she felt sympathy for her. Although Jaspar clearly wouldn't have lost much sleep had Lady Lark died with the king's men, she was a wasp caught in Leonel's web.

Leonel halted before her. "Get up!"

She was slow to respond, as if her mind was elsewhere.

"Now!" He grabbed her forearm and wrenched her up.

She tried to get her feet under her, and might have if not for her cousin's disgust. He released her, sending her facedown on the floor. "Stay, then!"

Kennedy felt her stomach fall through her. If Jaspar looked much beyond her nose, she would see what was under the bed.

"I'm sorry." She lifted her head. "I'm so"—she sobbed—"frightened."

*Don't look this way. Anywhere but here.*

"Then you are of no use to me!"

Jaspar's eyes swept up the bed, but before Kennedy could give thanks, Jaspar did a double take.

With the assassin, Moriel, Kennedy had known fear, but it paled in comparison.

However, Jaspar didn't announce her discovery—at least not in words. She tilted her head, frowned.

Kennedy shook her head on a snowball's chance Jaspar wouldn't reveal her.

"What is it?" Leonel demanded.

A dead silence followed, each second that passed sweeping Kennedy nearer the fate Leonel planned for her. Thus, it came as no surprise when his boots turned toward the bed.

*Get a grip! You've been through worse than this—come nearer death.* The reminder of the tumor filled Kennedy with determination. She scrambled opposite Leonel's approach, but he was a step ahead of her. He heaved the mattress back and landed it in the path of her escape.

"So there you are."

She flipped onto her back and looked up at him through the ropes strung across the bed frame.

He hunkered down. "The Lord looks kindly upon me."

"You mean the guy in the red suit sporting horns and a tail? That would be the devil."

He laughed. "Perhaps." He drew his meat dagger and tapped its edge. "Come out, Nedy Plain."

She looked to Jaspar. Though the woman had risen from the floor, her expression was not one of pride at having landed the big fish. She looked cornered.

Kennedy returned her gaze to Leonel, prayed she wouldn't get knifed the moment she came out. "All right." She scooted toward him.

When she cleared the bed, Leonel straightened and stepped back. "Get up!"

As she rose, the rope trailing her wrist brushed her palm. *Hello.* Unfortunately, Leonel was too near, but if in stalling him she could put some distance between them...

"Will you answer me one question before you stuff me down the garderobe?" she said.

"What would that be?"

She took a step back. "Why John and Harold?" Though it followed that with the boys out of the way Fulke would become earl, thus elevating Jaspar with him were she his wife, what gain for Leonel?

"Of what do you speak?" He looked genuinely puzzled. "Surely you know I had naught to do with Crosley's scheme."

True, but—

Leonel was off-guard. As much as she longed to pursue this night's atrocity, she stepped back and swung with all of her strength. The rope on her wrist whipped across Leonel's cheek, staggering him back and causing him to release the dagger.

Kennedy started for the door, only to falter in recalling the key's rattle when Leonel had locked it.

A moment later, he tackled her to the floor. She twisted around. An eye for eye, wasn't that what they said? She bunched a fist and missed her mark by a cheekbone.

"Witch!" Leonel reached for her arms.

Pain cramping her hand, she flailed and landed an elbow to his nose. It snapped his head back, sprinkled her with droplets of blood, and made him howl.

If that didn't bring someone running, nothing would.

Kennedy shoved him off and bolted for the dagger amid the rushes. Out of the corner of her eye, she saw that Jaspar had yet to move. Kennedy snatched up the dagger and spun around.

A hand to his nose, Leonel staggered upright.

She extended the dagger before her with one hand, beckoned with the other. "The key."

He lowered his arm. Rivulets of blood coursing his lips and chin, he said, "Do I die, so shall you." He stepped toward her.

She looked at the dagger. Acting out a violent movie she had seen years ago, she slashed the air. "I'm warning you!"

Her threat was punctuated by the sound of footsteps and raised voices.

"It's over," she said. "Don't make this worse than it is."

"What goes?" someone shouted from the corridor, then rattled the door. "Open, else we shall beat it down!"

Leonel glanced behind. "It can get no worse for me, Nedy Plain, but it can for you."

"I won't let you win, Leonel."

He took another step toward her, his gaze shifting between the dagger and her eyes. "I do not ask permission."

The door strained in its frame, wood cracked and popped.

Kennedy waved the blade again. "Then don't keep me waiting." Such daring for one trying desperately to avert a meltdown.

Leonel was poised as if to take up her challenge when he stilled at the sound of another voice.

Fulke was here, only feet away.

Leonel smiled the same disarming smile that had greeted her the day of her arrival at Castle Cirque. Who would guess that such a handsome, congenial face could disguise a terrible monster? "I will keep you waiting no longer," he said and lunged.

Though Kennedy knew she should let him stick himself on the dagger, she jumped back. And back she kept going until she came up against the table. What possessed her to trade the dagger for the basin was the realization she couldn't kill. But it proved the better choice and fitting revenge for the blow he had delivered her after dumping her in the garderobe. She swung the basin and struck him on the temple.

She gaped as he fell, shocked that it had worked. How ironic that, just as Lady Lark had knocked him senseless at Castle Cirque, so had Kennedy done at Brynwood. The man was in sorry need of a helmet.

Jaspar put an uncertain foot forward. "Leonel?"

With an explosive crack, the door burst inward.

# 29

*Their meetings made December June.*
*Their every parting was to die.*
*~ Alfred, Lord Tennyson*

Kennedy looked up. Blue eyes met green. "Fulke," she breathed.

He stood in the doorway, stared long and thunderous at her, then at Leonel who lay at her feet. The ire was still there when his gaze swept back. Worse, even.

As Kennedy felt the beginning of tears, Jaspar came to life as if someone had plugged her in. She dove into Fulke's chest and began jabbering between sobs.

His gaze never leaving Kennedy, Fulke gripped the woman's arms and thrust her toward one of his men-at-arms.

"Fulke!" Jaspar cried.

Three strides and he was at Kennedy's side. He didn't touch her, but searched her face, and with such seething she imagined he was determining what form her punishment would take.

"I know you don't want to hear this," she said, "but please let me—"

"Not now." The wrathful air fell from him. He touched her torn sleeve, gently brushed a finger beneath her swollen eye. "I am sorry, Nedy."

Then his anger was for the man at her feet?

"'Twas Leonel who wore the wyvern, was it not—that given him by Baron Brom?"

She nodded warily. "Yes, on the other side of the medallion I did not see."

He looked at her temple where Leonel's booted foot had left a lump. "I was a fool. Can you forgive me?"

Her heart swelled so large she feared it would burst. "There is nothing to forgive."

"Aye, there is." He folded her into his arms and held her as near as he could. For nothing would he lose her again, he silently vowed as he breathed her. Whether she was a witch, a dream, or come from six hundred years not yet lived, nothing would keep him from her.

She lifted her face and looked at him through shimmering eyes. "You believe?"

"Aye, sweet Nedy, I am beginning to believe in witches."

The smile in her eyes wavered. "I am not a witch."

"So Crosley tells."

They had spoken?

"Very well, then," Fulke acceded, "a dream."

"Nor that. Nor mad. My name is Kennedy Plain and I am real. I—"

"I know. I need time, is all." Time to believe himself worthy of such a miracle. Time to put away Limoges that he might look to a future with her. Time to lift the burden of the king's medallion from about his neck.

"Time," Kennedy murmured. "It looks like I'm going to have plenty of it."

"My lord." A man-at-arms stepped into the chamber. "Sir Leonel awakens."

Fulke pulled back from Nedy and threaded his fingers with hers. He looked to the man-at-arms and glimpsed Lady Lark, Marion, and his mother in the corridor. When he had returned to the keep and followed the din abovestairs, had they been there outside the door? Had he pushed past them? He didn't recall, for all his thoughts had been on Nedy and the feeling that she had returned and was in danger.

He started toward the door. "Deliver the miscreant to the tower. And his cousin with him."

Jaspar shrieked and tried to free herself from the soldier who held her. "Pray, hear me, Fulke. Upon my word, I was not of this. Only this day did I learn what he had done."

He halted. "You knew naught of the medallion? That of which he surely boasted?"

Her eyes widened. "I...when you asked of it, I could not say."

"You could not say 'twas your cousin who paid assassins to murder the king's men? Whose intent it was to kill Lady Lark? Nay, Jaspar, I do not believe you. Leonel did it for you, and he shall not bear punishment alone."

"Aye, he did it for me, believing I might wed you as 'twas to have been in the beginning." Pain contorted her face. "But more, he did it for himself upon my promise I would see him lord of Cirque once you and I wed. Had I known what he planned..."

Fulke stared at her. If it was true she hadn't known, what *would* she have done had she been privy to Leonel's plans? Unfortunately for her, he was not certain she would have put an end to them. "Methinks I cannot believe anything you say, Jaspar."

Nedy gripped his arm. "In this instance, she's telling the truth. She didn't know."

Why did she defend a woman who had behaved so ill toward her? "How do you know that?"

She opened her mouth to answer, but closed it until the men-at-arms had carried their prisoner past her and through the doorway. "I overheard their conversation. When Lady Jaspar confronted Leonel about the attack, he warned her that if she told you, he would say she had ordered him to do it."

"Be it so, she could have revealed him when I asked after the wyvern." He looked to Jaspar. "Why protect a man who would do what he has done?"

"I had to." Her jaw trembled, and she lowered her head. "Leonel is my brother."

Not what Fulke expected. Lover, perhaps, but brother? "What falsehood do you tell, Jaspar? All know he is your cousin, that your mothers were sisters."

It was some moments before she lifted her chin to brave him again. "Aye, but we are also brother and sister."

Fulke did not care for the only conclusion to be had.

"Tell your man to release me," Jaspar beseeched, "and I will reveal all."

Fulke motioned for the man-at-arms to unhand her.

Jaspar smoothed her gown, touched quivering fingers down her thick braid, then clasped her hands before her. "Nine months after my aunt came to live at Laverre following her husband's death, Leonel was born of her deception and my father's." Her chin creased. "I resented Leonel for years, but he adored me, followed me about, begged my friendship. When my mother died, and later his, we had only each other. We drew near." Tears soaked her eyes. "I cannot say I love him with any measure of my heart, only that I care for him."

Her sincerity surprised him.

"He shall hang?" she asked.

There were many ways for a man to die. Somehow, Fulke doubted the king would let Leonel go so easily. "I cannot believe the king would allow him to live, Jaspar."

She pressed a fist to her breast. "And of me? Do you believe what I have told?"

Only because of what Nedy had revealed. He looked to where she stood at his side and stole a moment of revel as he beheld her eyes. "I believe you, Jaspar, but now is not the time to speak of your place at Cirque." Later they would talk. Not that her fate required much thought, for there was only one thing to do if she remained at Cirque—wed her to one capable of withstanding her cunning and repressing her affinity for discord. Unfortunately, such a man might prove difficult to find.

He looked to the man-at-arms beyond Jaspar. "Accompany the lady to her chamber. She is to remain there until I send for her."

Jaspar dragged her gaze from Fulke to Nedy. "I do not like you, Nedy Plain, whoever you are. I cannot." Her voice splintered. "But I thank you." She stepped into the corridor.

Fulke squeezed Nedy's hand. "Come, I wish to be alone with you."

She smiled. "I would like that too, but what about Mac? He's—"

"I came from him to you. He told me much that I would not allow you to speak." Much that Fulke had finally allowed himself to believe. "The physician is with him now, and this eve he shall sit at my table with John and Harold."

Her smile sparkled like stars upon night. "Thank you."

As he drew her past those in the corridor, he met Marion's gaze. It was lit with approval and happiness, whereas Lady Lark's was of bewilderment. As for his mother, from her eyes to her nose to her mouth and chin, disapproval reigned. But he did not seek her blessing for the woman with whom he would spend his life. Did she give it, grandchildren would abound about her skirts, did she not, time would surround her loneliness at her dower property two days ride to the north. No more malice would he suffer beneath his roof. It was time to heal and be healed.

The setting sun painted the walls of the lord's solar in orange bled with pink and cast a golden glow on the canopied bed alongside which Fulke and Kennedy stood.

Fingers still meshed with hers, he raised his other hand and stroked her cheek. "I feared never to see you again, and now you shall be my wife and bear me sons and daughters."

She smiled. "Is that your way of asking me to marry you?"

"Does it need to be asked?"

Kennedy's breath stirred wildly at the love in his eyes he had yet to speak. "No, but still I would like to hear it."

He caught her hands between his. "Nedy Plain, will thee wed me come the changing of the leaves, the whispering of the breeze?"

Autumn, and so poetically written on the air—as had been written the words he would never carve into the walls of a prison cell. "You do know I'm not noble?"

His gaze never wavered. "You are more noble than any woman who has ever perched a crown upon her brow. Tell me 'aye,' and I will take you to wife this eve if you wish."

Though she swelled with hope, Graham's mother threw a shadow. "What about your mother? She won't approve."

"Think you I must needs have her approval?" He shook his head. "I do not."

It was the same as Graham had said, though not in so many words.

Fulke drew her nearer. "Does my mother put aside her bitterness of a life she hated, her visits shall be welcome. Does she not, no part of your life will she touch."

Was it wishful thinking that made her believe him as she had tried to believe Graham? Or was it his eyes that held steady, echoing a vow never to be broken? All that and more. "I believe you. But what of Lady Lark?"

He carried her hands to his lips and kissed her palms. "She has decided to enter the convent, and does she determine otherwise, I shall convince her father to wed her elsewhere."

"Then it's true that King Edward is her father."

Fulke frowned. "How come you by that?"

"The conversation I overheard between Leonel and Jaspar. He taunted her with it."

"Then 'tis as Lady Lark told—her captor knew of her relation to Edward." He nodded. "Aye, Nedy, 'tis true."

"But if the king is her—"

"Edward will grant me my desire. And I desire you. You know it already, but I will say it. I love you, Nedy Plain."

She closed her eyes, sowed the seeds of his words throughout her memory that she could call upon them when she was a very old woman.

His mouth brushed hers. "All I would do for you, no matter the cost."

Those words, never to be carved into a stone wall, leapt at her. But now he would not die for her.

"Will you marry me?"

She lifted her lids. "With my whole heart."

He lowered his head and opened his mouth on hers.

Kennedy thrilled to his kiss. No sweeter taste had she tasted, no greater need had she needed.

He cupped her face in his hands, with his fingers gently brushed her swollen eye and the lump at her temple.

"Pinch me," Kennedy whispered against his mouth.

"Do what?"

"Pinch me. Anywhere."

Still, he didn't follow. She supposed he wouldn't. She pinched her thigh.

"What do you, Nedy?"

His voice rang loud and clear, meaning she was still here, as was he. She looked up. "Pinching myself."

"For what?"

"To see if I am only dreaming. It's a silly thing we do where I come from to test whether a person is dreaming or awake."

He almost smiled. "And?"

"I'm still here. I'm not dreaming. You're real."

"I am relieved. You will tell me more of this world from which you come?"

"Now?"

"If I am to wait 'till our wedding night to have you in my bed, I will need a distraction."

She laughed. "And a better place to tell my tale than here."

He led her to a chair before the fireplace. As they would have days... months... years ahead of them, Kennedy began at the beginning, a regular Scheherazade.

She couldn't sleep, at first because of Fulke's proximity that stoked her senses even while they lay apart on the bed where they had moved when enough of the tale was told for one night. Later, it was the chill creeping about the room that kept her awake. And now it was fear of the pull. When it came, she must be conscious. And if it didn't come soon? Dread it though she did—the fear that she might not escape it—she wanted it over with so she could go on with her new life. She had to believe she would.

"Nay," Fulke muttered.

It was too dark for her to make out his features where he lay on the opposite side of the bed. Was he awake?

"Fulke?"

A sound rumbled from his throat.

A dream, then—rather, a nightmare, or at least something disturbing. Kennedy moved nearer and stroked his bearded jaw. "Wake up."

He grumbled.

"Fulke." She shook his shoulder. "You're dreaming."

He drew a sharp breath. "Nedy?"

She caught the bare light reflected in his eyes. "It's me."

He pulled her so tightly against him it was as if he meant to absorb her through his skin. "You are here."

"I am. Was it a very bad dream?" she spoke into the crook of his neck.

His tense silence revealed a vulnerability she had not previously seen in this warrior. But then, as she knew well, dreams could be powerful, sometimes enough to change lives—in her case, give life.

"'Twas of fire," he said. "John and Harold in the midst of it, smoke pouring from beneath the door."

A chill deeper than that which breathed through the open windows pricked Kennedy's arms.

"I could not reach them." He pulled back and she felt his gaze search the dark for her face. "Amid blackened walls, you came to me, held me, then disappeared like summer snow."

Then it wasn't a dream, but a memory of that other past which her return would have wiped clean?

"I waited on your word that you would return to me, but you did not. Then death came for me."

"How did you die, Fulke?"

"A noose, tighter and tighter 'til dark dragged the light of day from my eyes." His hair brushed her cheek as he shook his head. "So real a dream I have never had."

She laid a hand to his cheek. "It wasn't a dream. John and Harold did die in the fire. In your grief, you sent for me the morning after—tomorrow—and when I left you it was to bring myself back to an earlier time that I might save your nephews."

His silence was thick.

"Do you understand, Fulke? What you believe to be a dream happened. All of it—as it would have had I not been able to return. But it's over now. Leonel can't harm John and Harold. They're safe."

"What of you?" he asked tightly. "Will you leave me again?"

*Would* the pull take her? Could she beat it as Mac had done? She had to. "Not if I can help it."

"Can you?"

"Mac did it. I can too."

"Then 'tis as he told, that you must die there to stay here."

"It's true. I have a brain tumor."

Fulke slid fingers through the hair at her temple. "Here the tumor is gone?"

Was he holding his breath? "I've never been healthier."

His tension eased. "You and Crosley ask much of me. However, as I am unable to find another explanation for all that has happened, I shall no more say 'nay' to you."

She huddled nearer.

He kissed her nose. "You are cold. I shall light a fire and we will sit and talk some more." He stood, and she heard his feet fall across the chamber. He opened the door, reached around it, and retrieved a torch from the corridor. Though weakened by its long burn into the night, it lit the chamber enough for Kennedy to take better note of it than she had earlier.

She dropped her feet over the mattress as Fulke moved before the hearth. The structure was large, its presence made larger by the thick mantel above the sheltering cavern. In fact, it seemed everything about the room was on a massive scale: armchairs, tables, stools, carved chests, tapestries and, of course, the bed—big enough to hold dad, mom, and a passel of children.

Kennedy touched her stomach, tilted her head back, and considered the canopy. With its sheer white fabric stretched overhead and falling in swells from the frame, it was all that was soft about the room. Something more was needed. Flowers would be nice. She looked to the floor and sighed. "Fulke?"

"Hmm?" He urged a fledgling fire with a poker, straightened, and kicked a scattering of rushes from the hearth.

"Why hay?"

"Hay?" He set the torch in a wall sconce to the left of the mantel, leaned down, and poked some more.

"The rushes on the floor. Except for in stables, I've never seen it used for floor covering."

He looked over his shoulder and grinned. "'Tis truly a different world in which you lived. Tell me, what is it you use there to keep the chill from the floor and scent the rooms?"

"Carpet is the top pick, but rugs over tile and hardwood are a good alternative."

His split eyebrow rose. "An entire keep carpeted? That I should like to see."

She laughed. "The average house is nowhere near as large as this. In fact, I'd guess four of them could fit inside your hall."

He leaned the poker against the wall and moved toward her. "Then they are quite small, though not as small as a peasant's cottage."

"It's all relative."

"'Tis what?"

She went through the motions of erasing the comment from the air and considered the rushes again. With the exception of the clearing around the hearth, they were strewn throughout the chamber.

Fulke halted before her. "You shall miss your carpet?"

"Not really, though it certainly isn't as dangerous as—"

*Dear God!*

# 30

K<small>ENNEDY COULD NOT</small> move for what might prove precious seconds. Like the historians, she had made an assumption. Perhaps a deadly one. Despite the malfeasance that hung over Sinwell, had no one ever considered the fire might have been an accident? It might not have been of Leonel's doing but of a stray spark.

"What is it, Nedy?"

She jumped up and darted past Fulke. "I may have been wrong."

"Of what do you speak?"

"Leonel...the fire."

When she reached the door, Fulke caught her shoulders and dragged her around. "Tell me!"

"It may not have been Leonel who set the fire. It may have been an accident."

Though his face moved from confusion to disbelief, he released her and flung open the door.

At a sprint, Kennedy followed him down the dimly lit corridor and up the stairs to the third floor where she had been brought in that other past. At the landing, they were met by a thready haze.

Fulke started shouting for his men, Kennedy praying as they ran to the first chamber from which the smoke issued. She halted alongside Fulke. He pulled his palm from the door, having assured himself there was no fire on the other side.

"Stay here!" He thrust the door inward.

Smoke puffed out—fed by a red glow in the darkness beyond. As he disappeared inside, somewhere in the room, a child coughed.

She couldn't just stand here! Vaguely aware of boots on the stairs that announced Fulke's men, she dropped to all fours.

Where was the bed? A memory of Fulke hunkered down amid the blackened ruins guided her as she crawled in under the smoke. The crisp rushes pricked her palms, but soon ash would be all that remained of the eager fuel. When she and Fulke came out, all this might be ablaze. A firebreak was needed.

She swept the rushes left and right, clearing a path as best she could. Though she kept low, the choking smoke wound her nasal passages and coated her mouth and throat. She wheezed and coughed.

"Go back, Nedy!" Fulke bellowed.

She couldn't—not only for the boys but for him. If any died, especially the king's daughter, he might yet carve words into prison walls.

"I have them both!" Fulke shouted as he passed nearby. "Curse it, Nedy!" He coughed. "Come out now!"

He had his nephews, but not Lady Lark. Though he had remembered that other past in the guise of a dream, he hadn't mentioned anything about the king's daughter, and neither had Kennedy gotten around to telling him of the woman's fate. Thus, he wouldn't know the lady was here until it was too late. But where was she? Had she been in bed with the boys? Pulled a chair alongside and fallen asleep?

Blinded by the dark and smoke and increasingly warmed by the fire that snapped up the rushes to the left of her path, she bumped into the bed. She dropped her face to the floor, sucked the bit of air there, and called, "Lady Lark!"

"She is not within," Fulke answered her.

He was wrong.

As Kennedy worked her way around the bed, sweeping her arms before her in hopes of landing a hand to a human form, Fulke's feet thumped the floor.

"Where are you, Nedy?"

She inhaled another breath from the floorboards and winced. Her throat burned, brain was turning to mush, and she felt as if she were floating away. *I am floating away!* It was the final pull, and it meant to steal her from Fulke.

"Nedy!"

"I'm here!" It came out weak, made her painfully aware that if she didn't succumb to the pull, the smoke would finish the job. The pull growing more insistent with each creep of her body across the floor, she continued forward.

"Go away," she pleaded. "Please, go away."

She touched legs, but not of a human. Head reeling, she groped a chair leg upward and, in the seat, found who she was looking for—until it registered that the thigh beneath her hand belonged to a man. And when he moaned, she knew. Not Lady Lark but Mac who sat beside the boys' bed, the past having been altered by his release from the tower.

"Mac!" Her voice sounded distant, her limbs felt disjointed. "You have to"—a cough barked from her—"get out of here."

He moaned again.

"Nedy!" Fulke shouted.

"Here!" Though she was losing feeling in her arms, she wound them around Mac, heaved, and landed on her back with him on top.

"What...?" Mac rasped like a rusted up gear.

Somewhere in the room, something fell heavily and was met by a leap of flame.

Kennedy shoved Mac off of her, crawled to his head, and positioned herself to drag him down the cleared path.

The pull yanked, determined to return her to her death.

*I'm not going!* But then, why was she drifting away from herself? "No!" she cried and, keeping as low as possible, gripped Mac beneath the arms and pulled.

"Nedy." Fulke was on his hands and knees beside her.

Though she knew he held her arm, his hand on her felt whisper light. She was losing the battle, about to slip through his fingers.

"We must—" He hacked and began pulling her from beside the bed.

She longed to throw herself in his arms, to cling to him, but she couldn't. "Not without...Mac."

"What?" Disbelief stilled him, urgency moved him. He felt past her and found Mac's inert form. He pushed her. "Go toward the light!"

She peered through the smoke. There was no mistaking the fire to the right, nor its intensifying heat that plastered her gown to her skin. But directly ahead, a light slashed side to side. Fixing on the voices beyond the room, she lowered her head and sipped tainted air. It was then she felt the pain stir behind her eyes and knew it was the tumor.

"Go, Nedy!" Fulke shouted across the yawning years.

She was leaving him. "Please, God, not now that I have found him."

As her arms and legs sprawled beneath her, she was pulled opposite. Up...up...Then suddenly forward, bumping against another figure. Mac? Was Fulke dragging her too? Not that she could stay...

Her heart broke, spilling its aching contents. The dream was gone. Or would soon be. All was lost.

"Nedy!" Fulke's voice echoed as if from across a deep canyon. "I have you. You're safe."

He could still see her? Was holding her? It seemed so, but as she was nearly outside herself, the rest of her would follow.

"I'm sorry," she whispered, then whimpered as pain tore through her head.

"Open your eyes! I will not lose you."

He seemed nearer. Was that his breath on her face?

"Fight it, Nedy!"

She longed to, but how? It was strong, would split her in two before letting her go. Another pain splintered her skull, bringing with it a strong sense of her mother's presence.

"Nedy!"

She thought it was Laurel's voice, but couldn't be certain. She hurt so bad.

"It's all right for you to go, baby. Jack's here with me."

Kennedy felt divided, in both places at once and yet neither.

"I'll be fine," Laurel said softly.

"Mom..." Kennedy squeezed the hand in hers—whoever it was.

"I love you, Nedy."

She sighed, and the tearing in her head went out on her breath. No more hurt. *Thank you, God.*

"Nedy!"

Fulke was still here? She reached herself backward, strained to feel him, to hear him.

"Do not leave me!"

Moisture fell to her cheek. Tears? For her? *Fight it!* she commanded the shallow breath in her lungs, the ebbing of her heart, the slowing of her mind, the weakening of her limbs. *So much to live for. Claw your way back.*

Claw she did, refusing to yield to the ease of death. She would go on—in another time, another place, but she would live. She would be the wife she longed to be, would stand beside Fulke and be his partner in life. She would make children with him, love them as she had been loved, teach them, see them grow to adulthood, hold their children. And Fulke would be at her side until she died a very old woman.

Voices. At first they were murmurs, but they grew louder and anxious, and somewhere she heard coughing and the sound of children crying. The boys? Soothing words spoken by Lady Marion. Mac's gruff speech.

Then breath. Kennedy gasped, filling her lungs with wonderfully cool air. Arms were around her. Fulke's face was near, his breath mingling with the smoke that clung to their bodies. Yet the pervasive scent was not repugnant, for it meant more than fire. It meant she was back.

"Look at me, Nedy."

It was as if her lids were sealed, but she forced them open. "Fulke," she croaked as his shadow-deepened face came into focus.

A smile lifted his mouth. "Aye."

Night was behind him, she realized as she caught torch light in his moist eyes—eyes that wept for her. She stared into them, warmed herself by their fire, and found herself there. She touched his bearded jaw. "I—" She turned her face away and coughed.

Fulke pulled her to sitting and thumped her back. When the coughing subsided, he eased her against his shoulder and pressed a skin of wine to her lips.

Nothing had ever tasted so good. As the moisture wet her mouth, she looked to the keep at Fulke's back. He had carried her outside, away from the smoke and fire that billowed from the third floor. Out of harm's way. Back to life—a life that would be so beautiful.

"Enough?" he asked when the last drop slid over her bottom lip.

She nodded. "Are John and—"

"The physician and Lady Lark are with them. They are frightened, but look to be well. Methinks Crosley will soon recover." He nodded to the left.

Kennedy peered beyond him, startled at the number of men and women who ran past toting buckets of water. Hard to overlook, especially with the excited din they raised as they rushed up the stairs to the keep, but until that moment they had existed only as white noise.

Mac was propped against the wall of the keep ten feet away. He sat in a circle of pulsing light cast by an overhead torch. Marion was beside him.

He grinned weakly. "You made it."

"I did, didn't I?"

"I knew you could do it."

She looked beside him to where the physician knelt alongside John and Harold. The little boys were wide awake. Though their sooty faces were tracked with tears, each clutched to his chest what looked to be an assortment of action figures.

"You saved them," Fulke spoke into her hair.

She tilted her face up to his. "Not without you. And Mac. It all began with him."

Regret rose on Fulke's face. "I was wrong in believing of him as I did."

"As he was wrong about you. But neither of you could have known."

He swept the hair back from her face. "I am a stubborn man. Can you make of me something more?"

She smiled. "I don't want to change you. The man who told me he loved me is the only one I want. You."

He lowered his mouth to hers. The kiss was short, but breathless. "As you are all I want, Kennedy Plain."

For the first time, he had used her uncut name. It sounded odd, as if it belonged to someone else. "Why did you call me Kennedy?"

"'Tis your name, is it not?"

"It is."

"Then surely I ought to use it?"

"I prefer Nedy." Not only had there been warmth and love attached to the familiar name by which her mother had called her since childhood, but the words of love that would nevermore be carved into stone had been for a woman known to him by that name. That was who she was.

"'Tis as I shall call you, then," Fulke said.

A shadow fell over them. "My lord?"

Tensing, Fulke looked up at the physician. "John and Harold?"

"They are fortunate. Neither they, nor Sir Arthur, ought to suffer any lasting ill."

"You would examine Lady Nedy now?" Fulke asked.

Lady. She was a lady. His lady.

"Aye, my lord."

Fulke looked to her. "I must needs leave you, though 'twill be for a short time only."

Her joy wavered. "Where are you going?"

"To assist with the fire."

And if she lost him to it? "Fulke—"

He pressed fingers to her lips. "I vow no ill will befall me."

Surely, having come this far, they would not now lose one another? She tried to smile. "I will hold you to that."

He kissed her again. "Rest, Nedy." He eased her off his lap and against the wall. "I shall come to you as soon as 'tis done."

Their hands touched, then he strode to the boys, spoke softly to them, and folded them into his chest. "I see you are fond of your soldiers," he said as he drew back.

John looked at his handfuls, then to Harold's. "Ever so. You do not mind that Sir Arthur allowed us to sleep with them?"

"I do not. Indeed, I am most grateful to him." Fulke glanced at Mac, straightened. "I shall return soon." He bounded up the steps.

Kennedy dropped her head back against the wall and looked heavenward. "I do not know why You did it, but I thank You for another chance."

It was some minutes before Kennedy's presence roused Fulke. When finally he lifted his head, his gaze was pained as if he remembered that other past in which she had come to him. "You are well?" he asked as he rose from the ashes.

She smiled. "More than well."

He crossed to where she stood in the doorway and lifted her hands in his. "I had hoped you would sleep the day through."

She might have, but the absence of his arms that had carried her to bed hours earlier had brought her to the gutted room. Searching his beloved face that contrasted sharply with the devastation behind him, she said, "I missed you."

His thumbs caressed the backs of her hands beneath the sleeves of her robe. "I am sorry, but I had to come back here."

"Why?"

"'Twill not surprise you, but I have seen this before." He turned and drew her into the room. "I have stood amid this ruin, though then I grieved."

Kennedy reveled in his warmth at her side. "It's in the past. Leave it there."

He surveyed the room, lingered on the hearth, and settled his gaze on the place where the bed had stood. "Aye, that is where it belongs."

Kennedy stepped in front of him. "I love you, Fulke."

He brushed his mouth across hers. "I love you, Nedy."

She beamed inside and out. In spite of their surroundings, she was touched by mischief. "And just how much do you love me, my lord?"

He raised his bent eyebrow, but when he spoke, it was with grave seriousness. "I would die for thee, Nedy Plain. A thousand times, I would die for thee."

# Epilogue

## Los Angeles, California

It wasn't possible. Still, she could dream as Nedy had done and find solace in the impossible.

Laurel caressed the page of the final entry. Though she had promised to read the journal, she hadn't until now, certain it would contain a poignant farewell sure to shred her threadbare heart. But today, a month after Nedy's death, she had braved it. Such a struggle it had been to make sense of the words, at first because of her reading impediment, but then because what Nedy had written offered too much hope for so little return.

Fresh tears threatening, Laurel looked to the boxes that held her daughter's possessions. There weren't many, but they filled the modest foyer of the home she had made with Jack. Eventually—not today, not tomorrow, not next week—a place would be found for them.

Laurel stifled a sob. She longed for this unbelievable tale of a second chance to be true, ached for Nedy's promise that a sign would be forthcoming.

She hugged the journal to her. What harm to believe—?

No. Denial would get her nowhere. Nedy was gone. This terrible grieving wasn't fair to anyone, especially Jack who deserved better than a woman who couldn't speak without her voice cracking, whose eyes were more pink than green, and who spent more hours in bed than out of it. It was time to begin letting go. Time to live, even if only for the memory of her daughter to fill the hole blown through her. She stood taller, put her shoulders back, and considered the journal. She would pack it away with the rest of the belongings.

The doorbell rang. Jack and Graham? The latter having kept his promise to help clear out Nedy's condominium, he had left with Jack a short while ago to bring back the final load. Guessing Jack had misplaced his key again, she crossed the foyer and broke her rule of never opening the door without first looking through the peephole.

It wasn't Jack or Graham, but a tall blonde man with bright green eyes, a questioning smile, and a halfway attractive face that placed him mid-thirties.

She gripped the door. "May I help you?"

"You are Laurel Jacobsen?"

A British accent. "Who's asking?"

"My name is Hunt Wynland."

Wynland? A shiver shot through her. "I—I'm Mrs. Jacobsen. What can I do for you?"

"I have something for you." His gaze slid past her to the room beyond. "It is of some import."

He wanted to be invited inside, but as well dressed and clean cut as he was, there was no guarantee he was harmless. Forget that his last name was the same as the Earl of Sinwell. He was a stranger.

Laurel put a hand out. "Do I need to sign for it?"

He reached into his jacket, withdrew a leather-covered tube, and extended it.

"What is it?"

"A message that has been waiting a very long time to be delivered."

*...a sign will be forthcoming.* Could it be? Or was she off her rocker?

"Mrs. Jacobsen?" Concern on his wavering face, the man reached to her.

— 327 —

She gripped the door tighter and tried to get her knees back under her, but she was slipping.

He came through the door and put an arm around her waist.

"I'm all right," she said, but it wasn't true.

Bearing a good portion of her weight, he navigated her past the boxes, into the living room, and eased her into Jack's recliner.

"I believe you're supposed to put your head between your knees and take deep breaths," he suggested where he knelt beside her.

She bent forward. When she finally came up, he asked, "Better?"

"Yes."

He smiled in a rather lopsided way. "I apologize if my visit has distressed you. I assure you, it was not meant to."

She nodded. "May I see it?"

He placed the tube in her hand. "It is very old."

She brushed a thumb over the dried, cracked leather. "Fourteenth century?" The words she spoke as if in casual conversation shook her.

The man's eyes widened. "Actually, the container is from the fifteenth century, but close enough. How did you know?"

"Wishful thinking. Who sent it?"

His eyebrows rose with apology. "It is said to have been written by an ancestor of mine, a woman by the name of Nedy—a many times removed great grandmother."

Laurel's heart fluttered. "Go on, please."

He gestured to the opposite recliner. "May I?"

"Of course."

He lowered into the chair. "It's a curiosity. For six hundred years that has been passed through the family under strict instructions that it remain sealed until this year and month." He leaned forward. "As the oldest son, it fell to me to open it two weeks ago. Though it was long thought to be a treasure map, as you will see, it is a collection of letters—addressed to you, Mrs. Jacobsen, at this place of residence." He grimaced. "Inconceivable, wouldn't you say?"

If she had been winning the battle against the reeling in her head, she had just taken a giant leap backward.

"Mrs. Jacobsen?"

She waved him down as he started to rise. "I'll be fine. Continue."

"There is not much else, at least, until you have read it. Then, I hope, you will explain some things to me."

Though part of her wanted to rip into the tube to discover its six hundred year old secret, she was afraid to believe. Hands quivering, she unwound the delicate thread that looped between tube and lid. Four figure eights and she set the lid back on its stiff leather hinge.

She stared at the irregular edges of the rolled sheets within, gently ran her fingers over them. She could have sworn she felt Nedy's hand upon them.

She turned the tube and tapped out the contents, then looked to Hunt Wynland. "I assume you've read these."

"I have. As I said, it's inconceivable." His gaze intensified. "But they *were* written six hundred years ago. Of that there is no doubt."

Laurel unrolled the sheets and stilled at the words that leapt off the parchment. "It's her handwriting!" She smoothed the curled sheets on her lap, for the first time in her life tackled the printed word with passion.

*Dear Mom,*

*It is the year 1373. As I write this, Christmas nears and a child grows in my womb. By early summer, I will be a mother.*

Laurel teared, felt joy bloom in her breast. A baby. Nedy a mother. Answered prayers.

*As you will have guessed from my journal, the father is Fulke Wynland, a man I love down to the deepest breath of my soul. A month after the fire at Brynwood Spire, we were wed. You will be pleased to know that John and Harold were in attendance, as well as Sir Arthur Crosley who wed Fulke's sister, Lady Marion, last week. Fulke and Arthur—or Mac, as I still think of him—are feeling their way toward friendship. Fortunately, the injury to Mac's leg has healed, leaving him with only a slight limp. I am well and happier than I ever believed possible, but I miss you and worry about how you are coping. For this reason, I am sending this sign across the years that you will find peace in knowing I did go on. I will continue writing letters so you will fully know the daughter to whom you gave life. I love you. Your daughter for all time, Nedy Wynland.*

Laurel dropped her chin to her chest. "I believe."

"Then it's true," Hunt Wynland murmured, though his voice remained tinged with disbelief.

She looked up and was struck by the realization her daughter's blood ran through him—thus, hers. "Providing I'm not dreaming, it's true."

He settled back in the recliner and gestured for her to continue.

There were a dozen letters detailing the major events of Nedy's life with Fulke and their children—two girls, two boys, and John and Harold. In 1392, John assumed the title of the Earl of Sinwell and Nedy and Fulke left Brynwood Spire to live at the barony of Trune. The final letter was penned in the year 1427 when Nedy would have been eighty-two. Fulke was still at her side, as were three of their four children, a multitude of grandchildren, and her first great-grandchild. Though her life was touched with sorrow as all lives are, it had been beautiful and fulfilling. That was all there was, meaning Nedy had not made it much beyond her eighty-second year. Still, she had far outlived twenty-eight.

Laurel dabbed her eyes, sighed, and rolled the parchments together. When she looked to Hunt, she saw his gaze was fixed on the knotty-wood picture frame on the table between the recliners. Since the reading of the first letter, he hadn't spoken. How long had he been staring at the mother and daughter picture taken seven years ago?

"That's Kennedy," Laurel said, "though I always called her Nedy."

His eyes swung to her, and though doubt lingered, he said, "I know. A portrait of her hangs at the Wynland estate."

And one day Laurel would see it. She knew it as surely as she breathed.

It seemed the most natural thing to reach to the man she had mistaken for a complete stranger. "Would you like me to tell you about her?"

He waged a palpable battle between belief and disbelief but, at last, clasped her fingers. "Tell me about our Nedy."

Excerpt

# THE UNVEILING

Age Of Faith: Book One

# 1

There was but one way to enter Wulfen Castle. She must make herself into a man.

Annyn looked down her figure where she stood among the leaves of the wood. And scowled. Rather, she must make herself into a boy, for it was boys in which the Baron Wulfrith dealt—pages who aspired to squires, squires who aspired to knights. As she was too slight to disguise herself as a squire, a page would be her lot, but only long enough to assure Jonas was well.

Still haunted by foreboding, though it was now four days since it had burrowed a dark place within her, she dropped her head back against the tree beneath which she had taken cover and squinted at the sunlight that found little resistance in autumn's last leaves. If only her mother were alive to offer comfort, but it was eight years since Lady Elena had passed on. Eight years since Annyn had known her touch.

A thumping sound evidencing the wily hare had come out of the thicket, Annyn gripped her bow tighter and edged slowly around the tree as her brother had taught her.

Though the scruffy little fellow had not fully emerged, he would soon. She tossed her head to clear the hair from her brow, raised her bow, and drew the nocked arrow to her cheek.

The hare lifted its twitchy nose.

*Patience.* Annyn heard Jonas from two summers past. Would she hear his voice again?

Aye, she would see him when she journeyed to Wulfen Castle where he completed his squire's training with the mighty Baron Wulfrith, a man said to exercise considerable sway over the earl from whom he held his lands.

Annyn frowned as she pondered the Wulfrith name that brought to mind a snarling wolf, her imagining made more vivid by the terrible anger the man was said to possess. Since before William of Normandy had conquered England, the Wulfrith family had been known England to France for training boys into men, especially those considered seriously lacking. Though Jonas's missives spoke little of that training, all knew it was merciless.

The hare crept forward.

*Hold!* Jonas's voice, almost real enough to fan her cheek, made her smile, cracking the mud she had smeared on her face as her brother had also taught her to do.

She squeezed her eyes closed. Thirteen months since he had departed for Wulfen. Thirteen months in training with the feared Wulfrith who allowed no women within his walls. Thirteen months to make Jonas into a man worthy to lord the barony of Aillil that would be his as Uncle Artur's heir.

The hare thumped.

Annyn jerked, startling the creature into bounding from the thicket.

*Follow, follow, follow!*

She swung the arrow tip ahead of the hare and released.

With a shriek that made her wince as she did each time she felled one of God's creatures, the hare collapsed on a bed of muddy leaves.

*Meat on the table*, Annyn told herself as she tramped to where her prey lay. Not caring that she dirtied her hose and tunic, she knelt beside it.

"Godspeed," she said, hoping to hurry it to heaven though Father Cornelius said no such place existed for animals. But what did a man who did not know how to smile know of God's abode? She lifted the hare and tugged her arrow free. Satisfied to find tip and feathers intact, she wiped the shaft on her tunic and thrust the arrow into her quiver.

She stood. A catch of good size. Not that Uncle Artur would approve of her fetching meat to the table. He would make a show of disapproval, as he did each time she ventured to the wood, then happily settle down to a meal of hare pie. Of course, Annyn must first convince Cook to prepare the dish. But he would, and if she hurried, it could be served at the nooning meal. She slung the bow over her shoulder and ran.

*If only Jonas were here, making me strain to match his longer stride. If only he were calling taunts over his shoulder. If only he would go from sight only to pounce upon me. Lord, I do not know what I will do if—*

She thrust aside her worry with the reminder that, soon enough, she would have the assurance she sought. This very eve she would cut her mess of black hair, don garments Jonas had worn as a page, and leave under cover of dark. In less than a sennight, she could steal into Wulfen Castle, seek out her brother, and return to Aillil. As for Uncle Artur...

She paused at the edge of the wood and eyed Castle Lillia across the open meadow. Her disappearance would send dread through her uncle, but if she told him what she intended, he would not allow it.

She toed the damp ground. If he would but send a missive to Wulfen to learn how Jonas fared, this venture of hers need not be undertaken. However, each time she asked it of her uncle, he teased that she worried too much.

Movement on the drawbridge captured Annyn's regard. A visitor? A messenger from Wulfen? Mayhap Jonas once more returned for willful behavior? She squinted at the standard flown by the rider who passed beneath the raised portcullis and gasped. It belonged to the Wulfriths!

Though the men on the walls usually called to Annyn and bantered over her frightful appearance, her name did not unfurl any tongues when she approached the drawbridge.

Ignoring her misgivings, she paused to seek out the bearded Rowan who, as captain of the guard, was sure to be upon the gatehouse. He was not, but William was.

She thrust the hare high. "Next time, boar!"

He did not smile. "My lady, hasten to the donjon. The Baron Wul—"

"I know! My brother is returned?"

He averted his gaze. "Aye, Lady Annyn, your brother is returned."

So, neither could the renowned Baron Wulfrith order Jonas's life. She might have laughed if not that it boded ill for her brother's training to be terminated. Though of good heart, he had thrice been returned by fostering barons who could no more direct him than his uncle with whom he and Annyn had lived these past ten years. Thus, until Uncle Artur had sent Jonas to Wulfen Castle, brother and sister had been more together than apart. Soon they would be together again.

Silently thanking God for providing what she had asked, she darted beneath the portcullis and into the outer bailey, passing castle folk who stared after her with something other than disapproval. Telling herself her flesh bristled from chill, she entered the inner bailey where a half dozen horses stood before the donjon, among them Jonas's palfrey. And a wagon.

As she neared, the squire who held the reins of an enormous white destrier looked around. Surprise first recast his narrow face, then disdain. "Halt, you!"

She needed no mirror to know she looked more like a stable boy than a lady, but rather than allow him to mistake her as she was inclined to do, she said, "It is Lady Annyn you address, Squire."

Disdain slid back into surprise, and his sleepy green eyes widened further when he saw the hare. "Lady?" As if struck, he looked aside.

Annyn paused alongside Jonas's horse and laid a hand to its great jaw. "I thank you for bringing him home." She ran up the steps.

The porter was frowning when she reached the uppermost landing. "My lady, your uncle and Baron Wulfrith await. Pray, go quick 'round to the kitchen and put yourself to order."

Baron Wulfrith at Lillia? She glanced over her shoulder at the white destrier. How could she not have realized its significance? The baron must be angry indeed to have returned Jonas himself. Unless—

William's unsmiling face. The lack of disapproval usually shown her by the castle folk. The wagon.

Not caring what her appearance might say of her, she lunged forward.

"My lady, pray—"

"I will see my brother now!"

The porter's mouth worked as if to conjure argument, but he shook his head and opened the door. "I am sorry, Lady Annyn."

The apology chilling her further, she stepped inside.

The hall was still, not a sound to disturb God and His angels were they near.

Blinking to adjust to the indoors, she caught sight of those on the dais. As their backs were turned to her and heads were bent, she wondered what they looked upon. More, where was Jonas?

The hare's hind legs dragging the rushes where the animal hung at her side, she pressed forward, all the while telling herself Jonas would soon lunge from an alcove and thump her to the floor.

"'Twas an honorable death, Lord Bretanne," a deep voice struck silence from the hall.

Annyn halted and picked out the one who had spoken—a big man in height and breadth, hair cut to the shoulders.

*Dear God, of whom does he speak?*

He stepped aside, clearing the space before the lord's table to reveal the one she desperately sought.

The hare slipped from her fingers, the bow from her shoulder. Vaguely aware of the big man and his companions swinging around, she stared at her brother's profile that was the shade of a dreary day. And there stood Uncle Artur opposite, hands flat on the table upon which Jonas was laid, head bowed, shoulders hunched up to his ears.

Annyn stumbled into a run. "Jonas!"

"What is this?" the deep voice demanded.

When Uncle's head came up, his rimmed eyes reflected shock at the sight of her. But there was only Jonas. In a moment she would have him up from the table and—

She collided with a hauberked chest and would have fallen back if not for the hand that fastened around her upper arm. It was the man who had spoken. She swung a foot and connected with his unmoving shin.

He dragged her up to her toes. "Who is this whelp that runs your hall like a dog, Lord Bretanne?"

Annyn reached for him where he stood far above. He jerked his head back, but not before her nails peeled back the skin of his cheek and jaw.

With a growl, he drew back an arm.

"Halt! 'Tis my niece."

The fist stopped above her face. "What say you?"

As Annyn stared at the large knuckles, she almost wished they would grind her bones so she might feel a lesser pain.

"My niece," Uncle said with apology, "Lady Annyn Bretanne."

The man delved her dirt-streaked face. "*This* is a woman?"

"But a girl, Lord Wulfrith."

Annyn looked from the four angry scores on the man's cheek to his grey-green eyes. *This* was Wulfrith? The one to whom Jonas was entrusted? Who was to make of him a man? Who had made of him a corpse?

"Loose me, cur!" She spat in the scratchy little voice Jonas often teased her about.

"Annyn!" Uncle protested.

Wulfrith's grip intensified and his pupils dilated.

Refusing to flinch as Jonas had told her she should never do, she held steady.

"'Tis the Baron Wulfrith to whom you speak, child," her uncle said as he came around the table, his voice more stern than she had ever heard it.

She continued to stare into the face she had marked. "This I know."

Uncle laid a hand on Wulfrith's shoulder. "She is grieved, Lord Wulfrith. Pray, pity her."

Annyn glared at her uncle. "Pity *me*? Who shall pity my brother?"

He recoiled, the pain of a heart that had loved his brother's son causing his eyes to pool.

Wulfrith released Annyn. "Methinks it better that I pity *you*, Lord Bretanne."

Barely containing the impulse to spit on him, she jumped back and looked fully into his face: hard, sharp eyes, nose slightly bent, proud cheekbones, firm mouth belied by a full lower lip, cleft chin. And falling back from a face others might think handsome, silver hair—a lie, for he was not of an age that bespoke such color. Indeed, he could not have attained much more than twenty and five years.

"Were I a man, I would kill you," she rasped.

His eyebrows rose. "'Tis good you are but a little girl."

If not for Uncle's hand that fell to her shoulder, Annyn would have once more set herself at Wulfrith.

"You err, child." Uncle Artur spoke firm. "Jonas fell in battle. His death is not upon the baron."

She shrugged out from beneath his hand and ascended the dais. Her brother was clothed in his finest tunic, about his waist a silver-studded belt from which a sheathed misericorde hung. He had been made ready for burial.

She laid a hand on his chest and willed his heart to beat again. But nevermore. "Why, Jonas?" The first tear fell, wetting the dried mud on her face.

"They were close." Uncle Artur's low words pierced her. "'Twill be difficult for her to accept."

Annyn swung around to face those who stared at her with disdain and pity. "How did my brother die?"

Was Wulfrith's hesitation imagined? "It happened at Lincoln."

She gasped. Yesterday they had received tidings of the bloody battle between the armies of England's self-proclaimed king, Stephen, and the young Henry, grandson of the departed King Henry and rightful heir to the throne. In spite of numerous skirmishes, raids, and deaths, it was told that neither man could claim victory at Lincoln. Nor could Jonas.

"Your brother squired for me. He was felled while delivering a lance to the field."

Despite her trembling, Annyn held Wulfrith's gaze. "What felled him?"

Something turned in his steely eyes. "An arrow to the heart."

All for Stephen's defense of his misbegotten claim to England.

She sank her nails into her palms. How it had pained Jonas to stand the side of the usurper when it was Henry he supported. And surely he had not been alone in that. Regardless of whose claim to the throne one supported, nobles vied to place their sons at Wulfen Castle. True, Wulfrith was Stephen's man, but it was said there was none better to train knights who would one day lord. If not for this silver-haired Lucifer and his thieving king, Jonas would be alive.

"He died an honorable death, Lady Annyn."

She took a step toward Wulfrith. "'Twas for Stephen he died. Tell me, Lord Wulfrith, what has that man to do with honor?"

As anger flared in his eyes, Uncle Artur groaned. Though Uncle also sided with Stephen, he had been aware of his nephew's allegiance to Henry. This, then—his hope of turning Jonas to Stephen—among his reasons for sending his nephew to Wulfrith.

Amid the murmuring and grunting of those in the hall, Annyn looked to Wulfrith's scored flesh and wished the furrows proved deep enough to mark him forever. And of Stephen who had pressed Uncle to send Jonas to Wulfrith? Whose wrongful claim to England had made the battle that took Jonas's life?

"Again, were I a man, I would kill your beloved Stephen."

While his men responded with raised voices, out of the darkness of his accursed soul, Wulfrith stared at her.

"Annyn!" Uncle strangled. "You do not know of what you speak."

"But I do." She turned her back on him and gently swept the hair off her brother's brow.

"Pray, Lord Wulfrith," her uncle beseeched, "do not listen—"

"Fear not. What has been spoken shall not pass from here."

Annyn looked over her shoulder. "My uncle is most grateful for such generosity from the man who bequeathed a grave to his heir."

Wulfrith's lower lip thinned with the upper, and his men objected more loudly, but it was Uncle Artur's face that stayed her. His torment pushed past the child in her and forced her to recognize it was not Wulfrith who staggered beneath her bitter words. It was this man she loved as a father.

She swallowed her tears. She would not further lose control of her emotions. After all, she was four and ten winters aged—a woman, though her uncle defended her as a girl. If not for his indulgence, she might now be wed, perhaps even with child.

She closed her eyes and drew a deep breath. When she lifted her lids, Wulfrith's harsh gaze awaited hers. "We wish to be alone," she said.

He inclined his head and looked to Uncle. "Lord Bretanne."

"Lord Wulfrith. Godspeed."

Despising the baron's ample shoulders and long-reaching legs, Annyn stared after him until he and his men passed through the door held by the porter.

"You should not have spoken as you did," Uncle said, though the steel in his voice would forge no sword.

Jonas's death had aged him, had stolen the breadth of shoulders on which he had borne her as a young girl.

Pressing her own shoulders back, she stood as tall as her four feet and some inches would stretch. "I know I have shamed you, and I shall endeavor to earn your forgiveness."

He mounted the dais and put an arm around her. "All is forgiven." He turned her to Jonas.

As she looked at her brother, a sob climbed up her throat. Reminding herself she was no longer a girl, she swallowed it.

"An honorable death."

Uncle's whispered words struck nearly as hard as when Wulfrith had spoken them. Though she struggled to hold back the child who incited words to her lips, she could not.

"Honorable! Not even eight and ten and he lies dead from serving a man who was more his enemy than—"

"Enough!" Uncle dropped his arm from her.

"Can you deny Jonas would be alive if not for Stephen's war?"

Anger met weariness on his brow. "Nay, as neither can I deny he would yet breathe if Henry, that whelp of Maude's, did not seek England for his own." He reached past her, ungirded Jonas's belt, and swept up his tunic. "Look!"

She did not want to, longed to run back to the wood, but that was the girl in her. Jaw aching at the force with which she ground her teeth, she dragged her gaze to the hideous wound at the center of her brother's chest.

"What do you see?" Uncle asked.

"A wound."

"And whose army do you think shot the arrow that put it there?"

*Henry's, but—*

"Whose, Annyn?"

*Henry's, but Stephen—*

"Speak it!"

She looked to her quaking hands. "Henry's."

He sighed, bent a finger beneath her chin, and urged her face up. "Stephen may not be the king England deserves, but until a worthier one appears, he is all there is. I beseech you, put aside Jonas's foolish allegiance to Maude's son. Henry is but a boy—barely six and ten—and unworthy to rule."

*Unworthy when he led armies? Unworthy when—*

She nodded.

Uncle stepped back. "I must needs pray."

As she ought to herself, for Father Cornelius told it was a long way to heaven. The sooner Jonas was prayed there, the sooner he might find his rest. "I shall join you shortly."

As her uncle turned away, Annyn saw the captain of the guard step out of a shadowed alcove. Had he been there when she entered the hall? Not that any of what had been said should be withheld from him, for he also had been like a father to Jonas. Did Uncle know of Rowan's presence?

She looked to her uncle as he traversed the hall and saw him lift a hand to his chest as if troubled by the infirm heart that beat there.

Panged by the suffering of the man who had been good to her and Jonas—far better than his brother who had sown them—Annyn silently beseeched, *Please, Lord, hold him hale.*

A moment later, she startled at the realization that she called on the one who had done nothing to protect her brother. Thus, it was not likely He would answer her prayers for her uncle.

When the old man disappeared up the stairs, Annyn drew nearer the table and reached to pull Jonas's tunic down. However, the V-shaped birthmark on his left ribs captured her gaze. Since it was years since the boy he had been had tossed off his tunic in the heat of swordplay, she had forgotten about the mark.

She closed her eyes and cursed the man whose charge of Jonas had stolen her brother from her. Wulfrith had failed Jonas. Had failed her.

When Rowan ascended the dais, she looked around.

The captain of the guard stared at the young man to whom he had given so many of his years, then a mournful sound rumbled up from his depths and he yanked down Jonas's tunic.

For fear she would cry if she continued to look upon Rowan's sorrow, Annyn lowered her face and reached to straighten the neck of her brother's tunic. If not for that, she would not have seen it. Would never have known.

She looked closer at the abraded skin deep beneath his chin. What had caused it? She pushed the material aside. The raw skin circled his upper neck and, when she traced it around, it nearly met at the back.

Understanding landed like a slap to the face. Wulfrith had lied. An arrow had not killed Jonas. Hanging had been the end of him. Why? Had her brother revealed his allegiance to Henry? More, who had fit the noose? Wulfrith who stood for Stephen? It had to be. And if not him, then surely he had ordered it.

Annyn whipped her chin around and saw that Rowan stared at what she had uncovered.

Bile rising, she stumbled past him and dropped to her knees. When the heaving was done, she wiped her mouth on her sleeve. "What will Uncle say of Wulfrith and Stephen now 'tis proven Jonas was murdered?"

Rowan sank deeper into silence, and she realized that, though Uncle's heart might abide the honorable death of one he had loved, Jonas's murder would likely ruin it, especially as he had sent her brother to Wulfrith in spite of Jonas's protests.

If not that she loved her uncle, she would have hated him. "Nay, he must not be told." Feeling as if she had aged years in these last moments, she stepped past Rowan and pulled the misericorde from her brother's belt.

Frowning over the pommel that was set with jewels to form the cross of crucifixion, she wondered whence the dagger came. She would have noticed such a splendid weapon had Jonas possessed one. Was it of Wulfen? It mattered not. All that mattered was revenge.

*Vengeance is not yours, Annyn.* Jonas's voice drifted to her from six months past when he had come home for three days. *Vengeance belongs to God. You must defer to Him.*

Her anger at the visiting nobleman's son who had set one of her braids afire had faltered when she heard Jonas speak so. He, who had so often shrugged off God, had found Him at Wulfen. Considering Baron Wulfrith's reputation, it had surprised her. And more so now, having met the man and discovered his lie about Jonas's death.

False teachings, then. A man like Wulfrith could not possibly know God. At that moment, she hardly knew Him herself. For days, she had prayed He would deliver Jonas home. And this was His answer.

She squeezed her fists so tight that her knuckles popped.

How she ached to make Wulfrith suffer for the bloodguilt of her brother's death. She knew vengeance was God's privilege, but she also knew it had once been the privilege of surviving family members.

Would God truly strike her down if she turned to the ways of the Old Testament? Revenge *was* the way of the world—certainly the way of men. Revenge begat revenge, as evidenced by the struggle for England's throne.

She nodded. How could God possibly deny her, especially as He was surely too busy to bother with such things himself? Were He not, He would not have allowed what had been done to Jonas.

Splaying her fingers on her thighs, she glared at the ceiling. "Vengeance is *mine*, and You shall just have to understand." A terrible, blasphemous thought crept to her tongue, and she did not bite it back. "If You are even there."

"Annyn?"

She looked to Rowan whose talk had turned her and Jonas to Henry's side—Rowan who would surely aid her. If it took a lifetime, Wulfrith would know the pain her brother had borne. Only his death would satisfy.

It had been necessary. Still, Garr Wulfrith felt the stain of young Jonas's death.

He reached for the hilt of his misericorde and too late realized he no longer possessed it. *That* had *not* been necessary.

Berating himself for the foolish gesture, he lifted a hand to his cheek where Jonas's shrew of a sister had scored his flesh. So the girl who looked and behaved like a boy had also turned. Though Artur Bretanne remained loyal to Stephen, somehow his brother's children had found Henry. For that, Jonas was dead. And hardly an honorable death as told.

Remembering what he had done the morning he found his squire strung from a tree, he told himself it was better that the truth of the betrayal die with the betrayer. No family ought to suffer such dishonor, not even a family that boasted one such as Annyn Bretanne. Thus, he had falsified—and now felt the brunt of God's displeasure.

*Save me, O Lord, from lying lips and deceitful tongues,* his mother would quote if she knew what her firstborn had done.

For this, Garr would spend hours in repentance and pray that this one lie did not breed, as lies often did—that after this day, he would know no more regret for having told it.

He looked over his shoulder. Though it was the receding Castle Lillia he sought, Squire Merrick captured his gaze. A promising young warrior, if not a bit peculiar, he and Jonas had served together in squiring Garr. At first there had been strain between the young men who both aspired to the standing of First Squire, but it had eased once Jonas was chosen. In fact, the two had become as near friends as was possible in the competitive ranks of the forty who sought knighthood at Wulfen Castle. But, as Merrick now knew, friendships often had false bottoms.

Garr shifted his gaze to Castle Lillia. He pitied Artur Bretanne. The man would be a long time in ridding himself of his niece, if ever, for who would take to wife that filthy little termagant who had but good, strong teeth to recommend her?

Of course, what man took any woman to wife other than to get an heir? Women were difficult, ever endeavoring to turn men from their purpose. However, as with all Wulfrith men who preferred warring over women, especially Garr's father, Drogo, Garr would eventually wed. Forsooth, he would have done so three years past had his betrothed not died of the pox.

He turned back to the land before him. Once Stephen secured his hold on England, Garr would find a wife of sturdy build whom he could visit a half dozen times a year until she bore him sons to raise up as warriors—men who stood far apart from ones like Jonas.

An image of the young man's death once more rising, he gripped the pommel of his saddle. How could he have been so wrong? Though he had sensed Jonas's allegiance to Henry, he had used it to put heart into the young man's training. After all, how better to make a man than to give him a powerful reason for becoming one? The aim was not to turn one's allegiance, though sometimes it happened. The aim was for the squire to give his utmost to his lord, which was of greatest importance in battle.

But the strategy had failed with Jonas—fatally. A mistake Garr would not make again.

Telling himself Jonas Bretanne was in the past, dead and soon buried, he released the pommel. As for Annyn Bretanne, she would put her loss behind her. All she needed was time.

# About the Author

Tamara Leigh holds a Master's Degree in Speech and Language Pathology. In 1993, she signed a 4-book contract with Bantam Books. Her first medieval romance, *Warrior Bride*, was released in 1994. Continuing to write for the general market, three more novels were published with HarperCollins and Dorchester and earned awards and spots on national bestseller lists.

In 2006, Tamara's first inspirational contemporary romance, *Stealing Adda*, was released. In 2008, *Perfecting Kate* was optioned for a movie and *Splitting Harriet* won an ACFW "Book of the Year" award. The following year, *Faking Grace* was nominated for a RITA award. In 2011, Tamara wrapped up her "Southern Discomfort" series with the release of *Restless in Carolina*.

When not in the middle of being a wife, mother, and cookbook fiend, Tamara buries her nose in a good book—and her writer's pen in ink. In 2012, she returned to the historical romance genre with *Dreamspell*, a medieval time travel romance. Shortly thereafter, she once more invited readers to join her in the middle ages with the *Age of Faith* series: *The Unveiling, The Yielding, The Redeeming, The Kindling,* and *The Longing*. Tamara's #1 Bestsellers—*Lady at Arms, Lady Of Eve, Lady Of Fire,* and *Lady Of Conquest*—are the first of her medieval romances to be rewritten as "clean reads." Look for *Baron Of Blackwood,* the third book in *The Feud* series, in 2016.

Tamara lives near Nashville with her husband, sons, a Doberman that bares its teeth not only to threaten the UPS man but to smile, and a feisty Morkie that keeps her company during long writing stints.

Connect with Tamara at her website www.tamaraleigh.com, her blog The Kitchen Novelist, her email tamaraleightenn@gmail.com, Facebook, and Twitter.

**For new releases and special promotions, subscribe to Tamara Leigh's mailing list: www.tamaraleigh.com**

Made in the USA
Charleston, SC
12 January 2016